49

W9-BXG-396

THE FAVORITE
DAUGHTER

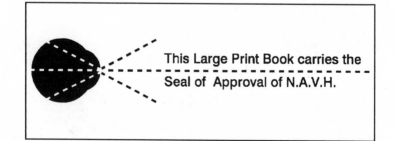

This Large Print Book carries the
Seal of Approval of N.A.V.H.

THE FAVORITE DAUGHTER

PATTI CALLAHAN HENRY

WHEELER PUBLISHING
A part of Gale, a Cengage Company

Farmington Hills, Mich • San Francisco • New York • Waterville, Maine
Meriden, Conn • Mason, Ohio • Chicago

LIBRARY OF CONGRESS CIP DATA ON FILE.
CATALOGUING IN PUBLICATION FOR THIS BOOK
IS AVAILABLE FROM THE LIBRARY OF CONGRESS

ISBN-13: 978-1-4328-6793-5 (hardcover alk. paper)

Published in 2019 by arrangement with Berkley, an imprint of Penguin Publishing Group, a division of Penguin Random House LLC

Printed in the United States of America
1 2 3 4 5 6 7 23 22 21 20 19

*To all those affected by the
memory-stealing disease
of Alzheimer's —
may we find a cure.*

Your feet will bring you
where your heart is.

Irish proverb

PROLOGUE

Memory is the seamstress, and a
capricious one at that.
Virginia Woolf, *Orlando*

The wedding for Colleen Donohue, Lena
to her family and friends, and Walter Littleton was ready to begin one spring afternoon.
The Lowcountry of South Carolina
preened, the temperature in the seventies
without a hint of the summer humidity that
would arrive soon, the river shimmering
with glints of sunlight captured in its crests,
the blooms of the azaleas and gardenias
competing for attention. The air was soft as
cashmere.

For this very day much dreaming and
planning had gone on behind the scenes,
starting with the gown. Lena's cream-
colored lace dress, originally worn by Aunt
Rosalind forty years before, had been re-
made for Lena's taller body. Her ethereal

and younger sister, Hallie, as the maid of honor, was adorned in a pale pink sheath dress with a circle of baby gardenias on her head, her straight blond hair falling to her shoulders. Lena's loose curls had been tamed for the day and pinned high under a pearl crown and a veil edged with tiny Swarovski crystals.

It was a small town, Watersend, South Carolina, nestled where the May River met the wide saltwater bay. The wedding was being held in the 1820s stone Episcopal church, full to overflowing. Although they weren't church members, everyone in town did favors for the Donohues, even the priest — for Mr. Gavin Donohue, to be specific. Lena watched from the bride's room window as outside the guests arrived in pairs and clusters. The ancient oak trees spread their gnarled limbs, offering shady protection, and sunlight filtering through the Spanish moss turning it to gossamer.

"A mass migration," Lena said to her mother, Elizabeth, who was fastening the last of the satin buttons at the back of Lena's dress. "I bet there's not one person left in town. If a stranger came through, it would look like a ghost town."

Elizabeth laughed, a sound as tiny as she was. "Well, you know your dad. He can't help but invite everyone. If someone walks into the pub, he's all a-chatter about his oldest daughter getting married to that endearing Littleton fella, and then he's off inviting them. I gave up counting long ago. The Oyster Shack just decided to cook enough Lowcountry Boil to feed the entire town. It's a safe bet." She gazed off. "Still not sure how they're all going to fit under that tent in our backyard, but . . ."

"It's wonderful there are so many," Lena said. "It's nice that people will witness this promise. It makes it feel more true, more of a sacred commitment. Even if they are mostly here for Dad."

"They are here for you, too, honey. You and your dad: two peas; one pod."

Lena studied her mother's face as she'd done all her remembered life, looking for a sign of what was missing, a gap that she'd always felt, wanting more and finding less. Was this closeness with her dad a source of pain for her mother? Or was Elizabeth merely stating the truth without subtext?

Elizabeth Donohue wore a blue lace dress that fell like waves around her slim body. She was impeccable in her appearance and mannerisms — her Virginia aristocratic heritage surrounding her like a perpetual shine. Lena had never seen her mother unkempt. Even her cotton nightgowns were ironed and coordinated with her robes. Meanwhile, Lena had trouble finding matching shoes.

Everything to do with the wedding planning had been annoying to Lena and she'd only endured it for her mother's sake — trying to please a woman who'd never had a *real* wedding. They all knew the story — how her parents had agreed that the money they'd spend on a wedding would go to opening the pub. The justice of the peace in Watersend had married them, Mother in the white dress she'd worn to her high school prom, and Dad in a black suit with a cobalt-blue tie.

Lena hadn't wanted all the nuptial hoopla; she'd merely wanted to say her vows in a simple dress, throw a huge party at her dad's pub, the Lark, where she'd spent most of her life at his side, and then hurry on with their adventuresome life. She and Walter had so much planned — children, creative work, travel and family gatherings — and sitting through prim parties and opening gifts with dainty oohs and aahs had not been part of her dream.

Thank God for Hallie, who had not only helped Lena maintain her patience through months of cutesy-pie smiling, but also knew enough to organize the wedding events down to the last toast said and confetti tossed. Lena, her head perpetually in the clouds, as their mother was always reminding her, wouldn't have made it a week into the spreadsheets and budget calculations. Hallie, on the other hand, dove into the deepest end of this wedding planning pool and arranged every small and beautiful detail. And now it was time; Lena had paid her dues in composure and her wedding day was here.

Hallie and Lena had spent the morning lazing in their childhood tree house, staring over the May River just as they'd done almost every Saturday of their early lives, and secretly during many midnight hours when their parents had believed they were asleep. When Mother had finally called them inside to have their hair and makeup done for the wedding, Lena had grasped Hallie's hands and declared, "Nothing will change between us. I am here for you and you for me — the Donohue girls forever even if my last name changes."

Hallie had cried, true-blue tears that wet her cheeks and rolled into the soft corners of her mouth. "It will change — you'll be married while I can't keep a guy around for more than six months."

"Do *not* cry! You'll find your soul mate, too. I know it." Lena had pulled her sister close. "And look at us. Some things will change, but not us, not you and me." And Lena had meant it; nothing, not even marriage, could separate her from her beloved sister.

"You won't be able to meet me at midnight to stare at the stars, watch for the shooting one," Hallie said quietly. "Not like before."

"We'll find new ways."

It was times like this when Lena would think how much younger Hallie really seemed — not immature as much as naïve. She'd never dated anyone seriously for more than a few months, and her shy insecurity kept her from the wider world, even attending college at the local satellite of the University of South Carolina. Hallie was living at home and finding jobs as a wedding organizer and party planner. Why did Hallie ever need to go anywhere else? she asked when pushed on the subject. She had everything she wanted right there. So, yes, Lena's marriage was putting a bit of a strain on Hallie's life cocoon.

Outside the bridal room door, the organ reverberated with "How Great Thou Art," one of three songs that the organist, a last-minute replacement, knew. "That's the third time she's played that song," Lena said to her mother. She leaned close to the mirror and once again checked her rosy lipstick. She didn't often wear makeup and her face looked dollish and plastic so she wiped some off just as the door burst open and her three bridesmaids entered bearing a contraband champagne bottle held high.

"You ready?" Kerry asked, her face especially bright and cheerful with too much blush and eye shadow. Count on her to sneak in the alcohol.

It was Sara who popped the cork and poured the bubbly into those plastic flutes that Lena so hated. They always cracked when she drank from them.

"Let's save it for after," Margy said. "Can't have a drunk bride."

Kerry made a dismissive sound. "One small sip for everyone!" She held her thumb and forefinger a hairbreadth apart and laughed.

Margy handed a flute with one splash of bubbly to Lena. "Let's cheer to a long and happy life with your great love."

"To stellar sex and forever together," Sara said.

"Sara," Lena said, and pointed to her mother with a laugh.

Sara pretended to whisper. "Oh, no. Doesn't your mom know about sex?"

Mother took the champagne bottle from Margy and poured herself a small amount into a real glass from the side table. No plastic for Elizabeth. "Oh, that," she said with a wink. "Our children arrived in pink and blue packages."

"Okay, enough," Margy said. "Let's cheer."

"Not without my little sister," Lena said. "Where's Hallie?"

No one answered, each glancing around.

"Mother, do you know where she is?" Lena asked, taking the champagne bottle and walking toward the doorway.

"Darling, I've been in here with you the entire time." Mother stepped forward and attempted to take the bottle from Lena's hand. "You're going to spill that on your dress. You *know* how you are."

Yes, Lena did know how she was: klutzy. And how lovely of her mother to remind her at that moment.

"I'll get her." Kerry headed for the door, in such a rush she almost knocked over the brass cross on the banquet.

"No." Lena shook her head. "Let me." Lena wanted to find her best friend, the other half of her heart. She opened the door

16

to an empty hallway, breathing in the aroma of mildew and incense. The ancient stone walls offered the impression of being in a castle far away, a place she'd never been. She took a few steps out and glanced left and right. "Hallie?"

Only "How Great Thou Art" answered her call until Mrs. Martin, Lena's second grade teacher, stepped out from the ladies' room and gasped. "Oh, my. Lena! You are so beautiful. Who knew you'd turn into such a lovely young woman?"

Lena laughed and smiled. "Thank you." One of the vagaries of living in a town you'd never left was the danger that people's memories of you at your most awkward age might be revived at any moment. Lena and Walter had gone round and round about where to live and had decided to stay in Watersend. He was new in town and she didn't want to abandon her family — a tight-knit group that both nourished and made each other nutty. His family had disbanded — his word — when he was nine years old and his parents had divorced. An only child, he was shuffled back and forth, here and there, without ever feeling at home anywhere. Until, he said, until he met the Donohue family. This was what he'd been looking for, this kind of deep connection and family life, right alongside the kind of love that swept him away.

It wasn't just love of family that made them stay in Watersend — logic was also part of their decision. Walter was a builder who could work anywhere and what with the Donohue family connections he could thrive in town while also finding work in both Savannah thirty minutes away and Charleston two hours away. Lena's job as a writer for the local newspaper would be enough for her until she started getting bigger assignments with more important news sources, which she had faith would happen soon.

Walter. His name made Lena smile, the quiver of rightness in her chest quickening. That he'd chosen her was still a surprise. Yes, they were getting married "too quickly," having known each other just eight months — six before he knelt on one knee and proposed, and two since they'd begun planning the wedding, which was easy for Mother and Hallie to arrange as just another backyard party. But love is love and *this* was love. It doesn't take long to plan a party in a place like Watersend, where the town is waiting at the ready for something just like this to happen, like the night sky waiting for the stars to appear.

Walter's distant — both in geography and in emotional support — parents argued about which of them would attend, so that, in the end, neither of them were present. His groomsmen equaled Lena's bridesmaids in number, and all of them he considered "brothers." Lena measured them with unease as she'd only met them the day before the wedding and found them both loud and annoying with their private jokes and vague assertions of Walter's partying past life. When Hallie had asked, "Are you sure?" Lena had told her, "You can't dictate love. You can't tell it when and when not to appear. You have to grab it when it comes — such a rare and wonderful gift."

From the moment Lena had met Walter Littleton from Atlanta, Georgia, she'd been adrift in feelings she'd never felt before — most strongly, the desire to share her life with someone else, with this *particular* someone else.

Lena was twenty-five years old, the age she'd always told her little brother, Shane, and Hallie she would be when she married. When she and Walter had burst through the door of the pub to announce their engagement that January night, Shane had laughed and said, "Right on time."

Now at the church, Lena's ballet slippers

— she'd refused high heels, convinced that she would fall in them halfway down the aisle — were smooth along the stone hallway as she looked for her sister.

The vestibule appeared ahead and Lena backed away. Legend and lore told that seeing Walter would be bad luck. She wanted to fully experience *that moment* — the one when she walked down the aisle and Walter eyed her all aglow with the veil wafting behind. Lena wasn't traditional by any means, but some wedding mythology was ingrained in a girl's mind, so permanently and elementally etched into the psyche that even she couldn't resist.

She turned swiftly and lifted her skirts to walk back down the hallway to the bridal room. The organist had shifted to her second song — "Amazing Grace." The pew dwellers would be getting antsy. It was five past the hour.

Lena pulled open two wooden doors to spy two empty rooms before she opened a third one where two lovebirds were entangled in an embrace so tight that Lena smiled at love so evident on her wedding day. They were kissing, the woman's face lifted to the man's. His hand was in her hair, pulling her close. His other hand raised the skirt of her dress so that white silk panties flashed. Lena almost turned away in embarrassment for intruding on such an intimate moment, but something in the scene didn't allow denial. The man's lips traveled down the woman's neck, and the flower crown Lena had created with her sister the night before fell to the floor.

A tiny woman with blond hair in a pink dress and a man in a tuxedo.

He was Walter.

She was Hallie.

Lena's belly turned to fire, ignited by the truth of what she was seeing. There Lena stood, a walking cliché: the sister betrayed on her wedding day. If it weren't so stunning it would be laughable. It was the annihilation of everything Lena Donohue believed in: true love, her family's protection, and her sister's fidelity. It was death, so why was she still alive?

The champagne bottle shattered on the stone floor, a bombshell of splintered glass and fractured reality as she dropped it in shocked pain. All that had seemed real was illusion; all solid ground fell away; all love dissolved into treachery. Only one pure thought exploded through her mind — *This is the end of everything good.*

CHAPTER ONE

May you never forget what is worth
remembering, nor ever remember
what is best forgotten.

Irish proverb

Ten Years Later

The problem with memories, Colleen
Donohue often thought, wasn't with the
ones she couldn't let go of, but with those
that wouldn't let go of her.

She was no longer called Lena; now she
was Colleen. She had long ironed-straight
hair, bright red lipstick, a loft apartment in
New York City and scant vestiges of a Lowcountry river running through her veins.
Gone were the curls and the sundresses, the
flip-flops and fishing poles.

Her apartment in Brooklyn was a studio
— functional, sunny and chic. Once a
Presbyterian church, the stone building had
years ago been divided into apartments.

Colleen lived in the smallest unit, in the far top corner overlooking Arlington Place. She'd once found faded photos of the church and believed her studio had been part of the old choir loft.

That August morning she knew better than to leave the apartment. Although the air conditioner strained, it still kept her space at a lovely seventy-two degrees. Outside, the city was almost intolerable, the heat roasting the garbage and wilting anything green and lovely. No one talked much of that, but it was why New Yorkers who had them left for their Hamptons homes or their seaside cabins. Colleen had neither; her job as a freelance travel writer kept her out of the city most of the time anyway. Yet she was home that day, having just returned from Mexico.

The rainy morning was sluggish and insolent, having its own personality it wanted to impose on Colleen.

She needed coffee.

It was ten a.m. Colleen wasn't exactly the type to jump out of bed and make a run for the day. She brought the day to herself on her own terms, slowly and carefully. How many office jobs had she turned down merely because she'd have to rise to an alarm, dress in something presentable and

24

chat inanely with colleagues over the tops of cubicles? Here, she rose at her own internal clock — sometimes early but usually not — and poured coffee before launching into her writing.

With her coffee cup and a stale croissant beside her, Colleen set to work on an article describing the Mexican resort. It was coming slowly. Too slowly. She hadn't yet found a hook for the reader, an overarching narrative that might turn a run-of-the-mill tourist trap into something special. They'd paid her to go. She'd indulged in the Presidential Suite and the spa treatments. She'd met a guy at the bar and enjoyed an easy flirtation. She'd taken the ecotour and suffered through a slide show. She'd drunk the house margarita and tolerated the mariachi band. Now she needed to craft words to turn it all into an exotic journey.

She tapped her fingers on the keyboard and words scrolled across the white space. Music from the apartment next door vibrated the wall — her neighbor's teenage son was home alone, obviously skipping school, and listening to the Grateful Dead. She rose from her chair and banged on the wall, knowing the gesture would be ineffectual. She turned up her own music, Nina Simone, coming from the wireless speaker on the kitchen counter version of her family's old turntable in the kitchen at Watersend. Why she wanted to re-create a place she'd rejected, she left that to her subconscious.

She glanced around her apartment and smiled. This place made her happy. As happy as the May River? her brother had asked her one day over the phone. Yes, she'd said, although it wasn't really true. Yet and still, this space soothed her. It was all one room — with a curtain that hung between the bed and the living space and a kitchen area with a long bar made of honed black marble. One couch of cream linen faced two bright blue upholstered chairs. The narrow windows framed in iron looked over the lanterns and sidewalks of her neighborhood streetscape. Everything inside her studio was in its place, unlike the cluttered family house in Watersend where the collections and remnants of years of Donohue life needed dusting and organizing. Here, photos of the exotic locales she'd visited were set on tables in matching white frames and hung in pleasing arrangements. The kitchen was stocked with pale blue plates and appliances. *This* space belonged to Colleen.

Two hours until her deadline. Procrastination usually spurred her toward productivity, but not now.

Hearing her phone ring and seeing her brother's name on her cell made her jump up to answer. God, she loved talking to Shane, hearing his voice across the miles; he and Dad were her last ties to the Lowcountry and she wanted to hold tight to both of them.

She answered on the second ring, imagining him at the family pub, the Lark, cleaning glasses behind the bar or meeting a delivery truck in the back alley. If Colleen closed her eyes, she could smell the hoppy aroma of beer; she could visualize the dark wood paneling glowing under the lantern lights and hear the clang of glasses, the call of patrons, and a fiddle being tuned in the corner. Nothing, not one thing in her life, was as familiar to her as the Lark.

"Sis." Shane's voice vibrated in her ear.

"What's up?"

"A lot."

"Is something wrong?" she asked, as she could tell his voice was off, something amiss. Colleen automatically placed her hand over her stomach, where fear seemed to wait to be awoken.

"There is," he said.

She heard the difference; his tone lower and quieter. There wasn't a joke hidden in his voice this time.

"Dad." Colleen walked to the window overlooking the street, brownstones across the way lit with the sun rising to midsky, and she rested her forehead on the glass. "It's Dad, isn't it?"

"He's been acting funny."

"He's always acting funny." She smiled as she invoked her dad's favorite entry into a sentence. "As the Irish say, when Irish eyes are smiling, they're usually up to something."

"This isn't about his funny sayings, Lena. It's complicated, too. And I don't know if I can tell you everything over the phone. You have to come home."

Colleen laughed, relieved now because nothing was *really* wrong with her dad. This was another ploy to get her to return home. Another trick. They'd tried many times before and in many ways — her niece Rosie's baptism; her other niece, Sadie's, first birthday party; her sister Hallie's pneumonia that was so threatening. Of course there were also the holidays and anniversaries and milestones of family life. She was accustomed to the pleas to return.

"Shane, what's going on?" Colleen walked the few steps to the kitchen, poured more coffee into her pottery mug shaped like an owl's face, one she bought in a city and country already forgotten.

"Dad's not doing well. Don't make me go over this entirely complex situation on the phone. I've tried to handle it without you, but now I need you."

"I've already made plans to come for his birthday party in two weeks. I can't come *right* now."

"Lena." He said the name she didn't use anymore. "It's been six months of fast decline. I've tried to figure it out by myself. Like you, Hallie is too busy to help and . . ." His voice trailed off.

He usually knew better than to mention Hallie's name, and now the dull pain crashed into Lena's chest. "Fast decline?" she asked.

"Yes. Forgetting names; losing things; getting lost . . ."

"It's just comedy-Dad — he's like that. He's always been like that: absentminded, stumbling along. Why is this time different?"

"I've tried to keep the worst of it from you, but I took him to the doctor last week. He believes it's Alzheimer's." He paused in the time it took Colleen's breath to gather in fear. "I need you to come home."

Dizziness enveloped Colleen and she sat on a stool as coffee sloshed from the mug onto the black marble counter. "You better not be mucking with me," she said, using her dad's only curse word, if it could be called a curse word at all.

"I'm not mucking with you."

Between brother and sister, this line was a solemn vow that they were telling the truth.

"It can't be," Colleen said, brightening for only a breath. "His sixtieth birthday is in two weeks, and that's too early. I know that —"

"Yes, it's called early onset."

"Why am I only hearing this now? I talked to him just a few days ago. He was fine."

"That's the thing, Lena. He's fine until he isn't. You only talk to him when he is. But when I received a late mortgage notice . . . It's a long story. Come home and I'll tell you everything." Shane had never been so direct. Maybe he was thinking that her arguments often won, that she always had excuses. Maybe this time her baby brother didn't want to hear them.

"Okay," she said softly. "I hear you. So what are we going to do?"

"I have an idea." His voice was resolute; she'd heard it before. "I have a really good idea."

CHAPTER TWO

The past is never just the past.
　　　　David Whyte, *Consolations*

Colleen stood at the window with the disconnected phone still in her hand.

No.

Not Dad.

Her brother had hung up on her, but not before telling her to text her flight info a.s.a.p. For tomorrow, he'd said.

Tomorrow.

"Oh, Dad." Her voice broke as she spoke into the silent apartment.

Gavin Donohue was the kindest man Colleen had ever known. He was the barometer of all things good and true; he was the most stable and loving presence in her life, and she missed him every day. If her brother was right — and he'd used the solemn phrase and incantation, so he must believe he was — then of course she must go home

31

tomorrow. If what he'd said was true, she didn't have the luxury of time, to amble home whenever she felt strong enough to face Hallie and the memories.

Memories. They were being destroyed in her dad's brain. Yet memories were why Colleen was in New York, the reason she'd left her family and the life she once thought she'd never abandon.

Then she did what she always did when her mind acted like a runaway train, like a rubber ball bouncing in a closed room — she grabbed a pad of paper and a pen from her Lucite desk and began to write a neat list. First, finish the article. Second, make plane reservations. Third, do not Google Alzheimer's.

Nothing good, ever, came from over-Googling.

The article was shit. Colleen knew it and yet she hit the send button anyway. "Mexican Fun in the Sun." Even the title was the worst. But she didn't care. Her heart hadn't settled for even a minute since Shane had called that morning.

It's all in the details — this was a universal law in the writing world, as unbending as a physics equation. Colleen had kept the focus on trivialities — the scattered sparkle of morning sun on the river; the gravel road with weeds forcing their way up in the ruts and grooves; the thickness of hotel room towels; the floral rug with vines that wriggled through the pattern like snakes. Well-chosen details added together made a vivid picture, and she gathered the minutiae and decided which ones to share, which ones would send a reader to plan a trip to the location she'd just vacated.

But the overarching narrative of her *own* story? Ah, she'd avoided that for years. It was easier to notice the smallest things in her forest than to rise above the treetops and gaze down to see the not-quite-green relationships and withering spaces.

And now? Her sight was fixed firmly on home and on all the emotional uncertainty a visit there would entail.

Colleen had learned to be happy in the years since the heartbreak that had caused her to run from Watersend. She made a good living and had enough friends to stay as busy as she pleased. Sometimes she sensed a glass wall stood between her and her pals, as she was never able to tell the full truth of why she chose New York, why she never went home. Avoiding all mention of family and home, there seemed to always be a piece missing in her relationships, as if by leaving out the subject of her family she'd left the bottle of wine at home when she arrived at a dinner party. She cherished her work and her apartment and someday — maybe someday — she would again love a man. Until then, she went on as many adventures as possible and talked to her brother and father at least once a week. To her sister she didn't speak at all.

Back at her computer, she typed "LGA airport to SAV airport" in the search bar and watched the flights scroll, one by one, then startled as her apartment buzzer squealed. She walked to the intercom and pressed the speaker button. "Hello?"

"Colleen, you can't ignore me forever. Let me in, love."

Philippe, the sort-of-boyfriend she'd been avoiding since her return from Mexico a week before. This was a relationship she needed to end, a discussion she needed to have about how she didn't feel the same as he did. He'd been so much fun, taking her to haunts and hidden places in the city she'd known nothing about, introducing her to an Italian social scene that kept her up until the early morning. She'd had a blast, but now he wanted more. More than she was willing to give. But his friendship, his ability to be fully present and listen, well, she did enjoy that part.

"Darling," she said, using his language. "Not now."

"I have croissants," he said. "Warm ones from Pastanos."

This man knew his way to her heart, or at least her bed. She pushed the buzzer and then opened her studio door to watch him stride up the stairs, but it was her neighbor she saw first: Julia, who wore multiply colored spandex and her bleached hair high in a ponytail, revealing the dark roots.

"Hello, Colleen," Julia said in her singsong voice as she pulled keys out of her purse. "How are you today? Not traveling right now?"

Here was the neighbor who watched Colleen's every move but had no idea what went on with her own teenage son. "Not right now." Colleen averted her gaze to see Philippe climbing the stairs with the telltale brown paper bag in his hand.

"Another friend?" Julia followed Colleen's gaze to the tall man in dark jeans and black T-shirt, his smile as wide as his face.

"Your son," Colleen said, "skipped school today." She greeted Philippe with a much warmer kiss than she would have if Julia hadn't been watching.

Julia slammed shut her apartment door

and in the wide hallway where a tenant had painted a bright blue mural of the Brooklyn Bridge, Philippe laughed. "Will you ever give her a break?"

"Not until she gives me one." She took the bag from his outstretched hand and together they entered her apartment. She grabbed the croissant and took a bite before they reached the kitchen counter.

"Colleen." Philippe grabbed a *Travel and Leisure* magazine from a leather bag slung across his body. "You did it!" He held it up and pointed at her name on the front cover. "Your name in big bold letters right here." He dropped the satchel onto a stool and the magazine onto the kitchen counter.

Colleen grinned and even had the good sense to blush a bit. Yes, finally her name had found its way onto the cover of one of the finest travel magazines. *Top Ten Tips for Traveling by Expert Colleen Donohue.* There it was, right next to the sailboat tilted against the wind in Barbados, directly under *Island Escapes.*

Philippe flipped open to the article and pointed at her professional photo — Colleen leaning against a pillar in some faraway and nameless place with an azure sea in the background. Her hair backlit and lifted lightly by what appeared to be a breeze but

had actually been a fan, appeared like a halo. She wore a sarong and sandals — "forced casual," she called it. "And your photo." He held up his hand for a high five. "Well done, my love."

"Thanks, I'm really proud of that piece."

"Well, the advice tips don't matter so much to me. It's the stories you wrote to go with them that make it interesting." He kissed her cheek. "I felt like I knew you better with each one."

Colleen ran her fingers along the edge of the counter. "How about the stories where I wrote about the travel mistakes I made?" she asked. "Was it too much?"

"Nope. Made it even better. I loved it."

"Me, too." Colleen nibbled on the end of her croissant. "If only my piece about Mexico had flowed as easily."

Philippe reached her side and pulled her close against his long, lean body. "You can ditch me if you must, but you have to tell me what's going on. It's like another woman replaced the one who left for Mexico. Did you pick up a virus there that changed your heart?"

He was endearing and funny. Why couldn't she fall in love with the endearing and funny ones? Why did they bore her? Why did she instead want to call Daren, the

guy who had constantly stood her up while they'd dated? She smiled at Philippe. "No, I've just been so buried in work, and I told you before I left — I'm not sure we're right together."

"You don't look so well." He squinted. "Have you been crying?"

My God, she had been. She touched the edges of her eyes. How had she not realized? "It's my dad."

"You have a dad?"

"What the hell does that mean?" She moved away, putting space between them. But she knew what he meant. She never talked about her family. "Yes, I have a dad. The best dad in the world."

"And what's wrong?"

"I'm going home to find out. My brother won't tell me much until I get there other than Dad might have Alzheimer's. So it's either the worst trick in the world to bring me home or . . ."

"No one would lie about that, would they?"

"Not Shane." She shook her head, crumbs falling from the croissant in her hand.

"I'm sorry, Colleen. What can I do to help?"

"There's nothing."

"And your mom?"

"Mother to me. And sadly, I lost her two years ago."

"You know what?" He paused and tilted his head in curiosity. "I know nothing about your family. Tell me about them." He moved closer to her, lowering his voice with the tender request.

She shrugged, wiping at the edges of her eyes to remove any further evidence of emotion. "It's not a complicated family as far as families go."

He laughed and with his usual dramatic flair threw his arms in the air. "All families are complicated. Two or twenty, they are all complex." He ran his hands through his messy curls. "So you can't fool me, Colleen Donohue."

She smiled before she knew she had. "True. I just meant that there aren't that many of us. Mother was an only child and she's passed. I never knew her parents; gone before I was born, because Mother was a late-in-life baby. Dad only has one sister, and she lives in Virginia. I don't have any cousins at all. I know this sounds crazy to someone from a family like yours — all those sisters and brothers and aunts and uncles; it's like you could have your own country."

"What about your dad's parents? Your

grandparents?"

"They were amazing, at least what I remember of them. They died when I was in elementary school. They used to come visit a couple times a year, but we never went to see them."

"That's weird." Philippe took a croissant from the bag and held it absently in his hands. "My favorite times were visiting my grandparents."

Colleen shrugged. "They loved coming to see us." She took the croissant from Philippe. "Now. Can we stop talking about this?"

He lowered his voice. "Let me be here for you." He came closer and moved to place his arms around her.

She allowed his hug with the shield of the croissant before her. "That's so sweet, Philippe. But I told you from the beginning I have —"

"No interest in a serious, long-term relationship." He stepped back. "I know."

"But you thought you could change my mind." Colleen had been here before, with men who thought she was playing games when she was telling the truth. "Listen. You're an amazing guy. If I had even the slightest inkling to settle down, it would be with someone like you. Maybe even you."

He took the pastry from her, placed it on the counter and kissed her, long and slow and luxurious. She allowed him to draw her closer to the unmade bed at the far end of the room, but stopped a few steps from the rumpled sheets. "Philippe, not now. You know I adore you, but I have to book my flight and figure out what's going on with my family. I'm a bit of a mess."

His dark hair fell over one eye and he brushed it away, his gaze set on her. "You're always a mess. It's one of my favorite things about you." He kissed her again.

"That's what my mother always said."

"You're a beautiful mess then," Philippe said as sunlight fell through the large windows forming a spotlight on the hardwood floor between them.

"Philippe, I have to go home tomorrow."

"And I didn't even know you had one."

Colleen looked at him and she laughed despite herself. "I don't have one, really. Home. That's a misnomer at best."

In a swift motion, Philippe picked up the magazine from the counter, flipped to her article and read out loud. " 'Number ten: When you return home, take with you everything you've seen and learned.' "

Colleen stared at Philippe, aware of the obvious: she didn't know what or where home was anymore.

"What happened," he asked, "that you can write about going home and yet never do it?"

CHAPTER THREE

Remembrance of things past is not
necessarily the remembrance of
things as they were.

> Marcel Proust,
> *Remembrance of Things Past*

She felt the air punched from her chest as Philippe held up that article, showing her words that had meant one thing when she'd written them and now meant something altogether new. She flopped onto the couch and he sat next to her, pulling her close. He didn't ask, but he didn't have to, because Colleen started to talk, to flatly tell the story she'd never spoken out loud, not once in ten years, the story of her wedding day.

"Holy shit." Philippe's voice held tenderness and compassion despite the profanity. "That *really* happened?"

"It really did." Colleen was dry-eyed. She'd once assumed that if she ever poured

43

out the story, she would fall apart, but maybe the narrative had dried out; maybe it'd lost its power.

"And then," Colleen said, "she married him."

"Damn." Philippe shook his head. "No wonder you don't like to get too close to anyone." He grinned, but Colleen didn't find the off hand joke funny. Not one bit. "Sorry, bad timing. So then what happened?"

Colleen found herself telling the rest of what she knew, what she'd heard from her brother, her parents, or worse, what had been in the texts, e-mails and voicemails from Hallie. Never, not once, had Colleen answered any of them. "I left. No, more accurately, I ran. I grabbed my already packed suitcase and drove away. Hallie is the one who sauntered into the bridal room and told everyone the wedding was off."

"Did she tell everyone *why?*" Philippe asked in a low voice.

"I have no idea. Then Walter announced in the packed church that I had left the scene — no explanation why, just that I had run." Colleen shook her head and felt oddly disconnected to the story, as if she were telling Philippe something she'd read in the newsfeed on her computer. "So then my parents had everyone over to our house anyway, because the food and drink had already been prepared under a big white tent in our backyard. The tent Hallie picked out with daisy chains, just like we'd made as kids, falling from the posts." Colleen shrugged. "Not that I blame Mother and Dad — you can't waste good food and liquor, I guess. It was a party without a bride and groom. At least Hallie and Walter had the good sense to stay away, or so my brother told me."

"Then they married?"

"Yes. The betrayal goes on and on. They tried to do it quietly — going to the justice of the peace in Watersend six months later — but nothing is quiet in a small town. First comes cheating, then comes marriage, then comes two babies in a baby carriage."

"I'm so sorry, love. What about your parents? I mean, weren't they livid with your sister? It seems like she broke up the family."

"If they were angry, and I'm sure they were at some point or on some level, they never told me. But then again, I didn't speak to anyone at home for a long, long while. When I finally did, they were just glad to hear from me and it wasn't a subject I would talk about. I've made it clear that I never, and I mean never, want to hear about Hallie or Walter or talk about them . . . so I'm not exactly sure what their feelings are about it."

"No wonder you don't want to go home."

"That's the thing, though." Colleen stood, her heart racing with this first telling of the sordid tale. "I *do* want to go home. I just don't want to see *her,* or Walter, or their offspring. But I do want to go home. I've been there a few times over the years, but there's always been this complicated scheduling nightmare of who comes and goes so I can avoid . . ."

Philippe stood and pulled her against him, brushed her hair away from her face. "Although I know the answer to this question, I'll ask anyway — would you like me to go with you?"

Colleen smiled.

He nodded, his mouth in a tight line. "You know, it's amazing that you can tell that tale without crying."

"It is, isn't it?" Colleen said as she touched his cheek. "Listen, you're so sweet for coming by with my favorite croissant and listening. I've never told it before and your kindness allowed me to let it out. Thank you. I promise I'll call when I return, but I can't focus on anything else but getting to South

Carolina right now." Colleen kissed him and walked him to the door. "I have to book a flight now."

"You're always on the next plane out. Is that how it's always going to be?"

"I don't know." She propped the door open with her foot.

He shook his head. "Someday, Colleen Donohue, I believe you're going to have to feel something." And with that he was gone, his shadow retreating down the dark stairwell, his back straight and his hand waving over his shoulder.

Feel something? Damn, she'd felt plenty, she wanted to tell him. Plenty enough to last a lifetime. Feeling things was overrated at best. She gently closed the door and went straight back to the computer, chose a flight, entered her credit card number and slumped into the couch to text her brother with the information.

"Whoa," she exhaled into her empty apartment. She'd told the story; she'd said it out loud; and now, like the aftershocks of an earthquake, Colleen felt the fracture lines inside her chest. There was an ache and need for her family that flowed over her with a panicked sense of lost time.

When you return home, she'd written in the article, *take with you everything you've seen and learned.*

But how could she do that?

This was a question most women would ask their mothers, but two years ago they'd lost a youthful fifty-eight-year-old Elizabeth Donohue to a silent killer — a brain aneurism that had sent her crashing to the family's dock while she was dragging a crab trap out of the water in preparation for a lawn party that evening. Dad had been cleaning the picnic table. Teamwork, they always said, was an important ingredient in a marriage.

As the Irish said, two shorten the road.

Dad had raced to his wife, but it had been too late. It had been too late the millisecond it happened. Elizabeth was gone, the rope still in her hand, a smile on her face and guests on their way for fresh crab.

Shane had called Colleen that time, also. His voice shattered in grief, he'd told her, "I already bought you a plane ticket home."

Colleen had been late, arriving only two hours before the funeral; a late season snowstorm had socked the Northeast and canceled most flights. When she landed, there was no one to pick her up so she'd called a cab and told the driver to take her directly to the church where the funeral service was being held, the same one where she'd once expected to be married. She'd texted Shane. *I'll meet you at St. Paul's. Keep Hallie away from me.*

"Lena," her brother had phoned to say in a whisper, Hallie obviously near. "You can't avoid her. It's our mother's funeral."

"I can. I will. I'm here for Mother, and for Dad. And of course for you. But not her. Not Hallie."

"She wants to talk to you."

"No." Colleen had closed her eyes so tightly that bright confetti burst in the darkness.

Somehow she'd managed to avoid her sister for a full two days, during the house visits, funeral and burial. Of course she'd glimpsed Hallie across the room with Walter, who kept her welded to his side, protective or possessive, who could say?

During this time, remembered arguments between Colleen and her mother had come to mind, one after the other in unrelenting succession, causing Colleen to feel both sick and nostalgic. Regret, that was what death brought in its disorienting wake. Why hadn't she been closer to her mother? Why hadn't her mother been closer to her? Why had they argued about everything from how she fixed her curly hair to her decision to become a writer? Why did they argue more

49

than Hallie and Mother? Death, she realized, also brought a litany of why why why, like a whining child.

Colleen had finally stopped the never-ending reel of questions. That was part of life's abrupt ending — there would *never* be answers. Nothing would be resolved.

There had been loving moments together, of course there had been. When Colleen's mother had rubbed her back as she coughed with the flu, when she'd kissed Colleen good night and brushed her hair off her forehead — little moments that added up to a quiet conviction that there was love present and available. Yet there was also always the quieter conviction that Mother loved the others better, that Hallie was the favorite Donohue daughter. Dad would adamantly deny this accusation and then collect Colleen in his arms and spin her around, saying, "Who wouldn't love everything you are?"

Colleen still didn't like to think about the day of the funeral. The deep sorrow pressing on her, the knowledge that whatever she felt she was missing from her mother she would never know or have, the weight of who they all used to be and would never be again: a complete family.

This trip home would have to be different.

If the siblings were going to help their dad, they couldn't ignore each other. But she damn sure wasn't going to run to Watersend with open arms and magnanimous forgiveness. Cautiously polite would be Colleen's goal — all for Dad.

Memories had originally kept Colleen away, and now that her dad might be losing his, she would return.

CHAPTER FOUR

Scars have the strange power to remind
us that our past is real.
Cormac McCarthy,
All the Pretty Horses

When Colleen finally slept that night, she fell into fractured dreams of childhood: pleasant, filmy dreams of when it had been the five of them, secure in their family and fast in the absolute certainty of their love. Dad, Mother, Colleen, Hallie and Shane on the banks of the May River.

When she half woke before the alarm sounded, a memory of the languid Sundays they'd spent together lingered in the luminous space between sleep and wakefulness.

Dad had always taught her that the natural world revealed the face of God; that spirit lived in his creation. This was all Colleen knew about religion. While her friends went to church on Sundays in their frilly sundresses and patent leather shoes, Dad ensured that this family kept the Sabbath in the landscape surrounding Watersend. Gavin infused their family rituals with a sense of the divine. "As the Irish say, what fills the eye fills the heart." Even now, his voice resonated in Colleen's mind.

Each Sunday they would embark on an outdoor excursion: a trip on the johnboat through the secret alleyways of marsh and sea islands, their faces raised to the wind; a dockside lesson on casting the shrimp net; or maybe a hike through the nearby nature preserve, booklet in hand, to find and name the majestic birds that fluttered and flocked there. There were treasure hunts in the parks, kayaking in the estuaries, hikes to hidden ponds.

When Colleen had first relocated to New York, she'd awoken on Sundays with such a profound sense of loss that she felt as sick as if she had the flu. When she finally realized what was ailing her, she'd started walking through Prospect Park on Sunday mornings to capture at least some of what she'd lost. But it hadn't been the same. Not one little bit.

The Lowcountry was a seductress, a holy and righteous one, but one nonetheless. She was irrevocably beautiful in her ever-changing seasons and personalities. She kept her secrets well hidden in the lush and meandering tidal river creeks that only a very few people knew their way around. Her dad was one of them — the waterways were as familiar to him as his own body: the river water his blood and the land his bones. It had been the same for Colleen.

Leaving her childhood home and family had crushed the last fragile bits of her already broken heart. Hallie had always been the first person Colleen turned to with everything in their lives. The cruel part about this heartbreak, the shocking part, was that the first person Colleen wanted to talk to about the betrayal was the betrayer.

Finally one Sunday, she'd wandered into Manhattan's St. Patrick's Cathedral and taken a seat in the back row. As the priest offered communion to the congregants, she had felt left out of every kind of family there was. It was time, she decided when the tears were spent, to create a life of her own. That was what everyone had to do eventually — make their own life. And so she'd moved forward, making friends, succeeding at her job, finding lovers and becoming involved with her little community, leaving the past behind.

■ ■ ■ ■

The Savannah Airport was as charming as ever. White rocking chairs in clusters, faux pillars meant to suggest a house of the Old South, and photographs of the marsh, oyster beds and river docks — all images that still evoked the word "home" in Colleen's mind, despite having worked so damn hard to erase it. What she wanted home to be instead? She had no idea. A first-class seat in an airplane? A studio apartment in an old church? A park in New York City? A hotel room in another country?

Dressed in jeans and a black T-shirt, her hair pulled into a ponytail, she tossed her backpack over her shoulder and dragged her small rolling suitcase across the concourse, the wheels popping and squeaking until she saw Shane sitting in a rocking chair reading the paper as if he were waiting on their back porch for her to finish throwing the shrimp net. "Hello, bro," she called out as she reached him.

He glanced up and smiled. Her little brother — the most adorable of the three of them, with his black curls and green eyes, an upturned grin that didn't show his teeth, and the small silver scar on his top lip from

55

when he'd taken Colleen's dare to kiss a crab.

"Well, hello, big sis." He stood and hugged her tightly and then stepped back. "No matter how many times you come home I'm a little shocked to see how different you look."

"Different?" She cocked her head and smiled. "Better, you mean?"

He kissed her cheek. "I mean without the wild hair and the sundresses and sunburned nose."

"Well, I'm here. So let's get started on your big idea, whatever it is. And you must tell me every single thing going on with Dad. I can't bear to think of him failing. I've hardly slept."

Shane took the rolling bag from Colleen and headed for baggage claim. "This is it." Colleen placed her hand on his arm. "I don't have another bag."

"*This* is it? Taking your own advice to travel light?"

"Yup." She grinned at his reference to her article.

"Colleen." Shane rubbed the stubble on his face. "You *are* going to be here for a while. This isn't a quick in-and-out. Not this time. I know you can work anywhere — no excuses."

"I know, Shane." She slipped her arm

through his.

Shane raised his eyebrows in question. He wasn't used to her being so agreeable.

Colleen felt the cold fingers of panic tickle beneath her throat. Her worst fear escaped in a quiet voice. "Is he . . . dying or something and you're not telling me?"

"No!"

"Okay."

Once in Shane's banged-up navy blue Jeep, Colleen settled into the seat and rolled down the passenger-side window, letting in a blast of hot, humid air. "Dang," she said. "And I thought New York was miserable in August. Now I remember why I've never come back in summertime."

"Sorry Dad's crisis didn't coordinate with your schedule."

Colleen studied her brother's profile. "Are you angry?"

"No," he said quietly as he maneuvered the Jeep out of the parking deck. "I'm sorry. It's just scary and I've needed my big sister."

"I'm here," Colleen said and reached to pat his shoulder. "I'm here. Now tell me everything."

While Shane drove the thirty minutes to Watersend, through miles of green marshland set against gray-blue estuaries, and under Spanish moss dangling from live

57

oaks, Colleen tried not to think about the day she'd driven away from this beloved place. She turned away from the scenery to her brother, who spoke.

"It began a few months ago. You know I've been living above the pub for a while now, so sometimes I don't go to the old house for weeks. One afternoon, a rare free one, I decided to take out our old johnboat. At the house I found three weeks' worth of unopened mail and a burner on the stove that had been left on for God knows how long. After that, things started to make sense — now he forgets names, repeats questions, wears the same outfit for days in a row, and more."

"Oh, Shane." Colleen set her hand against her heart. "What if that burner had caught something . . ."

"Don't even play the what-if game right now, Colleen. It's too terrible." Shane turned left to drive over the Savannah bridge, a sailboat of a structure winging its way over the moving waters of the Savannah River, dividing Georgia from South Carolina. Below on the right were the spires of the grand dame city and to the left the smoke-chugging port of Savannah. Colleen held her breath as they crossed — an old childhood habit from when Shane had told her that ghosts could get them if they took a breath while crossing a river.

"Welcome home," he said as they passed the wooden sign declaring they'd entered South Carolina.

"Go on about Dad," she said. "I want to know everything before we see him."

"Looking back, Lena, I believe this dementia has been happening for a long while, a slow decline, and Mother covered for him. You know how they were — so tightly knit together. I think she made sure we didn't know, or maybe she herself didn't want to know. Either way, she concealed it."

"That makes sense. She would protect him from anything." Colleen leaned back on the seat and watched the landscape fly by — the wooden stands selling fresh shrimp, trees crowding the road alongside ramshackle cottages on the two-lane highway. "We will figure this out together."

He took a breath and then paused before asking, "Did you know Hallie moved from Savannah? They're only ten minutes away now, at the edge of town."

"Yep. Dad told me."

They were silent for a while as the mere mention of her name created open spaces, timid pauses. At a red light a few miles from town, Shane turned to Colleen. "Hallie is meeting us at the pub," he said. "Dad's having lunch with some old buddies and we'll catch up with him at home later."

"Hallie? Can't that wait?" Colleen wanted to find her feet first, to take a breath and inhale the Lowcountry air, to hug her dad before she had to face her sister.

"Lena." It was a one-word admonishment.

"I go by Colleen now. You know that, Shane."

"Not with me you don't."

Colleen let the comment rest and inhaled the briny scent of the marsh as she began to take it all in, as if she would be required to write about the spruce and pine proudly shooting toward the sky, about the summer green grasses and the hand-painted signs announcing fresh shrimp, peaches and strawberries. She held her hand out the window and let it roll with the wind, dipping and rising. She and Hallie had done that as children — perched on opposite sides of the backseat and put their hands and arms out the windows to pretend the car was a plane.

"You'll cut off your hand when a truck passes by," Shane said with the grin that all the girls had fallen for since he was a young child.

They laughed, easing the tension that had

filtered between them. The line was what he'd told them when they were young — always so logical, their little brother.

"Lena," he said as she pulled her arm back into the car, "it's happening fast."

"What do you mean?"

"Even though Mother might have hid it for a while, he's now gone too far, too fast."

"For example?"

"I've had to take his car keys." Shane's voice cracked on the last word. "He thinks the car is in the shop. But twice he became lost and once he hit a light pole. It was time. I also discovered that the bank was about to seize the pub. Dad hadn't paid the mortgage in almost a year. A year!"

"What?"

"I've caught up — it's all fixable. But there are other things, too. There were late notices. Packages unopened."

"Didn't you realize anything weird about him before this? It doesn't make sense."

"I did, but here's the thing — I just thought he was being his eccentric self. You know, changing subjects midstream, never finishing a sentence, making inappropriate jokes to the customers, losing his keys. But then the bigger things started happening — forgetting what day it was. Asking where you were, like you were upstairs."

"My God, this breaks my heart." Colleen swallowed past sudden tears. Her sweet dad had been looking for her in the next room when she was eight hundred miles away.

"I finally took him to the doctor, trying to convince myself maybe he was just getting sick or had low iron or something, because the truth is that a lot of the time he seems okay. But then something will happen, like he'll put his cell phone in the dishwasher at the pub or pour a beer into a whiskey glass. Nothing big, all things that can be explained by distraction."

"I found my earrings in the silverware drawer the other day," Colleen said. "I took them off when I was unloading the dishwasher and —"

"I know," Shane said. "That's what I told myself, too. But the tests came back. Early-onset Alzheimer's."

"Have you told him?"

By then Shane had arrived at the pub, and he maneuvered the Jeep in the alleyway to the sign that announced, *Owner Parking.* "Of course I've told him." Shane shifted into park. "But he doesn't believe me and he thinks he's fine and doctors are quacks."

He placed his hand on Colleen's shoulder. "I have an appointment with a specialist at MD Anderson Cancer Center in Jacksonville. I need you to take him."

She smiled. "Ah, that's why I'm here."

"Partly, yes. I thought if I told you on the phone you might not come."

She shook her head. "Of course I'd come. I want to take him. I want to help."

He faced her before opening the car door. "There's more to it. I need you to chip in. We decided to get this test — it's called a PET amyloid plaque-imaging scan. A mouthful, right? Anyway, it's one of the only tests that will give a mostly definitive diagnosis and insurance doesn't cover it. It's still considered experimental, but . . ."

"Why isn't it covered?"

"Because even if it shows the plaque, even if it's there, there's nothing to be done about it. There aren't any medicines or treatments . . ."

"Plaque?"

"From what little I understand, that's what Alzheimer's is essentially — plaque and tangles in your brain cells. It's more complicated than that, but that's above my pay grade."

"Oh, God. Yes, of course I'll help pay. Yes." Tears gathered and Colleen pressed her palms to her eyes. "This is so scary."

Shane nodded and she knew he didn't trust his voice, what it would sound like

63

with fear and grief mingled. Together they climbed out of the car and Colleen stood in the parking lot of the Lark as waves of emotion — joy, melancholy, regret and something that felt vaguely like peace — swept over her until she remembered her sister. "When does Hallie arrive?" she asked quietly.

"She's probably inside waiting," Shane said. "Let's go, sis."

"Give me a minute."

"I've given you years."

Chapter Five

Memory is never a precise duplicate
of the original . . . it is a continuing
act of creation.
Rosalind Cartwright,
The Twenty-four Hour Mind

The Lark was housed in an eighty-year-old
brick and tabby building that had always
been a pub, as far as Colleen knew, although
it had once been known by another name
and owned by another family. Her dad had
baptized it the Lark some thirty-five years
ago, after his favorite Irish poem and song.
He and Mother had just married when they
bought the place and Colleen was only a
twinkle in their eyes.

Colleen ambled slowly around to the front
of the building, wanting to see its face
before entering; Shane followed.

The name was writ large in a golden
Celtic font across an emerald-green frieze

above the pub door. The single front door was arched and painted a bright red with dark green trim. The slate roof sloped with a single chimney pot poking up like a submarine tower from a sea of dark shingles. A brass knocker forged into the Claddagh design — two hands surrounding a heart — hung in the middle of the door. It was a home to many and definitely to the Donohue family. The Lark's facade was as familiar to Colleen as the smile of her dad's face.

"It never changes," she said to Shane and leaned against his shoulder.

"I hope it never will. It feels like the only stable thing right now."

Colleen kissed her brother's cheek. "We'll get through this. He's here with us. That's what matters most."

Shane gave her that look, the one that let her know he didn't agree but wasn't going to fight with his big sister. Colleen pulled out her ponytail, feeling her hair come loose around her face. "And the hair puff begins," she said. "Welcome to South Carolina and a hundred percent humidity."

Shane laughed as he pushed open the front door and together they entered the main room of the pub. She was all of her ages when she walked through that front door — from childhood to preteen to adolescence and beyond. Memories pulsed like electricity.

Dark wood was blushed golden by low-slung lanterns casting their glow across the floors and tables. The back wall glistened with the starlight of glass barware and bottles lined on wooden shelves. Posters announcing bands and singers, some events past and some coming soon, shared space on the walls with signed photos of small-town celebrities. Strung across the back of the bar, pennant flags announced the countries from which they'd received visitors through the years. The flags flapped with the breeze when the bartenders were busy behind the lacquered bar.

Colleen looked at her brother. "The bar stools. They're new."

Leather bar stools were lined like the bottles on the shelves, ready for the customers that would come later in the day. Behind the bar, the shiny brass taps with their rounded heads were ready to dispense the requested brand of beer.

"Yep. It was one of the many things Dad did before I took over the finances. He found the stools on eBay and bought a load of them. Brand new. Leather with brass nailheads. He misunderstood the terms of sale

— thought the price for one of them was the price for the lot of them."

"Oh, God. Sounds like something I would do."

"Yes, but something you would do and remember doing."

Colleen walked to a stool and ran her hands over the smooth leather. "They sure fancy up the place."

"No one here likes fancy; they want things to stay the same. They want to feel that when they're here time doesn't pass."

Colleen nodded. "I get that." She glanced around the room. The pub was empty of patrons — it wasn't open yet, and only memories lingered in the corners, having their private life. "I need a beer," she said and walked behind the bar, grabbed a tall mug and expertly poured herself a Guinness, tipping the glass so that the white froth would rise to the top, evenly skimmed. It was a task that took both patience and skill — a true Guinness, her dad had taught her as a child, took exactly 119 seconds to pour from a tap.

"You still got it," her brother said.

"Whoa, miss, can I help you?" A tall guy in a baseball cap, muscles bulging like a fake costume under a too-tight T-shirt, entered from the back room and approached Colleen.

"Oh, Hank, this is Lena, my sister," Shane said with a laugh. "Don't tackle her." Shane looked at Colleen. "This is Hank, our bouncer, bartender, manager and all-around do-anything-I-need guy."

Hank gave a bow and salute. "Mighty fine to meet you. You're a legend around here." He pointed to the slow draw of the beer against her glass.

"A legend?" Colleen didn't look away from the glass until it was full and then she tilted it to allow the foam to settle. She hadn't tasted Guinness since the day she'd left — avoiding it as the memory spark it could be. She took a long sip and then instantly regretted every day she'd ordered anything else.

"Yes, indeed," Hank said. "A woman who could outbartend and outwit every man in the place."

"False," she said with a laugh, but enjoying the compliment. "It's just talk. I spilled more beer than I served."

"That, too," Hank said. "I heard that, too." And then came a holler from the back for someone to check on a delivery. "A pleasure," he said and was off.

Colleen then turned to see a woman

slouched at a corner booth, someone she hadn't noticed when they'd arrived. Only the woman's back was visible. Scattered over the round tabletop were notebooks, a calendar and stacks of paper. Her head was bent over the papers, the long stretch of her neck hidden beneath a cascade of blond hair. A thick dark Guinness sat untouched beside her, the white foam atop it not yet dented by the first and best sip.

Hallie.

A quiver of both anxiety and expectation ran underneath Colleen's ribs. She had no idea what to do or say — the ingrained habit of turning away, of slighting her sister, was rising. But she had to find a new way of being with her if they were going to help their dad.

Colleen came from behind the bar just as Hallie turned around. They stared at each other for a moment, a still point in the room. It was the first time their eyes had found each other since that moment in the church ten years ago. Colleen didn't budge, her mug of beer wavering in the air halfway between her lips and her elbow. Her sister looked older, but of course she would. Her eyes were puffy; she'd been crying. But still she was pretty in the way she'd always been: small mouth, small nose and round brown eyes just like their mother's. She wore glasses now — tortoiseshell.

Colleen walked the few steps toward her sister. "Hi, sis." Colleen spoke first and didn't break her gaze.

Hallie's brows drew together in a question. "Hello, Lena." Her greeting was tepid at best.

"How's it going?" Colleen exhaled the question.

"Huh?"

Colleen shrugged. "Okay, that was dumb. I just don't know what to say . . ." She didn't even try to fake a smile.

Hallie shook her head and motioned for them all to sit. "I have some stuff for us to go over for Dad's party."

"Already? Can't we take a second to . . ." Colleen didn't know what exactly they needed to take a second to do.

"Not really," Hallie said and glanced at their brother. "The party's only two weeks away. And on top of that we must figure out Dad's health care and his finances because any second now you'll bolt, and Shane and I will be left holding the bag."

"I'll bolt?" Colleen exhaled the words with a cough of disgust. "Are you kidding me? That's how you want to start this, when I'm here to help?" Hallie's comment was a preemptive strike and Colleen knew that — she was being told she'd ignored her sister for *far* too long.

Hallie waved away Colleen's retort. "There's a lot to do."

She was right — there was a lot to do. The table was littered with calendars and lists and pages highlighted with various colored markers. Hallie, the organized one; she always had been. Even her college degree was in hospitality management — event planning her specialty. One calendar was labeled "Family" and the other "Dad's Party." On one were slots for ballet and art camp and babysitters, and on the other were slots for caterer, band and guest list. Then there was the large blue folder labeled "Medical."

"Let's get started," Shane said. "Now that the happy reunion is over."

Neither sister laughed or addressed his, once again, terrible joke. He tried again. "As the Irish say, be sure to taste your words before you spit them out."

"Shane!"

"Shane!"

The sisters said his name in unison.

An awkward silence passed and Shane spoke up. "Okay, well, we can't let someone else make decisions for Dad. This is up to us. We have a lot to talk about, to unravel. And listen, this is going to be a *great* party. We haven't given a big bash in a long while. I think the last time the town saw something like this was when that movie from Hollywood filmed and opened here. We want to make it special. Aunt Rosie and Fred are coming in. Old friends of Dad's from Virginia. Probably half the town. I don't know how the hell we're going to keep it a secret, but there's a lot to do."

Colleen nodded. "We've got this. We're all here together. This is ours to figure out. This is *our* family."

Hallie set her glasses carefully on the table. "*Our* family? *Now* you want to call it yours?"

Colleen opened her mouth for a quick retort, but was silent. For years, Hallie had begged for reconciliation, and Colleen had ignored her, shunned her. Sure, in the privacy of Colleen's room or in the middle of a dark night, she'd thought of the terrible things she wanted to say to her sister, but she'd never uttered any of them. Now she felt those withheld words rising and she did her best to swallow them.

There was a reason she'd avoided even a single discussion with her sister: the way she felt at that moment, dislocated and free-falling. She couldn't bear it. This *exact* feeling was what she'd avoided for a full decade. "Don't do this." Colleen spoke in a whisper.

"Lena?" Shane said and placed his hand on her arm.

Colleen turned her head slowly to her brother. "Take me home to see Dad. I want to see him *now.* "

Hallie brushed her hand through her hair and began to gather her papers. "Of course you're going to run. That's all you've ever done."

"Are you kidding me?" Colleen stood and stepped back, emotions swamping her. "You didn't give me any choice. What, you wanted me to hang around to watch the never-ending betrayal?"

Hallie didn't answer, but she didn't back down either, staring at her sister.

"Hallie, you forced me to leave; you betrayed me; you broke my heart — and now you point the finger at me?" Colleen shook her head. "I'm here to help Dad, not fight with you."

"*I* forced you to leave?" Hallie's voice broke, a crack in the hard facade of anger. "I begged you to come back; to talk to me; to let me explain. I tried to . . . apologize. Do you realize this is the first time you've even said my name?"

Colleen leaned forward and placed her hands on the back of the chair. "Do you realize I had to leave behind everything and everyone I loved?" Colleen pushed at the chair, making a harsh scraping sound.

"You obviously have things you want to say to me." Hallie glanced away. "No matter how sorry I am, it won't matter to you so go ahead. Get it over with. I've waited a long, long time."

"I do, but not now."

"Yep, you'll leave now, saying you love us but never coming back, never meeting your nieces or seeing your family."

"I do love . . ." Colleen's words were choked; she was losing grip on her tightly held control.

"If you'd loved us, you wouldn't have run. You would have stayed, listened. Maybe you'd always wanted to leave."

"Hallie." Colleen felt dizzy. "That's not true. You . . . you betrayed me. You were the only person in all the world I believed would never, but you did." She held up her hand. For ten years she'd slammed her mouth shut against her emotions. "Not now." She began to walk away, slowly, carefully, as if she might trip on the very words that had spilled from her mouth.

Shane piped up. "Whoa. You're not going

75

anywhere, sis. It's time for me to tell you my idea," he said as Colleen made for the back door, her heart hammering.

"Can't wait to hear it," Colleen called over her shoulder, "as most of your ideas are good ol' trouble. But right now all I want is to go home."

"All right, but I can't leave right now." Shane dug out his car keys from his back pocket. "Here." He tossed them to her and she grabbed them in midair. And then he let out a noise that sounded like a grunt their old dog used to emit when he fell from the bed to the hardwood floor. "God help me get through this with the likes of you two."

CHAPTER SIX

Every act of memory is to some degree
an act of imagination.
Gerald M. Edelman and Guilio Tonini,
A Universe of Consciousness:
How Matter Becomes Imagination

Dad still lived in the family home and as
Colleen drove Shane's rattling Jeep toward
it she intuitively knew every bend in the
road. Long leaf pine, magnolia and live oak
lining the street reached up and over, forming a canopy. She passed a wooden stand
where peaches were piled in pyramids,
golden and ripe, as an engine revved in her
chest, mimicking the Jeep. She had no time
to stop. Something must be done.
Something.
Anything.
She pressed harder on the gas pedal and
the car lurched around the first corner. The
siren was annoying, but Colleen drove to

the right to allow the police car to pass. Instead the blaring lights flared in the rearview mirror and Colleen parked on the soft sand shoulder under a tree and dropped her forehead to the steering wheel. She did not need this.

The knock was quick on the driver's-side window and she rolled it down to stare into the face of a high school friend, Brad Young. "Oh, Brad!"

"Driver's license and insurance," he said so sternly that she laughed.

"Seriously?" she asked and tucked her hair behind her ear. Maybe he didn't recognize her.

He nodded, his blue hat bobbing. He straightened the billed cap and stared at her.

"Brad. It's Lena Donohue."

"I know, Ms. Donohue."

"Stop with the formality," she said, aiming for a flirty, fun grin. "I know I was going too fast; I was trying to get to my dad."

"You were going sixty in a thirty."

"Oh . . ." She cringed. "I'm sorry; I didn't realize. It's been a hell of a day, and I was rushing." She paused. "I just flew in and I think my driver's license is in my suitcase. I don't drive much in New York and . . ."

"I know where you live, Lena."

"So I guess you can take me to the

Watersend pokey. I was going thirty over, and I have no license with me. This is Shane's car and I have no idea where the insurance is." Colleen opened the driver's-side door and stepped out to stand next to Brad. She put her hands behind her back. "Get it over with."

He tried not to laugh but she saw the curl of his smile as he shook his head. Together they walked to the back of the Jeep and leaned against the bumper. Cars eased past, slowly, the occupants craning their necks to see what was happening. Perfect fodder for gossip at the Bible study group or book club, for the neighborhood lawn party or bridge club.

"How's your mama?" Colleen asked.

"She passed last year." He placed his hand on his chest and patted over his heart. "It was a tough good-bye."

Brad, a friend since second grade, had been a small kid who excelled at the violin, who'd kissed Hallie in truth or dare in seventh grade and beat Colleen at the archery contest at Summer Fun Day in the town square. And she hadn't known his mama had passed.

"I am so sorry. I never heard." She touched his blue-uniformed arm and squeezed.

"How could you know?" he asked. "You left a long time ago."

"I come home sometimes," she said. "And I wish someone would have told me."

He took off his dark sunglasses and gazed at her directly. "If you come home, no one knows about it."

"I scoot in and out."

"We sure do miss you around here."

"Thanks, Brad. But . . ." Colleen shifted her feet, dry dirt scattering like bugs, and she looked down the road, focused on anything but the reason she hadn't returned: cars passing, a buzzard swooping down toward prey she couldn't see, the sound of the palmetto leaves swaying against each other in the breeze in music like rain on a tin roof.

"I know. We all know. But still . . ."

"How's Cindy?" Colleen asked after his wife, a woman he'd met in college, a woman Colleen had never met. She wanted to change the subject, avoid references, however indirect, to Hallie.

"She's great. We have two kids now. Did you know that? Two boys."

"That's really sweet. I'm so glad."

"You know, you were always such a good friend. So much fun."

"I still am." She smiled but felt the edges

80

of it slide toward falseness. Was she still a good friend? Was she still fun? Some people might disagree.

A squawking noise emanated from a radio in his car and he nudged off the bumper. "Need to go."

"No ticket? No arrest?"

He laughed. "Slow down. Remember where you are now."

The flaring police lights came back on, the siren emitted a quick squeal and Brad drove away, leaving Colleen at the roadside. *Remember where you are.* But in his deep southern accent, which seemed to have become pronounced in her absence, he might just as well have said, *Remember* who *you are.*

Colleen leaned against the bumper of the Jeep, closed her eyes and raised her face to the naked South Carolina sun. She and Hallie had always believed that it was their sun, made for them, shining on them.

I know who I am, don't you worry, mister, she wanted to holler at Brad's fading tail-lights. *I'm a New Yorker. A travel writer, and a damn good one.*

After a dismal job hunt spent traipsing up and down the streets of New York that first spring, from one interview to another, the spent cherry blossoms dusting the sidewalks like pink snow, Colleen had refused to give up and go home. She'd been relentless, undeterred, returning again and again to those who'd told her no, as if the intimate rejection of her sister and Walter had padded and softened other rejections, rendering them inconsequential in comparison. Eventually, she'd landed her first job, writing for the *Daily News* about local getaways for New Yorkers. She'd sold her engagement ring at a pawn shop and got by on small jobs until, one by one, in what felt like agonizingly slow succession, she'd been hired for better jobs, and bigger publications, able to leave Maggie's basement.

In the decade since then she'd compiled a record of every locale she'd visited and every article she'd written. For a long while she'd collected bumper stickers, not to put on a car, but as a reminder of where she'd been. Now she carried in her mind a watercolor montage of travel. She couldn't tell someone if she'd gone to Poland before or after London, but she could describe the emotional impression of each city, each landscape imprinted in her personal geography.

If she wanted the longitude and latitude, the name and coordinates, of every place she'd been, she could dig through piles of papers and notes and final published articles. But what she actually remembered was visceral and palpable. The window of her hotel room in Zermatt had framed the Matterhorn as it thrust from the earth in a pinnacle of glory, its snowy crown white and glistening. At a Navajo dance around a campfire in Arizona the flames had seemed to lick the stars, wanting to eat them alive. At the observatory at Mauna Kea in Hawaii the earth had faded away, overtaken by the sky with its multitude of stars and bringing to life the ancient belief that gods were hidden within the constellations.

What she'd wanted from those travels was to *become* someone else altogether, not to crawl out of her body but to claw her way out of the memories that threatened to define her. Somehow she believed that if she constructed a rich, full present and an even more exciting future, she could bury the past.

But it hadn't worked that way.

No excursion or new setting had soothed her heartache; no first-class flight or five-star hotel had defined what "home" meant to her. Her job had blessed her with adventure and purpose, but it had never done what she'd intended — sew up the torn places where her family's absence was felt.

Without her express permission, her heart continued to seek what she'd lost, what she couldn't stop loving.

Her family didn't know this side of her — the professional, voyage-trekking woman who'd experienced people and places they'd be hard-pressed to imagine. But didn't they still know her better than anyone else? Who cared what her eyes had seen or her body had sensed if those experiences had no connection to what really mattered?

One place she'd never been; one job she'd never been assigned from any magazine — Ireland. And always her dad asked, "Ireland yet?" And she would tell him, "No, Dad, the next one is Argentina." Or it could have been California or Idaho or Maine. They weren't *always* exotic locales, but they were continuously fascinating.

Colleen stepped into her brother's Jeep and drove another few miles before pulling into the family home, up the long pebble driveway with the overgrown azaleas crowding the edges. She hadn't seen them in bloom in years. If pressed, she couldn't remember the colors of the blossoms.

The front of the one-story white brick house faced the street and stretched out sunbathing on the wide green lawn where ancient oak trees spread their limbs like a crocheted blanket across the sky. Spanish moss hung from those trees, catching and holding on to the summer light, hoarding it for the coming fall.

The driveway curved from the road to one side of the house between the house and detached garage. In that space, Colleen parked the Jeep and stared directly into the backyard, where the sloping green lawn rushed toward the river. A dilapidated tree fort clung to the largest oak with the last of its rusted nails. The back of the house possessed a small screened-in porch on the left side and to the right a set of three stairs and small concrete porch covered by a striped blue awning where a screen door opened to the kitchen.

Colleen absorbed all of this in the time it took to blink twice, and then it was the tree house her gaze sought by instinct. Nestled between the branches of an old oak, the tree house was tilted, half-drunk. The roof had long ago collapsed. Dad had once mentioned fixing it up, bringing it back for the nieces, but nothing had happened except that the tree reached higher, and the house inside of it had warped with the growth. Colleen turned away, feeling the swish-wash of sorrow for all that was lost. Then her gaze found the dock of her memories and dreams, hovering over the pewter water.

She found herself at the end of the dock before she knew she'd decided to walk that way, sitting with bare feet dangling and her red high-tops by her side. A midday shower threatened in the gray clouds that blurred the horizon like a flock of black birds. The water crested and fell to the rhythm of an outgoing tide. It was all so familiar, so achingly familiar. Would it always be this way for her dad or would even this place become strange, just another dock, another river, another tide? Things were special in their specificity to the soul, this much she knew.

This was where her childhood had taken place, where her dad had taught her to throw the shrimp net and fish with live bait. This was where she'd experienced her first kiss, where her mother had told stories of mermaids and sea creatures that Colleen believed in longer than she believed in Santa Claus. This was where Walter had proposed . . .

With a jolt, she stood and wrapped her arms around her belly for protection, as if the memory could punch her.

Walter stood at the far end of the dock, his hair awash in twilight and a big smile on his

86

face. Colleen walked toward him, wondering how she'd been so lucky as to love a man like him. Sure, she'd had her fair share of good-looking and wonderfully goofy boys in high school and college, also experiencing heartbreak and angst that echoed a Taylor Swift song, but Walter was in a category all his own: both funny and sincere, both manly and sensitive. They'd met at a fundraiser for a museum in Savannah and had barely left each other's side during the six months they'd been dating; an invisible cord connected them.

She'd heard about love at first sight, of course. She'd read about it. But she hadn't believed in it until Walter. They didn't fight. They didn't disagree on anything that caused more than a moment's pause — he didn't like avocados and she put them on everything; she despised salmon and he knew twenty-five ways to cook it. But even those small things had made them laugh. "Let's eat avocado and salmon every night to prove our love," he'd once said.

That evening as she walked toward him on the dock, Colleen felt her heart quicken. Something was different — his shoulders set back and a determined smile on his face as if he were posing for a photograph. When she reached him, he took her in his arms.

"This is your favorite place in the world, right?" he said.

Look how well he already knew her.

"Yes," she said and kissed him. "Here, and the pub."

Then he dropped to one knee as if she'd written a childhood play about a romantic proposal, and he'd read it. "You are the woman for me, Lena Donohue. I love you, and you alone. I never dreamed I'd meet someone like you. All the days I have, I want to spend them with you. Will you please spend the rest of your life with me?" Then he handed her a perfectly gorgeous aquamarine ring, square cut with tiny diamonds surrounding it because somewhere along the way she had casually mentioned that she didn't want a big diamond and adored aquamarines.

"We will stay here in this magical land, create our own little family. You won't have to leave your river, and I will never leave you."

Colleen dropped to her knees also. They would always be a team, just like her mother and dad: equals. And it would begin with her in front of him, not looking down at him. The sun set just as she said yes. He'd timed it perfectly. And somewhere in the yard, Mother took the photo that Walter had asked her to snap at just the right moment.

It was a photo Colleen had had printed the next day and placed in a silver frame to set on her bedside table. On the wedding day, after she'd returned to the house to grab the suitcase she'd packed for their honeymoon to Napa Valley, she'd thrown that picture into the river.

CHAPTER SEVEN

Memory, once waked, will play the tyrant.
C. S. Lewis, *Till We Have Faces*

"Lena." Her dad's voice called out and Colleen turned to smile as he headed toward her. He appeared as he always had — robust and on fire, his cheeks ruddy and his grin wide, his clothes loose and his steps longer than his short legs gave the impression they could be.

He looks the same. That was Colleen's first thought. There wasn't anything different about him. Shane was wrong and he'd tricked her into coming there with some cockamamie story about Dad's mind fading.

Short and round, the shape of him. His thick hair had thinned hardly at all, still dark and wavy, though now infused with silver. He ran his hands through it and reached Colleen in a few steps. His green eyes — so green they almost seemed painted on, gazed at her. He threw his arms around her and held her fast. He was only a few inches taller than Colleen, and her face rested on his shoulder. "What are you doing here, my Lena?"

"You didn't know?" she asked. "Shane didn't tell you I was coming for a few weeks?" She stepped back, holding his hands.

"Yes! Yes." Dad nodded and hugged her again. "I've been working on the garden and just totally forgot. Now don't you go thinking that one little forgetting means that quack of a doctor was right. Of course I remembered you were coming. I've been counting the days."

"I only decided yesterday."

"Then I counted one day." He squeezed her hand. "You're staying here, right? Not some hotel like last Christmas?"

That was a good sign. He remembered that at Christmas she'd stayed in the creaky old bed-and-breakfast — Auntie Mae's — on Main Street. The one with mildew in the shower and the snoring man in the next room and the breakfast of packaged biscuits only partially warmed. She'd stayed there, and tolerated it, because Hallie and Walter and their adorable girls had decided it was the Christmas to let Santa visit Grandy's house. They'd coordinated their visits so that Colleen didn't go to the house until they'd left for their own home for a rest and naps. Colleen had carefully stepped over the children's new dolls and toys and tutus they'd left for their return that night, and enjoyed the afternoon with her brother and dad.

"Nope, no hotel for me, Dad. I'm staying here."

How could he look so normal while plaque grew over his brain neurons? She had the impulse to shake his head, loosen the tangles. How could they be standing on the back lawn with the river flowing by and the sun moving toward the horizon and far off a seagull crying out while something interrupted the connections in Gavin Donohue's brain?

"Dad." Colleen touched his cheek. "We're going to find a way to stop this."

"Stop what?" He looked out to the river as if something were arriving that he could not see — a storm or a ship.

"Whatever is happening, we won't let it. And I'm so happy to be here, but I'm also starving." She smiled at him. "Airplane peanuts didn't quite do the trick." She thought of her beer, sitting at the pub, with only a sip taken from it.

"Well, my little lark, then we must go to the grocery because the cupboard is bare. I was going to eat at the pub myself."

"Let's go inside and see if there's anything I can rustle up." She wanted him to herself for a little while even if she hadn't rustled up anything in longer than she could remember. She wanted to assess the situation without Shane or Hallie standing by with their mournful expressions, with their know-it-all facts about a relentless disease. She looped her arm through her dad's and kissed his round cheek.

"You can surely try." He fell into step beside her.

Halfway to the house, their feet denting the soft summer grass and the world quiet, he faced his daughter. "I know you came here because Shane and Hallie guilted you into coming, what with my diagnosis. But you don't have to be here if you don't want to be. They're wrong about it all. I just have a head too full of too much and sometimes I forget things."

"I *want* to be here, Dad."

"No." He shook his head. "You don't. I know that. You haven't wanted to be here since that terrible day. I understand. I wish it was different." He paused and stared at the dome of sky. The thunderheads that had been building at the horizon had arrived and were starting to sprinkle warm raindrops. Then he gazed back to her, his eyes soft. "I've wished for you to return, but not this way. Not because something *might* be wrong with me. I want you here of your own desire."

"Dad." She took his face in her hands and kissed his forehead. "I am here because I want to see you. If the doctors are wrong, or the doctors are right, we'll find out. But I'm here for *you!*" She tugged at him. "Let's get out of the rain."

As they entered the house, the warmth of her childhood home embraced her. A fragrance, one she'd never been able to label, sifted around her. Toast with butter, she'd once told Hallie. No, Hallie had said, clean laundry. Salt water. Soil. Whatever it was, the elements combined into an aroma both primal and Donohue.

A loud clap of thunder, a shuddering of the world outside, and both Colleen and her dad jumped at the sound. Fat raindrops fell onto the wide windows and ran down to dimple the view outside. "We just made it." Her dad pressed his hand against the window. "This house has always protected us."

Colleen stood next to him. "Dad, it's a

great house. And a great home."

His gaze fell to hers. "It is, isn't it?"

"Yes. I should come more often. I love it here. The way the doors creak and the metal roof sings in the rain. I love the way the record player still roosts in the kitchen with a pile of LPs. I love the way the attic fan whirs me to sleep. I love . . ."

Her dad smiled, but sadly, as if his mouth wanted to both grin and frown. "You must miss it. I think of that often. How very much you must miss it. If I'd have left — if I'd ever left this world we built from scratch, I think a part of me would have died."

"But, Dad, you didn't grow up here. You set off and built your own life. You came here — you and Mother — and started your lives. Bought the pub. Had a family. It didn't kill you to move from Richmond. It won't kill me to build a new life also."

"I had to leave, Colleen. You didn't."

"You *had* to?" Her mind raced in tangles of its own, reaching for something new it didn't yet understand, something unfamiliar.

"As the Irish say, if there is a way into the wood, there is a way out."

"Dad." She said his name on an exhale. "Will you ever stop saying that? Saying, 'As the Irish say.' "

"I hope not."

And the hope, so simply stated, was suddenly as important as any wish uttered in that small piney kitchen with the electric stove and the white-painted cabinets and the childhood initials etched with a pocketknife into the wooden table, initials that had earned each of them a time-out in their rooms.

Colleen tamped down the sadness that could quickly turn to grief and opened the old refrigerator — a white Kenmore with magnets of every variety stuck to its door. The anthropology of the family could be charted in those magnets: inspirational quotes from her mother's collection; Irish shamrocks and leprechauns; names and phone numbers of house services. Then there were the faded photos of their childhood faces in class pictures and on outdoor excursions. Brighter photos of Rose and Sadie. Attached behind the magnets were notices, notes and invitations to parties and weddings that had long since passed. "Dad," she said, "we could probably take some of these down."

"They keep me company," he said with a grin. "I like to see all those names and pictures up there."

"That's sweet." She peered inside, hoping

to find enough to assemble a small lunch, and instead found a refrigerator fully stocked. "Dad!" She turned to him. "You said there wasn't any food."

"I did?" He glanced inside.

"Yes, you did."

"Well, looks like Ms. Boone has been here."

"Ms. Boone?" Colleen grabbed a white butcher's-paper package marked "Turkey" and a bag of sliced Swiss cheese. Mustard. Mayonnaise. Lettuce. Tomato. She placed them all on the dark green linoleum counter that hadn't been changed since the day her parents had moved in.

"You know, the housekeeper," he said and went to the cupboard to pull down a loaf of white bread and hand it to Colleen.

"I don't think I've met her. Is she new?"

He was quiet for a moment, staring at the rain streaking down the windowpane. "I think so." Then he turned to Colleen and fear passed over his face. "I bought the groceries yesterday. Or was it the day before? With Shane. In anticipation of your arrival. I totally forgot. Ms. Boone has been gone for a while now."

A nervous thrumming filled Colleen's chest. He'd forgotten, but then he'd remembered that he forgot. "You have all my favorite things. Thanks, Dad."

She busied herself. Toast the bread. Spread a thin line of Duke's mayonnaise and a thin one of mustard. Lick the mustard off her fingers. Wipe the tomato juice from the counter. Add a tomato slice. Then his voice asked, "Do you have a man in your life?" He took a seat at the kitchen table. "Anyone you love?"

"No." Colleen set the sandwiches on her mother's flowered thin-china plates. If you are going to have fancy plates, you must use them, Mother used to say.

"I worry about you, little lark." Her dad placed a napkin on his lap. "I want you to love someone. To *really* love."

"I have loads of love, Dad. I love you. I love Shane. I love life and my job and adventure . . . I have friends in New York, and I love them, too."

"And you love your sister." He leaned forward and placed both hands on the table. "I know you do."

"Oh, Dad."

He took his sandwich in both hands and held it, but spoke before taking the first bite. "Love isn't to be parsed out, Lena. It is to be spread wide. When a heart is damaged, it only hurts more to shut it down."

"What Hallie did was more than damage

98

— it was betrayal."

"I know about betrayal." Then he dropped his sandwich onto the plate and stood. "And I know about forgiveness. Wait here."

"What?" Colleen stood.

"Hold on," he called from the living room and moments later appeared with a framed photo in his hands. "This" — he handed it to her — "is more important than any man. No matter who was engaged to him first. No matter anything at all."

Colleen took the wooden frame, upside down in his hands, and turned it right side up. There they were: Colleen and Hallie at six and seven years old. They'd never been the kind of sisters that others said looked alike — in fact, they were opposites in many ways. Colleen with her dirty blond, unruly curly hair. Hallie with her white blond hair that was so straight it might have been ironed every morning by their mother, just like her dad's shirts. Colleen with the heart-shaped chin and Hallie's squared off with dimples. Hallie with brown eyes, and Colleen's like their dad's — green and deep set and almond shaped. In this photo, they were facing the camera laughing with their mouths open and their heads thrown back. A burst of sunlight behind them, a setting sun, was caught in the camera lens.

"Christmas Eve," Colleen said.

"I think so. Your mother knew where and when every photo was taken. I only know that it shows love. A lot of it. And you can find it again. I believe that."

"Dad." Colleen exhaled and placed the frame on the kitchen table. "I remember. I can even tell you what we were doing that night — putting food out for the reindeer on the dock, leaving cookies, too. We laughed because you told us that Santa would be using leprechauns that year to deliver the presents. I remember it all, Dad. But it doesn't change what happened *after*."

"Yes, it does. Every memory changes what happens now and later." His sandwich was long forgotten. "If it's true what the doctors say, if it's true that I will lose my memories to some plaque in my brain, I know this — memories influence everything. And what am I without them? I have no idea. But yours — your memories, my little lark, use the good ones."

"Dad."

He set his hand on her arm. "Just forgive. And state that forgiveness."

"You seem to always be blaming me for leaving. What about blaming her for what she did? Can't you see my side? Don't you ever get mad at *her*?" Colleen closed her eyes, tried to center her emotions to right.

"Of course I did. I struggled with it; I used harsh words I wished I could take back. Hallie had to also forgive me for the things I said to her and Walter, the blame I cast on them."

Colleen held up her hand. "I don't want to hear about it. I'm sorry I brought it up." She turned away. In a small way she'd been able to pretend Hallie and Walter didn't exist as part of the family she left. Yes, she knew it was the truest form of denial, but we all do what we can to survive.

Dad continued over her thoughts. "But what use is that blame to carry around? What use is that?"

"I don't carry it around . . . I don't think. But it hurts to see her, Dad. Can't you understand that? It hurts to even see her with him."

"I know your pain. I do. The loss of someone you love can tear a hole in the soul. But can you not imagine that Hallie must hurt also? She lost *you.*"

"She chose to lose me. She made her choice. There might not ever be a way to reconcile. Some things are just too far gone . . ."

"Just try."

CHAPTER EIGHT

I don't know how much longer
I have to know you.
                    Lisa Genova, *Still Alice*

It wasn't Dad's fault that he was able to choose the good parts and overcome the bad ones. He didn't sit in Colleen's heart and mind to witness the hell parts. Hallie had been Colleen's best friend. They were only eighteen months apart in age. Almost Irish twins, their dad had always said, and yet not once had their mother laughed at this joke. Whenever he said it, her laughing mouth went into a line as straight as a stick, and she walked away or changed the subject. She didn't much like talking about private things, and how often and when they might or might not have had sex to produce two children so close together was embarrassing to the prim Elizabeth.

A few times she'd seen Dad embrace her

to assuage the comment. "I love you, Betty," he'd say and with his finger under her chin, he'd tip her face up for a kiss.

He was the only one who was allowed to call her Betty. He was the only one given access to her private thoughts. But that was okay with Colleen and Hallie because they had each other, and then soon, a little brother to pass around and dress and feed until they grew bored of him and their mother gladly folded him into her arms.

They absorbed their dad's proclamation seriously — they were twins of a certain sort. It confused them later when Colleen went off to kindergarten and Hallie had to stay home and play alone with Shane. Colleen remembered, even now at thirty-five years old, the desolate feeling of being in school without her sister. She felt half-finished, as if she'd forgotten her arm at home. When it was time to open her Clifford the Big Red Dog lunch box on the first day, she burst into tears. The teacher, the lovely Ms. Hannity, thought her homesick, but she was merely Hallie-sick. Hallie had put a daisy in her little snack baggie. It was the first time ever that she'd eaten lunch without her sister. Who would eat the pickles off her sandwich?

That very afternoon they'd plotted that

either Colleen must act dumb and be held back a grade or Hallie must be *very* smart and advance a grade. Neither ever happened, but their plan had given them hope after that first afternoon spent separate from each other.

The next morning, in her brother's apartment above the Lark, Colleen sorted through a pile of photos on the kitchen table. The pictures afforded an odd variety of time travel back through Gavin Donohue's life. Some were black-and-white, some color, some torn and faded and others obviously newly printed. Colleen sifted through them and felt a tremor below her chest: her dad's life in photos.

Shane sat across from her, sipping a cup of coffee. It was ten a.m. and he'd just stumbled from bed, his hair matted on the left side and sheet marks on his cheek.

"Rough night?" she asked him.

"No, just late. There was a tiebreaker in the dart competition and old Mr. Ballew would not forfeit the title without great agony. How was your night after you left the pub?"

After spending the afternoon with her father, she'd driven him to the Lark, where she'd spent the early evening.

"It was great to see so many people — who doesn't want to run into their prom date and their second grade teacher in a bar?" She grinned. "I got a bit overwhelmed and went back to Dad's."

"Overwhelmed?"

She shrugged. "All the times I've come home over the years, I haven't really hung out here. I like the Lark when it's empty — just us, you know? None of my best friends — like Margy, Sara and Kerry — even live here anymore. I haven't talked to or contacted anyone in ten years." Colleen shook her head. "Ten years. My God, how did that go so fast?" She paused and stared at her brother as if he had the answer to the dilemma of time. "Anyway, I just wanted to go home and sit on the dock and catch up on work e-mails and edits until Bob brought Dad home."

"Do you talk to those girls at all? Your bridesmaids?"

Colleen shook her head. "At first it was too embarrassing. They called and texted and Kerry even tried to visit me in New York, but I guess people can only be shunned for so long. I thought about trying to get us all together last year, but then realized that they hadn't called in years and might not want to hear from me at this

105

point." Colleen pressed at her temples and felt the weird lightheadedness that signaled embarrassment, a warning sign that she had inched too close to the past. "Let's stop talking about this." She tried to smile at her brother but felt the tremble in her lips. Leaning toward the table of photos, she asked, "So, what's all this for?"

"When Hallie gets here, I'll explain."

Colleen yawned, covering her mouth and slumping into a chair. She'd slept the night in her childhood bedroom, if sleeping was what it could be called. She'd tossed and turned on the sagging mattress and when she had faded away, it had been to fragmented images of the life she'd left behind.

"Lena?"

"Yes?"

"Are you okay?"

She nodded. "I think so. What time is Hallie coming?"

"About fifteen minutes," Shane said and walked to the coffeepot to pour another mugful. "I know you've asked me to never discuss this with you, to allow our relationship to remain separate, but I have to say something."

"Of course you do."

"You have to mend this with her. It's been ten years. They have a beautiful life and a great marriage and two girls — your nieces, by the way, who you will adore if you give them even a second of your time. You can't pretend they don't exist."

"Did you and Dad plot ahead of time to gang up on me? And did you *both* conveniently forget about her part in this?"

"We didn't forget. We don't forget. We've been here for a decade without you. We've had the long nights of regret and misery with Hallie." He rolled his head around his shoulders, loosening the tension. "She knows how we feel — the way we all are now didn't come easy. There were years of tension and heartache. But forgiveness and family won out."

"Forgiveness." Colleen felt the sweat on her palms, the uneasiness in her chest. "Why does that word make me feel like I want to crawl out of my skin, Shane? Why does it make me feel like I am falling into the dark place where I'm sleeping in a friend's basement and drinking vodka like water? It's just a word."

"Maybe because you can't separate forgiveness from forgetting. Listen, sis, I'm not saying you have to be best friends with her again. I'm not saying you have to trust her. But we're here for Dad, and a little grace and kindness might ease the tension for everyone. Being angry and rude doesn't change a damn thing that happened ten years ago."

"I hear you." Colleen settled back into the seat, feeling something akin to relief, something like exhaling or falling asleep after a long day. She didn't need to be best friends with Hallie again. She didn't need to trust her. She just needed to release the fist of anger in her gut, the defensive way her heart added another stone to the wall around her heart at the mere mention of Hallie's name. "I will try," she said. "For Dad."

Shane raised his mug in a toast to her. "Okay, I'm going to jump in the shower. If Hallie gets here before I'm out, be nice." He winked at her before shutting the bathroom door.

When Colleen had awoken that morning, listening to the sounds of her dad in the kitchen preparing his one poached egg and two pieces of bacon, she'd promised herself she would not react to Hallie, not get caught up in the maelstrom of the past. But promising and doing were, of course, not the same damn thing. Then she'd entered the family kitchen to greet her dad, sit with him while he ate and waited for the sheriff, Bob Macken, to come pick him up to go fishing. Shane had worked out a complicated but crafty system of friends who stopped by every day to check on Gavin, eat lunch with him or take him out until it was time to go to the pub.

As the waterfall sound of the shower came muffled through the bathroom door, Colleen poked around her brother's apartment. This had once been a room for rent — a cheap bed and bath with a storage room attached. But Shane had fashioned the space into a home. He'd salvaged old hardwood floors from a demolished bank — thick pine with knots as wide as fists. The kitchen cabinets, which he'd found in a dumpster, had been pulled from a remodeled house. She remembered the Christmas when he was covered in sawdust from stripping the paint to expose the beautiful pine underneath.

The place was small — an L-shaped kitchen and an oval wooden breakfast table open to a square area with one large denim-slipcovered couch, a pine trunk as a coffee table and two easy chairs. A TV hung on the far wall between two windows whose glass panes were divided by white-painted mullions.

On the east-facing side wall an old stained glass panel, left from when the pub was called McNally's, hung from a chain over another window. Sunlight slanted through the McNally family crest, creating puddles of red and green and yellow on Shane's hardwood floors and up the far wall.

She wandered back to the kitchen table and sat to leaf through the photos. From a glassine envelope she took out two images: Dad as a child standing with an unknown man in a military uniform; then Dad as a young man in a dark suit, sitting on a stone wall alone. Behind was a field of green and undulating hills — his time in Ireland after college, she surmised. Why had Shane gathered all of these photos? For a collage to be displayed at the party?

Shane emerged from the bathroom wearing worn khakis and a white T-shirt, his wet hair making dark marks on each shoulder. "You approve of the new place?" he asked and spread his hands wide.

"You've done an amazing job with this apartment, little brother."

"I'm not done yet," he said. "I plan on replacing the oven as soon as I can. I found a vintage black Viking on eBay."

"How do the ladies in town like it?" Colleen asked.

"Don't let them up here much," Shane said. "You know how it is. Married to the pub, as they say."

"Love just mucks you up anyway."

"So cynical you are now." He shook his wet hair so droplets splashed her face and T-shirt.

She reached to lightly smack his arm, but he dodged her just as he'd learned to do through the years. "I'm not cynical at all. Just a bit more realistic than the girl who left here."

"Does that help, Lena?" Shane grew serious, his smile lost and his hands grasping the edges of the chair.

"Huh?" Colleen knew what he meant, but hoped she could change the subject.

"Does all your travel help to keep you from becoming mucked up with love?"

"I love my job. I don't know that it helps in that way, but I adore discovering new places and absorbing all I can about them, then trying to put my experiences into a story for the people who won't ever get to travel there. I've been to places that make this world seem small."

"This world?" He held out his hands to hold Watersend in his palms.

She laughed. "No! I mean the entire world. When you travel, it seems smaller, all of us connected by water and land. That's all." She paused. "No place is small. Not this town, not any place I've visited. They're all connected, and all unique and all the same. No matter where I go, people want to talk about love, relationships, how special their home is. We aren't so different, really."

"I know traveling can be fascinating, but I just wondered if going all over the world keeps you from missing us, from missing Watersend."

Colleen weighed the question. "Yes, it does help," she said just as the click-snap of the front doorknob caused them to turn together.

The door opened and there stood Hallie. She hadn't knocked, was obviously accustomed to coming and going in Shane's apartment. And that quickly, Colleen felt left out. Even if it was her choice to disappear, she felt as though they'd been sneaking around behind her back. She found her hand placed protectively across her stomach, and she had a sudden need to be alone, very alone.

"Good morning," Hallie said cheerily, apple cheeked and forced-friendly with cups of Revelator coffee in a cardboard carrier, lifting it high. "You know I hate your coffee, Shane." She smiled at him and he smiled in return and Colleen watched their easy way.

"You hate anyone's coffee but theirs," Shane said.

Hallie headed their way with a fake smile. "I'm so excited about the new things I've added to the party. We're doing sparklers and poppers when he walks in. There will be party favors to take home — small bottles of whiskey! Jameson's agreed to donate. And the fiddle band canceled a big gig to be with us."

"Whoa!" Shane laughed and held up his hands. "Great ideas, Ms. Bubbly. But don't bring that coffee to Colleen when she's near the photos."

"*You* have coffee near them." Colleen pouted and pointed at his mug on the breakfast table.

"I'm not *you,*" he said with a grin, and Hallie laughed with him as she handed Colleen and Shane the extra coffees.

"Not funny," Colleen said, but the edges of her mouth turned up before she took a sip of the scalding drink. Some things didn't change — yes, she spilled and tripped and broke things. "Thanks for this," she said and lifted her cup to Hallie. Was it a peace offering? Probably not. It was best not to read into anyone's motivations; it was best to stick on a smile and get through the tasks at hand.

"So what's *your* great idea?" Hallie dropped her satchel on the floor, not making eye contact with Colleen and asking Shane.

Colleen looked at her brother. "Those four words of yours — 'I have an idea' — have gotten me into more hot water than anything in my life."

"I know. But this time for the good." Shane straightened and smiled. "We're going to save his memories. We will be his memory keepers."

"Do you know of a treatment? Something new? I know there's loads of research and . . ." Hallie's voice rose in a tone Colleen recognized as hopeful. For as little as she knew about her sister now, who she was and how she lived, it was odd to know the tone of Hallie's voice as clearly and accurately as if she'd typed up her feelings and handed them to Colleen to read.

Shane shook his head. "Nothing like that. We can hope and we won't give up, but this idea has to do with his party in two weeks. After meeting with the doctor and reading about this horrific disease I know this much: it steals your memories."

"Yes," Hallie said. "Steals. It's like a thief. A horrible, evil thief." She removed her glasses and set them on top of the photos to press her fingers gently into the corners of her eyes.

"So we're going to save them for him." Shane clapped his hands together like a coach about to describe a winning play. "I've spent weeks going through the piles and boxed photos in the attic. Mother was halfway through organizing them when she left us." Shane took in another breath. "So they're all in one place, but they're mixed up. Because Mother and Dad both grew up in Richmond, many of the photos overlap. I'm not sure which ones are his and which are hers. But I don't think it much matters."

"No," Colleen said. "I don't think it does. They were together since they were — what? Thirteen years old?" Colleen ran her fingers over the pile of photos. "How did you choose these from all the boxes and envelopes in the attic? This is a labor of love." She looked at him. "You're a good son."

He shrugged. "He's a better dad."

"Yes," she agreed. "He is."

Colleen sorted through the images that had been so carefully dated and organized while Hallie watched her, not touching any of them but gripping her coffee cup with both hands. A small clip had been attached to each photo with a scrap of paper that told the name of the other person in the photo and the date.

Shane spoke up. "So what I did was choose the ones with him in the picture."

"But if a memory is gone," Hallie said, "how will a photo help? If it's gone it's gone."

Colleen chose a labeled photo: Aunt Rosalind, 1979. "How did you know all the dates and names?"

"Sometimes I would casually ask Dad, but Mother mostly had them in boxes by year and I just figured out the rest myself. If I didn't know the information" — Shane lifted the glassine envelope from the table — "I didn't include it. I've chosen twenty photos for the book, and that's where we come in." Shane said this with a huge smile, the lopsided one that convinced all the girls to believe anything he said.

"*We* come in?" Colleen asked.

"You two are going to work together." He paused for the full effect, but neither sister reacted. "You're going to choose a labeled photo and then interview the other person in that photo. Of course there are a few you can't do that with — like our grandparents who are gone — but mostly you can. You can visit or Skype or just call, but you will show or describe the photo to the other person and ask them to tell you a story about the day depicted in the photo."

"Brilliant," Hallie said.

"I've had a thick leather scrapbook made. Each photo will take a page and the story will go next to the photo. Dad can read the story, see the photo, and even if his memory is gone, it will be recaptured for that moment, for that reading." Shane's voice cracked unevenly and he bent his chin toward his chest, rubbed the back of his neck, avoiding eye contact.

"Shane," Colleen said quietly, "this is the most beautiful gift. I'll do anything I can to help."

He nodded. "You're the writer, Lena. You can create each story to say what it needs to say. I want to gather some small part of his life this way. To *keep* his life this way. Even as he loses most of his days, I want to give *some* of them back to him. And you, Hallie, you're the organizer. You can help Lena while you're planning the party, as well as write out the timeline that will go in the front of the book."

Colleen ignored the use of "Lena" — it wasn't worth the fight and this was about Dad. Completely about Dad.

Hallie placed her coffee cup on the table and clapped her hands together, folded them into a prayer pose and placed them under her chin, propping it up. This old

117

gesture, one of sincerity on Hallie's part, caught Colleen's breath. How many times had she seen Hallie do this as a child? A million or more, most likely. She could blame the sting of the hot coffee on her tongue and back of her throat, but the sudden urge to cry had nothing to do with the coffee at all.

"Ah," Hallie said. "That's why you asked me to start putting together a timeline of Dad's life."

"Yep, he'll be able to see his life as a journey, each major event marked on the timeline. You're so damn good at those things."

Hallie nodded. "Got it."

"This is a ticking clock," Shane said. "If we want to create a decent memory book, we're going to have to ask him questions even as his answers are slowly disappearing."

"What do you mean?" Colleen asked, clearing her throat and her mind of sticky memories clinging to both.

"I'm told that Alzheimer's is characterized by what is called retrograde amnesia. It takes the memories cluster by cluster, going backward, erasing the most recent memories first . . ." Shane's voice caught on the last word.

"Oh, God." Colleen sat hard on the chair. "Can't something stop it?"

"No. Not that they know yet." Hallie shifted her gaze to the photos on the table. "I don't mean to sound know-it-all, but we've lived with this a bit longer than you, and it's just that we know there's nothing that breaks the cycle."

Anger flared, a little piece of kindling always ready to be lit right beneath Colleen's ribs. The words, so quick they came to her tongue, but she swallowed them, almost choking on their bitterness. What she'd wanted to say had something to do with why they'd lived with it a bit longer, and how Hallie had lived with Walter and then a nice list of curse words. But instead Colleen saw her dad's pleading eyes asking for Colleen to forgive, and instead of speaking, Colleen stared at the photos.

"Now let's get to work." Shane sifted the photos under his hand.

"But we'll do other things, too, right?" Colleen asked. "Maybe that doctor will have some answers."

"What doctor?" Hallie asked, looking only at Shane, her hands gripped in small fists on top of the table.

"The one at MD Anderson; I asked Colleen to take him."

"I'm going, too." Hallie opened her fists and set both palms on the table, lifted her eyebrows in the same way their mother had done when she was adamant, when what she said was "the end of the discussion."

Colleen couldn't stifle her laugh; the siblings turned to her. "Sorry." She shrugged. "I just can't believe how much you looked like Mother right then — with the lifted brow and the earnest proclamation."

Hallie stared at Colleen for a moment and in that space — that gap between what was said and what would be said — Colleen held her breath.

"I know." Hallie almost smiled. "Sometimes I can't believe the things that come out of my mouth when I'm with the girls; it's like Mother snuck inside me."

Colleen exhaled. "Yes."

Shane leaned forward. "Then it's set — you two take him to the doctor; start the interviews; plan the party. I'll keep things running here."

"Because we don't have any other life?" Hallie asked with a smirk.

"Not right now you don't." Shane stood up. "This, right here, our family, is your life."

"Well, then, as a family we have one

problem to figure out." Hallie held up her hand as if in surrender. "I thought I could figure it out alone, but I can't."

"What's that?" Shane asked.

"His timeline. I'm trying to get it right, but there are spots I don't understand unless I ask him, and that will give it away."

"Well, sis, you have exactly thirteen days to figure it out." Shane tapped on her bag overflowing with papers and notes. "Somewhere in there is the answer."

Hallie shook her head. "Something is missing."

"I think the photos will help," he said.

Hallie's gaze fluttered between her sister and brother. "All right, but I'm afraid it's already too late — that he won't be able to tell us the truth."

Shane lifted a photo of Dad and Bob fishing. "I've discovered he's most lucid in the familiar places — so maybe you can talk to him at home or in the pub or out on the river." Shane then turned to reach into a high cabinet and bring out a leather-bound book that he plopped onto the table. "Here's the book," he said. "The clasp is a seashell I found in Dad's bedroom. I think it was Mother's."

"This is amazing," Hallie said in a voice full of wonder, the tone she'd have used when Colleen told her a story about the mermaids that might live in the river behind their house.

Colleen opened it. Thick creamy paper had been hand-sewn into the spine. On the first page was an image of Dad on the day of his birth, a black-and-white photo of a crumpled baby in a bassinet who looked more like a shrunken old man than a newborn. He was wrapped in a white blanket and only his little face with his squinted eyes and furrowed brow appeared. A blurry sign was posted on the end of the bassinet with BOY writ larger than his name. In neat calligraphy next to the photo read:

Gavin Aengus Donohue
April 16, 1956
Richmond, Virginia

"We are going to fill the rest of these pages," Shane said.

"His life full of love," Colleen said. She paused to find what she was trying to say as she looked at the photo that had already been pasted in, as the weight of the beautiful and terrible past, and the unknown future, swelled inside her. "Alzheimer's can't take away that — not the love."

CHAPTER NINE

The leaves of memory seemed to make
A mournful rustling in the dark.
Henry Wadsworth Longfellow,
"The Fire of Drift-Wood"

The siblings continued to sort through the photos until the glissandi of a harp brought Colleen's glance around to search for its source: Hallie's cell phone on the kitchen table; her ringtone with one word on the screen: *hubby*.

As Colleen's stomach lurched upward, she rose and hurried to the bathroom, which was still foggy and warm from Shane's shower. She slammed shut the door and inhaled the fragrance of soap and shaving cream, a memory aroma of her parents' bathroom, a comfort.

Damn. Damn. Damn.

The word "hubby" should have brought images of Walter, but oddly it hadn't. It brought forth, steaming from the past, another time when Colleen hadn't been chosen, a brief slice in time when she knew their mother loved Hallie first and best. When there was solid-as-the-ground proof that Hallie was the favorite daughter.

The backyard had glittered with fireflies, the sun flirting with the edges of the horizon, holding tight to the day just as Lena, Hallie and Shane were. They ran barefoot through the soft grass, catching those lit-up bugs and scooping them into Ball jars, the metal tops having been poked full of holes by Dad's awl. It was a contest — who could grab the most fireflies? Colleen was losing because with each capture she felt a twinge of guilt; she didn't want to trap beauty in a jar, although release would come at night's end.

Only Dad had joined them in the backyard that night, since Mother volunteered at the library. They were laughing — Colleen couldn't remember why — when a black police car appeared in the driveway. All three children stood as still as though they were playing freeze tag. A cop car wasn't good, right? Their gazes flew to one another, as frenetic as the flies in their jars.

Mother climbed out of the back of the car, her arm in a sling and a Band-Aid over her

left eye. Panic filled Lena at the sudden realization that the woman who held the family together could herself come undone.
Nothing was certain.

The policeman stepped out also, removing his blue hat and holding it over his
chest; smiling, he nodded at Gavin and the
children. Then Mother bent over, placed
her hands on her knees and called for her
children, for *two* of her children. Hallie and
Shane bolted to their mother and she
gathered them to her while Dad sidled over
to Lena and wrapped his arms around her.
She shuddered. Something more than an
injury was awry in the world that, only moments before, had been warm, safe and
secure. Then, as if slapped, Mother gazed
up and called for Lena. "Come here, my
big girl."

It had been a minor car accident, a fender
bender caused by a teenager driving his
daddy's truck without permission. They'd
had a good laugh about how Mother's car
had to be towed while the tanklike truck
drove away without a mark. An ambulance
had squealed into the town square in response to Mrs. Farley's 911 call from the
post office. The paramedics had justified
their presence by giving Elizabeth a sling
for the bruise on her right wrist and a Band-

Aid for the small cut that had nothing to do with the accident and everything to do with a mosquito bite she'd scratched too often.

All was well, but Colleen never forgot the moment when her mother initially called for two of her children, and not for the third.

Now, standing in Shane's bathroom, Colleen felt the aftershocks of the memory; a shaking of her internal world. It was like picking up a mended pottery mug that had been glued together, pouring hot liquid into it and watching it break again.

Shane banged on the door. "You okay in there?"

"I'm fine. That coffee hit me wrong. I'll be out in a second." With deep breaths, Colleen stood in front of the mirror and squeezed some of Shane's toothpaste onto her finger. She rubbed it on her tongue and swished water around her mouth and then spit it out, watching it flee down the drain. If she was really going to stay and help her brother with this project for her beloved dad, she must find a way to get control of the emotions that swelled and surged with every prod. "Get it together," she said to her image. "Right now."

She opened the door and joined her sister, who averted her gaze, and her brother, who had a plan to save their dad. "Okay," Colleen said, "tell me everything the doctor told you about this disease. I need to know before we do one more thing."

Shane sat and slumped with the weight of this discussion, as if it was a bag of concrete held between his shoulder blades. "This has been killing me, Lena. But I've been the one dragging Dad from doctor to doctor until we landed at the neurologist."

Colleen collapsed on a chair. "I feel so . . . left out."

"I think you left us out a long, long time ago." Hallie spoke while staring at the table, not meeting anyone's eyes.

Colleen had every perfect comment to return — she'd had years to perfect those comments — and right now she would say, *I think you were the one who left me out on my wedding day. Least that's how I remember it.* But instead she stared at her sister, screwing her back molars together so tightly that she felt the tension in her scalp. "Don't," she said to Hallie.

"Say it," Hallie said, her mouth quivering. "I'm ready. You've held it in all these years and I want you to say it *all.* Say everything cruel you've ever wanted to say. Please say anything you want. I just can't stand the silence anymore." She wrapped her arms around herself as if in protection of what might come next.

Sure, there'd been times throughout the years when Colleen *had* practiced the speech she should have uttered in the back hallway of that church with the champagne puddling at their feet and soaking through her ballet slippers. Once, Colleen had learned the word "heartseer," which meant the pain of missing someone so desperately that it felt like an illness. For years, that word was the one she used to describe how she felt about her sister, and of course Walter.

On sleepless nights when she missed the rushing song of the river outside her window, when she wanted to weep, Colleen would replay the scene in the back hallway of the church, and in her imaginings she'd always found the words she could have said — always new, always fresh and never spoken.

The questions she'd carried, baggage as heavy as the rocks that they'd piled at the water's edge to keep the river from encroaching onto the soft earth of their backyard, rose again. *How did you two get together? How did you fool me? How?*

But now, with her sister in front of her, Colleen dug into the debris of the past for different words. "I just want to help Dad.

Not fight with you. Please."

Hallie's stunned expression was no different from the one when she'd been discovered in that tiny alcove room with Walter — pain and shame melding together with half-closed eyes and quivering lips. "What?"

"I don't want to do this anymore. I don't want to be mad and sad. I don't want to have to run away from the home I love so very much. I'm exhausted of it all. Let's just accept that we will never be close again — but we can be polite. That has to be good enough."

Shane slammed his hand on the table, the photos scattering. "No, that is not good enough. Not good enough at all."

Hallie bent, plucked up a fallen photo and placed it gently on the table. She opened her mouth to speak, but nothing came out; she slumped back defeated, her cheeks red as if she'd just finished running a race.

Colleen stood then. "I think I need to go." She felt it — the urge thrusting her out the door. *Run. Get out. Don't look.* It was a voice she'd been heeding for a long time.

Shane placed his hand on her shoulder. "You are *not* leaving here, Lena."

Colleen hugged him and grabbed a photo of her dad and Aunt Rosalind from the pile. "I'll take this one. But right now I am leaving. I don't want to fight or talk. I can't. I'm going to the house. This evening I'll bring Dad to the pub instead of Bob."

Gavin routinely arrived at the pub by three thirty in the afternoon. His days had always belonged to his family, but the evenings eternally belonged to the Lark. Other dads were present for their kids at bedtime and for soccer games and ballet recitals, but Colleen, Hallie and Shane had considered themselves lucky because their dad was around for breakfast and rides to school, for lunches and summer mornings on the johnboat.

And of course the pub belonged to all of them.

As soon as school let out, all three would rush to the Lark, located within walking distance of both the junior high and high schools, which were housed in drab brick buildings side by side. When they were younger, Mother would pick them up from the pub while other mothers sat in car pool or walked to the school. Often Colleen would beg to stay and do her homework there, and Mother usually allowed this. By fifteen years old, Colleen knew the difference between whiskey and bourbon and could distinguish the aromas of various

130

types of gin. She wasn't allowed to taste anything until she was sixteen, but by eighteen she could identify a brand of whiskey blindfolded. This particular skill had impressed more first dates than she could count.

Colleen knew the way to the Lark from every spot in town — a touch-point as familiar as her childhood home. And she drove there now with Gavin in the passenger seat.

Gavin stared through the windshield, his hands flat on the dashboard in some muscle-memory need to place his hands on a steering wheel. "When the heck is my car going to be ready?"

"I'll ask Shane," Colleen said and hoped her dad couldn't see her face flush as she swallowed past the thickness of the lie.

"And when is your husband coming back to help me clean out the shed?" Gavin twisted in his seat and gently touched Colleen's arm. "He promised he'd finish with me weeks ago. Such a good man, that Walter, always chipping in."

Colleen neared the stop sign and stepped too hard on the brake, both of them lurching forward into the safety of their seat belts. "Whoa!" Gavin pressed his hands into the dashboard.

"Sorry, Dad." Colleen took in a deep, shaky breath. "Walter is not my husband."

Gavin squinted at her and set his mouth in a straight line. "Of course he's not. Why would you say that? I know that."

Colleen stared at her dad until the car behind them honked and she gently, very gently, pressed the gas to move forward, and then swerved the Jeep to miss a pothole. They both shimmied to the right, Gavin grabbing on to the side door handle. "Sorry, Dad, I don't drive much at home," she said.

"This is home."

"I don't drive much *in New York,* is what I meant." They passed the bookshop and the market, the café and the medical clinic, the bright awnings of the downtown stores flashing by like kites.

"Wait," he said and pressed his hands to the side window. "Where are you going?"

"To the pub, Dad." Colleen stopped at a striped yellow tape stretched across the road and attached to two gas lanterns: construction crews blocked Second Avenue.

"But this looks . . . wrong." His brow furrowed.

"Sorry?" Colleen glanced left and right. "Dad, I'm taking Blue Willow because Second is closed."

"Oh, yes." He leaned back on the seat.

"Construction drives me crazy. Makes the familiar seem unfamiliar. Sometimes it feels like I left for years and just returned."

"I know." But she didn't. Yes, there were a few new buildings, two just-opened bars and a small strip mall. A couple of old warehouses had been converted into modern apartment buildings. None of these should have confused him.

A minute later, Colleen parked in the back lot of the pub and her dad jumped out of the passenger side with the agility of a younger man. Colleen stayed buckled in, watching him go through the back door without glancing back to see if she was following. Maybe he'd already forgotten her. If he forgot her, would she disappear? Without her dad's memories of her, would she exist at all? A hollow place inside her echoed with his absence not yet real, but clearly soon it would be. It was like watching the sun shrink below the horizon — there and bright and full of colors until it was gone, only darkness remaining.

"No," she said to the empty car. "No."

Needing preoccupation, Colleen checked her cell. There were a slew of group texts from her girlfriends wanting to know if she'd like to join them for happy hour. She'd forgotten to tell them she'd left town.

Then another few from Philippe — he adored her; he missed her; he hoped her time at home was going all right; he was thinking of her. She didn't answer because she didn't know what to say.

She sent quick texts letting her friends know she was out of town . . . again.

Colleen climbed out of the car and stood in the sweltering heat, closed her eyes and drew on her internal compass that allowed her to focus when all was going awry. But focus didn't arrive; instead, Walter did.

CHAPTER TEN

Explore memory as the place where our
vanished days secretly gather and . . .
the passionate heart never ages.
  John O'Donohue, *Anam Cara*

The pickup truck swerved into the parking
lot, into the second owner's spot, marked
Leprechauns Only. The man at the wheel
wore Ray-Ban sunglasses and a smile; he
was either talking on the phone or singing
to himself, Colleen wasn't sure which. He
didn't see her; that much was clear. But she
damn sure saw him. Walter Littleton.

Somehow he'd been frozen in her mind,
an image as firm as a statue. He'd become
someone to despise, Exhibit #1 of all men
who cheated and lied, so much so that she'd
almost forgotten how *real* he actually was.
Colleen took two steps back, mostly hidden
behind the Jeep. But she didn't need to hide
— Walter was preoccupied and hurried.

He held a cell phone in his hand and from where she stood Colleen saw the earpiece dangling from his ear to the cell. He laughed and simultaneously opened the back door to his truck. Two little girls, both in tutus and T-shirts, spilled out and ran for the back door, small backpacks — a pink one shaped like a pig with pointy ears where the pockets would open, and a red one designed as a ladybug — flopping on their shoulders. Walter hollered good-bye and I love you to them and returned to his call. The girls were inside before Colleen could register their faces and decide which one was Rosie, which one was Sadie.

There stood the man who was supposed to be *her* husband. Those little girls — they were both she and Hallie as children, and they were also the children she was meant to have had with Walter; they represented a life lost with the man who drove the pickup and laughed on the phone. They were her nieces; her sister's children; Walter's daughters.

His hair was thick and tousled; nothing there had changed. His dark curls caught in the breeze and tangled as he skimmed them back from his forehead. His jeans and boots hinted that he'd come from a work site, dark mud on the side of his left leg. His red

T-shirt declaring *Littleton Construction* was tight on a body that had not gone soft, not one bit. It was the smile, the damn smile, that left Colleen momentarily unnerved. She anticipated feeling the particular grief of her insides folding up, closing inside of her like a shell, but it didn't come.

His voice slid past her, the words unintelligible but the sound familiar. Then Walter climbed back into the truck, still talking, and drove off. Just like that. She didn't throw rocks at his truck, cry or lose her breath. She merely stood still, waiting for her heart to find its rhythm again, and then she walked inside the Lark.

The pub's back room had always felt like a secret, a place only the family and employees were allowed, where boxes and dirty glasses and bottles were untidily shoved onto shelves and into bins. Shane was bent over a box, yanking off the tape with a zipping sound, and Colleen wanted to tell him that she'd just seen Walter and the world hadn't tilted off its axis, that she was breathing in and breathing out and that was just that.

Instead a small voice called out, "Aunt Lena!" and Colleen glanced down to the source behind Shane — to one of the little girls who'd jumped out of the pickup truck.

Which one? The child peered from behind Shane's leg. She wore a bright pink tutu, garish and torn in places. Her white T-shirt was adorned with a picture of a princess; Colleen wasn't sure which one. The little girl's hair hung in a long braid over her shoulder, a mimic of the princess on the shirt.

Colleen's blood rushed to her face: was this Rosie or Sadie? Rosie was the name she and Walter had chosen for their firstborn, her aunt's name. Hallie had taken even that. Did she even know she'd taken it? Had Walter told her? The betrayal, a gong sounding in a canyon, echoed on and on and on.

"Rosie?" Colleen bent, her hands on her knees, to lock gazes with the child. It was like looking into her sister's eyes.

The girl nodded and grinned before stepping out and placing both her hands on her hips. "I knew it was you. Mommy showed me pictures."

"She did?" Her niece was the cutest girl she'd ever seen, in many ways a replica of Hallie at the same age but more brazen. Hallie had been shy, reticent, always waiting for Lena to make the first move.

"Yes, and she tells us stories all the time. I know everything about you."

Hallie told stories about Colleen? To her

children? This took a minute to absorb, and all the while the little girl stared at Colleen until she spoke, patient in her waiting. "I doubt that," Colleen said with a laugh. "Now, who is that princess?" Colleen braved a touch to Rosie's shirtsleeve.

"You don't know who Anna is?" Rosie's mouth dropped open and her eyes widened.

"Seems there's lots of new princesses lately. I get confused."

Rosie's smile was Walter's, lifting high onto each cheek, leaving Colleen shaken as if a tiny tremor passed under the floor of the pub. She turned to Shane for help.

"Anna is the princess sister in *Frozen,*" he said, as serious as if he were explaining the difference between distilling and fermenting whiskey.

"Ah, yes." Colleen looked at Rosie again. "I didn't know her name."

"You haven't seen *Frozen?*" Rosie asked, as incredulous as a seven-year-old could possibly be.

"Nope. How about we watch it together?" Colleen suggested.

Rosie gazed at Colleen, tilted her head. "Why don't you ever come visit us? Mom says you never come home. I want to catch shrimp with you. Mom says you're better at it than she is."

"Rosie," Shane said. "Go find Sadie before she gets into trouble."

Rosie didn't break her gaze with Colleen. "He always says that when he wants me to go away." She scowled and ran off, her tutu bouncing, through the swinging door that led to the main area of the pub.

"Adorable, like you said," Colleen admitted as she stood straight and stretched her back.

"Precocious, too," Shane confirmed.

"If she was sent here to charm me, it worked."

"Not sure if that was the purpose, but Hallie is out there waiting on us."

"To do what?"

"So the two of you can get started on this project."

"This project." Colleen dropped both hands on her brother's shoulders and glanced around the room to check that her dad hadn't walked in. "We can still do it, but I think the doc appointment will tell us a lot — maybe there's a new treatment."

"Okay." He nodded with a slightly crooked smile.

Colleen knew that damn smile. It was the same one he used when he wanted to brush off a flirting girl he had no interest in. The same one he'd used to placate one of her childish temper tantrums, or convince their mother he wouldn't do the forbidden something he intended to do anyway.

Colleen removed her hands from his shoulders. "Don't patronize me, Shane."

"I'm not, sis. I'm just exhausted."

"I'm sorry you've had to bear this burden without me. But you know, it's odd. He seems okay for a long while and then he'll say something that doesn't make sense."

"Like?" A new voice joined their conversation and there stood Hallie. She looked tired, her eyes sinking into dark circles and her hair tied back in a knotted mess. "What doesn't make sense?"

Colleen tried to smile at her sister, attempted to get past the habitual inclination to cringe and withdraw. "I was telling him that sometimes Dad seems fine and then he doesn't. On the way here, he seemed lost but blamed it on the construction."

"He does that about once a week — blames the construction," Hallie said and then turned to the squeals of her daughters, who barreled into the back room, bouncing off each other like pinballs. The second, smaller version of Rosie was also wearing a tutu, but hers was red and not quite as tattered.

"Is this *her*?" Sadie asked Rosie, speaking

around the thumb in her mouth.

"Yes, dummy. Can't you tell from all the pictures?"

Sadie nodded. "She's prettier in pictures."

Colleen couldn't help it — she laughed, until Shane joined in, and then Hallie.

"What's so funny?" Sadie asked.

"You, silly." Colleen leaned down to her second niece. "Hello, I'm your aunt Colleen."

Sadie sidled farther behind Rosie, as if she needed a shield. "I thought her name was Lena."

"It is," Rosie confirmed and then turned to Colleen. "We made this for you at summer camp." She held out a plastic stick covered with silver glitter and bright ribbons of every color.

"Oh?" Colleen took it, avoiding the lumps of glue by holding it between two fingers. "Thank you so much."

"It's a magic wand," Rosie explained.

"I've always wanted something magical." Colleen waved it in the air; glitter scattered, clinging to whatever it touched.

"I told you," Rosie said to Sadie, giving her the littlest shove. And then there they were in her memory, herself and Hallie as little girls. She was telling Hallie, "I told you so," and Hallie was grinning from ear to ear. Just like these little ones, Hallie and she had worn ratty tutus and believed that life's glittery path would lead them to become princesses — Cinderella and Sleeping Beauty — who would be saved by men's kisses. Look how that had worked out.

"I think I need a drink," Colleen said and held her wand high.

"It's only four in the afternoon." Hallie placed her hand on top of each little girl's head to protect them from their happy hour aunt.

Colleen waved her glittering wand. "It's magically five o'clock. Thanks, princesses." She set out for the bar in search of her dad and a whiskey.

The pub was mostly empty except for Mr. Brown, who sat in the same seat he'd occupied in Colleen's memories. A widower even when she was in high school, he drank whiskey sometimes and other times just water, staring at the TV above the bar and making conversation with whoever crossed his path. His bald head as polished as the bar top; his gold wedding ring still on his left hand.

He glanced up. "Well, hello there, Lena Donohue."

"Hi, Mr. Brown." Colleen reached his side and offered a hug. "How are you?"

"About the same as I always am. How are you, dear? How is the big city treating you?"

"Wonderfully, actually."

"We miss you 'round here. We all do."

"That's very sweet of you to say. It's good to see you, too." Colleen smiled and walked away as he returned his attention to the soundless baseball game. This was the way of the Lark — tradition built in as firmly as the bricks and mortar, as the beer taps and bar counter thick with shellac. This pub — just as the marsh behind her house — held the invisible geography of her memories.

At a side table, empty whiskey glasses next to them, two men in baseball caps were deep in animated conversation. The words "mayor" and "bullshit" and "roadblocks" slipped out in loud proclamations. Yes, Colleen also remembered this well — the men and women who argued about politics or religion or family or ex-lovers then went right back to being friends again. It was as though this place allowed the venting without the consequences. Well, most of the time.

Her dad, they all knew, had tried to replicate a true Irish pub in the Lark and maybe he'd succeeded, but surely those pubs didn't have cobia fishing trophies on the wall, sand between the floorboards and the sweet-sour aroma of pluff mud that would never dissipate no matter how many scented candles were lit. Those pubs on the Emerald Isle didn't display the South Carolina flag — featuring a palmetto tree and crescent — hanging on the wall next to the University of South Carolina baseball team photo signed by every player. No, Dad might have tried to imitate the *idea* of an Irish pub, but the details made this place exactly what it was — a Lowcountry home for many.

One other man stood at the bar, and Colleen quickly sized him up — midthirties, maybe early forties; the dim light obscured too much of his features to tell for sure. His hair was dark and tousled like he'd been out on a boat all morning. He wore fishermen's shorts and a faded red T-shirt announcing a long-gone event at a bar in Savannah.

A guy in a pub in the middle of the afternoon was obviously there to drown his pain, most likely heartache. She'd become an expert at guessing why men and women were at the pub, a game she used to play when bored while washing glasses behind the bar. But what this guy would soon discover was that heartache could never be drowned. It had to be buried alive.

■ ■ ■ ■

It had been two weeks since the wedding, two weeks since Lena Donohue had loaded her car and driven to Greenwich, Connecticut, to her friend Maggie Marlow's house. Maggie hadn't been able to attend the wedding, what with a two-year-old at home and no real help. Maggie had been her college roommate and now lived in a place where her husband took the train into Manhattan each day, and she tried to fit into a life she'd decided she was made for. Maggie also had a pullout couch in the basement and bottles of vodka.

Lena's drive from Watersend to Connecticut had been accomplished in a fugue state punctuated by tears and recrimination, of roiling anger and slamming her fists on the steering wheel. She hadn't stopped to sleep or eat, only to refuel the car and use the dirty restrooms at convenience stores that all looked alike, selling junk food, beer, soda and beef jerky. She spent most of the drive reviewing the wedding and the weeks leading up to it in obsessive loops. When had her sister and her fiancé found the time and privacy to become lovers?

Colleen had been out of town only once

since the engagement — a weekend spent traveling with her father to check out pubs along the East Coast. It was their annual dad-daughter trip and they always came home with new ideas, some innovative way to streamline the ordering or to attract new patrons, although new patrons were rarely truly needed. After the wedding, Colleen was going to stay and help run the pub whenever she wasn't working for the local newspaper; she and Walter had even discussed adding a microbrewery with their own brand of Lark beer.

As the ribbon of highway had disappeared under her tires, the signs and exits a blur, Colleen tormented herself with endless questions. When had Hallie and Walter hooked up? Had they been running around together this entire time? Had her sister always hated her and only pretended to admire and love her? Was Hallie getting back at her for being older and being, well, so freaking bossy?

And Walter. My God, Walter. Loving him seemed to be stapled onto her bones, infused in her blood, so much a part of her body that she would never be able to stop feeling it. Yet, he chose her sister. The only thing she knew to do was run — get away from him as far and as fast as she could even as her body and her heart beat with the need for him.

It seemed impossible to hate the very same person she desired. A cauldron of toxic, contradictory emotions bubbled inside her. During that drive (and in the years following) the love sometimes won out and she wept with grief; other times, hate and rage took over and she seethed.

Fourteen hours of such fruitless thinking, of angry expletives and ignoring her ringing cell phone, passed before she pulled into Maggie's driveway and stumbled to the pullout bed. For the next two weeks, Maggie listened and Colleen ranted.

Colleen's family did not retreat so easily. They all called, one after the other, in hourly increments and quick sequence. They left messages. They texted. Colleen refused to tell them where she was. Let them worry. She answered her dad once, told him she was safe and asked him to give her time to grieve.

The vodka did its job on most nights, plummeting Colleen toward a deep, dreamless and amnesic sleep. But that vodka, it fell down on the job by the time dawn leaked through the small square window across the room. Then Colleen's mouth felt like it was made of the black ash at the bottom of her dad's grill. Her head felt like a bowling ball too heavy to lift and her throat was lined with broken, sharp oyster shells. She could have handled all of that, but the *remembering* did her in every time. She'd awaken, curse the obvious hangover and then pull at the threads of blurry memory in a continuous effort to understand *why*.

Oh, yes, she'd think. I drank most of Maggie Marlow's vodka because I'm in Connecticut to forget that my sister and fiancé are in love.

Had they taken advantage of the wedding already in place and walked down the aisle together? Had they eaten her shrimp and grits, drunk her champagne? Said the vows she and Walter had practiced at the rehearsal? Gone on the honeymoon to the wine country of California?

Colleen wanted to know, yet she didn't want to know. She wanted to call Shane or her parents and ask. But above all — shimmering on top and below and around those questions — was an imperative need to forget.

When two weeks had passed, Maggie urged Colleen to come out with her to the local watering hole. "You have to get out of my house," she joked with a wink. "Actually, I have to get out of my house and

149

you're my excuse, so let's go."

It was a pretty town, a northeastern version of Watersend, with Tudor style replacing coastal shingle-style homes. The streets' gaslight lampposts and iron sidewalk benches were reminders of home. And it was a damn Irish pub that Maggie chose, obviously trying to be comforting, bringing Colleen somewhere that felt familiar. But how could Maggie have known that emotional triggers hid on every street corner and inside every lit window? When Colleen walked into the dimly lit bar she felt she were floating, untethered from her life, dizzy. This was a pub, but it wasn't the Lark. She was Colleen, but she wasn't engaged to Walter. This was a small town, but it wasn't Watersend.

Maggie met up with her crowd of friends and Colleen found herself alone at the bar impressing a guy with red hair in a blue suit, with a white hanky in the pocket, with her knowledge of whiskey. "It's a single malt from one of the last family distilleries in Scotland. The name means 'Valley of the Deer' in Gaelic."

He was handsome in a buttoned-down way, as if he'd never put on worn jeans to go out on a johnboat or strained to hold a fishing pole against a struggling catch. His qualities might have come pre-packaged in a fluorescent-lit man-factory.

"Whiskey is a science with you, is it?" he asked as she downed her third.

"An art," she told him.

"You can't be from around here."

She fell into his smooth voice, his sense of humor and, hours later, his bed.

That next morning she awoke with a hangover worse than she'd ever had, one that barreled through her with such force that she finally understood the truth: she could not drown the pain; it knew how to breathe underwater.

So she'd learned to swim.

CHAPTER ELEVEN

You think you have a memory;
but it has you!

John Irving,
A Prayer for Owen Meany

The fiddle player was tuning up in the back left corner of the Lark. Colleen went behind the bar, grabbed a bottle of Glenfiddich and a shot glass. Just one shot to soothe her nerves after meeting the adorable nieces, who were still bolting around the pub like Hallie and she had done as children. Hank gave her a clownish nod and a salute.

The guy at the bar — the one she was sure was drowning his heartbreak — leaned across the counter. "Are all the customers allowed to serve themselves?"

Colleen downed the shot. "I'm not *really* a customer."

"You're a bartender who drinks on the job?" he asked, still smiling, and leaned back on his bar stool. His gaze turned into a squint. "Wait, I know you."

He was awfully jolly for a guy with a broken heart, and awfully sober for one drowning his sorrows. She'd summed him up incorrectly.

"You do?" She leaned over the bar and poured him a shot from the same bottle. "On the house."

"Yes, you're a Donohue."

A Donohue.

No one had said that to her in so long, she felt an unexpected rush of warm family sweetness.

He nodded, but slid the shot glass back toward her. "You can have it."

He wasn't heartbroken. He was happy and go-lucky, a mischievous type. What was he doing in a pub in midafternoon?

"How do you know that?" she asked.

"Research."

"You're researching the Donohues?" She wrinkled her forehead. Did she know him? "Why the hell are you doing that?"

"Not the Donohues per se," he said with a grin. "But the pub, the Lark. South Carolina is talking of making it a historic landmark." He leaned forward, a sly smile on his face like he held a delicious secret. "Did you know this was the first structure built in Watersend? The home of the founder, Mack Turnbull? When he'd finished building his home on the river, he turned this into the town pub, what he'd always meant it to be."

Colleen laughed and slapped her hand on the bar. "Seriously? No. I had no idea."

"Yep. It was more important to him than the library or the town hall. He believed it would be the central hub of the town. And damn if he wasn't right even all these years later. So I've been looking at old photos and records, and I recognized that smile of yours."

Colleen set her palms on the edge of the bar. "So what does it mean to be a historic landmark?"

"It means a lot, actually. Historical preservation keeps us grounded in who we are as a town and as a state and even as a country. The past defines us. It matters. And we need to preserve it."

He was so earnest she almost laughed, but that would have been cruel. She also wanted to tell him that there wasn't any problem with preserving the past around these parts — it was as natural as greeting everyone you passed. She also wanted to tell him that she had spent the last ten years trying to do exactly the *opposite* of preserving the past.

But instead, she smiled at him. "But don't you think some history should be let go? Knocked down. Destroyed?" she asked.

He laughed, this guy who wouldn't take her shot and who smiled at her like he already knew her. "But some things shouldn't be destroyed. And if we can get a historical marker for your pub, it will always be preserved."

"What about when it's better to turn something old into something new?"

"Well, that's part of what we decide."

They were having two different conversations, two separate rivers rushing parallel, and Colleen wondered if he realized that, if he knew she was talking about something other than the structure where they stood. "But save it if you must. It's a good old building. No one is trying to take it down."

"Someone," he said, "is always trying to take down old things. Trust me. Might not be now, but . . ."

Colleen eyed him — was he serious or teasing her? She spied the scar on his left ear that extended in a silver hairline to the edge of his cheekbone and crinkled when his cheeks rose with his smile. The drink warmed her and allowed an easy smile before she glanced over to see Hallie approaching the bar, her two girls twirling in their skirts. "Here comes another Donohue," she said to the man. "They're everywhere."

He turned and watched Rosie reach the stool next to him and crawl onto it.

Sadie stood behind Hallie and peeked out to tell Rosie, "You ask her."

"Aunt Lena," Rosie said, placing her little elbows on the surface of the bar, settling her face into the cradle of her hands, "can you come for a sleepover tonight?"

She and Hallie had done the exact same thing as children — Hallie pushing Colleen forward to negotiate with their parents. *You ask,* she'd say. *You ask.*

Hallie caught Colleen's gaze and unsaid recognition flew between them, wings flapping both in the air and in her chest. *Don't betray your sister someday,* that was what Colleen wanted to say to Rosie. Instead she came from around the bar to speak to the child. "Oh, I have to stay with Grandfather in his house. I promised him."

Sadie clung to Hallie's skirts and spoke to Rosie, pretending Colleen didn't exist. "Don't make her come. We don't know her yet."

Colleen laughed despite herself, the sound startling little Sadie into retreating further. "I'm not scary, I promise."

"Sadie." Rosie spoke in a grown-up voice and jumped off the bar stool to pull her sister from behind their mother. "Don't be such a scaredy-cat. See? She's pretty and she's nice."

Hallie laughed, but then stifled it quickly, taking her daughters' hands. "Aunt Lena needs to stay with Grandy."

"But," Rosie said, "we want to have a tea party and make bead necklaces with her."

"That sounds like great fun," Colleen said, "so let's find another time to do it."

Rosie looked at Sadie and stated loudly, "Sadie, that's what grown-ups say when they will *never* play with you."

"Oh! That's not true," Colleen said. "I have a magic wand now and I can make anything happen."

Rosie brightened and grasped a handful of Sadie's tutu. "See? She'll play with us."

Hallie was quiet during this interchange, but a small smile played on her lips. She tried to quell it; Colleen saw her try, but it wasn't working. Rosie and Sadie were playing the two different parts of Hallie — one ready to play and the other scared of drawing near to Colleen.

"Rosie," Colleen said, "will you scoot on back and tell Uncle Shane I need him? Sadie, can you go help your sister?"

"Okay." Rosie grabbed her sister's hand and together the two little girls ran off.

Colleen faced her sister, moving a bit away from the man who was researching their building. Hallie spoke first. "I know that not even a magic wand could force you to spend the night at my house."

"You're right. Why would I do that? It's absurd."

Hallie leaned closer. "I know we have to work together to help Dad and we will, but I want you to tell me all the things you've wanted to say. I can feel them, Lena. Like snakes running under your words — all the angry, hateful words you never said."

"Why does it matter now? Really? It doesn't."

Hallie brushed her bangs out of her eyes, reminding Colleen of the time her sister cut her bangs to the roots in the mistaken belief that this meant she would not have to grow them out. She'd been six maybe? "It matters to me," Hallie said. "I want you to say it all. And I want you to let me say things, too. You didn't reply to one letter or text or e-mail. I don't even know if you read them. But I have things I really want to say, that I want you to understand."

"You said all you needed to say when you married Walter. When you said, 'I do,' you said enough."

Hallie slammed her hand on the bar. Old Mr. Brown turned toward them and Mrs. Baxley, the librarian just joining her book club, took a few steps toward them and then seemed to think better of it. The historical society guy stared up at the TV as if he didn't hear or see a thing. Hallie continued, unaware of anyone else in the bar. "You can be self-righteous if you want, but you made choices, too. And not one of them had to do with love."

"Are you serious? Is Walter telling you to say these things? Is he totally in control of that head of yours? My God, you betrayed me in the most embarrassing way one can, and you have the nerve to say *I* made choices?" Colleen tried to lower her voice, but it rose anyway.

"You chose. You ran. You didn't listen. If you had cared about either of us at all, you would have at least . . ."

"At least what, Hallie?"

"I don't know. But not cut us off. You left the people you loved the most and rode off on your white high horse."

"From what I remember, I drove away in my beat-up Volkswagen ashamed and humiliated and heartbroken. Not quite the same thing as a white horse."

"I know." Hallie closed her eyes. "We'll never see eye to eye again. I hoped for so long. I prayed even. But what I broke can't be fixed. I see that. All we can do now is help Dad. Do our very best to put it aside, not let the volcanoes inside us erupt every time we get together."

"You're not the same," Colleen said in a low voice, taking a step toward Hallie. "You don't sound real; just spouting all the things you think you *should* say like a programmed robot."

"Of course I'm not the same. How could I be? And you . . . you not speaking to me for so long? It broke something in me."

"And you don't think you shattered something in me?" The anger felt fresh and vivid now; it was awakened and appearing as a fire from far, far below.

Hallie averted her eyes, let her chin drop to her chest. "I know. I know. You hate me and I deserve it." And with that, she was gone, slipping to the back room.

Colleen stood alone for a minute, or maybe it was ten, she wasn't sure, slowly breathing in and out. The faces in the pub blurred; the sounds of glasses clinking and somewhere a cell phone ringing seemed faint and far away. Finally, the man she'd spoken to at the bar, the one she'd forgotten was sitting only a few bar stools down, spoke. "Family feud?"

"What?" Colleen remembered him then. "No. Not a family feud. Just a sister feud. Big difference."

"In the photos I've seen, you look thick as thieves."

" 'Thief' being the key word."

"Huh?" The man crinkled his eyes in confusion; he shifted on the bar stool so his legs lengthened and she could see how tall he would be when he stood.

"Is eavesdropping part of your historical job?"

"Sorry. Promise I wasn't listening in — it was kind of hard not to hear. Guess I'm not that good at jokes." He grinned. "I never was."

Colleen turned away as the fiddle player tested the microphone and set up, beginning a tune. Colleen's chest thrummed with the memory of the song, of singing it with her parents. It was a comedic ballad that always had the crowd singing along with hand movements and rowdy cheers.

Colleen closed her eyes to absorb the tune. She knew the words — the song about the unicorns with the roaring chorus and the hand motions. It was a song the Donohues had jumped around to or sung

161

at the top of their lungs with their hearts in their voices in between doing homework on the back tables of the pub before it opened.

"Don't you forget my unicorn," sang the eavesdropping man next to her in an off-key voice. ✦

Colleen's surprise made her laugh out loud. "You know this song?"

"Who doesn't?"

"Most of the world." Colleen realized she didn't know his name, this man who knew the unicorn song and the history of the pub and her name. "And it's not fair that you know my name and I don't know yours."

"Oh, I'm so rude." He bowed his head and tipped an imaginary hat. "I'm Beckett Cooney. Would you like to see some of the old photos of this place?"

"What?"

"Old pictures of the Lark. Old ones of the past owners and your family and . . ."

"Is that a pickup line?" she asked. "Because it's terrible."

"Isn't it working?" He grinned at her. "But no, I just wondered if you wanted to see some of the past. Sometimes we know about it, but it's different altogether to *see* it."

"I've had enough of the past to last a long, long time. My brother, Shane." She pointed at him. "He might want to see the photos and know everything about this place. He runs the pub now."

"Yes," Beckett said. "I've talked to him."

"Well, it was a pleasure to meet you." Colleen nodded at him and set off for the front door just as it opened and in walked Brad Young, dapper in his police uniform. He caught Colleen's eye and smiled with a wave. Yep, Watersend exactly — you couldn't escape your past or your mistakes, even if they'd only happened the day before. Colleen waved in return and wound her way through the familiar maze of tables to the front door.

Chairs were set upside down on the tables waiting to be set up, their legs sticking up like miniature tree trunks in a man-made forest. Soon a bartender and waitresses would wander in wearing green polo shirts with *The Lark* and the emblem emblazoned on the breast pocket. They would take down the chairs and hum along to the fiddle player, set condiments on each table to accompany the few menu items that hadn't changed in fifteen years. Shepherd's pie. Fish and chips. Pub fries. A mixed salad for those who cared. But no one came there for the food. They gathered for the music and the camaraderie and for Gavin and his wisdom and his terrible jokes and to hear him say, "Well, as the Irish say . . ."

From across the room, Colleen heard Hallie's voice as she called to her children, "My adorables, let's be on the move."

Colleen froze in midstep, her heart catching on the phrase. She glanced backward; Hallie was walking with a hand stretched out for each child. Their gazes caught and the sisters stood still and quiet in the slice of time that couldn't belong to anyone else. No one could know what hidden doorway was opened to another time as Hallie repeated a call and a gesture their mother had said and done until they were too old to hold her hands, old enough to be embarrassed by the phrase "my adorables," grown enough to roll their eyes at each other and run from their mother, holding only each other's hands.

The girls and Hallie reached Colleen's side, and Hallie said softly, "I know." Then she opened the door, and afternoon light shot through in a single burst and then scattered across the room. In identical movements the sisters brought their palms to their brows to shade their eyes. Hallie stepped into the light and closed the door, leaving Colleen inside.

THE MEMORY BOOK

INTERVIEW WITH
AUNT ROSALIND AND UNCLE FRED

The color photo of Gavin and his younger sister, Rosalind Donohue Parsons, lay on the kitchen table in the Donohue home. In the photo Dad and Aunt Rosie sat together at a round table covered with a bright blue tablecloth. A centerpiece of balloons and flowers dominated the right side of the image. Behind them hung a banner announcing 1979 and HAPPY GRADUATION. Gavin wore a black graduation gown, open to reveal a dark blue suit with a wide green-and-blue-plaid tie. His long hair touched his shoulders. He was smiling and his arm was cast over Aunt Rosie's shoulder. She was wearing a flowered dress, and her hair was pulled into a high ponytail, yet her bangs were overpuffed and shadowing her face. Her blue eye shadow was the brightest thing in the photo.

Colleen dialed Aunt Rosie's number, and she knew the drill — Aunt Rosie, Dad's only sibling, would answer the phone and then call for Uncle Fred before placing the call on speakerphone. Together they would scream into the receiver while the radio or TV blared in the background.

"Hello?" Aunt Rosie's pack-a-day deep voice was warmly familiar to Colleen.

"Aunt Rosie, it's Colleen."

"My lovely Lena. Let me get your uncle. He will be devastated to think he missed a chance to talk to you."

The predictability of her aunt's reaction cheered Colleen. She settled back in the chair and glanced around the family kitchen. It sure could use some updating, but why bother? Wasn't it fine as it was? She thought of the man she'd met at the bar — Beckett — and what he would think of people's constant desire to throw out the old in favor of the new.

Then Rosie and Fred were both on the phone, hollering their greetings. Colleen explained the memory book they were making as a surprise for Gavin's birthday, and asked if they would help.

Rosie spoke up first. "Your brother told me your dad is having some memory problems. Is he okay, Lena?"

"Oh, Aunt Rosie. He *is* having problems.

That's part of the reason for the memory book. But we're managing it, getting him the best help."

"Oh, he'll be fine, my dear. No one in our family suffers from memory issues. We all meet our maker in other ways."

Uncle Fred cleared his throat and let out what was probably a laugh but sounded more like a coughing fit. "Go on, then," he said. "What can we do for you? We're very excited we'll see you soon."

Colleen described the photo as best she could, and then waited.

Rosie spoke softly through the lines; remembering the day long since passed seemed to erase years from her voice. "Oh, Gavin's graduation from the University of Virginia was spectacular. All he could talk about was his upcoming trip to Ireland. He was convinced he would find the Donohues' castle and we'd all turn out to be royalty. There was shrimp cocktail and martinis. Your grandparents hired a four-piece band with trumpets. Trumpets, I'm telling you — it was fancy for sure. Your mother — well, she spent most of the day crying about him leaving the next morning. Poor thing."

Uncle Fred's voice sounded deep and resonant. "How come you can't remember to pick up the dry cleaning but you remember your brother's graduation day so perfectly?"

"Because I love my brother and I don't love the dry cleaner. You be quiet and get back to your Golf Channel that's so exciting. Anyway, Lena, we celebrated in grand style at the country club and your dad kissed Ms. Elizabeth good-bye and off he went to Ireland."

Uncle Fred chimed in, "A shame what happened then. Poor Elizabeth."

Colleen stared at the photo. Her mother wasn't in it — wasn't even part of the background. "A shame?" she asked.

"Oh, pay him no mind. He's still thinking of her terrible death. We all are, dear. We miss her very much."

"I miss her, too, Aunt Rosie."

"Well, darling Lena, we will see you soon."

Colleen hung up the phone and felt her skin tingle in irritation at Aunt Rosie pitying her mother. There was nothing about Elizabeth Donohue that warranted the word "poor," that was for damn sure.

Colleen set her mind to typing the story, imagining her dad at college graduation, and headed for his European trip, so full of adventure for whatever might come next in his life.

CHAPTER TWELVE

Nothing fixes a thing so intensely in the
memory as the wish to forget it.
Michel de Montaigne, *Essays*

Seated in the Donohue family kitchen, Colleen hit save twice, always twice, on the third story she'd written that day from interviews with the folks in her dad's photos. Aunt Rosalind had been the last. The first photo was of a baseball team circa fifth grade showing Gavin and his best friend, Nick. She'd spoken to Nick's mother and learned that Nick had died in a car crash fifteen years ago, but she'd relayed a story of the time Gavin and Nick tried to build a baseball diamond in the backyard by burning the grass into a diamond shape using gasoline. What trouble they got in, she'd said as she laughed.

For the second photo, of Gavin standing in front of a schoolroom blackboard with high school history teacher Mr. Tuttle, she'd been able to find and speak to the man who'd instilled in Gavin his love of Ireland's past and its poetry. Writing the mini stories came quickly and easily to Colleen, and with each phone call she'd felt she knew her dad a bit better, loved him a lot more. Why did children find it so hard to accept that their parents' lives began well before their children were born? Now, discovering Dad before he was Dad felt both jolting and exciting, as if she were learning even more about her own life.

This would be Colleen's third night at home, and she was well into accomplishing her tasks for Shane. Somehow she'd managed to avoid Hallie and the girls for a full twenty-four hours, but that wasn't going to last but a few more minutes.

The aroma of peach cobbler filled the house. This was the one dish Colleen knew how to make and each time she baked it, she felt calm and right with the world. Sometimes she baked it and never ate a bite, giving it to a neighbor or friend. Everything else in the kitchen was a mystery, her every attempt to follow the simplest recipe, with only four ingredients, becoming an inevitable failure. She was reminded of chemistry class when she blew up the Bunsen burner and was sent to the principal's office for "not following directions."

Her dad had picked her up from high school that afternoon and told the principal, "Yes, that might be the theme of her life: not following directions."

When she'd slid into the car, the edges of her hair singed and smelling like they did the morning after a campfire, she'd started to cry. "I'm sorry, Dad. I didn't do it on purpose."

"Little lark, why would I want a daughter who always follows directions? As the Irish say, bless your little Irish heart and every other Irish part."

"Dad!"

"That includes your clumsy need to forge your own path."

Colleen had known that if it had been any of her other friends, they would have been in deep trouble with their dads. But not hers; he turned the worst of her into a positive, into another small aspect of his daughter to be celebrated and honored.

Colleen went over to the oven and leaned down to open the door, inhaled the sweet aroma of the peaches she'd bought at a roadside stand bubbling under a pastry crust. She slipped on hot mitts and pulled out the baking dish, setting it on the stove to cool. Somehow Shane had convinced their dad to miss an hour or so at the pub that evening so he could eat supper with his children at home. Colleen was cooking. Which meant she was reheating a store-bought chicken-and-poppy-seed casserole, steaming broccoli and baking the cobbler.

The needle on the old record player, a black box set on the side buffet, spun around with a Frank Sinatra LP that her dad kept on it. More albums in faded dust jackets filled a box under the buffet. But Sinatra was just fine for now, his voice a soothing embrace — *"Fly me to the moon."*

"Lena?" Shane's voice called out as he entered the back door. "My God, it smells good in here." He entered the kitchen and gave her a hug. "Peach cobbler. Please never leave."

She kissed her brother's cheek. "Anything for you. And you'll be pleased. I've finished three stories today."

"Well, that doesn't mean you can go back to New York early. And I'll be needing more of this."

"One can't live on cobbler alone. Trust me, I've tried."

He headed to the fridge. "Hallie and Dad are on the way."

Colleen spun around, hitting the side of

the cobbler pan and burning the edge of her pinky. She shook her hand in the air. "Shit." Then she looked at Shane. "Is Walter coming?"

"Only the girls." He fished a bottle of beer from the refrigerator and popped the top against the underside of the counter. He took a long swig, and then pressed the cold bottle to his forehead. "You know, of course, that you'll have to see Walter at some point."

"I saw him yesterday."

Shane's eyebrows rose. "You did?"

"Don't worry. He didn't see me. I didn't do anything; I didn't say anything. It was weird. He wasn't . . . Walter, if that makes any sense. He was just a guy, a guy I used to know." She smiled. "So when I see him, I'll behave."

"Behave? That's not really your forte." He laughed and Colleen twisted the dishrag into a thin rope and snapped his arm with it.

"Ow. Damn, sis."

"You're not funny."

"Oh, yes, I am."

Colleen made a face at him. "Will you watch the timer for the casserole? I want to walk to the river for just a few minutes before dinner. Maybe even cast the net."

"Will do."

Colleen took her own bottle of beer from the refrigerator and headed out the back door, allowing the quick slap-slam of the screen door to echo across the yard. The grass was soft beneath her sandals and she tossed them from her feet to one side of the stairs. The loamy earth shifted beneath her toes and she ambled slowly to the dock. At its end stood a gray heron, his neck curved in a majestic C. His wings were tightly wrapped around his body as he stared to the horizon.

Colleen stepped carefully, playing a familiar childhood game — to see how close she could get before the bird flew away. She'd always envied the herons' ability to be utterly themselves, and completely at one with their landscape.

"Each of us is unique," her dad had said to her one afternoon in a reverential voice on the dock, as they watched a pod of dolphins swim by in an achingly beautiful choreography. "Who would choose to be anything but what they are created to be?"

And Colleen had vowed, all those years ago when she was twelve years old, to be *only* herself, exactly what she was meant to be. But that promise had been lost with all the others because she'd invented a *new* Colleen. And who was to say that this new version was exactly the one she was supposed to be? Maybe there were many selves she could be; maybe it wasn't so static and unwavering. She could become someone new and then another someone new. There was no marble-cast Colleen, defined by someone else and then carved. And yet, and yet, there was a truth that had to be tapped, a real Colleen that needed her voice to be heard among the louder voices of expectation. What was that? Who was that?

She approached the dock on tiptoe, and made it only two steps before the great heron spread its wings and rose from the edge of the dock. Its feathers gray and speckled, white and dense, spread before her. A lump rose in her throat at the beauty. She swallowed it with a swig of beer and watched the heron skim across the river before settling on a sandbar exposed at low tide. The oyster shells created a crusted edge around tall summer-green spartina grass. The heron standing on its stick legs seemed to stare at Colleen with a message she would never understand.

She set the beer bottle on the built-in wooden bench and opened the rusted metal box that contained fishing equipment. The shrimp net lay puddled in the bottom tangled and damp. She withdrew the net and shook it out, droplets of water splattering across her cotton tank top and shorts, ones she'd found in the bottom drawer in her old bedroom. Who had used the net last? Dad never would have put it back in the chest so tangled and wet — it was a strict rule: clean it; dry it; wrap it.

Here was another hint that Dad's brain was failing. Even as she stood on the dock and Hallie drove him there for dinner, those neurons were twisting; plaque was growing along the axons like moss between the stones of their walkway, slowly, inexorably.

Colleen hoisted the net onto her lap as she took a seat on the bench. Her fingers began disentangling it, pulling here and stretching there in an intuitive motion. If only she could do the same to her dad's brain. If only she could reach in and . . .

"Lena!" his voice called out from across the yard. She waved at her dad and then stood as her nieces ran toward the dock, still wearing their tutus from the previous day. Rosie reached her first. "Will you teach us? Will you? Mom said you would."

"Teach you what?" Colleen smiled at the sheer enthusiasm, uncontained and free.

"To throw the net."

"Your dad knows how," Colleen said with a bite of bitterness she wondered if the girls could hear.

"Not as good as you," Rosie said. "Mom said so. You're the best."

Colleen held up the net. "Well, this one is too tangled to throw. We'll have to do another one later or wait until it's untangled."

"It doesn't work when it's tangled," Sadie said, tears forming in her blue eyes, eyes just like Walter's.

The little girl's words flew like the heron across the river, settling into the crevices of Colleen's fear. *It doesn't work when it's tangled.*

Without thinking, Colleen drew the little girl to her and wiped away her tears. Surprised, Sadie at first went rigid and then flung herself off Colleen and against her sister. As Colleen contained her slight hurt at Sadie's rejection, she heard Rosie say in a too-grown-up voice, "We'll fix it, Sadie. We will."

The dinner table was lively with overlapping conversations and the ringing laughter of two little girls who had their own jokes and method of communicating. Rosie engaged with Colleen, but Sadie still shrank back. Hallie had brought wildflowers, from the same roadside stand where Colleen had found the peaches, and set the bouquet in their mom's favorite blue glass vase in the center of the table.

They were getting along just fine, but it all felt so tremulous, so fragile. It would take one wrong word, one wrong motion, and it could all go badly. They trod carefully, talking of not much important and engaging the little girls as distraction. When Shane was finished eating, he nudged away his plate and settled into his seat.

"Don't go back to the pub," Colleen said. "Let's all stay here."

Hallie raised her fork in the air. "You used to say that all the time when we were kids, trying to keep Dad from going to work. 'Let's all just stay here for this *one* night.' "

"But this time I mean it." Colleen stood and began to clear the table; she piled dishes one on top of the other, held two glasses loosely between her fingers. "Even though I know the answer is always the same." Colleen set the plates in the sink, but her fingers slipped and the water glasses fell, hitting the porcelain farm sink and shattering with a startling sound. For a slice of a second she was back in the church alcove, the bottle hitting stone. She jumped back and grimaced, staring at the shards of glass sprayed across the counter and floor.

"It's not a party until Lena breaks something," Hallie said with a laugh.

"Speaking of parties, I heard a joke today," Dad said.

"No!" all three siblings stated in unison.

"Yes, yes," the nieces cried.

Colleen wiped glass from the sink and counter with a paper towel and tossed it in the trash before heading to the broom closet.

Their dad was the worst joke teller in the world; they all knew it. He missed punch lines. He left out the important parts. He tried again and again and the family had come to both love and dread the jokes he brought to the table.

"Tell me!" Rosie cried out, standing on her chair and raising her own magic wand, similar to the one she'd made for Colleen but with more sparkles, if that was possible.

"Why did the physics teacher break up with the biology teacher?" Gavin paused and smiled in anticipation. When it was silent, he blurted out, "Because there was no chemistry."

All of them laughed, partly in relief; he'd actually told the joke correctly.

Shane stood and held the dustpan for Colleen as she swept the glass shards into its basin. "It's fiddle night, and we need to get back. I left Hank in charge and that's only good for a couple hours, and then it's like leaving the pub in the hands of a friendly golden retriever."

"I'm coming tonight." Colleen tossed the fragments into the trash can. "I'll finish these dishes later. I want to be with you guys, not here by myself while the house makes noises in the dark."

"I have a joke." Their dad stood from the table and clapped his hands together.

"Is it better than the last one?" Shane asked as he ran water over the dishes.

"The last one?" Dad furrowed his brow and shook his head. "Okay, here goes. Why did the physics teacher break up with the biology teacher?" He paused again, just as before, and smiled. "Because there was no chemistry."

Their laughter was forced and disjointed.

"See?" he said. "I *do* know how to tell a joke."

"Yes, Dad, you do." Colleen wiped her hands on the dish towel and swallowed her rising grief.

"Grandy," Rosie said with her wand in the air. "You already told that one."

Gavin looked at Rosie and tousled her hair without comment.

Rosie turned her attention to her aunt.

"Aunt Lena, stay here and play with us."

"I promised Grandy I would help at the pub."

"Please!" Rosie sidled near Colleen and pulled on the edges of her shorts. "Just until we have to go home." Sadie, still not quite sure of this aunt who had suddenly showed up in their lives, backed away.

"Let's not go home." Rosie fluffed her tutu. "I like it better here."

Hallie placed her hands on top of both blond heads. "Girls, Daddy is waiting at home."

"I have a joke." Their dad's voice filled the room in a bellowing voice.

Silence fell. The LP hit the end of its recording, the swish-swish-swish of the needle.

"Dad . . ." Shane walked toward Gavin standing with his palms set on the kitchen table and a smile on his face.

Gavin continued. "Why did the physics teacher break up with the biology teacher? Because there was no chemistry." He raised his arms in a V for victory because he'd just told the best joke of his life.

No one laughed, the room quiet with discomfort and the record continuing to circle silently.

"Why can't I ever make my family laugh

at my jokes?" Gavin smiled good-naturedly and ambled toward the door. "And you wonder why I take my jokes to the pub."

CHAPTER THIRTEEN

Memory is a pulse passing through all
created life.
David Whyte, *Consolations*

They couldn't see her watching and for that
reason it felt very much like a movie. *The
Family:* that was what the movie would be
called, Colleen surmised. She sat on the
back stoop of the house, under the awning,
covered in shadow and quiet. It was late
morning and the day hadn't heated up to
its full potential and yet sweat trickled down
her legs and between her shoulder blades.
She held the morning newspaper, the one
she'd once written for all those years ago,
the one she'd meant to bring out to her dad.
Now it was scrunched in her lap, the pages
fluttering with the morning breeze.

Her dad stood beside the shed on the left
side of the backyard, handing boxes to a
man in work khakis, T-shirt, baseball cap

and muddy boots — Walter. The nieces were bouncing around like the ground was a trampoline, talking to them both. Walter took each box from Gavin and set it on the picnic table, then ripped it open. He took out objects one by one — a saw; a fishing reel; a hammer; a rusted knife — and laid them on the table. It was obvious they were sorting what to keep and what to toss.

And they were laughing. Slowly their words floated toward Colleen.

"Dad," Walter said, "what about the fishing competition in November? We could enter that one. It's a father-son one, but we can get away with it, don't you think?"

Gavin laughed and clapped his hand on Walter's shoulder. "I think we've gotten away with it for quite some time."

The girls yanked on Walter's hand, begging him to spin them around until they were dizzy. He grasped each girl in turn under the arms and spun and spun in a big circle, her legs flying out, until she begged to be put down. Afterward, the girls grabbed each other's hands and walked tipsy through the grass until they both fell down, rolling together like puppies.

The words they spoke started to overlap as Colleen understood that just because she'd ignored the growing family, just because she'd shut out any information about them at all, it hadn't meant they weren't close-knit and loving. To pretend otherwise had been consoling but foolish. Now reality played out on her childhood lawn, next to the dock where Walter had proposed.

Shane was right — Walter seemed to be a good dad. He leaned down when he spoke to his daughters. He was gentle. His laugh was deep and real. He had taken time off work to help Dad clean out the shed, and he wasn't doing it in a grudging manner.

She pulled her knees up close to her chest and sat as quietly as she could, watching a family that belonged to her but wasn't hers at all in any way that made sense. She cast the blame on Walter, on the man who stood in the sunshine calling Gavin "Dad." If he hadn't fallen in love with Hallie. If he hadn't betrayed her. A conversation from long ago floated across the air of the past. Walter telling her how he had always wanted a family like the Donohues, how when he was a child he'd lain in the bunk bed in his dad's apartment or in the pullout couch at his mom's guest house behind her friend's house, and dreamed of a family just like Lena's. He'd made them up, he'd said, and then found them living on the banks of the May River in South Carolina. Now maybe, just maybe, none of this had anything to do with love but with Walter finding and needing what he'd missed in childhood, with believing in a fantasy.

But then again, Colleen thought, as the heat of the morning mixed with the flame of anger, if that was true he would have just stuck with Colleen. So yes, love had something to do with it. He chose the second daughter. Her hands gripped the newspaper so tightly that it tore, the newsprint bleeding black on her damp palms.

Regret, she discovered, tasted metallic and bright, like biting onto a piece of tinfoil. She wanted to cry but she didn't dare — what if one of them looked over and saw her? She stood up quietly, wanting to sneak back into the house, back to her computer and her e-mails and her quiet world.

It wasn't fair, really. Walter and Hallie were the betrayers and yet they were the happy ones? It wasn't supposed to work that way. But not much worked the way it was "supposed" to work, because if that were true, her dad would be sharp and bright, playing trivia games at the pub and bantering about local politics instead of being confused about day and time and place.

"Aunt Lena," Rosie's voice called out just

as Colleen stood to enter the house. The child ran full bore toward Colleen, her arms out for a hug that was half a lawn away.

Escape was not an option.

Colleen received Rosie's hug with her own. "What's up?" she asked.

"Daddy is letting us skip art camp today and taking us to the water park in Savannah. Wanna come?"

"Where's your mom?" Colleen glanced around.

Rosie lifted her first finger and crooked it, wiggling it to draw Colleen near. She whispered, "She's doing things for that party that's a secret."

"Ah!" Colleen brushed the loose hair from Rosie's face, feeling again the childhood familiarity of her smile. "I won't say a word."

Colleen stood up straight and turned toward the group, where Gavin and Walter glanced her way but didn't move, not one inch, as if posing for a photo. Gavin smiled, but Walter's face appeared warped as though half of it wanted to smile while the other half was unsure.

Colleen wouldn't make anyone participate in an awkward moment, least of all herself. She opened the back door and entered the kitchen, Rosie trailing behind wondering if

Aunt Lena liked water parks and long slides.

Safe inside, with the door closed, Colleen smiled at her niece. "I love long slides like you do. But I have to help with the secret party, too. Okay?"

"Do you think it will be Grandy's last party?"

"What?" Colleen's voice pitched high and Rosie stepped back at the change in tone.

"I heard Mommy say that to Daddy. That maybe it was his last party, and she wants it to be so perfectly perfect. It's not his last, right?"

"Oh, Rosie, I don't think so. Your mom just wants things to be good for this one. I know one thing for sure — it is his last sixtieth birthday!" Inside Colleen seethed at her sister's carelessness. Yes, careless, that was what Hallie was. With hearts and sister-hood and love.

Rosie nodded and jumped up and down on her tiptoes, reaching for something unseen. "Someday I'll be tall as you, right?"

"Most likely taller," Colleen said and bent to face Rosie.

"Because I want to look like you." She touched the edge of Colleen's shorts, pulled on a loose thread. "I hope I do."

"Oh, sweetie." Colleen sat on a kitchen chair and faced Rosie. "You are going to be beautiful in your own way. Your own Rosie way."

"You think so?" Rosie pulled her shoulders back, stood taller.

"You already are."

The footsteps and voices of Gavin, Walter and Sadie drew closer and Colleen kissed Rosie's cheek and escaped to her bedroom, closing the door as quietly as she could.

Shane's voice joined them; he'd arrived to pick up Dad. And although she couldn't hear the words, what was important were the sounds. Sounds of family. Laughter. Cross talk. Doors opening and closing.

Colleen sat on her bed and took out her computer — she would focus on work, not on what was happening in the kitchen, not on what was happening in a life that wasn't hers anymore. If she decided to walk in that kitchen right now, there would be awkward silence. And it would be her presence that caused the change — her appearance in her own family. She slammed her fist into the soft mattress and then flopped back in bed to stare at the white ceiling fan going around and around, dust darkening the edges of the blades and shadows flipping.

She allowed her thoughts to ricochet from scene to scene, from memory to memory, without ever sticking on any of them; they would not go away or leave her alone, but she treated them lightly, easily — they were butterflies; they were fuzz from a blown dandelion; they were dust. How was she to continue avoiding and holding disdain for a man who was so kind to her beloved dad?

A soft knock sounded on the door and she sat up. *Please God, if you hear me at all anymore, do not let this be Walter.*

"Yes?" she called out.

"Little lark, may I come in?"

Colleen stood and opened the door to her dad. "Of course." She swept her hand for him to enter the room. "What's up?"

"You ran away just now. I saw you there, right there on the stoop, and then you went inside and hid in your room." He shook his head. "We can't be this way, little lark. We cannot."

"I didn't want to make it awkward while everyone was having fun. It's okay for me to step away once in a while, especially when it's weird."

He stared at her for a beat too long. Maybe he'd forgotten why it was weird. Maybe he wanted to say something that was stuck in his synapses. Maybe he was confused and had already forgotten why he was there. But no matter the reason, he finally spoke softly. "Your mom would not want this unforgiveness. She would not."

And he walked away.

"Mother," Colleen corrected, calling after her dad's retreating back. "*Mother* would not have wanted this unforgiveness."

But he didn't turn around; he didn't say another word.

That evening, the fiddle player was going strong, the strings singing, and Celtic music echoed across the room in strains of longing and melancholy — a specialty of the Irish. The room was almost full and it was only seven on a weekday evening. Colleen glanced around as she entered, having returned to the Lark after sharing dinner with Gavin and Shane. She watched as the historical preservation guy, Beckett, stood at the other end of the bar laughing with a cluster of men and women. He held a glass of water and his grin spread all the way to his eyes, maybe even to his forehead. Colleen looked away and headed to the back room with Shane.

"You can't be hurting for money. This place is hopping," Colleen said.

"Not hurting, but even one bad week could do damage. Dad mismanaged things badly before I got hold of the accounts. I'm still paying off the bills for supplies we

191

didn't need."

They were headed toward the back swinging door when two women waved at Colleen from the left side of the room. Colleen squinted, trying to adjust to the lighting. Ah! High school friends. What were their names? She dug far and fast. "Lena, Lena!" the blonde called and wound her way through the tables to reach her, giving Colleen a hug thick with the aroma of vanilla perfume. "It's me, Marie, from Latin class."

"Yes, hello." Colleen grabbed Shane's arm in a motion not to leave her. "How are you?"

"Oh, my God, I saw your article in *Travel and Leisure.* There I was right in the Savannah Airport and I thought, good Lord, that can't be our Colleen Donohue, the one who left ten years ago and never spoke a word to anyone again. But damn straight, I looked it up and it was you." She paused and glanced around the pub, checking if anyone could hear her. She twirled a flock of bleached hair at the side of her face and then tucked it behind her ear with a flirty tilt of the head. Yes, Shane stood a few feet away. Then she returned her attention to Colleen. "What a fascinating life you've had. Those stories were great. No wonder you left."

The other woman, with darker, shorter hair and wearing cutoff jeans with the ragged strings hanging down, had reached their side. "That's not why she left." She smiled almost savagely and Colleen spied orange lipstick on her teeth. "Do you remember me?"

Colleen stared through the makeup and tight clothes and grinned. "Yes, we were in Ms. Sparks's class together for calculus. Your brother, Jimbo, he was, what, a year younger?"

"Yep. He married Merilee; they live up the road with four kids."

"Four." Colleen shook her head.

"And" — the woman leaned closer — "we were in the school play together — *Annie,* remember? I was Annie."

"Yes," Colleen said. "I remember. Good times." She glanced at Shane and then at the women. "I have to go now, but so good to see you both." As she walked off with Shane she mumbled, "It's true, there are ghosts in the Lark."

Shane laughed and pushed at the swinging doors to the back room. "They're definitely not ghosts. Their happy hour drinking might be keeping the pub alive for another day. They are most definitely regulars."

"I believe they come here for you as much as for the drinks. I see how they look at you."

"Lost cause."

Colleen stepped through the open door he held for her and then stopped. "Shane, have I become a story?"

"What do you mean?"

"I know how things are here — not only in the town but also at the pub. Stories are told and retold; town gossip and all that. You know, the sister left at the altar. Am I one of those town gossip stories? I must be, because that woman just —"

"I don't know. And even if you are, who cares?" He winked. "Might do the pub some good."

Colleen gave a light punch to her brother's arm. "You're so mean." She nodded toward the main room. "Hey, there's some guy out there who's researching our pub for the state historical society. Have you talked to him?"

"Yep. Good guy. He goes all around South Carolina to save buildings. He's a real history buff and loves it here."

"Why does it do us any good for him to label this a historical site?"

"Tax breaks." Shane smiled. "We can use any break we can get."

"Break?" Hallie asked as she entered the back room to join them.

Colleen glanced behind Hallie. "Where

are your girls?"

Hallie dropped her satchel onto the back counter. "Walter is putting them to bed at home, to much protest." Her smile dropped and her face grew serious. "How are your photo stories coming?"

"I did three more today. But I don't know if we can do this — you know, make sense of a life that isn't ours." Colleen looked back and forth between her siblings.

Shane made a dismissive gesture. "We don't have to make sense of it. We only have to record what we can so he can look at the book, see it and read. If there are blanks or inconsistencies in what someone tells you, you can casually ask Dad about what he remembers, too, until he can't remember anything at all. Don't push too hard or get him upset."

"Well, maybe digging up old memories isn't such a great idea." Colleen addressed her brother. "Everyone remembers things differently. Each memory goes on top of another memory, changing it all."

"That's the point." Shane clapped his hands together. "There are the facts of the photo and then the narrative of the photo. I want him to have both. Historical fact. Storytelling truth."

Colleen was silent for a moment, weighing words that might come out wrong as they often did. "But maybe it's better if some things are forgotten."

"No!" Shane's voice rang out louder than usual. "Memory forms us. What are we without it? We aren't a biography. We aren't a list of facts. We are memories. They are the shape of our souls."

The sisters stared at him, their baby brother spouting a philosophy that made him sound like their dad.

Shane took a step toward them both. "We don't get to choose which ones to give back to him either. Just because they confuse us doesn't mean they aren't important. They are all his and we will save them for him as best we can."

Hallie sat on a chair and exhaled. "The shape of our souls."

"Yes," Shane said emphatically. "They are."

Out in the pub, the fiddle player was now playing "The Lark in the Clear Air."

"Has anyone ever asked Dad why he loves this song so much?" Hallie asked.

Shane shook his head. "Weird that I've never thought to ask why."

Colleen felt the memory slip up on her like a warm blast of air. She and Hallie had been in the tree house playing jacks, the rubber ball bouncing as they grabbed the jacks into their palms. Mother and Dad were below on the lawn folding beach towels. Dad whistled the tune, the ever-present tune that infused their lives. Mother's voice had risen. "Enough of that infernal song, Gavin. For God's sake, enough."

Colleen shook off the remembrance and glanced at her brother, something important brewing under the bubble of memory. "Let's ask him. Okay?"

"Okay."

Hallie picked up her purse and pulled the strap high on her shoulder. "I'm going home. I need to finalize some last-minute details." She paused. "I don't believe one person has RSVP'd with a decline, so I will have to get permission from the city to block off the street. And the bar won't be able to handle it either — I have to find a few bartenders and put out an outdoor keg and bar. Do we decorate with photos . . . ?" Her voice trailed off as if the details were drowning her questions.

This was exactly how Hallie had planned Colleen's wedding — with the same frenetic energy, the same obsession. Colleen had let Hallie do the work; she'd handed it all over to her. My God, she'd handed it *all* over — groom included.

"And" — Hallie clapped her hands together — "Dad's timeline still isn't coming together right."

Colleen exhaled, as if by breathing deeply she could calm her sister. "We can help with whatever you need."

"No." Hallie clutched the top of her satchel as if the timeline might jump out and into Colleen's arms. "I've got it. I'll meet you at the house early tomorrow for the drive to Jacksonville. Walter can take the girls to day camp and we can compare what we've learned from the interviews."

The swinging doors swished open as Hallie attempted her exit, but Hank entered lugging a crate of dirty glasses and banging into her. "Just what I need in this crowded area — more Donohues," he muttered.

Hallie juggled and maintained control of her papers and then stormed out, pushing past Hank while Colleen stifled a laugh. She turned to her brother. "I know you want to say something. I see it all over your face, but just keep it to yourself for now."

He tossed his arm over her shoulder, drew her close. "I know you only want to look at the terrible things Walter's done. I get that. But he's *also* a good man. He's been a great father; a big help to Dad around the house, fixing things and just hanging out. You can't just shove him into the monster category and keep him there. There is good in him. Even you wouldn't have fallen in love with him if he was so terrible."

"He fooled me." Colleen looked away, squelching the desire to be stern at the one person in all the world she did not want to be stern with — her sweet brother. But damn.

"Maybe he did, but please just cut him a break so that you can cut your sister a break. Please. He just bought Hallie the cutest cottage at the edge of town and fixed it exactly how she wanted. He's good to his family."

"I hear you," Colleen said. "But have you forgotten what else he did? Have you conveniently forgotten?"

Shane eyes filled with the flash of tears, brimming but not falling. He pulled his sister into a hug. "I have not forgotten, Lena. I haven't. I'm just desperately trying to keep us all together right now. I'm sorry."

Colleen let her head rest on her brother's shoulder, felt a simple peace that came with that love. "Now can we stop talking about it?"

"Yes." He kissed the top of her head and released her as they returned to the pub from the back room.

A young woman with perfectly placed lip liner and a tight pair of jeans walked toward Shane smiling and they were soon in conversation, Colleen left alone in the middle of the room. Sometimes when she entered the pub she felt like she was diving into a warm lake, a place of relaxation and ease that was meant just for her — maybe it was how others felt when they went to a spa. The only thing that compared was sitting at the edge of the river at twilight.

She knew a few of the clientele that evening, the deep voices and the accented laughs of her dad's old friends. Now the younger crowd had slipped in behind them, making the pub as much theirs with their iPhones glowing and their selfies taken at the bar. The faces weren't so homogeneous anymore either. It wasn't New York, but it wasn't the old Watersend either.

A few people called out Colleen's name and others waved. She slipped behind the bar and poured herself a Guinness, the foam even with the top. Hank returned and tipped his hat. "Nice job."

"Anytime you need an extra hand, you let me know." She shot him a grin before sliding onto a bar stool next to a young couple that was obviously on an awkward first date. She smiled at them both and spun around to face the room.

"You look so intense," Beckett said as he appeared before her.

"That's me, intense."

"I don't think that's true." He smiled and nodded toward the group she'd seen him with earlier. "I was just about to leave when I saw you."

Beckett grabbed a free bar stool two over, dragged it next to hers and sat. "So where do you live now, Colleen Donohue?"

"New York City. Brooklyn, to be exact."

"Wow. You left here to live *there*?"

"I did."

"Why? Must have been a hell of a job offer to ditch this place and this pub and your family."

"No. A hell of a something, though." She tried to smile but instead took a long swig of beer.

"A hell of a something." He leaned forward. "I can't wait to find out what that *something* is."

"Oh." She laughed. "That's not happening."

"Really?" He raised his eyebrows and threw back his head, raised his water glass and clinked it with hers. "Cheers."

Colleen tilted her head. "Can you toast

with water? I thought that was against the rules."

"Not in my book." He patted the bar and then his shirt pocket as if looking for a book.

"Oh, you have your own book?"

"I do. Maybe one day I'll let you read it." He extended his hands across the bar. "You know where 'cheers' came from?"

"No, but I have a feeling you're about to tell me."

"In medieval times, two men would clink glasses together before they took a sip so that the liquid would splash into each other's drink and that way they would be sure the other hadn't poisoned their drink."

Colleen's eyebrows rose. "Well, aren't you a fount of knowledge."

"That's me. A fount of useless historical information."

The fiddler began a jig and for a moment the pub patrons all quieted in appreciation of the musician's skill. When they resumed their chorus of conversations, Beckett held out his hand. "Dance?"

"Oh, no." Colleen shook her head. "There's a gaggle of girls over there. I'm sure one of them will dance. I'm not a . . . dancer."

"Who doesn't like to dance?"

"I didn't say I didn't like it. I said I don't

do it. At least not in public."

"Oh, let it go." He grinned and placed his water glass on the bar. "Just follow me." He took her hand and she did just that — followed him.

The last time Colleen had been on a dance floor it had been to learn the waltz for her wedding day. Another thing she'd avoided since then. Not because the memory was so painful, but because she was a terrible dancer. She tripped. She stepped on feet. She banged against people. And worst of all, she looked ridiculous.

But she followed Beckett onto the small square of plywood that Shane had put down only hours before to make a dance floor. The jig, called "Blarney Pilgrim," vibrated with a simple rhythm. Beckett pulled her into his arms and against his body in a quick movement. She blushed with the immediacy of the motion, with the nearness of him. He took two quick steps and carried her with him, leading her in a way she'd never been led on a dance floor. Their steps fell into a rhythm and, without much trying, she was dancing.

She relaxed into the steps and the music, allowing memories and tension to slip away. Forgetting, she thought, wasn't so bad after all.

The Memory Book

Interview with Bob Macken

The photo was torn at the corner like it had been ripped from a scrapbook. It was a color image — Gavin stood on a dock at the marina with his friend Bob Macken, the sheriff, their upright fishing poles beside them, their silhouettes long on the wooden planks. The men squinted into the sun.

Bob Macken now sat across from Colleen at a corner table in the local café. He held a cup of coffee in hands scarred by a lifetime of hard work. His face was leathery and dark with a ring of pale skin around his forehead where his police cap or his baseball cap or his fishing hat sat except, like now, when he was inside. His blue eyes met Colleen's gaze.

"I don't know where you found this photo. I'm not even sure who took it," he said.

"I don't know either." Colleen looked at this man she'd known all her life. "But it's one that

Shane chose."

"I think Shane might have taken it, actually. He came to get your dad from the docks that day. He was so worried about him. It was the one-week mark after your mother's death."

A tremble of regret passed through Colleen's chest. She had left so many problems to her brother. But Shane had assumed the brunt of obligations.

Bob continued, his coffee growing cold. "This photo, it's in half-light."

"What do you mean?" Colleen leaned closer.

"When a photo is at half-light, part of the image is dimmed." He brushed his hands together. "I'm an amateur photographer, so I'm just showing off my knowledge a bit."

Colleen nodded. "Go on."

Bob's hand, calloused and freckled, wavered over the photo. "It's the light we see at dusk or dawn, and it doesn't reveal everything, only a portion of what would be in the photo if it was in full light. Sometimes a photographer deliberately slows the shutter speed for effect, but here it's actually dusk. That day we left at dawn and were out on the river all day. Not much was said between us." Bob paused, turning his coffee mug in his hands, around and around, and then added a packet of sugar. Finally he looked up. "We traveled our way through marshes that your dad knows as well as his own backyard, and then we went out into the ocean, which we rarely did. We'd packed beer and sandwiches, but your dad didn't eat or drink a thing all day, until I became concerned. Then he caught a record-breaking cobia, only to release it, saying he could not bear one more death on God's earth. He'd suffered too many losses. He threw that fish back into the ocean. It was the only time I ever saw him cry."

Colleen placed her hands over Bob's, gave them a squeeze. "Too many losses?"

Bob stared off behind Colleen as though he could see into that day he and his best friend had gone fishing. When his gaze returned to Colleen, it was filmed with unshed tears. "Yes. Too many losses."

"More than Mother?" Colleen knew the answer. Yes, of course there was more than Mother; she, too, had left her dad alone in Watersend.

But Bob didn't say this; he merely nodded and coughed. "We all have losses in our life. All of us."

"What were the ones that broke Dad's heart?" Colleen asked, her pulse beating in her throat. These were the unseen memories she wanted to tap — the ones not captured in a photo.

Bob smiled at her and finally took a sip of

the coffee she'd bought him. "I thought you just wanted the story of the photo."

"I want everything, Bob. Everything you know."

He shook his head. "I've known you since you were a baby. Isn't that amazing?"

Colleen nodded. "Yes."

"But you've been gone for quite a while now, Lena."

"I know, but I'm here now." She took the photo from Bob's hands and slid it into the envelope where the others lay one on top of the other.

"Yes, you've come home for your dad." Bob smiled. "It's hard watching him lose his memories. Gavin's been a good friend to me. You'll let me know if there's anything I can do."

"You're already helping by adding to this memory book, by helping us gather as many of his days as we can in one place."

Bob knotted his hands in a prayer clasp and set them on the table. "It's a worthy goal. And I'm sure what you gather will mean something to him, but we all have private memories, ones we share with only a few people if anyone at all. And what of the memories we shared only with those who are already gone? For your dad, those will be lost forever." He glanced at the phone on his waistband, which was buzzing. "I must go now, Lena. But please let me know if you need anything else."

"I will. And thanks so much." She paused and then added, "Half-light — allowing in only enough light to see what one *wants* to expose."

"Exactly." He held his phone to his ear and walked briskly from the café, leaving Colleen with his words that hinted at something about her dad she could barely see out of the corner of her eye.

CHAPTER FOURTEEN

"Sure, everything is ending," Jules said,
"but not yet."
Jennifer Egan,
A Visit from the Goon Squad

Birdsong woke Colleen and for a moment
she was confused — in New York her windows closed against all noise. But she'd
woken up, of course, in South Carolina. She
rolled over and opened one eye to spy her
childhood bedroom, the one she'd shared
with Hallie, the one her mother had left
unchanged once the girls had become
estranged. A bulletin board was covered
with swim team ribbons and class photos
and dried flowers from dances already
forgotten. On the white wooden desk they'd
once shared was a Ball jar full of pencils,
pens and Magic Markers that were most
likely dried out. Watersend Cougars' red
and white pom-poms hung from one side of

the dresser mirror. Keeping everything intact had been part of Elizabeth's attempt to bring the girls back together, a kind of magical spell that their mother believed would inspire reconciliation; if she kept their things together, she could bring their hearts together, too.

She'd been wrong.

But she'd never given up. Every single phone call ended with Mother asking, "Have you called your sister?" and Colleen answering, "Of course not, Mother." This question had been asked over and over in various forms and each time neither Mother nor Colleen would bend.

"Will you at least try?" Mother would ask. "For me? For Dad?"

"I will do anything for you and Dad. Anything in all the world but that."

"You can't stay mad at her forever, Lena."

"I'm not mad, Mother; I just don't want to speak to her."

The conversations went round and round like this until the evening Colleen exploded, the words bursting from her as she stood in her kitchen in New York, jet-lagged and off her guard, with the cell phone on speaker. "Mother. Have you ever, even once, been upset with Hallie? Have you ever, even once, tried to see it from my point of view?

Have you ever, even once, loved me enough to understand how this must feel?"

The phone had gone silent and Colleen heard Dad, who was on the extension listening in, release a long-held breath. Colleen dropped her head into her hands and waited for the rebuke, for the harsh words from Mother in her strictest voice. But instead she'd only replied, "Yes, I have understood."

And with that the line had gone dead. The subject had never been raised again.

Colleen shook off the memory and rolled over to take her e-tablet from the bedside table, flip it open as the jaundiced light flashed on. She hadn't worked much in four days — and although this usually caused a little flutter of panic, she'd been too consumed with all things Dad to think about work. But there were bills and rent to be paid; e-mails to answer; edits to be done. Not that she lived paycheck to paycheck, but close enough that she couldn't wallow in Watersend and forfeit a month's work.

The e-mail tab blinked and Colleen clicked on it, quickly scrolling through the spam and the sales pitches and the special deals at Anthropologie and Neiman's as she looked for hints of her next assignment. There were a few offers — two to cover a music festival in Texas and one to write about a rodeo in Montana — but the one that caught her eye was from a Ms. Fisher and had the subject heading *Your Ten Tips.* She clicked on it first.

Dear Ms. Donohue,
We have been big fans of your travel articles for some time, and when the Ten Tips was released in *Travel and Leisure* it became our favorite. It was as informative as it was entertaining. We here at Penguin Random House would like to discuss ways for you to possibly turn your column into a travel memoir. Your writing is superb and your wit engaging.

Colleen stopped reading and almost laughed out loud — at first glance she'd misread *memoir* for *memory.* No, they did not want her memories. Well, at least not the ones that haunted her.

A memoir? About travel?

The idea — one she hadn't consciously considered before that minute — seemed as perfectly suited for her work as the travel itself. She hadn't had as much feedback about anything she'd written as she had the ten tips article, in which she'd shared her own stories — of the mistakes, foibles and embarrassments she'd experienced on the road. She'd exposed her life to make the points more salient, and something in the article had resonated with readers.

She wrote back quickly.

Dear Ms. Fisher,
   Thank you so much for the kind words. Your idea is intriguing! The stories behind the stories. Let's talk soon.

Colleen typed in her phone number and hit send.

She smiled as she closed her computer. She had other things to think about today. She and Hallie were taking Dad for the scan; hope simmered alongside dread. Colleen rose from bed, showered and dressed in quick order, a little spring in her step from the "superb writing" compliment.

"Dad!" Colleen called as she entered the kitchen. Morning light slipped into the room through the slats of the wooden blinds, casting yellow stripes onto the hardwood floor. Across the room Colleen spied the red-hot eye of the stove burner. "Dad?" she called again as she turned it off.

The house was empty; she could feel it. Where was he? Had she spent too long on her work? God, no. If something had happened to him because she'd focused on . . .

She wouldn't think about it.

The back screen door popped against the wooden frame as she exited to the backyard. At the end of the dock, Gavin's silhouette was set against the blue morning sky. He squatted as he untied the johnboat from its moorings. It was a small boat with a center console and a bench seat, the once-bright green paint now faded to an almost mint-colored hue. When she and her siblings were small, all five in the family had fit neatly in the boat, but now only two or three at a time could sit comfortably. Colleen burst into a run, calling out, "Dad!"

He turned quickly, coming off balance and falling to the splintered decking. He landed on his left side and let out a grand stream of curses. Colleen stopped, as shocked as if he'd hit her. That couldn't be her dad. She'd never heard him curse, not once. As a teenager, she'd thought he'd said "shit" one time but he'd laughed it off and denied it. "Cursing," he'd said, "is lazy. It's better to find the right word."

She'd never been able to follow that example, believing that sometimes a curse word was the right word.

Colleen quickly reached his side and bent to him. "Are you okay?"

He glanced at his daughter with a blank

stare and then maneuvered his body to sit and shake his head. "Silly me."

"Does anything hurt?"

He tented his legs, rose to a squat and then held out his hand so she could help him stand. "Lena, my little lark. What are you doing here?"

"Remember, Dad. We're taking a day trip today. You, Hallie and me."

"Oh, yes!" His eyes lit up. "I was just headed out in the boat for a quick net of shrimp before I went to the pub. I totally forgot."

They both glanced at the water then, as the johnboat, loosed from its mooring, bobbed away from the dock. Colleen caught the rope, a slithering snake, just in time. She pulled the boat back and retied it using the bowline nautical knot she'd known ever since she could walk onto the dock alone.

"Ready?" She turned to him and smiled.

"Where we headed?" he asked and rubbed his hip where he'd fallen.

"Jacksonville, Dad. I am taking you to see a specialist so we can figure out what's going on."

"Oh, yes." His face brightened. "Thank God for you, my sweet Colleen. You'll know what to do. They can't be right. I feel . . . too . . . normal for something so catastrophic to be happening."

He'd called her Colleen. This never happened. Little lark. Lena. But not Colleen. She placed her hand on his arm, reassuring him. "Dad, it seems that someone losing their memory wouldn't use the word 'catastrophic.' Let's go see this doctor."

His smile fell and he closed his eyes. A soft sound of something near to sorrow escaped his lips and then he smiled as if he'd gone off into a dream.

"Dad?" she asked.

His eyes popped open. "Just a nice memory that rolls in on your name," he said.

"What was it?" Colleen wanted to know. Anything that could evoke such a nostalgic smile would be something to put in the memory book.

Gavin shook his head. "Not now. Let's head to Jacksonville."

"We have to wait for Hallie; she's coming, too."

His grin reached all the way to his eyes, and she knew what it was: hope.

Colleen's hands were tight on the steering wheel of Hallie's minivan; she wasn't accustomed to making long drives, but Hallie had insisted so she could work on her satchel full of papers while they traveled.

Dad was in the passenger seat, fiddling with the knobs, trying to find a radio station. The floorboards were strewn with crushed crackers and empty juice boxes, discarded doll clothes and one empty *Toy Story* thermos rolling around.

"I don't know why we're doing this when we could be spending a perfectly lovely day together out on the river," Gavin said. He flicked another button on the radio and the *Beauty and the Beast* sound track burst forth: *"Be our guest, be our guest."*

Colleen pushed the off button. "Dad, we need to know what's really going on."

"I can tell you what's really going on." He paused. "Nothing."

"Good, then let's find out."

"It sure is nice having you here," Gavin said as he stared out the window, his hands folded in his lap. "I always believed you'd come home, like the time you ran away as a little girl and returned hours later."

"Dad." Colleen's chest tightened. "I didn't run away when I was little."

Hallie leaned forward from the backseat. "Oh, yes, you did. When Mother bought me a new pair of pink sneakers. You were so mad she didn't get you a pair, although you didn't need them, you packed up and left."

"I never . . ." Colleen paused. Hell, she

had, hadn't she? She'd forgotten about how she'd filled her Barbie suitcase with all her sundresses and a bag of Goldfish crackers. "My sneakers were blue. I wanted pink ones." She shook her head at the absurdity.

Hallie laughed with satisfaction, nudging the back of the driver's seat with her knee. "I remember you stomping down the hallway dragging your little suitcase. I was screaming at you, crazy with fear that you would really leave but too scared to go with you. I'll never forget it."

"I came back once I ate all the Goldfish and my shoulders were so sunburned I thought I'd been lit on fire. I came home and you were huddled on the stairs exactly where I'd left you. I tripped over you in the dark."

"We just can't stay out of each other's way, can we?" Hallie said. The sisters were quiet for a long moment, and inside that moment was childhood, and love.

Dad clapped his hand on the console. "We're a family and families by nature cannot stay out of each other's way."

The truth filled the car and the remainder of the drive was easy and quiet as they listened to country music radio stations come and go along I-95. Dad talked about the local high school winning states in baseball and a long-gone Braves game from before Colleen was born. Hallie worked on her never-ending checklists — the RSVP list; the caterer's food offerings; the outdoor furniture vendor who didn't have enough chairs but would find some. She didn't talk out loud about any of it, telling their dad it was school forms for her daughters. Meanwhile Colleen drove carefully, staring through the windshield, and heard her dad's words over and over, caught and echoing in Hallie's minivan.

Families by nature cannot stay out of each other's way.

It had been a two-and-a-half-hour drive to MD Anderson in Jacksonville, Florida, and the offices inside gleamed like a new kitchen and smelled like disinfectant and Band-Aids, that particular aroma of childhood skinned knees.

As the doctors tested their dad, imaged his brain with the spanking new technology and drew his blood, Colleen and Hallie were left in a private waiting room where old magazines and acidic coffee kept their silence company. Time dragged, trying to pull itself through dread.

Dad had once told Colleen that time was different for the Celtic people — that they didn't worry about *not* having enough of it or how to use it or if they wasted it. The quality of the experience, he'd said, determined the sense of time. She wanted to tell him that she understood what he meant now — because here, time stretched and warped. The past was compressed and became an amalgam of everything they'd ever done together; the present stretched past its limit, and the unknown future felt dark.

When Colleen had left Watersend on the afternoon of her wedding day, time had been her friend — she'd known that as the clock ticked forward, her pain would ease. She'd needed time to rush on, to swiftly turn into the future days when she wouldn't hurt so badly. And it had happened. The last ten years hadn't so much flown by as moved along in a frenetic need to get somewhere else. She'd gone from angry to ashamed to despondent and all the emotions in between. Where had she landed now? At avoidance? It had taken years for her heart to stop reaching for what she had lost but could not help loving still.

Now, God, now she wanted time to stand still, to stop stealing her dad's memories, to allow them to be quiet in its paused breath.

But time was not her servant.

Colleen peeked over at the papers Hallie worked on diligently — this time a set list for the band. "I can't believe we're going to get away with this — with throwing him a party and he doesn't know?"

"I think he knows." Hallie smiled. "More than a few patrons have slipped up and made a vague mention, but he ignores them."

"Maybe it's too much. Maybe we should cancel the party and just focus on helping him."

"Are you kidding?" Hallie pointed at all the papers. "This is going to be the highlight of his year. Of many years. What he does and doesn't remember and know won't take away from the party at all. It's a celebration of his life."

"Yes." Colleen nodded, not wanting to argue. "Have you figured out the timeline?" She tried to keep her tone light and breezy.

"No. We're going to have to ask him. Lena, it concerns the year before you were born, after Ireland. The dates on the photos don't match the date of your birth or when they bought the pub."

"So, this is about me?" Colleen's eyebrows rose with her voice.

Hallie exhaled through pursed lips as if she'd just run a race. "Isn't it always?" She waved her hand through the air. "Okay, just joking." She grimaced. "A bad joke."

"Very bad," Colleen said and rolled her eyes. "Okay, how are we going to ask him?"

"I was thinking we'd go out on the boat — me, you and Dad." Hallie's eyes shimmied away from Colleen's, a quick movement. "I know you'll say no, but I think it will get him to relax and remember, be receptive. It's been a long, long time and he asks for you so often . . ."

"He asks to go out on the river with us?" Colleen straightened up, feeling a tug on her chest as if Hallie had just caught her with a fishhook and reeled her in.

"Yes."

"Okay, then we will."

Hallie shut a notebook and brought her gaze back to Colleen, or at least near her. "I know I haven't said anything yet, but that article you wrote about ten tips for travel is really good. I didn't know any of those stories about you."

Colleen spoke carefully. "Thank you. That's nice of you to say." For the moment she kept to herself the e-mail about possibly writing a memoir; she wanted to savor the idea and even when she did speak of it, Hallie would not be the first one she would tell.

"You know," Hallie said, pulling out a large binder labeled "60th Birthday," "I've read all your articles, or all of them that I know about. Not sure if I've kept up, but I've tried."

"Really?"

Hallie nodded. "It's quite the life you live now."

She always seemed to be having two conversations with Hallie. Colleen took a deep breath, decided not to delve into the hidden meanings. While she was weighing her words, her phone beeped — a text from Philippe: *I believe you now, Colleen. It's been a pleasure being your friend. Take care of yourself. Good-bye.*

Colleen let out a long puff of air and deleted it. She could try and talk to him about it. She could appease him with a few words of adoration, but none of it seemed worth it at the moment. And what good would it do to keep him near? She didn't feel the same as he did. She was done.

"Anything important?" Hallie asked lightly.

Colleen looked up. "Not really. A guy in New York." She shrugged as her phone beeped again — this time a text from Beckett.

You busy tonight? Would love to see you.

Hallie laughed. "A guy who's not giving up?"

"No, a different guy this time."

"See?" Hallie leaned forward and spoke as if they were companions again in the tree house making a daisy chain together. "You can have any guy you want. That's always been true."

Colleen stood up, stashing her phone in her back pocket and swallowing her sudden fury. With effort, she pushed down the urge to vehemently deny her sister's statement, to call her a liar, to declare that she'd only ever wanted *one* guy.

"Listen, I'm going outside for some fresh air. If the doc comes in, will you text me?"

"You were out of town." Hallie folded her hands on her lap, her fingers inside her knotted fists like when they were kids and would play "here's the church and here's the steeple, open the door . . ." and then they'd wiggle their fingers for the people.

"What?" Colleen was a few steps from the door.

"When Walter and I began talking."

Colleen paused, wanting to run but suddenly unable to move, her feet glued to the faux-wood floor.

"He came over to drop off a bouquet of gardenias for Mother; he'd heard her say she loved them. We arranged them in a vase and then we started talking. That's all I did, Lena. I wanted to get to know my future brother-in-law."

"Oh." Apparently nothing was going to stop Hallie from unloading her tale of love and marriage. Colleen's ears buzzed. From somewhere far away Hallie's voice continued.

"He asked me about the party I was organizing for the Shepherds' anniversary, and gave me great ideas for a company picnic I was stuck on. We talked and talked. He had such good ideas and then he quoted a line from Shakespeare . . ."

Colleen startled and held up her hand. "I bet I know what it is."

Hallie shook her head. "No. This was between us. I never told you."

" 'Now, my fair'st friend, I would I had some flowers o' the spring that might become your time of day; and yours, and yours.' "

Hallie's lips parted, trying to pull in air. "How did you know?"

"Because he quoted the same line to me on our first date." Colleen felt something elemental shifting. "I found out later it's the only one he knows and whenever he's around flowers . . . he uses it. So what hap-

225

pened then?"

"That can't be true. Now you're just trying to be cruel. We shared our stories and he loved the same poets I did; he loved to talk about the meaning *behind* things."

Colleen interrupted. "Like how the universe expands, and how we're made of stardust and how time means nothing without space and how we have a purpose in life and we are meant to be here carrying our own blueprint . . ." Colleen spouted the long-remembered conversations she'd had with Walter, the ones that had kept her a little bit in love with him even as she hated him.

"Yes." Hallie's voice faded. "He loved to talk about things that mean something. Really *mean* something." Her voice sounded strangled. "Did he talk about those things with you?"

"Of course he did, Hallie. Do you think you were special and he saved all his best stuff just for you?" She was being harsh and she knew it. "He drew you pictures, too, right? Little drawings of your daily life? He sent articles and photos that would mean something to you, to *only* you, right? And only he knew you that well."

"Yes." Hallie's mouth shaped the word, but Colleen didn't hear her voice at all.

"Me, too, Hallie. Me. Too. And he was doing all of this with you while I was engaged to him? You never thought to tell me?"

"At first I believed he was just trying to be a good brother-in-law. You know, get to know the little sister. Then I realized that I was waiting for his next e-mail or call or for him to stop by the house to see you. I realized I wanted to hear from him. I was falling in love with him. So I told him I couldn't talk to him anymore. I told him." Hallie stared over Colleen's shoulder as if Walter was even now standing behind her sister.

"Really? You told him you didn't want to talk anymore, but you could play tongue hockey with him on my wedding day?"

Hallie's gaze snapped back to Colleen. "That's so gross."

Colleen bit her lip in an attempt to keep from laughing. "I have no idea where that came from. Sorry."

"Lena, I've been carrying this around and although you don't care anymore, and you don't love me anymore, I need to tell you. I've been trying and trying to tell you. For years I've been trying to tell you, and you've been cruel and cold."

"Just keep going."

Hallie closed her eyes; she couldn't look

at Colleen while she finished her tale. "So I *did* tell him that we had to quit talking, that I could never betray you, but the truth is, I couldn't stop. It was like a sickness. I fell in love with him so quickly and yet I loved you with all my heart. I was devastated. I couldn't stand to break your heart. I would have rather broken my own."

"Really?" Colleen's tone was sarcastic, biting.

"Yes, really. Walter and I talked about it for hours."

"While I was fretting over bridesmaids' dresses and chocolate cake with buttercream icing, you were talking to my fiancé about how he needed to stay with me even though he loved you? My God, this story just gets worse." The buried devastation began to rise like a tide. Her hands tingled; her stomach roiled. The truth didn't always need to be told, did it?

"No. It wasn't like that. He did love you — a lot. We just found this deep connection and we didn't know what to do with it."

"Seems to me you knew exactly what to do with it — or it looked like it in the church alcove that day."

"That was our first kiss." Hallie covered her mouth, wiping off that same kiss. "He'd said he agreed with me and that he loved you and wanted to build a life with you, but he wanted just one kiss. Just one."

"And you agreed?"

"I'd never felt that way about anyone, Lena. Ever. I didn't know what to do. I didn't know . . . what to do."

"So you thought kissing was the best answer."

"It was wrong. I know that. I've always known that." Hallie shook her head, her hair falling into her face. "I've lived with the consequences. We all have. It was wrong and I made a mistake and if I could go back in time I would warn you. I would warn myself. I would change everything. But I can't."

"Warn me?"

Hallie retreated then, her face closing in.

"Hallie, he seduced you the exact same way he seduced me. He used the same Shakespeare quote. The same bullshit 'we are all one in the stars' stories. He dug into that vulnerable little heart of yours and made a nest. Just like he did to me."

"You hate me."

"No. I don't hate you. Maybe I did for a time, or at least I tried. But mostly I've just been avoiding the pain." A moment of silence fell between them. Finally Colleen asked, "Was it worth it?"

Hallie stared at her sister for the longest time, as if she had never once considered this question. "I have Rosie and Sadie," she said. "How could I answer with anything other than a yes?"

"Was *Walter* worth it, Hallie?"

Hallie's mouth formed a tight little corkscrew, her eyes closed. "I know it started badly, but we've made a life and a good marriage. We have two little girls, Lena, your nieces, who are part of us, me and you the same."

So of course he was worth it, Colleen mentally finished for her sister. He was Walter with the resounding laugh and the twinkle in his eye. He was Walter who tuned in when you spoke, who remembered everything you loved and then showed up with it in his hands. He was Walter who knew how to touch a woman. He was Walter with the quick wit and the engrossing conversations.

No, Hallie hadn't needed to answer the question.

Chapter Fifteen

The past beats inside me
like a second heart.
John Banville, *The Sea*

Colleen took a long walk through the hospital grounds and tried not to think about Hallie's story, but of course she did, letting the images ricochet off her memories, fireflies trapped in a jar. An hour later, her sister texted her to say the test results were in. Colleen bolted back to the waiting room and arrived just as Dr. Ray entered in her green scrubs. Here, now, Colleen told herself, she would believe what she was told; she would no longer deceive herself by fabricating other possibilities.

In that private room, Dr. Ray grabbed a chair and brought it to face Colleen and Hallie. Gavin was in the exam room getting dressed so they had a moment or two alone.

"The scan shows significant amounts of

amyloid plaque. Along with his previous tests, I can say with assurance that your dad has mid- to late-stage Alzheimer's disease."

The proclamation dropped into the room like a heavy rock with no way to move it. There was no more faking it. No more denial. No more maybe, couldn't-be, not-Dad.

"Where do we go from here?" Colleen's voice was weak. Hallie sat still and quiet, her hands folded in her lap.

"We have new medicines now, but the clinical trials are only for patients in an earlier stage," Dr. Ray said. "They have not proved to be effective at the stage your father is in."

"Why did it take so long for us to know?" Hallie spoke up, her hands now flying through the air. "We thought it was just plain forgetfulness."

Dr. Ray nodded. "Do not blame yourself. You can't do that. This disease will be enough of a stressor on your family."

Hallie asked the question Colleen was wondering. "Why is he going downhill so fast? I thought it took years."

"Sometimes when someone is very intelligent, has a strong social network and higher education, the symptoms are masked for longer. So what looks like rapid deterioration is merely the symptoms finally becoming obvious. And didn't he recently lose your mother?"

"Yes, about two years ago," Hallie confirmed.

"Grief and change in routine can make it worse. And she was probably protecting him, helping him."

Colleen stood then, the information pulsing through her. "How long do we have?"

"No one can say. But he's definitely moving into the late stages." Dr. Ray softened her voice. "Has he had outbursts that are out of character?"

"Yes." Colleen couldn't deny it. "Just this morning he said a string of curse words that I'd never heard him use. He thinks cursing is lazy."

"We don't know," Dr. Ray said, "whether the aggression and agitation are because of damage to centers in the brain or aggravation at the memory loss. Even so, you must expect more of it. I'm sorry."

"So not only will he lose his memories of who he is and who we are, but he will become someone else at the same time?"

"No. He will *not* become someone else. He's still your dad. His brain is being damaged, and this will cause him to lose memories and act differently. But you have to

233

remember he is still the same man. You must do your best to keep that in your heart." Dr. Ray nodded toward the door. "He should be dressed and ready in a minute. You have plans to make. You need to consider arrangements. I'll put you in touch with a social worker to discuss safety, where he'll live and financial concerns. You have a lot ahead of you, but I know you both have a devoted brother. Gavin is lucky to have such a strong family network. I understand he owns a pub and is close to the townspeople? He is well respected?"

"Yes." Grief grabbed Colleen by the throat. The family. The town. The pub. She'd given them up and now they would help her dad.

Gavin's voice reached them just as he stepped into the room. "Well, are you all in here talking about me behind my back?" He was dressed and carrying his shoes in his hand.

Hallie went to her dad and hugged him. "Dad, put on your shoes."

"They are on." Then he glanced at his hands and laughed. "On my hands." Gavin sat down and looked at Dr. Ray. "Okay, give it to me straight."

Dr. Ray recited what she'd told the sisters while Gavin sat quietly, his shoes on his lap.

"So it's true."

"Dad, we will do *everything,*" Colleen blurted out.

He looked at her with an expression she'd never seen — he was frightened. "*Everything* will not be enough. I know that is true." Gavin swiped his hand across the table and magazines scattered; his shoes fell from his lap to the floor.

"Dad?" Colleen stared at him. He was aging quickly, the confusion etching his face with worry lines. Regret washed over her with the sensation of being punched in the stomach. She should have spent more time with Dad. Asked him about his life. Asked him . . .

His gaze slowly shifted to Colleen and then to Hallie as he slipped on his loafers. "If this becomes a hardship on you two or your brother, you must let someone else take care of me."

"What are you talking about, Dad?" Colleen fought back tears. "We aren't giving you away because —"

"I won't be me."

Colleen twisted her hands together, knotted them together. "You will be you. You will. You're the one who tells me about the Celtic world of the soul. That won't change. Your soul doesn't have plaque on it."

"You must know this, my girls. As I become just this body, as my memory doesn't serve you or me, you can never doubt my love. I need you to promise me that."

"I promise, Dad," they both answered, almost in unison, catching each other's gazes. They were together in this; finally in *this* they were together.

He folded his hands in his lap. "It's time to go back to the pub. I sure can't miss trivia night."

"Dad, there's never a night you can miss."

"That's very true."

They made it back from Jacksonville with Dad snoozing or humming to the radio as if they hadn't just heard the worst news possible, as if his mind was already sliding toward oblivion in a good-natured way. Of course this wasn't true — all three of them were hurting, holding the devastating news tight to their own selves like an invisible wound. What was there to say?

This time Hallie drove while Colleen sat in the backseat next to the sticky gummy bears in the side seat and a half-full juice box on the floorboards. She stared out the window, wishing for something perfect to say, something that would anchor them in the right now, but she found nothing but an old memory that rolled in asking to be known.

How old had she been? Maybe six, or even as young as five years old.

She was practicing throwing the net, her small hands around the edges of the nylon, the small silver weights like beads she liked to roll between her fingers. Dad stood behind her and held her arms as she imitated his movements, a slow dance as they threw the net in an arc over the blue-gray water. Together they pulled it out of the water and inside was a pile of squirming shrimp, translucent and thrashing against the constraints of the net.

"Let them go," Colleen hollered. She released her edge of the net as twenty or more shrimp fell to the dock. Their whiskers, what she called the antennae, tickled her feet and she began to kick them into the water. Her feet slid and the shrimp plunked into the dimpled river, sinking to the depths where she believed they would rejoin their family.

"Lena, love." Dad took her hands. "What are you doing?"

He didn't prevent her from throwing them back. He didn't yell. He just asked.

When one lone shrimp remained, Colleen plucked it from the dock and stared at its small beady eyes before tossing it into the outgoing tide. She turned to her dad. "We can't take them away from their family. What if the sister is looking for her brother or the little girl looking for her mother?"

Dad bent to Colleen and took her in his arms, pulled so closely that she smelled his aftershave and the salty brine of their river that ran through his heart and straight to her own. "You are so like your mother." He hugged her tightly, rubbed her back before releasing her to look into her eyes.

"Mother doesn't like to catch them either," Colleen said and wiped at the tears. "She only likes to cook them. I can't kill them, Daddy. I just can't."

"They were given to us for eatin'. They're a gift from the river. We aren't separating anyone. They don't have families like we do."

"If anyone ever took me from my family; if I were caught in a net . . ." Colleen threw her arms around him and he lifted her up, carried her back to the house.

"We'll try again another day because you are very, very good at throwing that net, Lena. It's a skill that takes some people years to learn."

Mother waited on the back step in her favorite navy blue sundress, her hair blow-ing in the breeze, all smiles and warmth. "Are you okay, sweetie?" She rubbed the top of Colleen's tangled hair.

"I just didn't want to take the shrimp I caught." Colleen was placed on the ground and she looked at her mom. "Dad said I'm just like *you.*"

Mother froze in place, the dish towel in her hand fluttering in the gust of an incoming storm. Her face looked different, Colleen thought. Funny. Then Mother began to cry, not with any noise but with tears that filled her eyes like the rain often did in the pitted spots of their backyard. She used the dish towel to wipe them away and turned back into the house, closing the door behind her.

Colleen looked at her dad. "Did I do something wrong?"

"No, Lena. No. She doesn't like to be reminded of their little deaths."

He hoisted his daughter onto his shoulders and walked around the side of the house.

"She doesn't love me like she does Hallie." Colleen stated this with conviction, as though someone had told her the fact and she needed to tell her dad the truth.

Gavin grabbed Colleen by the waist and swung her from his shoulders to place her on the ground. He bent to look directly into her eyes, which were the same color and shape as his own. "That is not true, Lena. Not at all true."

"Yes, it is." Colleen shrugged. "But it's okay because she does love me, just not as much."

"Why do you say such things?"

"I just know." Colleen skipped off and called back to her dad, "Are you coming?"

It was later that night, when everyone was asleep, the creaks of the house settling, acorns falling on the porch like footsteps, when Colleen sneaked out of bed to watch the full moon rise over her river. She wanted to watch just until it reached the top of the live oak, and then she would go back to bed, but she was stopped dead in her tracks when she heard Mother and Dad whispering in the kitchen.

They were talking about her.

"I try, Gavin. I do try. I love her very much. You know that."

And with that, Colleen ran back to bed, forfeiting her view of the moon as she buried herself under the covers. She didn't want to hear one more word. Not one. Even as a child she understood — it was best to believe what she was told to believe, not what she overheard.

CHAPTER SIXTEEN

Memories were like the tides.
Mary Alice Monroe,
Beach House Memories

Shane met Colleen, Hallie and Dad at the pub's back door. His face was set with tight control, his fists clenched at his sides. A cloudless sky was turning the early pink shades of twilight, the air still and hot. "What did they say?" No preamble, no greeting.

Gavin answered. "It's not good news, son, but it doesn't change anything. I'm going to walk into my pub right now and enjoy trivia night. I'm going to have my one whiskey. I'm going to love you and love Hallie and love Lena. Nothing about that changes." He nodded at his children and opened the back door and disappeared inside.

Hallie pointed after him. "Let me go with him. Colleen can catch you up." She slipped

241

inside with her satchel and her papers and her ponytail flapping.

Shane exhaled and leaned against the building, his hands jammed in his pockets. "Just damn. Tell me everything."

"First, before I forget — when I got out of the shower today, the stove burner was on and he was about to go out in the johnboat."

Shane rubbed his temples. "I knew this was coming. We have to make plans now."

Colleen went to him with a hug. This was the boy she'd held when he scabbed a knee or became scared during a thunderstorm. This was the boy she'd taught to hook a worm and throw a net. "I've missed you so much," Colleen said into his shoulder.

"Me, too, sis. Me, too."

"Shane." She stepped back. "We *are* running out of time. Your idea to catch his memories — we have to do it now. The doc said there's no question . . ."

The sound of the squeaking hinges stopped Colleen's statement and Gavin emerged. He propped open the back door with his foot and in his free hand he held a garbage bag. He took a few steps toward the dumpster and threw the bag in before turning to his children. "Is something wrong and I don't know about it? You look so serious."

Twilight filtered through the Spanish moss, spilling light like strained honey onto their dad's face. He squinted at his children. Shane took two steps toward him. "Dad, we were just talking about your doctor's appointment today."

"My doctor's appointment?"

Shane and Colleen exchanged glances. "Yes, Dad. We went to Jacksonville today."

Gavin rubbed at his face, wiping away a film of forgetfulness. "I'm sick, aren't I?"

"Not sick." Shane came to Gavin's side. "Remember? It's Alzheimer's."

Those two words next to each other hit Colleen: Remember plus Alzheimer's equals Irony.

Gavin's face broke into sadness. "Ah, yes. Well, that's a hell of a thing to have, isn't it?"

Shane's voice shook. "We're here, Dad. We are here for you."

Colleen looped her arm through her dad's and, together, they walked inside. Colleen cut through the back room and into the main area to sidle to the edge of the bar, with Shane on the other side. Gavin joined a group of friends at the dartboard and his boisterous laughter could soon be heard across the room. Colleen spoke to Shane in almost a whisper. "One thing the doc told me is that ritual and familiarity are two of the most calming forces for Dad. So having him here is good for him."

"We have to talk to Hallie and make plans," Shane said. "We have to . . ."

He abruptly quit speaking and Colleen followed his gaze to the front door, where a man entered the pub. Backlit in the setting sun he appeared as a silhouette, a cutout. As the door shut, he walked toward the middle of the room and his form became clear, the sunlight a spotlight: Walter.

He caught Colleen's gaze.

She wanted to tear her eyes from his, to run, to at least move, but none of that happened. She froze.

She realized now that in her memory he'd been taller. How could that be? Damned unreliable memory. He, too, stopped still, standing halfway across the room.

"Oh, shit," Shane said softly enough for only Colleen to hear. "Just what we need."

His blue eyes. She could see them from where she stood. His wavy dark hair. His mouth was open in surprise, and her gaze was drawn to his lips. Those lips that had kissed her everywhere.

Her heart paused and then she was swept

back in time: She was in a bridal veil with Swarovski crystals sewn by hand into swirling patterns. She was holding a bottle of champagne. She was sick and dizzy, and she couldn't move one step toward or away from him. How had she thought she was *now* okay?

A hand grabbed her arm, pulling her backward. "Lena!" It was Shane.

An electric shock ran from her brother's hand to her heart and jumped it back to life. She shook her shoulders to free herself from her brother and took long, purposeful steps toward Walter until she stood in front of him.

"Hello, Walter." She would be the strong one. She would not show weakness. She would hold her head high. He would never, ever know how much he'd hurt her. And even more, he would regret his rejection of her.

"Hi, Lena. Lordy, you look exactly the same. You're so beautiful." He smiled, so charming.

"You're despicable," she said, low and quiet, her hands stiff at her sides.

For all the practiced speeches, for all the times she'd imagined this moment, for all the eloquent words she'd manufactured in her journal and in her mind, those were the two words that fell from her mouth.

Walter burst into laughter and spread his arms wide. "There's my girl."

"Your girl?" Colleen's voice shook.

"You know what I mean."

"I don't think I do."

"I mean you haven't changed. Full of fire and spit." He reached forward for a hug.

Colleen, so stunned she couldn't react, allowed him to put his arms around her. He squeezed tightly and she froze until he released her and stepped back. "I'm hoping we can all be a family now, Lena. I hate that it's your dad's illness that brought you back, but let's all try."

"Try to be a family?" She repeated his words as though he'd been speaking in another language, and she was translating.

"Well, we are, aren't we?" He winked at her.

He winked!

Nausea rose so quickly that her body finally took action and she ran for the back room, through the swinging doors and out to the alleyway.

In the pub parking lot, taking gulps of fresh air, Colleen's body-memory flew back in time. She sensed Walter's mouth on her, his words and his promises as fresh as though he were saying them now. She bent over and placed her hands on her knees, drew in a deep breath.

She and Walter in bed together, a rumpled white comforter tangled between them. Sunrise filtered through Walter's bedroom window, which faced east toward the river that, in turn, flowed right past her own house. She reclined sideways, her elbow bent with her head propped in her palm. Walter trailed his fingers along her neck and then down her body, his lips following. "You're my family now," he said.

"We're a package deal," she told him, the desire rising again. She folded her leg over his to pull him closer and closer still. "Do you realize that if we floated along the river from here, we'd end up right at my family's dock? We're tied together by water."

"Meant to be," he said.

She felt him hard against her thigh and again they made love with the fervor of those who believe they will never get enough of each other. Their bodies were the same as the river outside, drawing them together with every tide.

A bang of the back pub door and Colleen shook herself from the vivid remembrance. She hated him. She wanted him. She loved him. No, she didn't. She hated him.

"Are you okay?" The voice startled Colleen and she stood quickly, becoming off balance and falling back to catch herself on Beckett's arm. "What?"

"I saw you run out, and I thought . . ."

"You thought what?"

"That you didn't look well."

Colleen tried to smile. "Just needed to catch my breath."

"Are you sick? Can I get you some water or something . . ." He reached for her hand and took it, lifted it to his lips to kiss her palm. So gentle; so sweet.

"It's not the kind of sickness that can be helped with water." She squeezed his hand.

"What is it then?"

"Memories," she said. "A sickening memory that came alive and then walked through the door; one I've tried to forget."

"*Trying* to forget never works." He smiled at her as if they were in on a secret together.

"Well, isn't that the hell of it all? My dad wants to remember and he can't. I want to forget and I can't."

"I'm sorry. Whatever it is, I'm sorry."

"So am I." Colleen shook her head and let go of his hand. "So very sorry."

"I know a great place to forget for a while, a place where we can see the stars. They give me perspective. Come with me?"

"If it means I don't have to head back

inside, then I'm good to go."

The back pub door swung open again, spilling a funnel of light onto the gravel driveway as Walter and Hallie stepped onto the threshold. Hallie crossed her arms over her chest; he gesticulated wildly. What world had Colleen fallen into that she had to watch this now? She pressed herself against the dumpster and pulled Beckett toward her. "Shh . . ."

"I saw you, Walter." Hallie's voice held back tears; Colleen knew the sound well.

"Saw me?" Walter's smooth voice, so seductive and calm, so caring and sweet.

"Hug my sister. I saw you. Did you kiss her, too?"

A great rip of laughter burst from Colleen. She slammed her hand over her mouth, but it was too late. Walter and Hallie turned toward her, moving out of the light to see Beckett and Colleen. "I'm sorry," Colleen said. "It's not funny, is it?"

"Not funny at all." Hallie stepped toward her sister.

"But it is," Colleen said. "Can't you see that? Nothing happened and look at how you feel. *Feel* how you feel." Colleen felt the veracity moving in waves, and she came closer to Hallie in the darkness. "Imagine you're in a wedding dress. Imagine you have no idea. Imagine . . ."

Hallie made a soft noise in the back of her throat. "We have children . . . we have a family."

"*I* was your family!" Colleen spread her hands wide. "We were your family. But you chose *him.*" The grief rose and Colleen turned to Beckett for help.

Beckett held out his hand and Colleen took it. "Come with me," he said.

Hallie stepped back to stand next to her husband. Colleen kept her eyes on Beckett. She allowed herself to be guided by his hand and the faint glow of the pub light. "Where are we headed?"

"Do you have to know everything?" he asked.

"Yes, I believe I do."

CHAPTER SEVENTEEN

Memory . . . is the diary that we all carry
about with us.

Oscar Wilde,
The Importance of Being Earnest

Nine Days until the Party

In the wee morning hours before her dad
awoke, Colleen sat cross-legged on her
single bed. Hallie's bed across the room was
empty and well made, the blue and white
throw pillows neatly stacked. Colleen set
her laptop on the pillows and began to
search for a list of alternative Alzheimer's
treatments. Brain games. Chanting. Vita-
mins. Vegan diet. CBD oil. Fish oil. Ginkgo.
Vitamin D. The list was overwhelming and
yet Colleen wanted to do something, to
show up at the social worker's meeting with
more than financial and insurance information. She wanted to have a list in hand —

what now? she would ask. What now? *Help us.*

The morning sounds of her childhood home waking had not altered during all the intervening years, a series of creaks and groans as familiar as her favorite song. Colleen had once imagined that the house was a living being, that secrets were hiding in the basement and that the heart of it was cached in a corner she hadn't yet found. Although even then she'd known and explored every inch of the house, still she'd believed in this fantasy. Dad had ingrained in Colleen the belief that in the Celtic world all things were alive. All had a soul. All had a purpose.

Settling back against the pink fabric headboard, she scrolled through e-mail, her eyes finding another e-mail to discuss the possibility of a travel memoir. Outside, the birds were waking with their choral crescendos and Colleen wondered — where would such a memoir begin? Where would it end? And under those questions was a bigger one, about how one could reach tip number ten about "going home" when one didn't know where home was. She couldn't say yes to this assignment until she knew what it meant for her, what the memoir would *really* be about.

Someone in the kitchen banged a pot and soft music, too soft to identify, came to her ears. Dad was obviously awake and starting breakfast. The aroma of bacon filtered into the room. Habits died hard. No matter how many times they'd lectured him on the evils of bacon, he arose each morning and put exactly two strips in the frying pan, just as his wife had once done for him.

Colleen didn't yet rise. She wanted to savor the memory of the night before when Beckett had taken her to gaze at the stars from a cove at the river. They'd lain back in a canoe without seats, an empty shell he'd left on dry land in anticipation of refurbishing it. He'd named the constellations as she tried to make out the shapes he saw: the Seven Sisters; the throne of Cassiopeia; the flying horse of Pegasus. They hadn't talked about much else and he hadn't asked why she'd been upset behind the pub or about the harsh words with her sister.

An hour into their quiet talk, she realized that if he did ask, she would tell him. But he was kind enough to let it be. Instead, she told him all about their dad, his mind being covered in plaque and tangles, his personality changing, the party and the memory book. After listening with quiet understanding, and sympathy, he took her home and

253

left her with one soft kiss; he never asked for or expected more. Unaccustomed to such reticence, Colleen almost asked him why he didn't like her, but she could see from the smile on his face and the gentleness in his kiss that he did.

This morning, he was taking her to the local historical society.

"Lena!" her dad called from the hallway.

"Coming," she called out.

She opened her bedroom closet and stared at the dresses and shirts, the pants slung over hangers and the sweaters folded on the back shelf, neatly and by color. Her mother had done this — organized Colleen's closet after she'd left — and it looked as though it had been waiting for her all these years.

The old sundresses looked inviting and simple. She ran her fingers over the various fabrics until she paused on a blue-and-white-striped dress, even now in style, and slipped it off the hanger and over her body. Yes, it still fit.

With a quick glance in the mirror and a brush of her humidity-curled hair, which she pulled back into a knot, she entered the kitchen to find Shane and Dad laughing at something on Shane's phone.

"You know I hate missing out." Colleen poked at her brother and peeked over his shoulder at a photo of a dog riding a bike. "Not that funny."

"Yes, it is," Dad said. "You gotta enjoy the little things, Lena."

"You look nice today, sis."

"Well, thank you."

Dad spooned a poached egg onto a plate and handed it to Colleen. "Special plans?"

She nodded. "Beckett is taking me to the historical society so I can see some old records about the pub."

"Old records?" Gavin held a spoon in the air and a large blob of egg fell to the hardwood floor.

Colleen jumped back to avoid getting eggs on her sandals and tried to ignore the fumble, one she might make herself. "Yes, you know — when it was built, who used to own it and things like that. He's gathering all the records that will support his proposal that it become a historic landmark. He said there are old pictures and I thought it would be interesting."

"Interesting." Gavin repeated her last word and stared off as if someone was standing behind her.

"Dad . . ." Shane's voice was soft and firm. "Remember? We're trying to get historic landmark status for a tax break. That nice young man you met . . ."

Gavin nodded. "Yes. But is it necessary? Why can't we leave it all the way it is?"

"Everything helps, Dad. And we won't be changing anything at all."

Gavin's face shut off, closed to his son and daughter. He set the plastic spatula on the burning eye of the stove's electric coil and walked away.

"Dad!" Shane grabbed the plastic utensil, now melting with long strings of black plastic stretching from pan to utensil, and waved it in the air. Colleen ran to the sink and turned on the water so Shane could hold it under the stream. A soft hiss was followed by the bitter stench of burned plastic.

"This can't go on." Shane's voice cracked as Gavin headed outside.

"I see that." Colleen's fingers tingled. "The social worker is coming to meet us day after tomorrow at your apartment. We'll make plans, and not just a scrapbook of memories."

"But still the memory book." His voice shook. "Still that."

"Yes." Colleen placed a hand on her brother's arm.

It was a color photo, faded by time as though it had been washed in the rain or by tears. The pub in the picture was a white thatch-roof building, squat and square, set against a landscape that must have been emerald in its time but was now like a weak green tea. The name of the pub was written on a circular sign over the doorway: O'Shea's. Was it the name of the owner, or maybe the owner before? Who knew? The doorway was painted dark green, the window sashes also. Two sets of rectangular windows were set on either side of the doorway, red awnings protecting them with swollen eyelids. In small, tight script words on the photo stated: 1980 County Clare, Ireland.

Beckett had fished the photo from a manila envelope with a pile of others, which they'd also placed on the pine table at the historical society. He stood next to Colleen and his hands sifted through them. Martin Burris, the long-term volunteer and history buff, a man whose bushy beard seemed to compensate for his bald head, stood back with his hands in his front jeans pockets.

"That photo you got there." Martin took a step closer to Colleen and tapped its center, almost knocking it from her hands. "Your dear dad brought that to the contractor to show him how he wanted the pub to look like in the redesign. He didn't go tear-ing out the brick and mortar, but he damn sure wanted to change its appearance. He would have added a thatch roof if they'd let him." Martin's accent, so deeply southern it sounded like a parody, made Colleen smile.

"Why *this* pub in Ireland?"

"I have no idea." Martin scratched his beard.

"What do you think?" Colleen asked Beckett.

He held another photo with a smile. "Think about what?"

Colleen held out the photo. "Why did he choose this pub to use as a model for the Lark?"

"Because it's good-looking? I can't guess about something a man did all those years ago."

"It's so interesting." Colleen sat in a chair, sifting through other images of the Lark during different stages of its life. "Why do we think to ask the most important questions when it might be too late for those questions?" She looked at Beckett. "Why don't we ask when it doesn't matter so desperately?"

"I don't know." He sat next to her and took her hand. "I just don't damned well know, but maybe you should try now — maybe it's not too late."

And in that instant, the one person, the only person Colleen wanted to turn toward was Hallie. This need, this primal and old desire, carried the pain of loss and the slightest whisper of existing love, appearing quietly and shyly from the past.

Yes, they would find a way to ask their dad — together, she and her sister would find a way.

CHAPTER EIGHTEEN

Time is an optical illusion — never quite
as solid or strong as we think it is.
Jodi Picoult, *My Sister's Keeper*

"I've never thought much about why it *looks* the way it does." Colleen stood in front of the Lark in the late evening. Above, an egret swooped toward her and Beckett, and then eased. When it landed lightly on the magnolia tree a few yards away, Colleen touched the edge of Beckett's shoulder and pointed to the pub to redirect his attention. "For me, it just *always* looked like this."

Beckett held copies of two photos — one of O'Shea's pub in Ireland and one of the Lark when it had been called McNally's. Colleen shaded her eyes and stared at the building. Dad didn't do anything accidentally. If he chose a pub from Ireland to replicate in South Carolina, he chose it for a reason.

"He never talked about it?" Beckett asked.

"I'm trying to remember. I don't know much about his life before I was born. Why don't I?" She shrugged and paused, tasting the unknowing with its hints of something larger. "He never went back to Ireland; he never took Mother there. He never visited again, so it couldn't have been all that important to him. I've never given his time there much thought. As little kids we think our parents' lives started when we came along. What I do know only has to do with how that journey to Ireland influenced us — you know, his funny sayings or once in a while a phrase or two about how it all felt there, how one day he wanted to take me."

"Not the family?"

"Huh?" Colleen shifted her feet, feeling the ground was moving with each new piece of information, each question. Shouldn't things be left well enough alone? Digging into the past never did much good; she sure as hell knew that. It only led to pain that had not faded, but lay in wait like one of those ridiculous fairy-tale dragons that slept until you roused it.

"Didn't he want to take the whole family, or was it just you?"

Colleen pulled at the strings of memory, yanked at the threads of the promise of an

Ireland trip. Was it once or twice that he'd promised? Maybe more? But one time — yes, when she and Dad had been alone in the pub washing glasses. She'd been twelve or maybe thirteen years old. They'd been singing together, but even the song had disappeared from her memory bank. What was it?

Whatever it was, she'd said, "I like 'The Lark in the Clear Air' better."

He'd set the glass he'd been washing onto the bar, which smelled like lemon polish, and put both arms around her to pull her close. She'd rested against his flannel shirt, which carried the aroma of salt and sea and whiskey. Her mother had often joked that she could sense him coming home not by the sounds he made but by the scents that preceded him. Colleen had rested into her dad as he whispered, "You're a chip off the old block, Lena. Someday I'll take you there, take you to the land of eternal green, and staggering cliffs you can't imagine even with the best of your imagination, to the land where fairies live in the knots of old oaks and the ocean is always thrashing itself against a land so beautiful there's not another like it."

Colleen stared off with this memory fresh in her mind — so quick and vivid in its entirety — as she answered Beckett, "I think he wanted to bring only me. I don't know why."

"Maybe he told the others, too, at a different time."

"Maybe." She smiled at him as he placed his hand on the brass doorknob. "Or maybe I'm special."

"Well, that you are." Beckett opened the door and together they entered the dimly lit space.

"I was joking of course." She shut the door behind them. "Of course I'm not."

Beckett stopped so quickly that Colleen bumped into him, their bodies touching. He wrapped an arm around her waist and pulled her in close. "Yes, you are."

Colleen blushed, felt the heat in her face and under her ribs, along her arms and thighs. Thank God for the dim light. She kissed his cheek lightly and let go to glance around the room.

Her dad stood behind the bar talking to a man on its far side, engaged in a conversation that had put serious expressions on both their faces. There were only six patrons, two couples and two women alone, scattered at different tables. It was too early for the crowd to be settling in, but this had always been Colleen's favorite part of the day, when she could be alone with her dad. He'd tell her an old myth or joke. He was always saving news from the beauty of the day to share with her — a dolphin that had visited the dock with its new calf; a phone call from his sister; a pub patron who had found true love; a sick person healed. He gathered these gems like Hallie had gathered oyster shells to place around their room.

"He looks so serious," she said to Beckett.

Together they approached the bar and Gavin spied them. His smile spread sure as a sunburst across his face. "My Lena!" he called out.

"Hi, Dad."

"When did you get here?"

"Just now." She pointed at Beckett. "I went to the historical society today. Remember, like we talked about over breakfast?" Then she remembered to quit using the damned word "remember."

He nodded in agreement. The man he'd been speaking to, Colleen recognized him — Mr. Dalton, her teacher from junior year algebra. She exchanged a few words with him and then he rejoined one of the women sitting alone at a table.

"Dad." Colleen sat on the stool that had just been vacated by Mr. Dalton. She would start over, make sure he understood.

"Yes?" He smiled at her and nodded at Beckett. It was a vacant word, a preconditioned response.

"Today I went to the historical society with Beckett here." Beckett took a bar stool next to her, reached under the bar to squeeze her knee in complicit sympathy. "We found such interesting photos."

"Photos?" His eyes lit as if someone had turned something on inside him.

Beckett pulled out color copies of the originals.

The door behind the bar swished open and closed, and Shane emerged, preoccupied on his phone. When he glanced up and saw them, he smiled. "Oh, hey. What's up?"

"We found these at the historical society." Colleen spoke softly and tilted her head at her brother in question. "Are you okay?"

Shane glanced at their dad, a sideways slide of the eyes that only Colleen would notice. "I'm fine. What are these?" He eased his way to the bar, pushing the photos under the domed light above.

"Dad," Colleen said, "one is a photo of the pub you used as a model for this pub. It's some place in Ireland."

Gavin slapped his hand on the counter and let out a laugh. "The old O'Shea pub in Clare. How many hours I spent behind that dirty counter, dragging the old kegs and cleaning after the brawls of the locals. Did you know it takes exactly 119 seconds to pour a perfect Guinness?" He looked at Colleen.

"I did, Dad. I did know that. You taught me."

He shook his head and lifted the photo closer to his face. "How long has it been?" His gaze found Colleen's and there seemed a desperate need for an answer. "How long?"

"I don't know exactly when you were there. But before I was born, so at least thirty-five years ago."

"Oh, my dear, you've always been a part of the pub."

"No, Dad. That's a different pub. That's not the Lark."

Her dad kept his gaze fixed on hers. She understood why he wouldn't look away; he needed to be grounded in that moment, to find his way back to reality. But it wasn't happening.

"Dad, that's another pub. Did you work there? At that pub in Ireland?"

"Yes, I did." He straightened and pushed the photo away. He glanced at the next one. "And this pub I found here." His smile was sad, a mere lifting of the edges of his lips.

"Is O'Shea's where you first heard 'The Lark in the Clear Air'?" That was Shane asking, his voice quiet so not to scare away the memories if he spoke too loudly. "And that's why you named this pub . . ."

"Yes." Gavin's smile was real then, reaching into the rivers of wrinkles at his eyes. "And it was my wedding song, indeed it was."

With that, he stood, turned quickly and moved to the far end of the bar to greet another patron, whistling his favorite song.

THE MEMORY BOOK

INTERVIEW WITH MR. BIVINS

Colleen held a sepia-toned photo. Gavin and Elizabeth Donohue stood in front of the brick pub holding a baby, less than a year old, wrapped tightly in a blanket, a head full of curls emerging from the folds. Another man, Mr. Bivins, the real estate agent, stood a foot away from Elizabeth wearing a dark suit and a file of papers that he held to the camera. Gavin's arm was flung over Elizabeth's shoulders and a grin spread across his face. Elizabeth, with a lacquered bob, held the baby in one arm and had slipped the other around her husband's waist. She wore a flowered sundress and large Jackie O sunglasses. Gavin wore a dark suit with a crooked green tie. Sunlight fell in long stretches, offering Gavin the appearance of being showered with light. In small script at the bottom of the photo, in the white band framing it, were the words

"January 1982."

Colleen sat at a long dark faux-mahogany table in Mr. Bivins's realty office, a table where clients signed closing forms and wrote checks for new homes or businesses. The air conditioner was set to arctic and Colleen ran her hands up and down her bare arms. Seated across from her, Mr. Bivins wore a black suit with a pale blue hankie poking from the top left pocket. His tie, also pale blue, had a stain of something resembling ketchup on the bottom corner. His face was earnest and round; rimless spectacles sat atop the red bulb at the end of his nose as he looked down at the photo.

After some chitchat about the weather and the new restaurant downtown, Colleen pointed to the photo. "You see, I'm wondering what day this was about. All of us in front of the pub and you holding those papers?"

"Closing day. We didn't think it would happen and that's why I have that silly grin on my face."

"Closing? I'm confused."

"Oh, the McNallys weren't quite ready to sell it, what with its success and all of that. But your dad, he was quite the charmer there, with your mom all smiles and your tiny little self only a couple months old when he bought it."

Colleen couldn't quite forge the connection

between herself and the small bundle in her mother's arms. Of course she didn't remember any of this — but there she was, part of the family history and pub from the get-go. Was this how her dad would one day feel when he looked at these photos and their stories? As though he didn't know the man in the picture? Colleen cleared her throat. "He bought it before I was born."

"No. Your mom was at home with you when he finally convinced the McNallys to sell. I remember that quite well. Your dad told ol' Bud that he'd worked in an ancient pub in a village in County Clare. He had ideas. Big ideas. Living all that time in a small village of thatched cottages, he knew more about *real* pubs than the McNallys ever could." Mr. Bivins's face settled into the wrinkles of his lifelong smile. "And it didn't hurt that your dad paid over market value. He was determined to own that pub. Nothing would stop him."

"Nothing usually does." Colleen paused. "But he moved here because of it, right? He'd already bought it when they arrived. The only pub he'd worked at before that was the one in Ireland."

"No." Mr. Bivins stared at the photo. "He spent months convincing Bud to sell. But didn't it become all he imagined it to be? It's a community. That's what he wanted — a community built around a gathering place. And your mother, always so quiet and polite, always holding on to your dad for dear life."

"But this couldn't be closing day. He bought it before I was born . . . it's why they moved here." She knew she was repeating herself, but maybe he didn't understand her, didn't comprehend the details.

"No, Lena. I remember as clearly as yesterday."

Colleen didn't want to argue with the older gentleman — there would be no use in that. She knew that stories changed with time, that even her own most vivid memories were unreliable — what time had it been? What day? Facts didn't matter so much as the overall impression. So if Mr. Bivins's timeline didn't match her dad's, then it was only the intention that mattered, the determination to own and run a pub in a small-town community. That was what was worth recording.

CHAPTER NINETEEN

Memory is an inner temple of feeling and
sensibility.

John O'Donohue, *Anam Cara*

Eight Days until the Party . . .
"It's falling apart." Hallie spoke to Colleen
and into the soft misty morning air and
pointed at the tree house.

They'd just arrived — Hallie and the girls
— to find Colleen alone on the back stoop
with a mug of coffee. The nieces hugged
Colleen, tripping over her and splashing her
coffee onto the concrete as they rushed
through the back door to find Uncle Shane.

"What?" Colleen looked at Hallie, wishing
she'd had at least ten more minutes alone.
She was unaccustomed to starting the day
with conversation. Living alone, she'd
learned to move more slowly into the world.

Hallie sat next to Colleen and pointed
again. "The tree house. It's fallen apart just

like us."

Colleen took in a long breath, inhaling the aroma of the coffee, the warm earth and salty air. "Hallie . . ." She hadn't seen her sister since the day before yesterday during the scene she'd witnessed between Walter and Hallie from behind the dumpster.

"It's true." Hallie swung her legs sideways to face her sister. "It's like the tree house couldn't take the passing years either. Dad once said he'd fix it for Sadie and Rosie, but he never did."

"It's just a tree house," Colleen said flatly.

"Maybe." Hallie brushed her hands through the air, dismissing the notion. "Or maybe it stands for everything."

In silence they stared at the crumbling structure. The tree house listed against the tallest branches, clinging to them with the last of its rusted nails. The floor was still intact but slanted, the roof long gone. Several of the board steps that had led to the top, nailed into the tree trunk, were still attached, but the lowest surviving one was too high to step onto, out of reach to gain a foothold.

"I'm sorry I got so mad the other night." Hallie stood when she said this, as if she meant to run as soon as the words left her mouth. "It hit me wrong to see Walter being so flirty with you. I was mad at him; at his stupidity."

Colleen shrugged, stared at the tree house. How had she not really looked at it since she'd arrived? It posed a danger — it needed to be taken down.

"I guess that's the end of that discussion." Hallie took a step down to the grass. "You're obviously not listening."

"I'm listening. I just don't know what to say." Colleen shrugged her shoulders, shifting her gaze past the tree house to the river. "I really don't. I just think we should never talk about Walter, or the past. I'm so sad about Dad. I have decisions about work I need to make; this party to get through; our memory book to finish. We don't need to rehash what we already know about us — let's just focus on Dad's care."

"Rehash it? Seriously?" Hallie slammed her foot into the soft grass, splashing a small spray of soggy dirt onto Colleen's legs. "Since it's the reason you haven't spoken to me or my girls in a decade, I thought it worth at least a few words. You didn't even meet your own nieces, my girls, until a few days ago."

"You told me your story. What else is there to say?"

"It's worth talking about no matter how

wrong or terrible I was. I get that it's my fault that you left, that you stayed away. But now is now and you're here and it's worth a few words."

"Okay then." Colleen stood. "Here are a few words." She cleared her throat and stared at her sister. "You broke my heart. You broke my spirit. Most of all, you broke my trust. I ran off, and yes, I *chose* to run off. I started a new life and avoided the pain the best I knew how. Maybe it was the wrong way to go about it, but I did all I knew to do. But now I'm back because I love our dad. He's in trouble and needs our help. I don't know anything more than that, Hallie." Her voice rose until Hallie stepped back, each sentence a shove, pushing her away. "I don't know *anything* else."

Hallie shook her head. "I don't either, Lena."

"*Please* stop calling me Lena."

"No." Hallie turned on her heel and headed into the house. "That's your name."

Colleen exhaled with frustration. It was "family meeting" time and she couldn't run; she couldn't leave. They'd told Bob not to come get Dad that day as they were spending the morning with him. Her coffee had grown cold and she tossed it into the grass before entering the house just as Dad's

275

words filled the kitchen.

"As long as poetry and myth are in the world, part of my memory will always exist." Gavin spoke as he held a photo in his hand. He stared at it, his eyes glazed over as he sat at the kitchen table.

"What, Dad?" Hallie asked from her seat next to him, her hand on his forearm in a protective gesture.

Gavin glanced to his daughter just as Shane came from the back of the house. "I might forget everything. Already I feel it leaving me. But if there is poetry, and there are stories about me, won't *part* of me still exist? I'm trying damn hard here to figure out what of me, aside from my body, will remain with you. If memory is the center of it all, what will be left?"

Colleen was quiet as she caught Shane's glance. How could her father be so lucid in one moment and so confused the next? The disease was as baffling as it was vicious.

The nieces weren't there to hear this; they were in the living room watching an animated movie about an old man and his house being lifted by balloons.

"Dad?" Colleen asked gently.

"Do we make memories or do memories make us?" He asked this paradoxical question as though he were asking what time

276

dinner would be ready.

"I don't know," Colleen said. "Maybe both."

"Maybe . . ." Shane chimed in. "Does it matter? We want to help no matter what it is."

"Listen," Gavin said. "I know why we're here." He lifted his head to meet Colleen's gaze. "To talk about me and my fading memory." He held the photo he'd been staring at. "But your brother brought this, and I just don't know why."

"Let me see." She glanced over her dad's shoulder. It was the faded color photo of Gavin sitting on a stone wall. Sheep, three of them with muddy bellies and bowed heads, stood in the background beside a creek. Boulders and rocks were visible below the water; rich green grass tufted the banks — it looked like every photo of Ireland she'd ever seen. Dad wore a suit and tie knotted so tightly that his neck wrinkled against the collar. A white flower was buttoned to his lapel and his smile was broad, his eyes crinkling at the corners.

"When was this taken?" Colleen asked.

"I don't know." He looked at her. "A long time ago." He paused. "You know I don't like being this late for the pub. I only trust Hampton so far."

"You mean Hank."

"Yes, that's what I meant." His face was so pained at his mistake that Colleen felt the embarrassment for him.

Hallie squeezed her dad's arm. "We love you so much. This isn't a talk about how you've done wrong but how we can help. You're going to need more care than you're getting right now. You can't live alone. And you can't . . ." Her voice cracked.

Gavin glanced away from Hallie, directly at Colleen. "You can live here with me." He clapped his hands together. "Problem solved." He stood from his chair. "Now I have to be getting on to the pub."

Hallie stood. "Dad, Lena lives in New York."

"I'm not a complete bumbling idiot. I know where she lives." His voice held the flint edge of anger not yet ignited. He closed his eyes and tried again. "But she can move back here." He took two steps toward Colleen, his face twisted with something she'd seen only when her mother died; some vital grief that couldn't hide behind a mask of any kind.

"I can't, Dad. I . . ."

"You can't? Why? You prefer to live in a tiny apartment all alone and avoid us?"

He'd never spoken to her like this — the

sudden sarcasm like barbed wire digging in. "Dad."

He shook his head, shaking free from the words that had just tarnished their house that had held kindness, love and warmth. "Will someone please take me to the pub? Whatever y'all need to discuss, I know you'll do without me anyway."

Shane stepped up. "Dad, it's only ten in the morning."

Gavin touched his son's face, such a tender gesture, before taking deliberate steps to leave. Just before he walked out, he picked up the photo once more. He stared at it, squinted; and then he glanced at his children, his eyes seeming to see something far away, misted with private memories.

He tossed the photo onto the table, and then he left with the quick slap of the screen door.

"He's obviously confused." Shane brushed his hands through the air. "I shouldn't have brought that one. It just doesn't have anyone else in it to ask and . . . I thought it might jog a memory."

Colleen stared at the photo. "That's the problem, Shane. You can't shake loose what's already gone. So it looks like what he does is create memories, or facts, to fill in the empty spaces. We can't make this harder on him. He's too embarrassed to say he doesn't know, so . . ."

"Should I go check on him?" Hallie asked, her hand already on the screen door handle.

"Leave him be." Shane rubbed at his weary face. "He'll probably go mess around in his shed or get the fishing pole . . ."

Hallie went to the window and pulled aside the green-and-white-checkered curtain. Their mother had sewn it twenty years before on her Singer machine in the spare bedroom, whistling and singing. With that image, Colleen felt so very young again, aware of a world full of possibility, buoyed by the certainty that she was both safe and loved.

Hallie glanced over her shoulder. "He went to the shed."

Shane also glanced through the window and then asked, "What progress have you made on the book? The party is in a week."

"Eight days," Colleen said. "And I have notes from four more interviews. I just need to turn them into stories." She set the photo on the side table once again. "So that's nine so far. How far are you, Hallie?"

Hallie spoke without turning toward them. "I've been planning the party. I haven't really . . ." She spun around. "I have two and that's it. I'm sorry. The party planning and the kids keep me buried. I still don't have permission to block off the street and if we don't get that we're —"

"I can call," Shane said. "The city commissioner owes me a favor anyway."

"Well, can you wiggle your nose and find me a pastry maker? I wanted shamrock cupcakes, mini ones, and the baker I hired said it was too much. So no, I haven't done any more interviews."

"That's eleven out of the twenty." Shane picked up the typed stories they had already completed.

"I'll do the rest in two days," Colleen said. "I can do that many, I think. As long as I can reach everyone."

"You don't have to do them *all*." Hallie set her palms behind her and onto the windowsill and then leaned back, her hair falling into her eyes. "I will do a few. I'm sorry." She paused. "Tomorrow I'll bring the timeline for us to go over after we meet with the social worker."

"What do you mean?" Shane asked.

"I'd like your help."

How hard could a timeline be for a man who'd led such a simple life? Colleen wondered. They weren't tracking ancestors without records or names. Smart-ass comments lurked on her lips, but the sadness in the room felt prescient, as if at any moment another piece of terrible news would wander through that slapping screen door.

Instead she said, "It's confusing, what some people say. But no one remembers things exactly right, do they? If you ask thirty people about the same night that happened thirty years ago, each person will remember it differently."

"Yes," Hallie said with an agitated flip of her hand in the air. "We never know the whole truth about a memory. It can be . . ." She took another breath, as if filling her lungs with courage. "Memories aren't *always* the truth. They aren't always true." She paused and glanced between her sister and brother while she bit the right side of her lower lip. "Let's try this." She glanced at her brother and then at Colleen. "Do you remember my thirteenth birthday party?"

Colleen closed her eyes, searched the past. "Help me out. Princess or circus theme?"

"Neither. It was the Olympics. We had little stations and we divided our friends into teams. You were the captain of one and I was captain of the other."

"Yes." Colleen opened her eyes. "Mother made the cake and it had the Olympic circles with your name straight across it. We had a piñata that looked like a gold medal and Dad made stations for high jump and sprint and then created fun ones like bean-bag toss and watermelon-eating contest."

"Yes."

"So we remember it the same. How fun it was. How nice."

"Do you remember which team won?" Hallie asked, tenting her hands under her chin.

"Yes. Yours." Colleen smiled.

"Do you remember what you did when it was time for the medal ceremony and Dad gave out the candy necklaces with a circle of chocolate in gold and silver foil hanging from the middle?"

Colleen shook her head, confident in her memories. "He didn't do that. You just won and we had cake and . . ." Colleen paused. "There wasn't a medal ceremony."

"Yes, there was. But you sulked off and went inside with your piece of cake and ate it alone in the kitchen until I started opening presents."

"No way." Colleen laughed and rolled her eyes toward Shane. "That didn't happen. First off, why would I do that? Second, I would remember it because that's just mean."

"It did happen. And it happened because you couldn't stand when I won. You were my best friend and biggest fan unless it meant I showed you up, even at my own party."

"It's not true."

"Except it is."

Shane stepped in. "Point taken, Hallie. We remember events differently. Interviewing these people or even asking Dad about an old photo isn't going to give us the facts . . . but it could give us a story that contains a more essential truth and allows him to see himself for a flash of a moment."

"I don't think that's her point, Shane." Colleen stared at her sister. "I think her point is that I can't stand for her to be happier than me or to have more than me. She's taken a very old and not accurate memory and used it to prove I'm a terrible person and that she is in the right. She wants to prove that my memory of the wedding day isn't fully true."

"Oh," Hallie said, her eyebrows drawn down, her voice low. "Your memory of your wedding day is factually correct. I'm just telling you that not *all* of your memories are true." She glanced at Shane. "And not all of Dad's are true either. And not all of his friends' stories are true. But a timeline *is* based on fact. It must be right."

"I get it." Shane sat down again. "Please

work together on this. Please."

"Why can't you do what Dad wants?" Hallie's words burst forth, rushing into the room.

"Me?" Colleen held her hand over her chest.

"Yes. Why can't you just come live with him?" She took two steps forward to face Colleen. There was no avoiding her now. They were almost touching.

Colleen stood her ground. "Why can't *you*?"

"Because I have a house and a family and —"

"A husband," Colleen said. "So because you have a husband and kids you don't need to move in, but because I have no one and nothing, I have to move in? Uproot my life?"

"That's not how I meant it." Hallie shook her head. "He loves you best anyway. You're his favorite daughter."

"That's ridiculous. And if it's true at all, then Mother loved you best — you were her favorite. And all of that doesn't matter. We *all* love Dad."

Shane stood and stepped between them, both taking a step back.

"I'm sorry," Hallie said and sat at the table. "I keep screwing this up. All I want is to help Dad and . . ." She paused and then looked at Colleen. "And fix things between us."

"You think embarrassing me in front of Walter was a good start? Yelling at him *about* me. About me!"

Shane made a groaning noise in the back of his throat. "Please, enough already with Walter."

Colleen composed herself. "Let's focus here. Shane, we'll meet at your apartment at ten tomorrow. We'll make a plan."

On cue to cut the tension in the room, the little nieces came rushing in. It was Rosie who spoke, but they both waved their magic wands in the air, glitter scattering like dust motes. "The movie is stuck. The little wheel keeps going around and around."

"It's the Internet," Shane said. "Let me reboot it."

Rosie waved her wand at Colleen. "Where's your wand, Aunt Lena? Maybe it will fix the movie."

How could she not smile? Was it their fault their dad was a cheating liar? Or that their mom was a betrayer? "Hold on." Colleen winked at them and ran to the back bedroom to seize her wand and returned waving it.

Holding hands, Rosie, Sadie and Colleen

tiptoed back into the room where the girls had been watching the movie and waved their wands with all their might, glitter catching in the morning rays that washed through the dusty windows. And just like that, the screen image disappeared and a moment later reappeared showing an old man and his dog running after a house being pulled skyward by balloons. They burst into laughter, the girls grabbing Colleen around the waist.

Colleen, of course, knew that Shane had booted the Internet just as they'd waved their wands. There was no magic.

The girls made whooping noises and plopped onto two small pink beanbag chairs, each labeled with one of their names in a loopy monogrammed script. Colleen's heart opened another inch or maybe two; she could almost hear the creaking noises of the rusted hinges. But it was *only* for the girls. When she turned to leave the room, Hallie stood at the doorway with a smile, big and bright.

"Hold on," Shane called from the kitchen. "I'll fix the Internet and then I have to go."

Colleen burst into laughter and Hallie stared at her in confusion. "What's so funny?"

Colleen held her wand high. "If only these worked with Dad."

CHAPTER TWENTY

Memory creates our frames.
      Dana Walrath, *Aliceheimer's*

Seven Days until the Party . . .
Often the world awoke when Colleen wanted it to sleep. She'd shared that sentiment with her dad one morning when she was very small. "Please tell Saturday to sleep in," she'd said. "I want to, and I can't if I think I'm missing something."

He'd laughed heartily. Now at thirty-five, lying in her childhood bed, her wishes weren't any different, and she yearned to make Dad laugh as he had then. She threw off the covers and stepped onto the knotted rug her mother had bought at a craft shop in Charleston. Colleen remembered the day. "Oh, darling, this is exactly what I've been looking for to match your room. Now your little toes won't be cold when you hop out of bed." She'd kissed Colleen's cheeks, then wiped the lipstick mark off.

Colleen smiled at the remembrance and closed her eyes for a moment, sent her mother some love and began the day with fatigue itching beneath her eyelids.

She'd stayed up most of the night writing stories from her notes and interviews. The stories mattered. All of it mattered and that thought had made her stay awake to get it done. From a day of interviews, she'd learned about her dad's aversion to ghost stories; his high school record for most home runs on the baseball team (a record still held to that day); how, as a toddler, he'd bang his head onto pillows when he was angry; how his first dog had been run over by a car in front of him (and the reason he'd never wanted another). They were just anecdotes from a normal life — but they were also all the parts of a man she loved, whom she loved more with each telling.

As she wrote, she'd included her own birth on March 2, 1981, in Richmond. Next was Hallie in 1983 and then Shane in '88. Her parents' wedding story was the one she'd struggled to put into words, as no one else had been there to tell her about it. She imagined how they felt and what was said. It was a simple photo that caught the moment in the courthouse when Dad handed

Mother a bouquet of wild roses. Neither of her parents had ever said much about that day, only smiled at each other with a shared look of private love.

When she'd finished, she gathered the pages and prepared for the meeting at Shane's. Dad was safe with Bob for the morning and Colleen girded her heart for what would come next, and then next.

Shane's apartment smelled like the local coffee shop. Colleen inhaled deeply as she stepped inside, shutting the door behind her. Hallie and Shane looked up from the paper-strewn table.

"Well, good morning to the two of you." Colleen reached into her bag, her finger snagging on an open safety pin somewhere in the recesses of all the random doodads she stored there "just in case." Then her fingers grasped the papers she was seeking. "I think I have something that will cheer you up."

"I don't think anything can do that," Hallie said with such sadness that Colleen wondered if she'd missed something.

"What's going on?" she asked.

"We're just going over the finances," Shane said. "Everything costs more than we could have imagined. We're going to have to share the burden."

"I'll do whatever I can." Colleen set the stack of stories on the table. "Tell me what you need and where we are."

"Well, Dad doesn't have long-term care insurance — he thought it was a waste of money — so we have to find out what that means. He's eligible for disability through social security, but it will be small." Shane spoke in a robotic voice as if reading off a teleprompter, his eyes askance at the far wall. Then he looked directly at Colleen. "His resources . . . our resources won't last more than six months if he needs in-home care. I hope the social worker has some answers, but we've all got to find a way to help."

Hallie held up her hand. "And we are not talking about memory care homes or anything like that. Not yet. Not now."

Colleen placed her hand over her chest, where she could feel her heart rolling, picking up the pace. "I will do anything I can. I will. I promise."

Shane pointed at the stories she'd dropped onto the table. "Thank you so much for this, big sis."

He bent over the pages, Hallie doing the same, their heads close enough to touch. Hallie's tangled hair was pulled into a ponytail at the nape of her neck, just as it had been when they were children and came off the johnboat. Shane scratched absently at his temples, leafed quickly through the pages without reading them word for word. He looked up first and smiled at Colleen; she felt warmth and a swooping feeling in her stomach — this was her family. *Her* family.

"Lena, this is simply amazing," he said.

"Well, thank you." She bowed with her coffee mug held high. "I stayed awake most of the night and it was like Dad was with me. I just wrote and wrote and the little vignettes came." She glanced at Hallie, who was sorting the pages, lining them in order one after the other. "You don't like them?"

"I do." Hallie looked up and Colleen saw the circles under her sister's eyes, dark and swollen. "But like I said, some dates are funky."

"I took the dates straight off the photos . . ."

"I know." Hallie stood and stretched, rubbing at her already obviously irritated eyes. "It might just be how tired I am. I'm preoccupied with planning the party."

"The party . . ."

"Yes." Hallie's unwavering gaze suggested she'd found her gumption again. "The

293

party. The one I am planning alone."

"So give me something to do. I'm here to help." Colleen broke eye contact to stare out the stained glass window. It was hard to look directly at Hallie; it was too much for Colleen to hold the gaze, as it caused her breath to catch, her heart to fly upward in a need for something that felt like reconciliation.

"No, you're not," Hallie said.

Colleen glanced back, but only looked at Shane. "What?"

"You know we don't have enough money to get a helper for Dad and you could stay."

"Not now," Shane said in a voice as firm as their mother's when they came running into the kitchen with muddy shoes. He looked up from Colleen's stories. "I'm reading these and I'm thinking about Dad, and I want you two to quit throwing jabs and punches."

"I'm trying to solve this." Hallie's voice came with a juvenile whine.

Colleen stepped forward. "You sound five years old, Hallie. For God's sake, we're all trying to find solutions to a challenging situation. Shane lives here in an apartment — he could move in. You have a family, so you can't. We can pool our money or look for other solutions, but me moving here is *not* the only possibility, so enough already."

"Maybe . . ." Hallie swallowed and sat. "Forget it."

"Maybe?" Colleen asked.

"Maybe we just want you here. Have you considered that at all?"

A knock on the door saved them all. Shane opened it to greet the social worker, Susan Clements, a tall woman confident in her stance, her shoulders back. She shifted the tortoiseshell glasses on her face and held out her hand to meet the three siblings as they introduced themselves one by one.

"It's nice to meet all of you," she said as she hoisted her loaded canvas bag higher on her shoulder. "I'm just sorry it has to be under these circumstances. This is my specialty — consulting on Alzheimer's. And it's always hard. There will be a 'new normal' for all of you that will be difficult to accept, but I'm here to help."

"Thank you," Shane said, and he stepped aside to show her into the living room. The siblings followed and they all took seats on the couch and side chairs.

Susan glanced at each of them and then spoke evenly. "This disease and its accompanying problems can bring out the worst in families. Old wounds can open as responsibilities shift. Let's try to let this bring out the best in us."

"Well," Shane said as they all sat facing one another over the pine coffee table, "we can certainly try."

"You see," Susan said, "with this disease the family is thrown off center."

Colleen thought, *We were already off center,* but she swallowed the comment and leaned forward to hear Susan.

"I'm here to give you coping tools." She held a folder. "First, there's paperwork to apply for help — there's government assistance in certain cases, community support services, and I can help you figure out what your medical insurance will cover. Once you fill out all these forms we can decide exactly what might help. You have to be patient, as the process can be tedious."

"We might be able to get help from agencies and you?" Hallie asked.

"Yes," Susan continued. "And decisions must be made about your father's driving, his living arrangements and his daily life. You must become aware of what will happen as the disease progresses. It is best to be prepared."

Colleen stood, feeling shaky, needing a breath from the barrage of information. "Would you like some coffee?"

Susan nodded. This woman with her facts

and her papers and her forms made Dad's disease more real in a way she hadn't expected. Colleen walked to the kitchen and poured coffee into one of Shane's dark brown pottery mugs with the pub logo etched on the side. "Milk or sugar?" she asked, welcoming the few minutes' reprieve.

"No, thank you."

Colleen handed the mug to Susan, who continued, "I know this stack of forms looks overwhelming. But everything you do will help. I have information on how to fully understand your own assets. I have brochures on care facilities, in-home care providers and more."

"It's a lot." Hallie slid the papers around the coffee table like a stack of tarot cards that could read their future. "Medical forms. Insurance forms. And what is this? A living will?"

"Yes."

"Power of attorney?" Colleen asked.

"While your dad is still mentally able, he *must* decide who will have the power to make financial decisions once he is unable. This is all the more important because he operates a business."

"Shane already has power of attorney." Hallie picked up a paper. "He signed it after Mother passed. You know, just in case."

297

"Just in case?" Colleen asked. "Or just because you told him to?"

"Because Shane runs the business." Hallie stared directly at Susan instead of Colleen.

Susan exhaled a long, jittery sigh as if she'd been through this many times and was hoping that, this once, she wouldn't have to face a bickering family. "And I need to tell you about these papers." She held a pile of photocopied sheets. "This is an article by Pauline Boss about the myth of closure. I want you to read it. Alzheimer's is a disease with a pattern of loss. It's unlikely that you'll experience the five stages of grief you've been taught. I don't want you to expect it. I've discovered that your experience may be more like what Boss calls 'ambiguous loss.' "

"Which is?" Colleen asked.

"Where there is a physical presence but a psychological loss." Susan sipped her coffee and allowed the silence to stretch beyond the comfortable.

"Now what?"

After another thirty minutes of explaining forms, Susan eased from her chair to stand, carrying her mug to the sink and placing it there gently before turning to the siblings. "Go over these papers and we'll meet later this week. I want you to absorb and read.

Most of what I said might slip right past you today. But I want to remind you of a few things. First, you must grieve. Second, you must somehow get yourselves onto the same page with the same plan. From there, we will move on."

She reached into the back pocket of her pressed khaki pants and placed three business cards on the counter. "Here's my number for any questions; otherwise, I will see you at our next appointment. And I can't tell you how sorry I am that you are dealing with this loss. This terrible loss." She took a few steps toward the door and then turned to face them all with her hand on the doorknob. "You must remember that your dad still has strengths. Many of them. And you can capitalize on those. He has a long history, a rich history. He has his routines and his loves and his loathings. Those don't disappear. Respect who he is. Look at what he can *still* do."

None of the siblings spoke after she left. They sat quietly and still, as if Susan had put them in time-out as their mother had done when they fought over the last piece of pie or whose turn it was in the front seat. Scarcity, their dad used to say, was not the way their family lived. There was and always would be enough for everyone.

Colleen began to leaf through the papers, her heart pushing against her chest with a need to leave the situation, leave the room, run . . .

But this time there would be no running. This time there was no friend in Connecticut who would allow her to sleep on a pullout bed. This time there was no man in a bar waiting to meet her. This time there was no clean and light-filled apartment in the far corner of a repurposed church.

"We have a lot to decide," Shane said. "Little by little. That's how we will do this. Take one step at a time." He held up a placard that Susan had left behind. "This looks like it will be helpful, maybe ease our frustration and his?"

Colleen took the card from him and read the ten rules out loud. "Don't argue; instead agree. Never reason; instead divert. Never shame; instead distract. Never lecture; instead reassure. Never say 'remember'; instead reminisce. Never say 'I told you'; instead repeat and regroup." Colleen stopped reading, although there was more. "We are going to have to learn a new way of being with him."

Shane took the card from Colleen and glanced at it. "Now what? Do we start this now?"

"God, I feel so bad for every time I've said 'remember' or corrected him or explained. I was only making it worse."

"We are doing the best we can." Hallie stood and began to pace the room, chewing on the end of her thumbnail. "First the party. Let's get that straight and then . . ."

Colleen burst from her chair, the tears she had wanted to shed freezing in her chest, her tears turning hard. "Are you kidding me? You are so obsessed with the party, I can see you just don't want to think about the most important things."

"If that's true" — Hallie drew close to her sister — "then you're the one who's spent ten years avoiding the deeper issues with the party that is your life. 'Just ignore it' seems to be *your* motto."

"Ignore it?" Colleen's voice felt not her own, but made of old resentment and anger and fear, and something even darker. "How could I ignore it, Hallie? Maybe I've stayed away from it. Maybe I've turned from it. But ignore it? Hell, no."

"Stop!" Shane's voice rang out and they both startled at their brother's reprimand. "Hallie, why are you so obsessed with the party? It's simple. You've done them before."

"Let's go over this timeline. I want to get it right and I can't. Something is wrong and you both act like you don't care."

"A slight overstatement." Colleen motioned to the pile of stories she'd spent all night writing.

"Since we didn't have time before Susan arrived, let me show you now." Hallie reached her slender fingers into a leather satchel she'd dropped onto the couch. She withdrew a pile of note cards. From where she stood, Colleen could see Hallie's loopy left-handed scribbling — a line or two on each card with a date on the top left corner. Hallie reached into her bag again, withdrew a roll of masking tape. She walked to one side of the kitchen, where she began to tape the note cards, one by one, on Shane's cream-colored plaster walls.

He didn't stop her.

Shane and Colleen watched their sister with wonder. This wasn't like her — the extremes of emotion, the barrage of words. Soon the cards were taped in crooked lines.

The first card was Gavin's birth and they went on in chronological order until 1979, when the dates were scribbled out several times. "Here." Hallie jabbed her finger onto the wall, at five or six cards. "Dad goes to Ireland, right? In 1979 right after his college graduation? And comes home after several months, immediately marries

Mother and moves here to buy the pub. Ten months later Colleen is born."

"Simple." Shane spoke quietly; anything else might send their sister off some emotional ledge.

"No." Hallie took a photo from her bag and set it against the note card. "This is Dad in Ireland and the date stamp says December 1980." She shook her head. "But he wasn't there then. He was here, with Mom, and then Colleen . . . a year later."

"Then the date on the photo is wrong." Shane took it from her hand. "Damn, when it turns a new year, I write the old year on everything for two months. Someone could have easily written the wrong date."

"It's stamped, not written, by whomever developed the film."

"That doesn't mean it's —"

Hallie cut Shane short. "There are more pictures like it. Think hard." Hallie tapped the side of her head. "Dad is lying to us. There's something he hasn't told us. This isn't dementia. These are cold, hard facts in front of us. Something is off."

"Does it matter?" Shane approached his sister carefully.

"Yes, it matters. It's our family. What if he's *lying*?" Her voice stuttered on the last word. "Dad doesn't lie, or I thought he didn't."

Colleen tapped the note cards. "So here's the thing." Hallie and Shane turned to her. "I found the same problem when I interviewed the real estate agent."

"Mr. Bivins?"

Colleen nodded. "According to him, the photo I showed him was taken on the day Mother and Dad bought the pub when I was about ten months old — in January 1982. But Dad always told us that he and Mother bought the pub before I was born. I thought Mr. Bivins was confused — that maybe it was just a picture from later and he got the dates mixed up."

Shane flopped into a chair. "So when did Dad really buy the pub, and why would he lie about that? And what was he doing in Ireland in December 1980, when we were always told he married Mother in May of that year?"

"Exactly," Hallie said.

"But do any of these dates matter," Colleen asked, "or is what happened in between the milestones what really counts, the blank spaces between each of Hallie's note cards? That's where his life was lived . . ." She pointed at the wall between the cards that stated, "Married Elizabeth" and "Colleen born."

Shane said, "Yes, but we need the markers to navigate, to . . . It's what we have."

"Then you figure it out. You do it." Hallie threw her now empty hands in the air. "I have enough crap to deal with. This is making me crazy."

"Enough crap?" Shane asked. "What does that mean?"

"Nothing." Hallie slumped onto a kitchen chair. "I just mean this." She took in a long breath to sustain whatever it was she wanted to say. "Look at all we must deal with. And I have two kids to take care of. Speaking of, I'm late. They get out at noon today from summer camp. I have to go . . ."

Colleen stared at her sister, who was obviously spent. It might have been years since she'd looked carefully at Hallie, but she knew the signs. They'd shared a bedroom for eighteen years, along with a house and a life and all their secrets. Colleen knew exhaustion when she saw it.

"Hallie." Colleen said her name gently.

Hallie looked up. "Yes?"

Colleen faltered. What was she supposed to say now? Something kind? Ask her sister what was really wrong? What was really draining the life out of her face and eyes?

She couldn't. What if the answer was, *You, Lena. You are doing this to me.*

"Nothing." Colleen turned away. "This is tough for all of us. We'll get through it."

As an alarm sounded on Hallie's cell, she departed to pick up her children and Shane headed downstairs to the pub. Colleen stood in front of Hallie's lopsided timeline. She had never once thought of her dad's life as a straight arrow from birth until now, as a bullet point list of when and how each event occurred. Instead, she'd thought of how he'd lived his life, the relationships he'd formed and all that he'd given. But now she focused on the notes, and on the dates.

In 1979 Gavin Donohue graduated from college and went to Ireland to travel for several months. He fell in love with a pub called O'Shea's and decided he wanted to own one like it at home. After working in O'Shea's he traveled briefly around the country and returned to South Carolina with myths and stories and a grand love of the Emerald Isle, along with a song he'd never let go of — "The Lark in the Clear Air."

In 1980, right after he returned from Ireland, he'd married Elizabeth in Richmond, Virginia, on May fifth — in a civil ceremony at the courthouse instead of in a fancy church wedding, so that they could use their money for down payments on a house on the May River and a pub that would be their livelihood. They moved to Watersend and began their life together.

In March 1981 Colleen was born in Watersend, which meant her parents had been married for ten months. All perfectly respectable.

And all so simple, until it wasn't.

Maybe because life never, ever followed an outline. Hadn't Dad always told them that he and Mother moved to Watersend to buy and open the pub? But if the dates were right on the photos, if Mr. Bivins was right, they'd moved to town before they had a thought of buying McNally's pub; Colleen had been born here in this place, but well before they owned the pub. According to Mr. Bivins, Colleen had been ten months old and Gavin started working at McNally's a couple months before she was born, which would make it about January 1981. If so, what had he and Elizabeth been doing between May 1980, when they married, and January 1981?

And there was still the question of when Gavin had really returned from Ireland.

Colleen placed her finger on the wall between the cards, wondering what had happened to her parents in the in-between spaces. Had they not moved to Watersend until after she was born? No. Colleen shook her head. Her birth certificate stated Watersend, South Carolina.

Why would their parents lie about when they moved here or when they bought the pub? What was the point in that?

Colleen sat on the couch and stared at the note cards dangling from the wall. Why would they lie, except to cover something up?

CHAPTER TWENTY-ONE

A pleasure is full grown only when it is
remembered.
C. S. Lewis, *Out of the Silent Planet*

Dust balls had made their home in the
corners of Shane's former bedroom closet.
It was there that Colleen began to pull bags
and bins off the shelves, moving piles of
clothes, shoes boxes and labeled plastic
containers to the floor in search of her baby
book. A double bed, dresser and desk
completed the sparsely furnished room,
which might have been suitable for a visiting monk. Shane had taken most of his
belongings with him, while Colleen and
Hallie's room still appeared as it had the
day Colleen had left.

Standing on the desk chair, Colleen finally
found the book she was looking for atop the
highest shelf; both Hallie's and Shane's
baby books lay underneath it. She grabbed

her book, covered in pink satin that was ripped and torn with the years of storage, nibbled by moths and caked in dust. She ran her hand across the top, where there was a painted image of a stork carrying a blanket laden with a baby wearing a pink bow on her head.

Considering the confusing dates associated with her birth, maybe it was true — maybe the stork had brought her precariously tipped in a blanket over to Watersend. How long had it been since she had looked at this book?

The last time had been with Walter.

They'd been sitting on the edge of her bed, going through old photographs and mementoes.

"I want to know everything about you," he'd said. "Every moment I missed. Every triumph. Every scar. Every story." And he'd kissed her.

Colleen shuddered; sitting on Shane's floor years later, she found that the memory had shifted from sweet to painful and had now become one of disgust. That is what memories do, she thought; the body's recollection transforms.

She slowly opened the baby book, a dried rose petal falling from its pages and landing on the floor. The first page's edge had faded to yellow and on it was written her full name and birth date along with a faded color photo of Colleen wrapped in a white baby blanket with only her red and crinkly newborn face showing. Colleen stared at the picture feeling no attachment to it at all — this baby had nothing to do with her, just another photo of a newborn in a hospital nursery.

Colleen flipped to page two. There she was — the photos she'd always known, the ones framed and hung around the house. Dad holding her on a chair in the backyard. Mother feeding her a bottle and smiling lovingly at whoever took the photo, her face flushed. A photo of Colleen in a crib, staring at a mobile of Winnie-the-Pooh, Eeyore, Piglet and Roo. Then what was amiss? This was the baby book of a loved and adored child — pages of photos and notes and records of her first word (boat); the date of her first steps (eleven months); her first solid food (bananas).

Colleen flipped through the book, page after page, looking for a clue that might tell her the full story, when it hit her hard, the realization like a sledgehammer on her chest. It was the beginning that was wrong. She turned back to page one and then page two. Her baby book went from day one to month two — there was nothing in between. No photos. No mentions of milestones or weight or shots, none of the details that filled the rest of the book.

How had she failed to notice this? Eight weeks unaccounted for. It didn't seem so big in the face of years and years of love and attention, yet also it seemed huge: a gaping hole. An empty space in which anything at all could have happened, anything at all that might change who she was. Maybe they'd been too tired to photograph or record?

Colleen closed the book and set it on the floor with a sense of the ground moving, as though the house had been tilted slightly, set slantwise on the property so the views to her beloved river shifted.

Without knowing how long she'd been sitting on Shane's floor, she heard him call her name.

"In here," she shouted, shifting her legs and glancing at the bedside clock to see that an hour had passed. Stiffly she stood, her left foot asleep and her right leg cramped. Shane was meant to go pick up their dad, who'd been out fishing with Bob all morning. Was it that time already?

Shane entered the room as she stood, her hand on the bedside table. "What are you doing? Cleaning out closets?"

"I was looking for my baby book."

"Why?" He walked into the room and bent down to lift the pink satin book from the floor.

"The note cards. You know, the ones on your wall. Hallie's right — something is off. I thought maybe I could find something in there."

"Did you?"

"There's nothing about me at all for the first two months. That is a book full of every milestone; every gurgle and coo and word and movement I made until I was three years old. And yet from birth to two months there is absolutely nothing."

Shane sat on the bed and opened the book, glanced at the first couple pages. "Where's mine?"

Colleen pointed to the closet. "Top shelf."

Shane reached up — no chair for him — and brought out a blue suede baby book, opened it and glanced up at Colleen. "You're right. It's odd." He flipped the book toward her, where there were photos labeled by age: One week. Two weeks. One month. Two months. And on and on.

"See? Where the hell was I from the first picture to the one of me at eight weeks old?"

"Had you never noticed that before?"

"No. Why would I?"

Shane sat next to her on the bed. "Well, I'm sure there's a perfectly reasonable explanation. Like maybe Mother was exhausted from opening a pub. Learning to care for a firstborn. All kinds of reasons."

"It's the 'all kinds of reasons' that gets me." She smiled at her brother. "I'd like to know which kind."

"Yeah, I get that. Me, too."

"And by the way, they weren't opening the pub yet. According to Mr. Bivins, Dad was working at the pub but didn't own it. So someone is lying."

"Or confused."

"Or that." Colleen stood and began to gather the boxes and bins to place back in the closet. Shane joined her.

"It's only two months," he said as he shoved a box into the back corner.

"*Only* two months." Colleen set her baby book back on the top shelf and shut the closet door. "But what if they were your two months?"

Shane nodded. "I would want to know. What will you do?" he asked as they walked back to the kitchen, where Colleen had made a makeshift office, her computer, notebooks and papers set out for a day of

314

making phone calls and conducting interviews.

"I don't know. At some point, I'm going to have to ask Dad. Just ask him. Do you think it's too late? He seems so lucid sometimes."

"I think it's worth a shot, Lena. I think we have to try. Or spend forever making up stories to fill in that empty space."

The day slipped away as Colleen sat at her dad's kitchen table and made four more calls: four more interviews with neighbors, teachers and friends about the photos that remained. These covered years she could recall herself, as it was the time from her eighth through twelfth grade years. Nothing new came to light in the conversations, just shared laughter and the usual confession of love for Dad. No one spoke of his diagnosis or his time in Ireland. This kept her mind far from the baby book; far from the unexplained spaces in the timeline.

Beckett called in the middle of her work and asked if she'd like to go out to dinner by the river. She agreed without missing a beat and continued with the stories.

When she'd finished, she sorted through the papers that the social worker had left behind. Hallie had divided the papers and marked them with sticky notes, assigning each of the siblings a task. *Call insurance company. Call local memory care services to inquire about at-home care. Make sure all financial records have been acquired.* It was a long list, an arduous list, and more than once Colleen thought about how very many people had to navigate this path alone. She was grateful — for the first time in a decade — she was grateful for her sister.

When she'd done enough for the day, she allowed herself to mull over the offer to write a travel memoir. Ten Tips? A Life of Travel? What would this book be, if anything at all? The idea began to move inside her without her permission, growing without her even paying it much mind. The minute she allowed her consciousness to touch upon the idea of writing the book, to draw close to it, she found that the seed had sprouted already. There were ideas and quotes and moments that came to her; in her mind she was already outlining the book.

Could she do it? Yes, it seemed she might. She had stories to tell, wisdom to impart, or at least wisdom that had to do with traveling. With her pen in hand, she began to scribble titles on a blank sheet of paper: *The Traveler's Guide. Girl Around the Globe. One*

More Trip. Land to Land. Sea to Sea. The World as Home.

She stopped, chewed on the end of the pen, a horrible habit she'd had since high school. What was she doing? She no more knew how to write a book than fly like the egret roosting in the backyard. But if the book was a series of humorous, insightful essays maybe she could do it. She paused, glanced up from her papers to see the pink light that signaled evening had arrived.

She rose feeling lighter than she had in months. Whether because of the thought of writing the book or her upcoming dinner with Beckett didn't matter.

THE MEMORY BOOK

INTERVIEW WITH HARRY WILLIAMS

The photo that Colleen showed Harry Williams, the Donohues' next-door neighbor, was of Gavin and Elizabeth as they stood together with Harry and his wife, Violet, at the edge of the May River, the flying egret behind them a streak of white against the blue sky. Harry owned the marina and had been close friends with Gavin since he purchased his first little johnboat.

Each of them held a clear plastic cup with a lime slice snagged on the edge. They were smiling. To one side a bonfire blazed with a metal plate above it where oysters were roasting under brown burlap. Other blurred people filled the background, drinking and talking. It was evidently a great party and Gavin's mouth was open in speech — telling a terrible joke, Colleen was sure.

Mr. Williams, who still lived next door to the

Donohue family on riverfront property, squinted at the photo, pushing his glasses down his nose for a better view. Colleen sat with him on his front porch, sweating glasses of sweet tea on the table between their wicker rocking chairs, the scene so picturesque she might have been in a photo op for one of her travel pieces on the South. The low tide sent the thick scent of pluff mud rising not only from the river but also from the boots Mr. Williams wore. His baseball cap, stained with black mud, was pulled low over his forehead.

"Oh, yes," he said in a thick voice that betrayed his smoking habit, "that was the oyster roast when Mickey fell into the fire pit trying to show off his fire-making skills. Quite the commotion. Good thing he was drunk enough not to feel it much. If you look now, you can still see the burn mark on his forearm. Lucky that's all that happened."

"And Mother and Dad?" Colleen asked.

Mr. Williams looked away from the photo with a wistful expression. "Oh, you know, Gavin was his usual fun-loving self. It was the second time I heard him break into Gaelic. Someone mentioned the drowning of a young boy over on Tybee Island during a riptide and he muttered a few lines before noticing he'd done so."

"In Gaelic?"

Mr. Williams nodded, setting his chin wattle into motion. "Yes. Surely you've heard him? It's only a few lines and he doesn't say them very often. I think I heard him three times in all the years I've known him. And always when he's had the extra whiskey. And always when something sad has up and happened."

"No, sir, I've never heard him speak in Gaelic. Are you sure?"

"It's quite beautiful, I'd say." He sat back in his chair, wiped the sweat from his forehead with a stained, once-white handkerchief he pulled from his back pocket.

"Do you have any idea what he was saying here?" Colleen took the picture back, feeling her own sweat start to trickle down her back and legs.

"Don't recall; sorry, my dear." He leaned forward. "Have you heard any news from the historical society?"

"Not yet, although I don't know why anyone would want to deny the Lark landmark status. I'll let you know. And thanks so much for telling me all about this party. I love hearing about the experiences Dad had when I wasn't here."

"And" — the older man leaned forward, removing his glasses to show only kind eyes — "why haven't you been here?"

"I'm here now." Colleen took a long sip of

tea and stood. "But you know I live in New York, Mr. Williams."

"Well, well." He stood also and shook her hand. "It's so lovely to have you home. I know how terribly and deeply your dad misses you."

Even as that sharp knife cut to Colleen's solar plexus, she smiled and bid Mr. Williams good-bye. She tucked one more story into the palm of her heart — Dad speaking Gaelic when he was sad — and waved good-bye. She walked across the soft grass, the border between their houses unmarked as she stopped by the tree house to lift her hand and place it on the bottom rung, glancing up and wondering if Hallie had ever heard their dad speak in Gaelic. Surely not. If Colleen hadn't heard it, then her siblings hadn't either. He was a different man with different people and as her image of him began to shift, Colleen felt off balance. What else didn't she know?

Nothing was simple, her dad had once told her. *As the Irish say, what's the use of being Irish if the world doesn't break your heart?*

CHAPTER TWENTY-TWO

Starting here, what do you want
to remember?
William Stafford,
"You Reading This, Be Ready"

Colleen climbed into the passenger seat of Beckett's old Audi. "This day went by so fast I barely went outside. Let's find a place to eat with a patio."

"Paperwork?" Beckett asked, looking down at her with his hand on the top of the passenger door.

"Loads of it, and diving into the past. Isn't that odd? Diving into the past making the present go by too fast?"

"In what way are you diving into the past?" Beckett shut the door for her and walked around to the driver's side.

When he'd settled into the driver's seat she said, "You know that memory book we're making for my dad?"

"Yes," he said. "Of course."

"Well, the situation is a little worse than I've let on. I thought the memory book was meant to remind him, but now I wonder if it's really just helping us know him better."

"How so, Colleen?"

"You know," she said, "everyone around here calls me Lena."

"So I've heard." He smiled as he stared out the windshield, guiding the car along the narrow, winding roads. They were quiet as he drove for only a few minutes; one left turn and two rights, and then he pulled into a gravel driveway shaded with a canopy of oaks. He put the car in park. "Would you like me to call you Lena?"

"No, I like Colleen now. I've been using it for ten years and become used to it. I can't get my family to switch."

"Why the switch at all?"

Even a few seconds without air-conditioning in a closed car was too much in the August heat. Colleen opened the door. "It's a long story." She swung her legs around and then stood before leaning in again to look at Beckett in the car. "Or maybe not so long. I just don't want to talk about it." She stepped away and then realized she didn't know where he'd taken her. "Where are we?"

Beckett stepped out of the car and faced her over the top. "My parents' house. I wanted to drop off my dad's tackle box before we go to dinner."

Colleen turned to look at the modest home. "You grew up here?" If he'd been in Watersend, how had she not known him?

He slammed shut the driver's-side door and walked around the car to pop open the trunk and withdraw a rusted red tackle box. "No. My parents moved here a couple years after I did. So they've been here about five years. My dad retired and when they visited me, they fell in love with the town. They packed and moved."

"From?"

"Michigan, where I grew up." He set the box on the ground.

"Michigan," she said. "I've only been there once, and it was in the middle of January. I thought I was going to die from the cold, that it would never leave my bones. I'd have moved here, too." Colleen fell into step with Beckett, heading toward the front door with a flagstone pathway beneath their feet. "So they moved here for you?"

"They'd like me to think so, but they moved here for the town. So far two of my siblings have followed."

"How many do you have?"

He paused on the doorstep, his hand resting on the brass knob. "Six."

"What?" Colleen burst out. "Six? Gosh, tell me they aren't all inside this house waiting to meet me."

He grinned.

Colleen flinched and bit her lip. "Sorry, that came out wrong. I'd love to meet your family. I'm just not prepared."

"I don't believe anyone is home except my parents and you can wait out here if you'd like."

Colleen touched his wrist, circled her fingers around it and then took his hand in hers. "I want to meet them. Six is just a lot. I have only two and I can't seem to manage all the drama between us."

Beckett kissed her cheek and then opened the door without knocking and called out, "Mom?"

Colleen had always wondered what it would be like to say "Mom," as it was always "Mother" in their house. The formality matched Elizabeth's personality, but under her breath at times when no one could hear her, Colleen had called her Mommy.

A tall woman, elegant even in jeans and a white T-shirt, came from the back of the house. She held a cell phone to her ear.

"Gotta go, bug. I'll call you later. Your brother, my favorite, is here."

Colleen stood stunned until Beckett burst into laughter and hugged his mom. "Nina loves when you say that."

"She's fuming right now, crafting an e-mail about my horrid sense of humor." The woman had long dark hair, a lined face free of makeup, and large blue eyes with eyelashes long enough to sweep up and almost touch her eyebrows. She hugged her son and then turned to Colleen. "Well, hello, sweetie, I'm Denise."

"Hi, I'm Colleen. It's a pleasure to meet you, ma'am."

The woman's smile bloomed larger and she set her gaze on her son. "Don't you just love the South? If I'd known I could be called *ma'am* I would have moved here long, long ago."

Beckett held out the box. "I brought this back for Dad. He said he wanted it for some tournament tomorrow. I'll put it in the shed."

"Just leave it in the kitchen for now. Come in and say hello to Dad, and Sylvia's here, too. Some mess with her job."

Colleen followed them down a narrow hallway, its walls covered in pale blue shipboard with photos of family and loads of boats, many different kinds of boats. The images were framed and lined in neat rows. They entered a small kitchen so green that Colleen almost squinted. The countertops were white, and the wooden table was painted one shade lighter. The fabric — on chairs and across the tops of the windows — was a green and white check reminiscent of the curtains in her own house. At the table sat an older man with hair to match the countertops, and a girl facing him. They were deep in conversation but turned their faces to Beckett and Colleen as they entered the room.

"Son." The man stood and hugged Beckett, effusive as if he hadn't seen him in months.

"Hey, bro." The girl wiggled her fingers at her brother and he bent over to hug her.

"Hey, sis. What's going on?"

"My boss. I hate him. Nothing new. You?"

He placed his hand gently on Colleen's arm and then withdrew it. "This is my pal Colleen Donohue."

Dad shook her hand first. "Welcome. I'm Bubba Joe."

"Dad!" Sylvia's voice rang out and she stood, jostled her dad with her elbow before turning to Colleen and holding out her own hand. "Hi, I'm Sylvia. And this is my dad,

Raymond."

"Ever since I moved south, I've wanted to be Bubba. Couldn't you have let it go for a few minutes? Let me live my fantasy?"

And then everyone was talking at once, while still somehow carrying on the conversation about the dinner they were having when the passel of siblings came in from Nevada next month.

"Where does everyone else live?" Colleen asked.

Denise rattled them off, top to bottom, where they lived and what they were doing. Colleen couldn't keep up. She glanced at Beckett, who shrugged and said, "You asked."

Within minutes they were back in the car. Colleen exhaled. "What a fun family you have. I'm a bit envious."

Beckett's face wrinkled in confusion. "You have a fine family from what I can tell."

Colleen felt the lurch of despair. How could she explain to this man that yes, it appeared she had a family, but she'd also willingly given up on being an intimate part of their tribe.

She grew quiet, running a finger along the passenger-side window, making tiny circles until Beckett parked at the Oyster Shack and they both climbed out. Once seated at a small outside table with a fan whirring overhead, Beckett said, "I feel like I've said or done something wrong. You've retreated."

Colleen shook her head. "I'm just not that hungry and . . ."

Beckett stood and held out his hand. "Come on. I'm not one to force a girl to eat. Let's take a walk instead. Maybe you'll change your mind."

"You can take me home." Colleen said the words she'd said so many times before when she'd felt the urge to open up, to crack the door that led to the room where all her sadness and grief were stored. Beckett wanted to talk about family. She did not.

"I don't understand." He exhaled and stepped back. "Listen, if you want to go home, I'll take you. But if I've said or done something to upset you, then you must tell me."

"No." Colleen shook her head, her hair falling from the clip that held it back. "It's my family. It's complicated, and seeing yours so funny and loving just brings up things I try my best not to dwell on. If I talk about it — it all comes rushing back at me and that is the last thing I want right now."

"We've had rough times, too, Colleen. Everyone does. I put them all through hell — that's why it's a big ol' joke that I'm the favorite. Mom doesn't say that because I've been the angel, or because anything is perfect."

"How so?"

"It's why I don't drink. I've hinted at that. I had a terrible problem in my twenties. I was arrested. I put them through hell and back, and then to hell again."

Colleen stared at Beckett — a man who seemed so together, with a family so intact.

"Come on," he said. "Let's walk on the riverfront and we'll eat if and when you get hungry."

After apologizing to the waitress and vacating their table, they ambled to the river park, where a sidewalk followed the curving shore of the rushing tidal waters. Gas lanterns and spotlights punctuated the darkness. "I'm sorry to ruin the night," Colleen said.

"So what happened, Colleen? What happened that you had to change your name and leave this place?"

She paused at the edge of the river and stared at the man who had asked her what no one ever had — the *real* reason. Other men had probed in different ways, but he'd nailed it: why did you change your name and leave this place? Tears bloomed in her eyes; a thunderhead of anguish built in her chest. And right there, with the exact right question asked, Colleen blurted out the truth. "On my wedding day ten years ago, I found my sister and my fiancé kissing in the hallway of the church. I ran. They married soon after. I've avoided this place as much and as often as I can."

"Oh, Colleen." He rested his breath on those words and then said softly, "I'm so sorry that happened. When she came outside with her husband . . . behind the pub, I figured something had gone wrong, but I didn't think . . ."

"I know. Who would think that?" Colleen's pulse bounced in her temples and she felt the flush of embarrassment begin to creep up.

"Did you have any idea?"

"None. Hallie had never betrayed me in the slightest. We were so close. So close. I didn't see it coming. I didn't suspect it."

"I don't mean to pry. Only talk about it if you want to."

"Honestly, I didn't have a clue. She was planning our wedding. Planning our wedding! She was picking out the flowers and the cake and the dresses and I guess she was also picking out her own groom. I didn't get a tingling sense of anything weird or wrong. I've gone over this a million times in my mind and tried to find the one place or time or hint. Hallie, up until then, had never had a serious boyfriend. She was naïve in a way. She'd never stopped living at home, even in college, and although she certainly wasn't simpleminded or anything like that, she was easily influenced by others."

Colleen rolled her neck around to shake off the ideas that had so long haunted her. "So he probably seduced her. But I've never wanted to know what happened." She covered her mouth with her hand as a laugh erupted. "No, that's not true. I totally wanted to know what happened. I just didn't want it to be Hallie who told me. Or my family — I was too embarrassed. So I've just made up my own stories, but I had no idea until she told me the other day."

"I can only again say I am so sorry. I know it must have broken your heart."

"Yes. But it felt like more than my heart. I felt like it broke . . . me. Now I come home only to see Dad and Shane. This week is the first time I've spoken to Hallie since it happened."

"You've avoided your sister for ten years?"

"Essentially, yes. It took careful planning, but I managed." She laughed, but he shook his head — he wasn't going to let her joke her way out of this.

"You know, if there's one thing out of a million I've learned it's this: when you are powerless over a situation, and everything rises in you to do something, to hurry and do something, sometimes there is just no fixing it. Sometimes there is . . ."

"Don't you dare say acceptance." Colleen closed her eyes. "Don't say it."

"Okay, I won't."

Colleen kicked at a fluff of Spanish moss that had fallen to the path. "I want a better solution than that."

He shrugged. "We all do."

"Actually I found a better solution than that — build a new and different life."

"Was it worth it to forfeit what's here?"

"Who are you? A counselor?" Colleen squeezed her hands into little fists, feeling her fingernails dig into the soft places of her palms. "See? This is why I don't talk about it. Now I'm being mean to you. I can't talk about this."

Beckett nodded. "I understand." He smiled, but his expression was sad, as if she'd let him down. God, she was tired of letting people down.

"No, honestly you don't understand. I think I have to go now, Beckett. I know my way home."

She set her feet to leave but then turned to see him still standing there, still looking at her with gentle kindness. "Why are you looking at me like that?"

"Like what?"

"Like you don't hate me. You should be mad as hell. I'm being . . . rude."

"I told you. I've been there. I get it."

"Been where?" Colleen took a few steps toward him.

"In the place where you don't want to accept what you must and so you try every damn thing in the world not to feel it or know it. I drank. Sounds like you run."

"That's not what's happening here."

He shrugged. "Then maybe I'm wrong."

"You are so frustrating!" Colleen's voice echoed across the plaza and she lowered it. "What happened that *you* had to accept?"

"I was driving and there was an accident, and the girl in the passenger seat, a friend, didn't . . . make it."

His words fell on her like a bag of wet sand between her shoulder blades, holding her immobile. "Oh, God, Beckett. I am so sorry . . ." And she forgot everything about Walter and Hallie. She touched the thin scar by his ear. "This scar, right? Tell me what happened. I mean, you don't have to talk about it. Here I am going on and on about a love affair and there you are with life and death and I'm . . ."

"No." He took Colleen's face in his hands, kissed her softly. "It *all* matters. I'm not saying my tragedy mattered more. I'm just telling you that I had one." His hands dropped to his sides and he was far off for a moment. "It was my fault. They told me over and over that it wasn't, that the rain and the dark night and the spilled oil on the road contributed." His attention returned to Colleen. "But it *was* my fault. I was preoccupied, fiddling with the radio, flirting with her, acting like a fool, and when the car started to skid I overcorrected. And I had been drinking and was set to drink even more that night — not drunk yet but damn well planning on it. I *see* it in my mind's eye every day. I remember it every day. I was careless and reckless and inattentive to anything but my own desires. And I will never stop trying to atone for it. I descended into a dark place for a long time — where the drinking was all I did or thought about. So I know how you feel — not the blame, but the inability to forget. You can't erase something that painful. I know."

"I am so, so sorry." Colleen felt a sadness that had nothing to do with her own life. "Isn't it strange?"

335

"What?" His voice broke free from the snags of the past. "What's strange?"

"What memories can be?" Colleen couldn't express exactly what she meant, but the thought hovered just beyond her consciousness, a gnat buzzing, a realization forming. "Memories are alive, and they can take over; they have their own life apart from us. But what are they really? Just some amorphous, dreamy things that shift with time, almost like ghosts. Still they cause us pain or happiness or they keep us from doing things or cause us to shiver inside and wake us in the middle of the night."

"Wow."

"Huh?" Colleen found his face in her sight again; she'd been staring across the river's blue expanse to the horizon, where green marsh grasses winnowed the sky from the water.

"That was beautiful. What you just said. I want to write it down."

Colleen tried to laugh, but laughter didn't want to join the conversation. Instead she offered Beckett a small smile. "I have no idea what I'm talking about. It's just that memories seem to be all we talk about these days — my siblings and me, I mean. How to save them; what they are; how to record them; how confusing they can be. And what are they, Beckett? Just some chemicals along a neural pathway?"

"No." He brushed back her hair and ran his finger along her hairline. "They are who we are, little strands of who we are, all tied together."

"Why can't we just pull out one memory strand, or ten or twenty for that matter, and keep only the ones we want?"

He didn't answer her, because of course there wasn't an answer.

Instead he told her, "I've only told one other person that story. It's mine. I don't like dumping it on people."

"I'm honored that you told me. My dad has this saying he's repeated for as long as I can remember. 'As the Irish say . . .' and one of them is, 'No matter how long the day, the evening comes,' which means, all things do end. But these bad memories of ours don't seem to have an end."

"Indeed." Beckett attempted an Irish accent that wasn't convincing. He laughed at himself and dropped his arm over her shoulder. In comfortable silence they took a few steps along the river walk. Colleen moved a few inches from Beckett, allowing his arm to fall from her shoulder, and they held hands.

Then quickly, a shiver ran up Colleen's

arm, and then down again. What was it? What was amiss? Something. Or was it that she was moving too close to Beckett too fast — alarms sounded inside.

There were so many people out enjoying the riverside at day's end. Two teenage boys ate something out of a paper bag. A set of three girls took selfies with their phones and then snapped them again and then again in various poses. A couple stood kissing, her arms thrown around his neck and tears on her cheeks. He consoled her with strokes on her hair and cooing noises.

So familiar: that stance and those noises. *Walter.*

Colleen squeezed Beckett's hand too hard. "What?" He paused in midstep and Colleen released his hand and pointed at Walter and the young woman with the bright red hair, so unnatural it looked painted on.

"That's him." Her voice fell as low as her quickly plummeting stomach. And the label came from habit. "My fiancé." She shook her head. "My brother-in-law."

"That's not your sister . . ." Beckett dropped his hands on Colleen's shoulders and spun her around to face him. "Don't get involved." Beckett then took her face in his hands, kissed her.

Colleen stared at him for a few breaths

and then broke free. "Of course I have to get involved. It's my sister." She twisted her neck to watch the train wreck, to see what she'd seen before as a repeating echo. But he was gone. Instead there stood a family of five, rough-and-tumble toddlers and two exhausted parents trying to get them to stand still for a photo next to the flagpole. The kids were having none of it.

There was no way Walter and the woman could have disappeared in that short time. Colleen broke free of Beckett and jogged the few yards to where they had stood only moments ago. She scanned the river walk, back and forth, and then looked toward the parking lot to see them climb into a bright red VW Bug — he in the passenger side, she in the driver's seat.

"Walter!" She hadn't planned on calling out his name; she hadn't planned on running toward the car. But she did.

The driver was quick on the pedal and the car gone before Colleen reached the pavement. Beckett was behind her in a moment. "Colleen . . ."

"I know that was him. He's cheating on my sister." Tightness gripped her chest.

"I'm sorry." Beckett's voice came sad and low in her ear.

"I have to go home. I have to tell her."

"Are you sure it was him? Are you *sure*?"

"Yes," she said with certainty now. "But what I'm not so sure of is if she'll believe me; she'll think I'm making it up to get back at her or . . ."

"I don't think it so much matters what anyone believes as long as we speak the truth, right?"

Colleen stared at this man she'd only come to know days before and smiled at him. "Who are you, Yoda?"

He laughed so deeply that Colleen could only smile in return.

CHAPTER TWENTY-THREE

Except for memory, time would have no
meaning at all.
Pat Conroy, *Beach Music*

Six Days until the Party . . .
Morning came with the sound of Colleen's
nieces' voices overlapping outside, and she
knew that her sister was at the house, and
she knew what she must do — tell the truth.
Colleen had slept as poorly as if she'd slept
on a bench at the river park where she'd
seen Walter kiss that woman. She rose with
dread and dressed quickly, poured a fortify-
ing cup of coffee and went to find Hallie
and the girls on the screened porch.

Rosie and Sadie sat on either side of
Hallie as she read to them from a picture
book that Colleen recognized from their
childhood — *Where the Wild Things Are*.
Hallie's voice lowered with great authority
and her girls laughed.

Colleen entered and they all looked at her, the overhead light falling onto their faces causing shadows that made the little girls indistinguishable from one another. "Aunt Lena!" The one on the left jumped off the swing and ran to her side. It was Sadie, the more reticent of the two.

"Hi, girls."

Hallie sat stock-still. "There you are. We were hoping you'd be up soon."

"Can I talk to you?" Colleen couldn't find small talk or jolly jokes for the little girls.

"Yes." Hallie shifted on the large seat and Rosie jumped down with her sister.

"Does this mean we need to go inside?"

"Yes, sweetie."

"Can we watch the iPad? Please?"

Hallie nodded. "It's in the kitchen."

The girls ran off quick as lightning. "The iPad with movies hidden inside — it's their favorite thing. I don't let them very often."

"I saw Walter." Colleen didn't want to talk about movies or iPads.

"Where?" Hallie asked as though she was as tired of his name as she already was of the day.

"At the river park."

"No, that wasn't him. He's out of town." Hallie shifted on the swing.

"He was with a woman, Hallie. A woman

342

who was crying and had her arms around him. He was consoling her, looking at her, and he kissed her."

"Nope." Hallie's facial expression didn't change. She rose to her feet and stood as still as the carved mermaid statue in the park, her face placid with denial.

"Yes."

"You're trying to make me feel the way you felt that day. You're trying to make me understand. But I've known, all these years I've known and I've tortured myself about it. You don't have to —"

"That is *not* what I'm doing. I'm telling you the truth." Colleen took a few steps closer. Hallie reached her hand out and for a moment Colleen thought she might slap her, but instead she grabbed on to the swing's rope to steady herself. "He's in Columbia, where he's supervising a housing project."

"No, he's with a women whose red hair is as bright as her VW Bug."

"Why are you doing this?" Hallie slapped her hand against the edge of the wooden swing and then flinched at the sting; she shook her hand out.

"I'm not *doing* anything. I'm telling you what I saw."

"Thank you, Lena." Hallie's words were

343

robotic, stilted. She turned quickly and entered the house, leaving the door ajar while calling out for her girls.

"Okay, adorables, it's time to go. We're taking Grandy grocery shopping." A pause followed and then high-pitched little-girl voices before Colleen heard her dad's voice join them and then the sounds of leaving.

Colleen sat on the newly vacated swing and shifted against the back pillow. Dad had had this swing made when they were in middle school — by an old friend who needed work, he'd said. He'd taken the friend a single bed mattress and had him build around it with nautical ropes hanging from the ceiling. If ever Colleen thought of taking a nap, she thought of this swing, of this musty-smelling mattress and the many blankets and pillows that had come and gone.

She closed her eyes. It had been Walter, right? Yes, of course it had. She hadn't imposed his image on some random man kissing a crying woman. Her memories might haunt her, but not under the bright lights of Watersend River Park.

Walter. The man she'd loved; the man she had held up against all other men; the man who'd married her sister. Charming and smart and full of adventure. And yet, and

344

yet, there he was doing to Hallie exactly what he'd done to Colleen.

"I'm finished!" Colleen set the final stories on Shane's kitchen table. "I finished this morning after Hallie and the girls stopped by and then took Dad shopping. So the book is done now, right?"

Shane grinned at her and leafed through the sheets. "I knew I could count on you."

"You did *not* know that." Colleen slapped his arm. "But you could."

He nodded while skimming the stories.

"Shane."

"Hmmm . . ."

"I need to tell you something."

He glanced up, a lock of hair falling over his forehead just as it had when he was a child, making him appear younger. "What is it?"

"Last night I think I saw Walter with a woman at the river park."

"You think you did or you did?" He set the papers on the table and gazed directly at Colleen.

She hesitated but knew the answer. As surely as she knew it was Walter in the alcove of the church. "I did. He was holding her, kissing her, consoling her. It was clear they were intimate. They drove away in her car before I could confront him."

"Just damn." Shane slumped into a chair. "I would never have thought or guessed this. Honestly, he's been like a model husband and father, a great son-in-law to Dad. Are you sure?" He held up his hand. "Don't answer that. Of course you're sure."

"You like . . . him?" Colleen leaned forward. "I mean, you two get along well and all that and you've never suspected this?"

"They're both under a lot of stress. Jobs. Kids. The move to the new house. Maybe it's the first time."

Colleen almost, but didn't quite, laugh. "*First* time?"

Shane cringed. "Second." He slapped his hand on his leg. "Just damn. I trusted him, too. He's been a help to all of us. He's been such a part of the family." He rubbed the back of his neck and shook his head. "It took a while for me to forgive him, you know? I blamed him for your leaving. I still do. But at some point I had to trust him for Hallie. What now?"

"Remember when Hallie said she was exhausted and had 'enough crap' to deal with? Maybe this is what she meant."

"Maybe, but they have a really busy life. It could have been a load of other things."

"Well, I . . ." Colleen stopped as the door handle made a clicking noise and Hallie entered the room, her satchel over her shoulder and a take-out coffee cup in hand.

"You what?" Hallie dropped her things on the table directly on top of Colleen's stories.

"Nothing." Colleen eased the papers from under Hallie's bundles. "Just need to finish . . ."

"Bullshit." Hallie took a sip of coffee and glared at her sister. "But right now I don't care what you were talking about, even if it was me." She sat at the table. Her hair was pulled back in a ponytail and she had a glazed look. Colleen had a vague sense her sister was seeing the river park and a red-haired woman.

"You okay?" Shane asked.

"The timeline." Hallie's words were robotic. "You know it's not right."

"It's not." Colleen glanced at her brother before turning back to her sister with a nod. "You're right, Hallie. But I think that in the memory book we have to give Dad the timeline he's always given us. It's what he told us, so it's what he believes and maybe that's the best we can do."

"The best we can do?" Hallie's face seemed to come alive again, her cheeks flushed. "It damn well isn't the best we can

347

do. And you know that. You just don't care."

"Don't care?" Colleen felt her voice rising and she checked it, spoke more softly. "I do care. I totally care. Listen, I found my baby book and it's like I didn't even exist for the first two months of my life. Of course I care. But the memory book is supposed to be for Dad, so he can look at it and see his life in some sort of narrative way, and if this is the narrative he told us, maybe that's the one he wants to remember."

"Maybe it doesn't matter what we *want* to remember," Hallie said, "but what is true. Isn't that what you want all of us to do? Face the truth?"

"No. I don't know what I mean." She glanced between brother and sister. "Have you ever wondered why we never visited Grandma and Granddad in Virginia? Or Rosie and Fred? I mean, I know we have a small family compared to most, but we never went to see them. They always came to us. We never visited Mother and Dad's town. We never saw where they grew up. We never *once* visited."

Hallie's eyes flitted to the note cards, back to Colleen and then again to her brother. "I never thought about that. It was just the way it was."

"Exactly." Colleen exhaled. "Just the way it was."

Shane lifted a folder from the table and then set it down again. "Maybe South Carolina was just more fun. It was Dad's home. He didn't like leaving it. We know that. Sometimes the most simple explanation is the right one."

"And sometimes it's not," Hallie said. "Right, Lena?"

"What's that supposed to mean?"

Hallie stood and walked to the wall where her note cards still dangled, looking as though one strong breath would send them all to the floor, where they might rearrange themselves in a new order. "My husband in a park when he's supposed to be out of town. The most simple explanation is that you were wrong. But it's not the correct explanation, is it?"

"No, it's not."

Hallie shook her head, breaking free of something invisible binding her, and rubbed her hands up and down her arms. She glanced first at Colleen and then at her brother. "We have to ask Dad. It's the only way. Nothing else makes sense. He has to tell us. Was he in Ireland for two years or one? Did he marry Mother in 1980 or 1981? That's the bottom line."

"I'd go by the stamp on the pictures." Colleen pointed to the pile of them on the table, the black-and-white, the faded color and the newly printed.

"Then you were born in Ireland."

"That can't be right. My birth certificate says Watersend. Unless my father isn't . . . Dad." She shook her head. "No. There has to be a logical explanation."

"Exactly."

Shane paced the room, running his hands through his hair. "We have a lot bigger things to figure out than that one year."

"Yes, we do. Like who's going to take care of Dad." Colleen was the one who spoke what they were all thinking.

"*We* are." Shane slapped his hand on his thigh, a sound that reverberated through the room.

"Well, we can face the truth or pretend it's not happening," Colleen said.

All these conversations, overlapping and underlapping, but all of them pointing to the same thing: a cold hard look at the truth.

Hallie shook her head. "You aren't talking about Dad. I know that. You're talking about seeing Walter with a friend and making me think it's . . ."

Colleen held out her hand to interrupt Hallie. "If she was a friend, she was a mighty friendly friend. I get that you don't want to admit the truth. Hell, I wouldn't want to see it either. But guess what — not wanting to see it doesn't make it go away."

"Shut up, Lena. Shut up." Hallie pushed at the back of a chair, the scraping sound like nails on a chalkboard. She slammed her fist on the table. Then her face went as still as a lake, turning from the rigorous and tumultuous river during a storm to something so still it was eerie. Her eyes were dry, her expression blank.

Colleen waved her hand in front of her sister's face. "Are you okay?"

Hallie's eyes didn't move, not seeming to be looking at anything. She spoke softly. "I guess there's no use pretending anymore, Lena. You hate me. Dad is disappearing. And my husband is a philanderer." She exhaled and her gaze didn't shift. "No more pretending."

Colleen sat as still as she knew how, unable to find the words or actions that might soothe this awful moment.

"Neither of you can say anything right now to make it better, so to relieve you of that burden, I'm leaving."

"Don't." Shane reached out his hand, touched her shoulder. "Stay."

Hallie looked at Colleen and then grabbed

her bag and left, the door clicking shut
behind her.

Chapter Twenty-Four

A man *needs* such a narrative, a
continuous inner narrative, to maintain his
identity, his self.

Oliver Sacks,
*The Man Who Mistook
His Wife for a Hat*

The pub buzzed with activity — a bridesmaids' party had descended, the women
ordering shots of tequila and wearing pink
T-shirts with the hashtag #gettinghitched.
As if getting married meant this poor girl
would be pulling a wagon for the rest of her
life.

Colleen felt that old ache again, the one
of betrayal, but this time it was for Hallie,
and it was a feeling she didn't want to have,
one she didn't want to indulge. Placing
another brick in that wall of protection
around her heart, she added some spackling
and walked through the screeching girls,

each laughing at the other in such high-pitched squeals that Colleen almost put her hands over her ears. Her dad sat at the far end of the bar, his head bent almost forehead to forehead with old Mr. Levin. Colleen knew his story, too: a widower who had lost his wife to lymphoma, who had sat on the same stool for the past twenty-five years, who drank only beer before his wife passed, and then afterward enough whiskey to kill him and need a ride home every night, and now only one shot a night. He twirled his whiskey glass. He nursed it. He sniffed it. He made it last as long as he could, and then he went home.

A doctor, an elegant woman with dark hair — Colleen didn't know her name — a woman who was new to town and had opened an emergency clinic, sat with the bookshop owner, Mimi, in the middle of the room, laughing and drinking a beer. Colleen waved at Mimi and both women waved in return. Tales of the town filled this pub as surely as tables, chairs and taps.

"Dad." Colleen said this gently. She didn't want to startle him. It scared her, the way she felt about Gavin's vulnerability. If her dad was easily frightened, if he couldn't find his way, how could she?

"Hello, little lark." Gavin smiled and

kissed her cheek. "When did you get here?"

"Just now. I was upstairs visiting Shane and . . ." Had he meant when did she get into town or when did she arrive at the pub? *Never say "remember"; never say "I told you"* — Colleen saw the words on the placard in Shane's apartment.

"Oh, yes," Gavin said with a nod. The noise level rose as the three-piece fiddle band began playing. Colleen thought again, as she had so many times, that although she'd never been to Ireland, if someone was put to sleep and awoke in this place, they would believe they had been transported to the Emerald Isle. At least as long as no one spoke in a thick southern accent or glanced at the photos on the walls.

As Dad walked away, Beckett approached. Colleen greeted him. "Hey, you. Sorry about last night. Not the best way to end a lovely date."

"Nothing to be sorry for. How is . . . everyone?" He glanced around the pub.

"Not so great. But how's the research coming for the historic marker?" She switched subjects quickly.

"Should be done in the next week or so. I thought it might make a good birthday present at your dad's big party, but it won't be ready in time." Beckett approached the bar and ordered a glass of tonic water with lime for himself and Colleen nodded that she wanted the same, as Hallie made her way toward them. She reached their side and put her hand on Colleen's arm. "We need to talk."

"I thought you left."

"I did, but . . ." She placed her hand on her stomach. "But I feel sick. I wanted to run away, find a place to hide, but I can't. I want to talk to you. I know that doesn't make sense and you can tell me to . . ."

"I'm here, Hallie."

Beckett took a few steps back and engaged quickly in a conversation with a man he knew on the next bar stool.

"You *are* right about Walter."

"For once, I don't want to be right." Colleen nodded but not with the satisfaction she'd thought might come.

"How it starts is how it ends." Hallie motioned to Hank and he brought her a shot of whiskey. She drank it and slammed the glass to the bar. "Right? How it started, with cheating lies, is how it's ending. How could I have expected anything less? It's my own doing."

"No, Hallie. It's not your own doing. It's his. You can see that, right? You didn't do anything to *make* him cheat."

"I've always felt that something was . . . wrong between us. Always, but I blamed it on you. Not *on* you, but on what I did *to* you. So I worked even harder to make our marriage great. I worked even harder to be a good wife and mother. I worked even harder to be . . . hell, I don't know, as amazing as you."

"What are you talking about?" Colleen took her sister's arm and gently guided her through the crowd, outside to the sidewalk and then to the river's edge.

Hallie was full on crying by then and Colleen put both hands on her sister's shoulders. "It's okay."

Hallie shook her head. "I'm not like you, Lena. I can't turn off my emotions. I can't stop because you say 'it's okay.' I've tried to be like you. All my ever-loving life I've tried to be like you." She pointed to the pub. "For God's sake, you're Dad's little lark. I've never even had a nickname."

"*Why,* Hallie? Why would you want to be anything like me?"

"Because you're just you."

"That makes no sense at all."

"You don't see it, do you?" Hallie's voice rose. The mingling couples and families and joggers and amblers all turned their faces toward Hallie and Colleen. But they kept on as though they were alone as they once had been, unraveling life's mystery, or at least their life's mystery.

"See what?"

"You're different, Colleen. You aren't like the rest of us. You're a little like Dad, the best of us, and then something more, something almost magical. The way your eyes shine brighter and how you gulp life by the mouthful, how when you put your full attention on someone they only see you, how you laugh and the sound falls through the air."

"It's the same as you, Hallie. I've always felt that way about you, too." Colleen couldn't quell the feelings now; tears filled her own eyes and a breach had been broken or crossed. Everything must be said at that river's edge.

"No. It's kind of you to say, but it's not true."

"We aren't the same, of course we aren't. But you're amazing. When you aren't trying to be someone else or . . ."

"Cheating with your fiancé."

"Yes."

"I'm sorry, Lena. I'm sorrier than I've ever been for anything ever. I've always suspected that the only reason he stayed with me was because he was caught. He denies it, but he wasn't going to leave you. He wasn't. If you hadn't seen us . . ."

"Well, I did."

"Ten years. Do you realize you haven't spoken to me in ten years?"

"I know."

"And you're so hard. So . . . hard. Like you're made of something else now. I hate it so much." A shudder passed through Hallie's body.

"I hate it, too." Colleen spoke the truth. She hated being so cold, but it was all she'd known to do.

"Then quit." Hallie looked up. "Be Lena. Please. You told me I was obsessed with planning the party so I didn't have to think about my marriage. And maybe you're right. But you're obsessed with your job so you don't have to think about us — your family here without you."

"That's not why. I love what I do and where I get to go and . . ." Colleen was defending something that was both true and not altogether true. Yes, she loved her job. But yes, she'd used it to avoid her family and the pain and the loss.

"All these years, I've known the truth about Walter. Deep down I've known." Hallie sat on the soft grass, her legs crossed.

Colleen sat across from her on bent knees,

her hands denting the moist grass, mud wet against her shins. "You've known?"

"Guessed at best. But, Lena, he's a good dad. A great man in so many other ways. We have a community and a life and the girls, the precious girls. I *needed* to believe he was faithful. I needed to believe that having him was worth the price of betraying you." She looked to Colleen, her eyes now clear and her voice clearer.

"We fool ourselves," Colleen said. "We fool ourselves to make circumstances tolerable. We fool ourselves to avoid the pain. We fool ourselves to make sure that life can chug along at its slow, grinding, safe pace. I understand. But you deserve everything good and true. So do I. We both do, and Walter Littleton wasn't and isn't either of those things."

"I've been at war with myself," Hallie said, her breath slowing as she calmed down. "One part of me convincing me to stay and that all was well, and the other part begging me to look and be aware." She shifted on the grass and gazed over Colleen's shoulder. "Do you have any idea what it is to be battling yourself? It drains you of so much . . . energy." She looked back at Colleen. "He's awful, isn't he?"

"He doesn't have to be all bad, Hallie. I

know the good parts, too, but you have to decide what you can and cannot live with."

"I know." Hallie took her sister's hands. "I love you. You know that, right? I didn't stop just because you did."

Colleen felt the thick sadness in her throat and tried to swallow. "I do love you, Hallie, but it's the trust that I haven't been able to find."

"I know." Hallie's gaze became unfocused. "My God, my girls will be devastated if I leave him. They think he's the bee's knees. Daddy this and Daddy that and Daddy here and Daddy there."

"He'll still be their daddy." Colleen was treading on unfamiliar territory, an un- mapped land she didn't truly understand because she didn't have her own children, and yet she could have just as well been talking about their own dad.

"You're the wrong person to complain to, Lena." Hallie hesitated before she contin- ued. "It feels like I'm losing everything that matters, except my girls. Dad's disease isn't a mistake he made. It's not his fault. Here, between us, this *is* my fault. It was a mistake that I thought was saving my own heart. I thought I was finding the love of my life, but I've never been able to forgive myself. How could I expect you to forgive me? Now

361

what, Lena? Now what do I *do?*"

"I have no idea." Colleen closed her eyes. "Except this — do not do what I did."

Hallie almost smiled. "No, I can't run away . . ."

"In a way you can. You can leave him. But you have family here, Hallie. A house. A home. Come back to it if you don't want the internal war of living with Walter."

The sisters sat quietly then, the voices of others rumbling past, a foghorn sounding far off and a baby crying from a stroller only a few feet away. But they didn't hear any of this, not with full awareness. They merely sat together in the silence between them, the silence that finally, finally spoke of sisterhood.

"What about you, Lena?"

"What about me?"

"What if you want to stay? What if you want to be here, too?"

"Hallie, if that happens, we'll figure it out. Don't use me as an excuse not to end your marriage."

Hallie took in a gasp as if she'd been hit in the solar plexus. "Yes, I've been doing that for far, far too long."

CHAPTER TWENTY-FIVE

We do not remember days,
we remember moments.

Cesare Pavese,
The Business of Living; Diaries 1935–1950

Five Days until the Party . . .

The johnboat tipped and bounced against the dock as Colleen, Hallie and Dad sat on the bench, so close together that their legs and knees pressed together. Shane sat solo on the driver's seat.

"Did we get a smaller boat?" Gavin asked as Shane pushed down on the throttle and the small motor pulsed to form a wake like the V of white birds flying across a pewter sky.

"No," Colleen said. Seated next to Gavin, she placed her hand on his knee as they tilted forward with the momentum. "We just grew bigger."

Gavin laughed and shifted his baseball cap

on his head, lifted his face to the sun. "There is no place on this earth as beautiful as the rivers and marshes of our land. You know that, don't you?" He asked this with his eyes closed so the siblings didn't know to whom the question was directed. They all answered in the affirmative.

"It is the scend of the sea for us now." Gavin leaned forward in the johnboat, upsetting the delicate balance. Each sister grabbed the side of the boat.

"The what?" Hallie asked.

"The scend," Gavin insisted. "You know, I've told you this before." His voice rose with the recent, increasingly frequent frustration of dementia sneaking in like fog in the night.

Colleen touched her dad's shoulder, squeezed it. "Remind us."

"Not send but scend." He spelled the different words. "The surge behind the boat — the surge behind our life. When the tide and the wind and the wave are all pushing us forward. That is now."

"Yes," Colleen said. "That is now." She understood he meant more than the wind and wave behind the boat, but of life's current toward something they could not stop, a momentum beyond their control.

Slowly Shane eased the bright silver johnboat into the larger river channel, where sandbars appeared and disappeared twice a day; where the shrimp weren't visible until you threw the net and lifted it with a great heave; where the water teemed with unseen life and slapped against the docks and shoreline with equal disregard. The humming motor and the swish-slap of river water on the hull lulled them all to silence. Colleen wondered what her dad and siblings were thinking, each with his or her own river of thought pulsing in different directions as complicated as the estuaries and creeks that spread from the main river, some reaching a dead end and others rejoining where they'd started.

Taking Dad out in the boat like this had been part of a well-laid plan. The night before, the three siblings had sat in the kitchen, playing an Ella Fitzgerald LP, and decided that the only way to understand the odd gap in Dad's timeline was to ask him. To gently ask him in a place that felt utterly familiar and wholly belonging to him.

The river.

The last couple of days had been rough on all of them — Dad getting worse not by the hour but almost by the minute. His spatial sense seemed to be deteriorating; he tripped over stairs and stumbled over his own feet. He time traveled at least once a day — asking when Lena would be home from ballet or when his wife would return from her afternoon bridge game with the ladies.

Another difficult choice had been made — Hallie and the girls would move in with Gavin. Although it seemed a simple solution, it wasn't. It was a decision fraught with heartache, and Dad asking again and again, Why? Why are you moving in? And Hallie having to explain again and again — I've left Walter. And their dad becoming concerned and upset once more.

But at this moment, out on the water, Gavin showed no concern for anything. His face was smooth and his grin relaxed, coming and going as easily as the clouds moving across the late afternoon sky. It was hot, yes, but they were accustomed to the August heat, and floating on the water was a perfect cure — the breeze whipping, the water cooling. A sailboat eased by and the man at the helm waved, and then a motorboat passed, pulling a pair of teenage boys on an inflatable tube, both screaming and loving the simple danger of being tossed off and into the water. The wake rocked them all back and forth as they held on to the sides of their own boat.

Shane slowed and drew near to one of the exposed sandbars, where spartina grass swayed, summer green and bent to the breeze. The tip of the sandbar, always exposed, was crusted with bleached oyster shells, tinkling like wind chimes in the wake of the tide. Shane expertly maneuvered the boat. There was the clanging of metal on metal as he yanked out the anchor and then the soft thud as he dropped it into the sand off the bow. From under the bench Colleen withdrew the cooler where she'd stashed a thermos of lemonade and bottles of water.

They jumped off the boat into the shin-deep water without talking, and with the practiced synchronicity of childhood. Hallie took the few steps to the sand line and dropped a blanket, stained and full of holes from its long and loving use. The rest of them ambled slowly to the blanket and then sat, chatting about the beauty of the breeze and what a stunning day it was for August when, without preamble, Hallie opened the discussion.

"Dad, we need you to tell us the truth about Ireland." She drew her knees to her chest in a silhouette so like her childhood self that Colleen thought maybe they had traveled back in time. Soon Mother would appear from behind the grasses carrying a wicker basket full of cut-up sandwiches, potato chips and apple slices, which would all soon be crunchy with sand.

"Hallie." Shane spat her name and leaned forward, digging his hands into the sand. "That's not the best way to start."

"Start what?" Gavin sat with his hands behind him, propping himself in a half-reclining position on the blanket. "Am I being ambushed here? Are you going to leave me on this island to swim home?" His attempt at humor fell flat and into silence.

Colleen sat cross-legged, her hands wrapped around a cold water bottle, her heart hammering. She didn't have a good feeling about this discussion. Some things were best left alone. Their dad was erratic now — sometimes fully Gavin and sometimes a man or young child they'd never met. He sang the lark song, humming or under his breath, all during the day. Something buried was pushing against the ground, forcing its way to the surface — a Lazarus of memory.

"I have never lied to you." Gavin's voice was strong. He seemed himself.

"I know." Hallie lowered her voice and wrapped her arms tighter around her knees. "But you haven't told us the truth about your time in Ireland."

"I don't know what you're talking about, my darling." He crossed one leg over the other and furrowed his brow.

"We want to know the full story. We love you and we want to know everything before you . . ."

"Before I forget," he said clearly. He removed his sunglasses so they all saw the tears that gathered in his eyes and didn't so much spill as seep into the wrinkles. "Oh, my children. I didn't mean to lie to you. Sometimes when we honor someone's request it hurts another. I never meant for such a thing."

"Then tell us," Shane said.

"If I tell you this story, I will betray your mother."

Colleen's pulse battered against her chest; the sun suddenly felt blazing and dizzying. *Don't, Dad,* she wanted to scream. *Don't change everything.* But she didn't speak a word.

"Dad?" Shane asked.

Gavin's gaze moved slowly to his son's gaze. "Oh, son. I'm going to lose this piece of myself, aren't I? Soon it will be gone and you will be feeding me with a spoon and I won't know your name, will I? That is now my destiny. So I have a choice, don't I? I can keep the story and allow it to be eaten alive by the disease or I can give it to you. Is giving it to all of you fair to you or to your mother?"

"Dad . . ." Colleen didn't think the words before she spoke them. "Your story is our story. Can't you see that?"

He held her gaze and then he said, "Perhaps you're right."

And so, Gavin Donohue spoke the tale of his Irish love. It was a slow telling, halting and starting again like an engine without enough oil. But the pieces of the story were intact — the story of his journey to Ireland, of meeting the first Colleen. Twilight fell long on the sandbar as the tide moved in, but it was Ireland that filtered into the Lowcountry evening air; the emerald world their dad took over an hour to describe. Fiddle music seemed to echo across the water. Galway Bay, winter whipped and fierce, raged at the sandbar instead of the calm May of Watersend, South Carolina. A pub, known dimly in a faded photo, sprang to life with boisterous County Clare villagers, with grief and love and laughter. And above all of this, and through it, "The Lark in the Clear Air" played on and on and on.

They arrived home in silence; enough had been said, the puttering of the boat and the whip of the wind were their companions. They docked and hugged each other good-bye without I love yous and see you laters, everyone absorbing what they had heard and now knew. When Shane and their dad had left for the pub and Hallie drove off to her children, Colleen slipped into her bedroom and began to compose the tale Gavin had told.

Yes, she thought, something had always been whispering, a certain knowing lurking at the edges of her consciousness, the gap of a secret where her mother's full attention might have been. Why had her mother insisted on calling her Lena, never by her full name? Now Colleen knew . . .

Colleen wrote so quickly that she mis-spelled words, shortened sentences. She would clean it later, but she needed to get it all down, everything her dad had said as best she could remember. The truth had struck her like a body blow and she still felt numb. Because she'd learned today that she had another mother, another woman to be called by the same name.

THE MEMORY BOOK

GAVIN DONOHUE'S STORY

Her name was Colleen O'Shea, and you met
on an unseasonably warm September day in
County Clare, Ireland.

As you stepped inside, the O'Shea pub was
resonant with the sounds of a woman playing
the fiddle and singing softly, *"Dear thoughts
are in my mind and my soul it soars enchanted . . . as I hear the sweet lark sing in
the clear air of the day."*

You'd stumbled into an evening of mourning
for a local couple who'd passed to the next
world only days before in a terrible car accident. The Irish mourn this way — completely
and with their entire being. There can be nothing held back. How else can one celebrate a
life? they asked.

The woman playing the fiddle was young
and lithe, dark curls falling over her left
shoulder and the fiddle propped on her right.

372

Her face was half-hidden behind the fall of her hair, behind the curls alive with her every movement. You saw her lips, parted in mourning for the sadness to escape. Her elbow flew up and down as her hand drew the bow across the strings.

You sat in the only free chair in the pub and, in reverence and awe, asked the man next to you, "What is her name?"

"Why you wantin' to know?" he asked in his Irish brogue, his eyes screwed tight in distrust and grief.

"Her music is so lonesome and beautiful. I wonder who she is."

"It's her mum and da that have passed. It was the last of her immediate family."

You looked at that woman who had lost so much and you wanted to save her from all tragedy and pain. You wanted to take that fiddle from her hands and take her in your arms. You didn't understand why; you had never seen her before that moment when you absently walked into a pub for a pint of Guinness. But who knows when a life will change? Who knows when a decision alters the course of all other decisions?

When she was finished, you went straight to her and introduced yourself: Gavin Donohue from America.

You believed you would be there for only

three more months, in that land of brilliant emerald and lush gold. You believed you'd tour, drink dark beer and research your family's heritage before returning to the life and the high school sweetheart waiting for you at home. But that's not what destiny had planned for you.

Within weeks, you canceled your flight home and you settled in County Clare with Colleen O'Shea. Gradually she told you of her homeland's history, its people, its music and its mythology. She fell in love with you as you fell in love with her, as the bow flitted across the fiddle strings and her voice rang out clear and resonant.

There was the awful pain of explaining this turn of events to Elizabeth, whom you loved and had promised to return to although you weren't yet engaged. You felt grief for what you left behind; you felt pain for Elizabeth, and yet you understood that you were answering a call to love in a way you never had before.

You were married on a cliff overlooking Galway Bay — on a windy day with thunderheads on the horizon. You weren't of her strict Catholic upbringing and couldn't marry in the church and yet her cousin, a Protestant cleric from town, performed the ceremony and you promised to love her for all your life. Together you settled into a small thatch-roof home that had once belonged to her departed parents. You took a job in her family's pub, where you'd met that night of her parents' wake, and started to have the tiniest bit of an Irish accent.

The Gaelic language slowly infused your speech until you learned enough to speak it in sorrow or joy — a few lines when needed.

Six months later, you discovered that the joy of that love had grown. Colleen carried your child and now she had a family again, and you were her family, and the child inside was her family.

You had goals and dreams — together you and Colleen would raise a family on the shore of a bay where your ancestors had originated before they boarded an immigrant ship and arrived on the shores of America to start a new life. You would help her carry on the family business.

Colleen went into labor on a frigid March day, two weeks early. Between labor pains and the stop signs that you ran, you rejoiced at the goodness of the world and the imminent arrival of your child.

The devastation happened quickly and without warning. Colleen lost consciousness when you were still within miles of the hospital. But maybe, you thought, this was normal —

the pain of birth and the loss of blood, which was evident on her dress, on the car seat. But it was too much blood, wasn't it? Too much.

They saved your little girl, but not your wife. Placenta previa they called it.

With all the love you had inside, you bundled up that little girl and you returned to your family in Virginia to begin again. You'd been gone for almost two years and you returned with a one-month-old baby daughter. The extended Irish family of O'Sheas understood your departure — there was no immediate family to keep you there. Your first love, Elizabeth, had waited. Yes, she'd remained true, always believing you'd return. Love, she'd said, brings home those who are meant to come home.

"I've always been yours," she said. "And I will still be yours."

But she had one condition — that no one would ever know of the great love from which your daughter, called Colleen after her mother, had been conceived. That no one could ever know that Colleen belonged to anyone but Elizabeth, and her name would be Lena. And she loved that baby as her own, and she promised that she always would.

You still loved Elizabeth, of course you did. Love does not always disappear; we merely make choices. Together, you and Elizabeth quickly married and packed to move to Watersend, South Carolina, swearing the small family to silence, and there you began again. You returned for your daughter, Colleen, so she could have a beautiful life. It was for your daughter that you didn't shut down. It was for your daughter that you pushed through grief and embraced a new beginning.

But you, Gavin Donohue, you carried those two years in Ireland within you as a force so divine and so life affirming that you opened a pub and named it after the song Colleen played that evening; the song that was sung on your wedding day, the song you see in your daughter's eyes. You honored your first wife, Colleen, in your heart while also honoring those with whom you chose to build your life, those you also loved deeply — our family: your wife, Elizabeth; your daughter, Colleen, called Lena; your second daughter, Hallie; and your son, Shane.

And that is the story of your Irish love, the one who molded your soul into the shape your family sees — a soul of the divine and the profane, of loyalty and betrayal, of life and death.

Chapter Twenty-Six

Memory is the scribe of the soul.
Attributed to Aristotle

"She's always been my half sister, at least by blood. She's always been all mine in truth and family, but not by blood." Colleen ran her fingers through her hair and leaned into Beckett's chest. They lay reclined on his couch in his small apartment across from the pub. He pulled her closer, and he listened, making soft sounds of assent. Only hours had passed since she'd returned from the boat trip; only hours since she'd discovered that the world wasn't exactly as she'd believed. She didn't look at Beckett while she told the story, but kept her eyes closed. "She died while giving me life; I was born in Ireland; someone who owed my grandfather a favor in Virginia forged my birth certificate here. And all of this was hidden to keep my mother safe, to preserve intact her reputation and the love she shared with Dad in the way she had always imagined it should have been."

"Oh, Colleen."

Colleen sat straighter and stared out the window at the inky night, the soft glow of the streetlights seeping into the liminal space between one day and the next, between this life and the next, between the story she'd been told while growing up and the truth she'd learned that day. "Yes, but we can't just make things up so we don't have to live with the truth. We don't get to do that."

"Many people do. And many people survive that way. It's not always so bad."

Colleen stood then, freeing herself from Beckett's arms. "I believe we have to live life as it is, not as we want it to be. *Acceptance,* right? Isn't that what you told me? Isn't that the way to an honest life?"

"Not everyone chooses an honest life, Colleen. And you can't blame them. Sometimes the truth is too much to bear. Go easy on your mother and dad."

Colleen sat again, slumped against him in what felt like defeat. "She changed *my* story so *her* story could look and feel better. I don't feel much like being easy on her right now."

"Then don't." He kissed her forehead and pulled her closer.

"The first Colleen died while giving me life. She died and I never knew she existed. Can it be true that somewhere inside I knew? Because now everything in the past takes on a new light — it makes sense — and it seems like I knew."

She didn't know how to explain this to Beckett, but all the times when their mother looked at Hallie with a certain eye and looked at Colleen with another, she'd known. When their mother told Dad that she was trying, my God, she was trying, she'd known. It was a different kind of trying than Colleen could have ever guessed. She wasn't making some meager attempt to be a good mother. She wasn't trying to survive motherhood. She was trying to love Colleen, who was the child of another woman.

"Are you okay?" Beckett asked.

"I'm not sure." Colleen sat and pressed her forehead to his, kissed him and then sat straight. "It wasn't my fault she couldn't love me the way she wanted."

"What do you mean?"

"It's not *my* fault that Mother couldn't love me as I wanted; it wasn't *my* fault that Walter cheated on me."

"How could it have been?"

"That's the thing. I always thought there was something wrong with me. Sure, there are loads of things wrong with me, but nothing that would keep a mother or fiancé from loving me. It was their hearts, not mine, that kept them far from me. I represented my dad's other love. Walter is and always has been a cheater, a liar and a manipulator — I wasn't so special. Just one in a long line."

She turned to Beckett as she felt something breaking open inside her chest, a fragile eggshell, flooding her breath with truth. "Do you know how very, very long I've tried to figure out what is so stinking wrong that my mother and my fiancé couldn't love me fully? I've made lists. I've tried to find the broken part of me that made them turn away from me. I have . . ."

Colleen fell back on the couch, lifting her face to the ceiling, where the whirling fan swirled the dust motes into a dance inside the evening light. "It was never about me at all."

"She just wanted to protect her life and love with your dad."

"Yes," Colleen said. "And maybe that's all she knew to do. I don't blame her. Or at least I think I don't blame her, but I'm glad

I know now."

"Does it change anything?" he asked. "Anything at all? Or is it just something you now know about your dad?"

Colleen closed her eyes, felt the information moving around inside her belly as a living thing. "Oh, yes, it changes things." She opened her eyes and glanced at Beckett. "I just don't know how yet. I just don't know how."

"I need to ask you something else . . ." He touched her hand and traced a circle on her wrist.

"What is it?" She took his hand.

"Do you still love Walter? Still want him back?" He averted his eyes, looking beyond her shoulder.

A noise that sounded much like a cough but was meant to be a laugh erupted from Colleen and she released his hand and leaned back, ran her hand through her hair and shook her head. "Hell no. The wounded part of me that wanted him has healed. There is nothing about him, even the good memories I hoarded for years, that I want anymore." She leaned closer. "If you'd asked me that question even a month ago, my answer might have been different. I might have *thought* I still cared deep down. But the minute I saw him, I knew that the scraped places of my heart had healed over and he held no allure for me. I waited for it — after I saw him — I waited for the shame and the sorrow to wash over me and discovered that the only thing that arrived was disgust. Absolute and pure disgust."

Beckett nodded and the smile she had already come to anticipate lifted his lips, the lips she suddenly and clearly wanted to kiss.

"And I've been wanting to tell you this, too . . . I've been asked to write a travel memoir with essays about my life and trips. And this new piece of information — it changes even that because if I didn't know this about myself, how could I possibly write about my life?"

"We live and write what we know when we know it, Colleen. You don't have to understand everything at once. Give yourself and all of this some time."

"I already feel like I've wasted so much of it, so much of time. I could have been here for my dad, could have . . ."

"Stop." He kissed her to stop the flow of would-haves and could-haves.

Colleen moved closer to him, allowing the comfort and ignoring the lying pinging messages inside, the long-held false belief that told her it was safer to run, to turn away.

CHAPTER TWENTY-SEVEN

Though lovers be lost love shall not;
And death shall have no dominion.
                              Dylan Thomas,
            "And Death Shall Have No Dominion"

Four Days until the Party . . .
She swept her nieces away to a lunchtime matinee the next day. Still, not one of the Donohue siblings had discussed what their dad had told them. Instead they all seemed to glance sideways at each other, waiting for one or the other to speak about it first. There were other things to attend to, other concerns. For now, Colleen was babysitting her nieces while Hallie met with a divorce attorney.

Movie theaters always made time stand still for Colleen. The hushed voices and soft seats, the bucket of popcorn with gooey butter, or what passed as butter, and the music of the opening credits enveloping the space.

This old theater had been here when she was a child and then had closed down for a while, but had reopened to great fanfare during the premiere of a movie that had been filmed in Watersend. Colleen had missed all the action, but Shane had sent pictures — one more hint that she was missing all the fun at home. Colleen was glad it was open and had air-conditioning and that she could try to be an aunt to her nieces.

It had only been the evening before when Colleen had learned about her Irish mother, when the world had tilted on its Donohue axis, and Colleen still hadn't found her balance. She sat between her nieces.

"What are you wearing to Grandy's party?" Rosie asked.

"I don't know yet. I haven't even thought about it."

Sadie's eyebrows rose in disbelief. "We decided a long, long time ago. We're wearing sister dresses. They're green with white bows and we're both going to braid our hair."

"Then maybe I'll get a green dress," Colleen said. "And a white bow. But you know it's a secret, right?"

"Uh-huh." Sadie kicked her feet back and forth an inch above the sticky floor. "We know how to keep a secret. Don't we, Rosie?"

"Yes, we do. Like we never told you that Mom said not to tell you that she cries because she misses you. We kept *that* a secret."

"Rosie!" Sadie kicked her sister. "You just told her."

"Oh." Rosie dropped her face into a prayerful bow. "I'm so bad. Don't tell Mom, please."

"You aren't bad." Colleen put her arm around Rosie and drew her close. "I won't say a word. And I cannot wait to see your green dress."

"And I can't wait to see yours." Rosie balanced the popcorn bucket on her lap, attempting to keep it from her sister.

"Guess I better get shopping." Colleen eased the bucket from Rosie's lap, took a handful for herself and handed the bucket to Sadie for sharing.

The lights dimmed and Colleen settled back into her seat, ready to escape her swirling thoughts. She'd been thinking of her mother who wasn't her mother, at least not by blood. Of her birth mother, gone before they even met. Of her dad loving someone else and losing her and still — and still! — living a life of beauty and kindness. And of her mother forgiving the betrayal. This right here had been why Dad had spoken of his understanding of betrayal, of the need to forgive. If Mother hadn't forgiven, if she had held and remembered in bitterness, their family would not exist. It was all too much to absorb or understand completely and immediately. *This family.* Colleen reached over and took the hand of each of her nieces, gave them a squeeze.

And Dad, too, had been able, somehow able, to love again. He'd had every reason in the world to shut down, to hide under some thatched roof in Ireland, bitter and full of whiskey, isolated from his family and those who loved him. But he hadn't. He'd said this to Colleen: "It was for you I was able to come back. For you I was able to keep my heart open to whatever might wait for me here. It was for *you . . .*"

For her. For Colleen Marie Donohue.

She wanted to take this knowledge and apply it like a salve to the past, to heal it and change it.

"Aunt Lena," Rosie whispered close to Colleen's ear.

"Yes?" Colleen shook herself free of her thoughts and looked at the screen. She'd been watching, but she hadn't seen a thing. It was still the previews.

"I have to go pee-pee."

"Okay, sweetie, let's go." Colleen took the little girl's hand. "You, too, Sadie."

Sadie popped up, the bucket of popcorn tumbling to the ground, yellow puffs scattering across the sticky floor to the row in front of them.

"I'm sorry!" Sadie dropped to her seat and bowed her head.

"What?" Colleen looked at Rosie. "It's just popcorn. No big deal." Smiling, Colleen stomped on a few kernels to make her point.

And then, as if someone had pushed a pause button, both girls looked at Colleen in relief.

Colleen first took them to the ladies' room and made sure they washed their hands, and then she bought a new bucket of popcorn. She bent over, hands on her knees, and told them, "I am the clumsiest person you'll ever know. I trip over my own feet. Your mom made the cheerleading team and since they felt so bad for me, they let me be the mascot. I can't dance. I drop things. So if you're spilling things, then you're *just* like me." Colleen wasn't sure how to speak to little girls, but truth seemed best.

"Grandy said you were nice. He was right." That was Sadie and she said it with a smile.

Rosie popped out her hip and placed her hand on it, so sure of herself. "And we're moving in with him. Did you know that, Aunt Lena? Now we'll live on the river just like you and Mom did when you were little."

"Yes, I knew that." Colleen kissed Rosie's forehead. "Now let's go enjoy this movie about . . . what is it?"

The girls responded in a chorus. *"The Jungle Book!"*

All during the film, Colleen thought of little but her dad. Mowgli danced through the jungle with monkeys and tigers and wolves, but Colleen saw a montage of her dad's life. Each and every memory now had a new color; a filter had been placed over them. Things made sense that never had before.

Either something is wrong with me or something is wrong with Mother. Colleen had said this to Hallie one afternoon on the swing set when they were probably ten years old. She heard her own voice saying it, a single thought that splashed into the afternoon.

"That's so silly." Hallie swung next to her, their legs pumping in unison, like everything they did in those days.

"It's true, though."

"Nothing is wrong with you." Hallie dug her feet into the earth to stop her swing.

389

"You're just being all melodramatic." She mispronounced "melodramatic," making it sound like "mee-lo dramatic," copying the word she'd heard their mother use every time Colleen felt something too deeply or was "too sensitive."

"Maybe," Colleen said and pumped higher and higher, wanting to make the swing wrap around the upper metal pole and back down again, the chain clanging as it flung her through the air. It never went that far, but she never quit trying.

In the movie theater, with the memory as bright and alive as King Louie on the screen, Colleen knew now: Mother had been trying to love another woman's child. She had been trying to *make* her heart do something, and one cannot ever convince a heart to love out of necessity.

She closed her eyes, the sound of "The Bare Necessities" filling the theater.

Colleen wasn't just her dad's child; to Elizabeth she represented the fact that Gavin had loved another woman, loved her enough to stay in a faraway land and start a new life. Colleen was more than just a newborn her dad had carried home. For Elizabeth, Colleen was a constant reminder of Gavin's betrayal.

It would take her a lifetime, Colleen knew,

to understand what it all meant. But with the clock running out on her dad's memory, she felt she was losing the chance to fill in the missing pieces of her earliest beginnings.

After returning home, Colleen relieved Bob of "watching" Dad and took her turn to sit with him on the wooden Adirondack chairs set in the grass in the yard, facing the river.

"Hey, Dad." Colleen patted his hand. "What are you doing?"

He looked up from a magazine and laughed. "Your sister gave me some puzzles to do. But it's made of numbers, not words, and it might as well be in Greek."

"Sudoku." Colleen took the pages from her dad and set them on the ground. "How are you feeling?"

"That's the worst of it, right? I feel fine until I realize I'm lost. Soon, I know, I won't know I'm lost, but for right now I do know." His voice was weak. "I have some things I want to say. Do you mind?"

"Dad, please. Say anything."

"It must have come as a shock, finding out about your Irish mother."

"Yes, and no. I always knew there was something . . . askew."

"Maybe." He stopped short and placed his hands on his knees, leaned forward to take in a long breath. "Maybe I should have told you sooner. But I promised your mother I would not."

"Dad, I understand all of that, and I understand your promises to her, and I know it was great pain for her. But why did she let you . . . keep my name?"

He flinched as if she'd slapped him, closed his eyes. "That was never up for discussion. It was your name. It was your mother's name." He opened his eyes and there was a flash of Ireland and fire and resoluteness. "I made my amends. I moved and I changed our life and I kept our secret. But your name belonged to you."

He stood and walked to the river's edge. Colleen followed, her heart in her throat, danger now seeming to lurk everywhere. It must be like having young children, always aware that the water was as much a danger as a comfort.

"We must stay on the water, my Lena. It is how we are connected to the place you came from, the place where you were born. That's why New York doesn't feel right to you."

"Dad, it does feel right. It's where my life is."

"Does it, though? Does it feel right?" He turned to her, his eyes bright as if someone had momentarily lifted a veil.

Colleen didn't answer because she wasn't sure anymore. Doubt had been creeping in for days. But this wasn't the time to disagree with her dad. It was the time to listen.

"Dad . . . go on."

"I don't know what I was saying."

"That there is a reason we must be on the river."

"Yes." He nodded, his jowls moving against the tight collar of his shirt. "Yes, indeed."

Then he was gone again, off into a land of nonsense and time travel, something about a baseball game he was late for and a shipment of kegs that hadn't arrived.

"Dad."

"Yes?" He looked at her and smiled.

"Thank you for loving me so well."

He gazed at her with utter tenderness and reached out his hand to take hers. "Lena, my little lark, never let your fears keep you from living your life or from loving. You can't run from who you are without losing your soul. Don't do it."

"I'm not running from anything at all. I'm just building a life away from here. Just like you did."

"Ah, yes, but are you building it out of fear or love? That's the difference." He leaned forward and took her face in his hands. "Do not settle for the mediocre to avoid pain."

"I hear you, Dad. I promise I hear you."

This seemed to satisfy him. The frenetic look that had flickered across his face mellowed and he was there again, her calm and amiable dad.

Colleen almost heard the ticking of the world's clock, the metronome of time passing, taking with it all that was precious of her dad's memories. But the damn clock's dark hands could never touch the essence of who he was with her, of the love that bound them together in ways Colleen had only dimly understood, in ways that her sister and her brother would never know, in ways that could never, even in memory's demise, be broken.

They sat back in the chairs. "Dad?"

"Yes?"

"You know how to speak Gaelic?"

"Yes, some I do."

"Why did we never know this?" she asked.

He rested his head back on the chair with a slight grin on his face as though she had just told him something lovely. His hand, with veins prominent under the wrinkled skin, the freckles evidence of his hours in the sun and the knuckles scarred from hard work and a few stray fishing hooks, held tight to hers.

"We all have our secret places, Lena. You are my *a stór, a mhuirnín,*" he said and closed his eyes. "My treasure; my darling."

Yes, secret places indeed.

CHAPTER TWENTY-EIGHT

Lord, keep my memory green!
Charles Dickens,
*The Haunted Man
and the Ghost's Bargain*

Three Days until the Party . . .

The next afternoon Colleen spent hours on the second floor of the small bookshop downtown, catching up with the owner, Mimi, and wondering how the elderly woman still managed to run a bookshop. But then she'd understood when she'd met her new assistant, Piper, a spitfire of a girl who was both funny and knowledgeable. Colleen had bought a pile of memoirs and started skimming them. She would take them home and look for the threads that bound the good ones together.

Piper had told her, "Well, to me, the good ones are the ones that tell the truth without ever blaming anyone else — just saying it like it is." Then she'd leaned forward conspiratorially, her small nose ring winking in the sunshine that fell through the tall windows. "I've read them all. I know it means I'm a nerd, but ask anything you want."

Colleen had thanked her, and thought that she could hang out in this store for just as long and happily as when she'd been a child. Because now, yes, *now* Colleen had a memoir to write — one about mothers and daughters and where you really came from. It did involve the ten tips, but so much more — it was about the journey of learning who she was.

She was also hiding. Hallie had made the quick and decisive decision to move to the Donohue home and today was the day. Shane had hired a crew and while Walter was out of town they were packing boxes and bringing them to May River. Walter knew they were leaving, but Hallie jumped on the chance to take what she needed without him over her shoulder begging her to stay or, alternately, cursing her for taking whatever it was she took. Colleen didn't want or need to be in the middle of that. Shane had hired enough men to get the job done. But this didn't stop her from thinking about it, from probing softly into the places that opened up with all the changes and realizations that had come into their separate lives.

If Colleen had married Walter, if she hadn't walked into that church alcove and seen what she'd seen, their demise would have happened anyway. In some other place. In some other time. With someone else as the woman who came between them. Eventually he would have cheated on her. She understood that now.

This was Walter's way, and perhaps it always had been. His bright and vivid charm had hidden a darker side, a need to sneak off for quick and furtive desire, a desire that burned and damaged. Colleen had had no choice but to see the truth in stark clarity that wedding day, but Hallie, she must have been living in the shadow lands where the truth was as elusive as a ghost. A rush of tenderness washed over Colleen and it was for her sister, for the exhausting futility of living in denial while clinging to an illusion.

Full of wonder at these new insights, Colleen began to feel the first inklings of what felt like gratitude. It was not she who must face Walter's excuses while protecting two young children and figuring out a way to keep the family together.

She had lost what she'd believed was the

love of her life on her wedding day; but she'd also been saved. She was not only grateful but also thrilled that she hadn't ended up with Walter.

What if someone had come to her at some point and said, "Look, here is what you escaped"? Would she have opened her heart again? Forgiven? Moved on? But no one had done that. Why hadn't she trusted life enough to know it was true?

If this memoir was to be written, she would have to understand the mother who was not her mother, and the woman who had given Colleen life while losing her own. Again she focused on her work. After what seemed like just a little while of writing and taking notes, she was stunned to look up and see that hours had passed.

After a few hours, she threw the books in her bag, along with her notebook, and hustled back to May River, feeling slightly lighter and significantly clearer. The way she'd happily lost track of time like that reminded her of when she was a young child and she and Hallie had played jacks in the tree house or sat in the corner of that same bookshop poring over the comic books their mother wouldn't let them buy.

Once home, Colleen came up short as she entered the living room. Stacked against the walls and piled four high in the middle of the room were brown corrugated boxes that had once held liquor and beer.

"It looks like we stole all the loot from the pub," she said.

Hallie and Shane stood next to the boxes, sweating in the August heat. Rosie and Sadie ran around in the playground maze, stumbling and laughing, their voices high in frantic need to ignore the reason they were actually there.

As Shane wiped the sweat from his brow with a blue dish towel, their dad's voice came from behind Colleen. "Hallie is moving in."

Colleen turned to see her dad in his work clothes, a pair of worn shorts and a white T-shirt whose every stain seemed to tell a story: when he'd painted the work shed; when he'd hung the wallpaper in the hallway; when he'd laid the bricks of the front walkway. In his hand he held a knife. He bent and zipped it across the top of a box. "Let's get you settled, my darling. Let's not be dragging this out and making you miserable."

Colleen glanced around the room. There was more here than would possibly fit in Dad's small house. "Did you bring everything? I mean . . ."

"I had to." Hallie's voice was strong. "We can shove it in the storage shed or garage or whatever. I left him all the furniture for now, but I had to get what I could or Walter would have . . ." She glanced at her little girls, who had come to a standstill in the living room.

"Is Lulu in a box?" Sadie asked in a small voice.

"Yes, sweetie. The box is labeled. I'll find her."

"She can't breathe in there. Get her out. Get her out right now." Sadie's voice rose higher and she began running from box to box, pulling at the tape, throwing aside her wand in an effort to save whoever or whatever Lulu was.

"It's okay." Hallie stood in front of Sadie and took her by the shoulders. "I put Lulu in a special box with oxygen. She'll be fine and she'll be waiting on your bed tonight."

Sadie accepted this and ran off with her sister, having been granted permission to draw with sidewalk chalk on the driveway, as long as they stayed away from the river.

Gavin walked around the room ripping tape off each box, peeling back the flaps and then moving on to the next one.

Hallie motioned for Colleen to meet her on the screened porch. When the door was shut behind them, the afternoon heat pressing down hard, Hallie said, "I haven't asked you. How were they at the movies yesterday?"

"Angels."

Hallie smiled. "I don't believe you, but I'm so damned tired I'll just have to accept it."

"No, really they were. They are truly adorable, and smart as little whips. I'm sorry . . . I'm sorry I missed so much of their lives."

"Well, you're here now." Hallie touched her empty ring finger. "I stayed as long as I could, Lena. This lie — he told me you were wrong about seeing him with that woman — was the last lie I will live with. To stay would be to betray myself and my girls."

Colleen's heart tripped over itself, landed in the pit of her belly. What had Hallie endured even before the humiliation of learning about his infidelity and the heartbreak of moving out of their home? Damn him. Two sisters. One man. Two little girls whose home was broken. And enough heartbreak and betrayal to sink them all.

Colleen took Hallie's hand. She was disappointed in her own reactions to what had been dealt her, what that river of life had brought to her and where it had carried her. She hadn't trusted it, not one little bit.

She'd taken things into her own hands, hardened her heart, set herself apart.

Was it too late to forgive? To become someone different? To love Hallie again?

Colleen reached through that sticky space between herself and her sister, to wrap her arms around Hallie and hold her close. It was a relief, holding her sister after pushing her away. It was a jump into a cool river on a steaming day; it was an exhale after holding your breath; it was falling asleep when you thought you might not. Colleen held her tight, held her just as she'd wished someone had held her many times during the past decade.

Hallie took a breath before asking the delicate question. "Haven't you wanted a family? One of your own?"

"Oh, Hallie. I have, yes, but each time I thought about actually doing it, I panicked. I was terrified of choosing unwisely, of being betrayed again."

"Then it's my fault." She closed her eyes, dropped her chin to her chest in prayer or confession.

"No." Colleen tapped her sister's chin until she looked up. "We each make our own choices; we each choose how we spend our hours. That's what I chose. Of course I've thought about it, but I've also been really, really good at avoiding thinking about it. When I'd have a birthday, I'd wonder, 'Is it too late now?' and then I'd move on."

"Don't." Hallie shook her head. "Don't move on anymore."

Colleen took a breath, wanting to find something wise and smart to say but understanding somehow that her sister had already said it.

The porch door creaked open and Gavin joined them. "Well, look what we have here. Now, let's go inside and get you settled," he said. "Let's make sure we have this cleaned up before your mother comes home. You know how she hates messes in her living room." He shook his head. "Good Lord, it's not a mood I'm up for tonight, what with Mr. Jacob's birthday party in the backyard."

"We'll get it cleaned pronto." Hallie hugged her dad. "Promise."

Gavin sauntered off, whistling.

Hours later, twilight arriving with its hues of golden light, the boxes had been either unpacked or moved from the living room; some were stacked in the garage and others in the back shed. Hallie and the girls would share Shane's room for now. Colleen imagined her nieces eventually spreading into her room the minute she returned to New

York, taking over the space and filling it with their frilly pink clothes, a new sisterhood in the same room.

Now the three Donohue children sat with Gavin at the kitchen table. The little girls had gone off with their daddy to dinner. He'd picked them up with a loud honk and they'd run out to jump into the backseat. Only Shane had risen to greet Walter, taking the girls' hands to escort them outside.

After Walter was gone, Hallie told them her ideas. "So I've done some more research and there are exercises you can do, Dad."

"Why do I need to exercise?" Gavin looked from child to child and then smiled. "Ah! I know what it is — I have that damned Alzheimer's. What exercises?"

Hallie held out her hand. "So this." She began tapping her fingers with her thumb, one-two-three-four, on each hand, back and forth. "Saying whatever mantra you'd like, Dad. Something in Gaelic if you please."

Gavin began to tap his fingers, saying *"anam cara"* until his tongue tangled the words and his tapping turned to only one finger over and over. He looked at his girls, the effort to continue too much after only a few tries.

"What does *anam cara* mean?" Hallie prodded.

"Soul friend." He turned away. "You know, sometimes I think if I grab the edge of a memory and pull it toward me, my life will stay with me." He stood then, his hands in fists at his sides.

"Dad." Shane kept his voice soft, to calm him, settle him.

"What?" Gavin answered, but suddenly he wasn't their dad. He was angry, his face red and contorted, his hand raised as if to pound the table. Then he turned and walked to the back door and outside, slamming the door hard.

The siblings stared at the closed door. "The memory book will help," Hallie said. "When we give him the book, it will help. I just know it. He can look at it and . . ."

Shane stood. "Maybe." He didn't look at his sisters but walked to the door and gazed outside its window as he spoke. "Or maybe I'm trying to convince myself I'm doing something, anything at all, when really nothing can be done. When really it's all meaningless."

"No." Colleen went to her brother's side and also stared outside. "It's not pointless. It's . . . Whoa!" Colleen froze, pointing out the window. "Dad is unmooring the boat."

Shane shoved open the door and ran, full sprint, to the dock. Colleen was fast behind him, reaching them just as Shane took the ropes from Gavin's hands. "Dad. Stop."

"It's my river." Dad pushed back at Shane, not hard but enough to startle them all.

"Not now, Dad. Not now. It's time to go to the pub. Hank has some questions for you."

Colleen knew this wasn't true, but if it kept their dad from the river, would a little lie matter? Was this what it had come to? Little lies to protect their dad's safety?

Gavin stood straighter.

Hallie ran to the dock, meeting them at its edge. "Dad . . ."

Gavin's face turned placid and a smile returned. He stepped forward, carefully, looking warily at the dock's splintered wood as if the boards were shifting and separating under his feet. He walked slowly, a shuffle more than a walk, until he reached his daughter. "When did you get here?"

"I've been here all afternoon. Remember? I'm moving back in."

"You left?"

"Yes . . . I married and . . ." Hallie pressed her lips together into a straight line. The explaining, it was exhausting. She exhaled as if she'd finally realized the futility. "Yes, I'm here."

Acceptance.

407

What an awful word, Colleen thought. What a giving-up helluva word. But it was the only one that applied.

She went to her dad then, put her arms around him and hugged him tightly. "I love you, Dad."

"Well, my little lark, I love you, too." And together they walked up to the house.

CHAPTER TWENTY-NINE

Sweet is the memory of past troubles.
Cicero, *De Finibus Bonorum et Malorum*
(On the Ends of Good and Evil), I, xvii

Gavin sat in the middle of the pub, his booming voice echoing across the dim room. Nightfall brought dark cover to the windows. The bar hostess walked from table to table lighting the tea lights. Colleen sat with her sister at a corner table, both sipping frothy Guinnesses and unable to find what they wanted or needed to say. Shane bustled about keeping the pub running. *Peaceful.* But Colleen knew by now what a fragile commodity peace was, how easily it could be broken.

"Then," Gavin's voice echoed, "the Yanks swept the World Series."

"What a night that was," another, deeper voice responded.

Colleen sipped her beer, and Hallie smiled

at her sister and motioned to her upper lip. "You have a beer 'stache."

Colleen wiped at her mouth and leaned closer. "I know this has been a long and crazy day, but do you have the finished book?"

"Yesterday I left it upstairs in Shane's apartment. I was afraid it would get lost in the chaos. But . . ." Hallie exhaled and fiddled with her ponytail. "You must go see it. It's amazing. Shane did an incredible job, and so did you with the stories." Hallie nodded toward the ceiling. "Go read it."

"I wrote most of it; I know what it says."

Hallie shook her head, strands of hair falling into her face. "But it's different when you see it all in one place like that — his whole life in words and photos. Birth to now. There are pictures of us as babies. Of Mother when she was young. Of this pub and our house and the river, which is the only thing that doesn't change. There's a continuity you can only see when you look at the larger picture."

"Then I'll go look at it." Colleen rose and then stopped. It hit her: the secret love story that had shaped all their lives was now on paper, not secret at all. "What did Shane do with the love story? Did he include it or leave it out?"

"He left it out . . ." Hallie shrank back. "I asked him to leave it out because of Mother. Other people will one day read that book."

"No." Colleen shook her head. "He'll know, Hallie. Somewhere deep inside, Dad will know that the story isn't complete. Just like I always knew." Inside Colleen's chest a galloping began, a herd of horses.

"What do you mean *just* like you knew?"

"I always knew something wasn't right between Mother and me. But no one told me what that *something* was. No one told me the truth. Dad might be losing his memory, but when he looks at that life story, there'll be an aching absence. He might not know in the way you'd define it, but he'll *know.*"

"What do you want me to do, then?" Hallie asked, spreading her hands wide and lifting her eyebrows above her glasses.

Colleen leaned down, her hands spread wide on the table. "I want that story included, that's exactly what I want. Because, Hallie, it's the truth." Colleen stood and placed her hand on her chest, over her heart. "By erasing that truth to make a prettier story, you erase part of who I am, part of who Dad is. And" — she spread her arms wide — "part of why this place exists at all."

"But we need to protect Mother."

Colleen shook her head. "What the hell are we protecting her from? Because you know, and I know, that making the story sound sweeter doesn't make it better. We can try and put all kinds of frosting and sugar on our lives, but I'm putting Dad's love story back into that book."

"His love story?" Hallie asked. "Of course you're part of that love story. Of course *you* are."

"What does that even mean?"

"It's why you want it in the book. Because *you* are part of it. You aren't thinking of Dad's reputation. Or Mother's wishes. Or Dad's promises to her."

"I'm thinking of all that and more. I'm thinking of Dad's life story. I'm thinking of how he is losing that life by the minute. I am thinking of . . . us. How we're half sisters." She took a breath. "You know, when I first came home, Dad said he knew about betrayal and about forgiveness. I didn't understand at the time. I thought he was talking about you and me, but he was talking about Mother. About how he betrayed her and she forgave him. Somehow he won back her trust. I want the same for us. I want to trust you again."

Hallie nodded. "I want that, too, more than I can say. But the memory book isn't about us."

"Hallie, it's always about us." Colleen turned and walked outside to breathe.

It was Shane who saw her leave and followed her out. Colleen spun around to face him on the sidewalk, the river running behind them, and took him by the shoulders. "You must put that story back in, Shane. You must. It's a choice between revealing Dad's life or hiding it." She paused and said, "Remember when we were talking about the interviews and you told me we don't get to choose which memories to give back to him? It's the same now."

Shane placed his own hands on top of hers and smiled at her. "Are you talking about yourself or Dad's memory book?"

Colleen didn't have to ask him what he meant. She had chosen to live her life by omitting part of her story, the painful part. And what had that done for her? She stared at her brother and answered his question. "Both; for both of us."

"I'll put it back in, Lena. I will include the love story, but you have to include all of your story, too."

"I'm trying, Shane. I am damn sure trying."

That night, she sat alone in her childhood

room with her dad's memory book and the sounds of a house she knew as well as the murmur of the river. Yes, she wanted to be alone with the book and the memories and the clanging of the past a constant din in her ears, but she also felt the warning pricks of desire that told her to move on. She wanted to hang out with Beckett. She wanted to tell him what she'd seen and heard that day. She wanted to rest her head on his shoulder and listen to his stories while he listened to hers. And that right there was enough reason to turn down the date. She could not and would not disappoint one more man, one more person, with her inability to go any further than where she was right then. With skill, after much adroit practice, she pushed aside the thoughts of Beckett and turned the pages of the book, reading the stories Hallie and she had written and gazing at the accompanying photos.

The heavy leather book with the hand-sewn crisscross stitching on the spine sat heavy on her lap. Dangling loose was the leather tie that had bound it all together with a seashell clasp. It was a work of art, just as her dad's life had been. But not even this book and its elegant appearance could in any way give her dad's life its due. It couldn't give him back his laugh or his way of moving through the world with a grin and a saunter. It couldn't show the twinkle in his eye or the quick wit that could conjure up a perfect retort when it was needed. It couldn't offer solace when loss knocked her over with a punch of grief.

So what was its purpose? What Shane had said from the beginning — to give their dad memories when they'd been erased, to fill in the blanks if only for the moment he read it or looked at it. At best, it would return him to himself. At worse, it would be just a pretty book.

Colleen heard the sounds of family: Hallie came home and put her children to bed. Shane dropped off Dad, and the swish of water in the pipes echoed as each one of her family readied for bed. There was the creak of floorboards, the called-out good nights. Colleen didn't leave her room for any of this. She stayed put, Dad's life book in her hands, and began to wonder — what would be in *her* book? Would someone have to skip over the last ten years, or merely put in the articles she'd written? Because the truth was, by the heart's standard she'd barely lived at all. She'd been perpetually busy and she'd done good work, but maybe she hadn't lived fully because she hadn't let her heart define her life. She'd let pain and avoidance shape her days and hours.

Finally she closed the book and her eyes and turned out the lights. She slept so lightly that she heard footsteps in the middle of the night, and the quick double sound of the screen door. Colleen smiled in her half-awake state. Just as they'd done when they were kids, Hallie was still sneaking outside to stare at the stars. It had always been the way Hallie calmed herself when she was struggling with hard times or decisions. The ritual settled her and she'd tiptoe back inside before anyone knew she'd been gone.

With the smile of memory, Colleen drifted back to sleep.

CHAPTER THIRTY

If you want to keep a memory pristine,
you must not call upon it too often.

Sally Mann, *Hold Still*

Two Days until the Party . . .
Colleen's computer screen glowed in the
bedroom's almost-morning light. She'd
woken early and checked her e-mail.

Dear Ms. Donohue,
We are ready for further discussions
regarding your travel memoir. When will
you return to New York so we may
schedule a time to meet?

The letter had gone on from there, with a
request for a prompt response.

She returned the e-mail with a note that
she would be home within the week and yes,
she would like to schedule a meeting.

She was wrong last night in thinking that

her life book was empty. These past ten years of *her* memory book would overflow with travel and interesting people and landscapes as exotic as any in the world. They hadn't been a waste. They'd merely been a different way of living from her siblings' and her dad's.

There were negotiations to be done, conversations to be had, but Colleen rose from bed with a smile and news she wanted to share.

Who would she tell first? Who would celebrate with her?

Her group of friends who had been texting her for ten days despite her failure to reply? Maybe, but probably not. Her family might see the memoir as a new preoccupation when she was supposed to be focused on them. Colleen clicked on the lights one by one as she made her way to the dawn-lit kitchen. With a Nina Simone record chosen, she turned the volume to low and began to assemble breakfast fixings.

For that brief moment, all was well with the world. Warm sun filtering through the checkered curtains and falling in dusty cones of light onto the linoleum counters made the kitchen hauntingly beautiful. Colleen was smiling when Hallie entered in her long leftover-from-high-school T-shirt with

Hello Kitty on it, fluffy slippers and a question that changed everything. "Where's Dad?"

"In bed." Colleen smiled at her sister, bleary-eyed and looking so young.

"No. His bedroom door is open and he isn't there."

A tidal wave crashed through the morning's peace and brought with it the flotsam-memory of something in the middle of the night. Footsteps. The squeak of the screen door. Hallie and the stars.

"Did you go outside last night? You know, like we used to . . . to see the stars." Colleen whispered the question, her pulse slamming against the bottom of her throat.

"No. What are you talking about?"

"Did you go out in the middle of the night to look at the stars?"

"No, Lena." Hallie's voice rose, and she burst into a run through the kitchen, out the door and into the backyard.

Colleen dropped the carton of eggs she held in her hand, perfectly oval blue eggs she'd bought from a roadside farmer just yesterday. They crashed to the floor, the shells shattering in a noise so soft it couldn't be heard over Nina's voice. The yokes broke, spreading yellow across the hardwood floor, but Colleen ignored the mess,

419

running into the backyard, following her sister to the dock where they both saw what wasn't there — Dad's johnboat.

"God. No." Hallie fell to her knees on the wood and picked up the dangling ropes. Then she spun to Colleen. "What time was it? What time did you hear someone get up?"

Colleen's thoughts spun back through time. Before she awoke and checked her e-mail but after she heard Dad say good night to Hallie.

"When did you hear him?" Hallie stood and grabbed Colleen by the arms and shook her as if to wake her.

"I don't know. I just don't know. I was half-asleep. I thought it was you . . ."

Hallie went running for the house. Her slippers had fallen off, one left on the grass halfway to the river and the other on the dock. Her hair flew behind her, tangled and matted with sleep. Colleen fled after her and they both burst through the kitchen door to find Rosie and Sadie standing in the kitchen, gazing at the broken eggs on the floor.

Colleen grabbed her phone and dialed 911. It took two rings, two eternal rings before someone answered, the voice nonchalant, casual as though Colleen were calling to report a lost stuffed animal. "Send help.

My dad, Gavin Donohue, disappeared in the middle of the night in his boat on the river. He has Alzheimer's . . . he's lost."

"Can you give me your address?" the voice asked so robotically that Colleen wanted to reach through the line and shake the woman.

Colleen rattled off the address and added, "Send someone now. And the Coast Guard needs to be notified. There's no time to waste. He might have been out there all night."

"All night?" It was Sadie's voice wailing so loudly that Hallie dropped to her knees and pulled her daughter close.

"It's okay. We'll find him. He knows these waters better than anyone. He can't be . . ." Hallie looked at Colleen, just realizing the most important part. "You heard him."

"What?" Colleen took one step toward Hallie, oblivious that she'd stepped into the broken eggs, lurching forward as her bare feet slid along the slick egg whites. She wavered, trying to catch her balance, then lost it and fell hard on her bottom, her hip grazing the corner of the cabinet with searing pain. She landed on the floor, her legs askew and her left wrist catching the fall. Another sharper pain shot through her wrist and arm.

Colleen let out a cry, drew her knees to her chest and dropped her head. She wouldn't scream in front of the girls. And it didn't matter, her silly klutzy fall; all that mattered was finding Dad.

"Are you okay, Aunt Lena?" Rosie rested her hand on Colleen's head, wiggled her little fingers on her scalp. "Are you hurt?"

Colleen looked at her niece and nodded. "I'm okay. I'm fine." She crouched before she stood and ignored the dull ache in her left hip, the knife pain in her wrist. "Hallie, call Shane." Then she ran outside as police sirens sounded in the distance, drawing near.

It took forever and only minutes for everyone to gather and work through the details. Kayaks and boats were sent out. Neighbors joined in and helped spread the word. Within thirty minutes, if there was a boat in Watersend, it was out looking for Gavin Donohue.

Colleen had paced the backyard, to the dock and back again, but now stood with her sister and brother at the water's edge, still in her drawstring-bottom and tank-top pajamas, her feet bare. Her wrist had swelled up to the size of a baseball, but she paid it no mind. She felt nothing but fear, an electric buzzing that filled her mind and body with panic. "He couldn't have gone far."

"Yes, he could have," Hallie said.

"He knows these waters." Shane ran his hands through his hair for the hundredth time. "He knows them better than anything in his life."

"He doesn't know them anymore, Shane." Colleen dug her toes into the dark soil, feeling the earth beneath her. "He doesn't know what he used to know. The maze of these marshes, they aren't like anything in the world. They change and shift. Dad has told us this a thousand times."

"But he's also told us that he trusts the river. He trusts it . . ." Hallie shuddered with the words.

"That's the problem, Hallie." Colleen's voice sounded flat and uncaring even to her own ears; she knew she didn't sound the way she felt. "He trusts the river, but the river, it can't trust him anymore because he's not Gavin. He's not the same."

"That makes no sense." Hallie dropped to a metal folding chair that someone had brought along with an untouched picnic basket loaded with snacks and water.

They were all being taken care of, but there was no way anyone could make the situation better. The nieces were inside with

Violet from next door. The Coast Guard was out. Food had been brought. Neighbors were on the water. A missing persons bulletin had been put out. They had fifteen hours of daylight — they would find him.

"You blame me." Colleen looked to her sister. "This morning, you blamed me. Like I could have prevented this."

"You could have." Hallie stared out at the river, speaking to Colleen without looking at her. "You could have gotten out of bed and checked who was awake in the middle of the night instead of just rolling over and going to sleep."

"Hallie." Shane's voice was deeper, already years older than he had been moments before.

"It's true, though." Hallie nodded, still not looking at them. "If she'd just gotten out of bed."

"I thought it was you. You always used to get up in the middle of the night and look at the stars. It actually made me happy, thinking of you outside, remembering those days. I didn't once think it might be Dad. I wasn't being lazy. I wasn't . . . being anything."

"It's not your fault, Lena." Shane rested his hand on her shoulder. "Blame the cursed disease. And you, Hallie. Stop pointing fingers."

Hallie nodded. "I'm an awful person." These words were said with such uncommon force that Colleen backed away, taking steps from her sister.

"No, you aren't. We're all scared to death." Shane exhaled and took two steps toward the dock before turning back to them both. "We will find him. He knows what to do. We will find him."

But they didn't find him. Hours passed and no one discovered him in a creek or estuary or sandbar. Harry from next door. His best friend from the marina who knew his favorite fishing holes. His buddy from the pub who lollygagged with him on Saturday mornings through the tidal creeks pulling crab traps out of the river. The Coast Guard. The neighbors.

Time stretched and collapsed. Minutes became hours. Hours were seconds. The sun moved across the sky and one sentence was repeated over and over by them all. "We'll find him."

By midafternoon, Beckett arrived in a small motorboat, coming in too fast and slamming into the dock before calling out Colleen's name. She ran to him. "Get in," he said.

Yes. At least she could be out on the same

waters as her dad, looking instead of waiting. She would be doing something aside from walking into the house, walking out, walking to the water and then to the grass. She hadn't had a single thing to eat. Egg whites had dried like sticky glue to the bottoms of her bare feet. Her thoughts flew everywhere — had her dad taken a thermos of water with him? A hat? Was he keeping out of the direct and glaring sun on this cloudless day?

"Your wrist." Beckett lifted her hand gently to look at the black-and-blueness of her hand and arm. "What happened?"

"I fell." Colleen gently pulled her hand away and cradled it as she settled onto the cushioned seat at the back of the boat. "Go!"

Beckett revved the motor. It was high tide, as it had been when Gavin left in the middle of the night. A cycle had already passed: a tide out and a tide in. "If he's out here, we'll find him," Beckett hollered over the wind and the water slapping the sides of the fast-moving boat.

The marsh passed by, the islands of green and waving grass, the maze of waterways, blue and gray and winding, isolating the islands from one another, keeping them apart even as they were bound together below the water. Each narrow, oyster-edged waterway led to another. Many people became lost in these waters, as the landmarks were few once you were in the thick of the estuaries. But Dad knew every landmark, every star and horizon view that would guide him home.

Home.

It was his mantra and his guiding light.

Where would he have gone? He never wanted anything more than he had — that was his way. He'd never wanted fancy. Even when he could afford it, he didn't want it. There was the time Colleen yearned for an expensive prom dress. The rest of the schoolgirls were sharing photos of their chosen gowns, making sure no one bought a duplicate — sequins and feathers; halters and taffeta. Dad had told Colleen, "Mother will sew you a beautiful dress. Who needs to cover up the real beauty of who you are, my Lena? No fancy dress can make a girl beautiful inside." And in the end, it was a simple satin shift with thin straps that looked fragile enough to break. It was a gown that other girls wanted and believed came from a fancy-pants store in Atlanta, which was what Colleen had told them.

"See?" Dad had said. "One doesn't need more to be more."

He hadn't taken off in the boat for something more or better. That wasn't the reason. So why had he gone? To prove that he could still navigate? Had his delirium put him in a dream? Was he looking for something?

She spun around to Beckett and placed her hand on his shoulder. "He's not in the marsh anymore. He's not in the river. He went to the open water."

Beckett pulled back on the throttle. "Why do you think that?"

"The open water, where this ocean leads to another. He talked about it; one of the last things he told me was that we were connected to *that* place by water, to the place where I was born by another bay. The place where Colleen, the first Colleen, died. And when I interviewed Bob Macken, he told me that the only time Dad went into the sea with his little boat was after Mother died. He went there for solace. Maybe he's gone there again."

Beckett pulled his phone from the storage compartment over his head and dialed quickly. "The police," he said to me before speaking into the phone. "This is Beckett and I'm with Colleen Donohue — I believe we need to quit looking in the river and head to the open water."

Something was said on the other side of

428

the line and Beckett answered, "Yes, I'm with his daughter."

Beckett hung up without another word and throttled forward again, heading toward the sea.

Colleen lifted her face to the wind, tasting the Lowcountry air she loved so very much. Someone could have put her in this boat with a blindfold and she would know where she was. The fetid pluff mud, the salt-soaked air and stinging aroma of rich sea life would tell her. This was her dad's lifeblood and he'd headed out into it when he hadn't known what else to do.

It hadn't been any different throughout her life. When Dad needed to think or needed to understand or decide, he'd take the boat out. Maybe he'd be gone for an hour, or maybe six, but when he returned so did his smile and peaceful way. He found himself out on these waters and somehow in the middle of last night, he'd tried to do the same again. He'd wanted Gavin back and he'd believed that he'd find himself out here as he always had.

She couldn't explain all that to Beckett. She could just point him to the outlet where the river met the sea.

CHAPTER THIRTY-ONE

Memory both is and is not our past.
James Gleick, *Time Travel*

Sunlight glittered over the surface of the water, tossing itself around the waves, playing. Splendor didn't fade in the light of danger, but instead seemed to taunt Colleen. Her dad had headed out here for exactly this, for the inherent beauty, and for the connection to the other side of the sea.

The immensity of the ocean overwhelmed Colleen and she let out a cry as she moved to the bow of Beckett's boat. She and Hallie had always talked of the universe's never-ending expanses. As children this had scared them. *So much out there. Too much unknown.* They'd talk about it and scare themselves and then cower beneath the covers together. No matter how big the universe, together they had their one little square on earth.

But now the sea felt larger than the universe, a place where it would be impossible to find one little dot of a boat and man who had been gone for at least twelve hours. Colleen stared over the water and then to the sky, wanting to beg the sun not to move, to stay exactly where it was until they found her dad. *Don't slide below the horizon. Don't take us to darkness.*

Above, the whap-whap sound of blades slapping through the air caused Colleen to look up. A helicopter. She glanced back at Beckett and formed a prayer motion, hands on her chest. Thank God for the helicopter, they would find him. She knew they would. Which didn't mean that she would quit looking, but now they had a better chance.

It was afternoon now — the sun was brutal and Beckett's small canopy offered little shade. He found two baseball hats in the bottom of a cooler, moldy and wet, but they both put them on, knowing the beating sun would do them no favors. There was an old curdled tube of sunblock and they both slathered cream on their exposed skin. But there was no turning back, that much was for certain.

Beckett throttled back and the boat came to idle, bobbing in the water as he walked to the front of the little Boston Whaler and took Colleen in his arms. "I don't know where to go. Tell me where he'd go. Is there a fishing hole? A quadrant?"

She shook her head against his chest. "No. He never left the river with me. He rarely left the bay or the marsh. All of his favorite spots were there. He liked to know the ocean was here, but he didn't take that tiny boat into it. Only once as far as I know."

"He would have run out of gas by now," Beckett said.

"Then follow the current." Colleen pointed east. "Follow that."

"Okay. Okay." Beckett let her go and stared toward the horizon, his eyes scanning just as Colleen's were.

"He liked the beach only once every year or so. He always preferred . . ." Her voice skipped over the next words like a rock skimming on top of the water in jumps and dips. "The safety of the river and bay."

"But not now."

"No." She turned to him and knew the wetness on her face was not the splash of ocean water. "We must have set something loose in him. This is our fault. We asked him all those questions and made him talk about the past, something he had kept safe in his own way, inside his own mind, and lived in his own secrecy. We should have left well enough alone. We unraveled something wound tight and, in his confusion, in his dementia, he went off looking for it."

"This is not in any way whatsoever your fault."

"It's my fault in more ways than one, Beckett." She looked toward the water, willing her eyes to see her dad's boat, his gray hair set against the blue water. "I heard someone get up last night and I should have gotten out of bed to check. But instead I rolled over, all happy and satisfied because I thought it was Hallie. I thought Hallie was going outside to look at the stars like she does when she's upset. I was wrong. So deadly wrong."

"How could you have known?"

"I could have checked. Taken five seconds to get my ass out of bed. I didn't think . . ."

"Stop."

"Go!" she said. "Keep going. He's out here somewhere. I know it."

When day began to fade from the sky and evening crept near, Beckett idled the boat and took her in his arms. "The day is almost over and I don't have lights on this little boat. It wasn't built to be this far out. There are professionals out here — we need to go back in."

Colleen could feel her body telling her to

do the same. They'd both guzzled the bottles of warm water Beckett had found at the bottom of the fishing bucket, and they'd had nothing to eat. Colleen had ignored her body's pleas for food and water, ignored the sharp and insistent pain in her hand and wrist, and urged Beckett farther and farther out, following an internal compass that told her they had to keep going.

She gazed out and there it was — she swore she saw a silver boat glittering in the far right corner of her sight, bobbing at the whims of the surging ocean. "There!" she screamed at Beckett.

He paused and tilted his baseball cap forward. "I don't see anything," he said over the wind. "Colleen, we have to turn back."

"Right there! Right there . . ." She pointed. "Three o'clock."

Beckett shook his head, not seeing what she did, and yet he drove toward her finger's direction. As they drew closer, she was more and more sure: yes, there was silver glinting on the waves. Then he saw it, too, and he gunned the boat to its limits. They bounced over waves his small boat was not made for, Colleen's spine jarring with each hit as the boat slammed against the current and she cradled her wrist in her opposite hand.

They reached the johnboat as the sky

darkened, as a brilliant sunset settled over the horizon behind them and the water turned a darker blue. The moon rose in front of them.

"Dad!" Colleen shouted as they drew closer. Over and over she called that one name. But no gray head popped up. No man waved at them in desperation. "Call someone." Colleen turned to Beckett as he eased his Whaler closer to the johnboat. "Tell them."

The boats bumped together and Colleen jumped from one to the next, landing crooked and falling on her bottom in the metal hull of her dad's boat, twisting her foot as she lifted her injured hand so as not to use it. There he was, lying flat on the bottom of the boat, his face hidden under the bench seat. "Dad. Oh, God, Dad."

She fumbled to her knees, ignoring the pain as she bent to see his face under the bench. He must have been hiding his face from the sun. Colleen placed her hand on his neck, something she'd seen done in movies and medical shows. This was where the pulse was, right? Yes, there was a slow lumbering wave beneath her fingertips that revealed a beating heart. His chest rose and fell, slowly but steadily.

She shook him gently. She said his name

into his ear. She tried to lift his eyelids but withdrew in horror to see his eyes were rolled back to expose the whites. She looked at Beckett, who was tying the boats together, lashing them with a rope from stem to stern.

"Is he . . . awake?" Beckett asked and peered over the bow.

"No. And I can't get him in your boat. We'll have to drag him. He's so sunburned, Beckett. My God . . ." A sob escaped just as the low hum of motors and horns drew near. The Coast Guard had arrived.

Beckett said, "I gave them the coordinates."

Men in blue uniforms and caps took over, hollering instructions, placing Gavin on a board and lifting him into their own boat, where he would receive medical attention. As Colleen watched, they expertly slipped in an IV and settled an oxygen mask on his face.

Beckett and Colleen climbed onto a second Coast Guard boat, as they had no light of their own to guide the way home. The men spoke in solemn tones. The boat with Gavin took off, rocking them all as they grabbed the edges and poles of the boat that would take Beckett and Colleen back to Watersend while the first would take Gavin to the hospital in Savannah.

He was alone; her sweet dad with his ravaged body on a stretcher, alone on that boat with strangers.

CHAPTER THIRTY-TWO

I think it is all a matter of love; the more
you love a memory the stronger and
stranger it is.
Vladimir Nabokov, interview,
BBC Television, 1962

Gavin Donohue lay supine on the hospital
bed, his toes pointing west and east under
the tented blanket. Machines beeped and
squealed and Gavin was oblivious to all of
it, his eyes closed and his body still. The
lines on his face had etched deeper somehow, the sunburn evident and flaming
around his face. His eyes were closed, the
lids puffy and red, the veins blue beneath
skin so fragile. His chapped lips were
covered with thick white cream. He
breathed — in, out, in, out — slowly,
intermittently, without any smooth rhythm.
Colleen stood with Hallie and Shane around
his bedside, all bearing their own guilt for

where their dad was and why and, Colleen knew, each sibling in some small way blaming the others. If this or if that or if only.

They stared at him, no one speaking, until Dr. Matthews entered — a tall, thin woman with dark hair and a white lab coat with iodine stains on the sleeve. She stood at the end of Gavin's bed, her hands placed evenly across the footboard, her stethoscope dangling from her neck. She cleared her voice before she spoke.

"You are *all* his children?"

"Yes," they answered in unison.

"I'm sorry, but your father's condition is critical." Her voice held steady as if this wasn't a damning verdict but something one said every day.

"Dad," Hallie said. "Dad, not Father."

Colleen knew why she corrected the doctor about something so trivial at a time like this — because it mattered. Dad always said it: names matter.

"Your dad." The doctor corrected herself and continued. "He was out on the water for eighteen hours or more without protection, which under normal circumstances would be bad enough, but this is much more dangerous."

"Why?" Hallie stepped forward. "You can't die of starvation and dehydration in that time. You can't . . . can you?"

"He drank seawater. Maybe a gallon or more of seawater."

"What?" Colleen asked.

The doctor nodded, her lips closed in a tight line. "He must have become confused. He headed out to open sea without water or food. When he ran out of gas, it appears he must have filled an empty water bottle over and over again with seawater. It happens. When people become disoriented and confused, they believe the water will help. Then the sunburn and hyperthermia disorientation make it worse."

"Why would he do that?" Shane's voice didn't sound like his. "You're telling me that if he hadn't drunk the seawater he might be okay?"

"I can't say that for sure, but we would probably be able to reverse the damage. As it stands, the salinity shut down his kidneys. His organs are failing; one by one they are failing."

"Stop them from failing." Hallie's statement seemed so logical, so absolute. *Just stop the failing.*

"We are trying." Dr. Matthews touched the tented blanket over Gavin's toes. "We are doing everything we can, but you need to be prepared. We can start him on dialysis, but not if his heart muscle has been damaged. We are going to get an EKG immediately. His breathing is erratic and his blood pressure is high." She paused.

"I don't get it." Hallie walked to the head of the bed, placed her hand on her dad's sunburned forehead, on the raging red skin that had become swollen.

"Seawater has almost four times more salt than our body's fluid. When there is a high concentration of salt in the blood, the salt is transferred by osmosis to the cells. The body tries to excrete the water through the kidneys, and then this dehydrates the body even more. When you drink saltwater you are actually doing more damage than not having any water at all. Your organs don't receive the oxygen they need, and that is where we are now. We're giving him fluids." She pointed at the bag hanging off a silver pole at his side, the tube winding its way through the beeping machine and then into a vein in the crook of his elbow. "But it's . . ."

"Too late," Shane interjected.

Hallie kissed her dad's forehead and then again looked at all of them. "I don't need a lesson on salinity or hyper-whatever disorientation. I meant I don't understand why he went out on the river in the middle of the night and drank gallons of seawater."

Shane made a small noise in the back of his throat. "He's confused, Hallie. You know that. There's no understanding the why or how. He just did. He wanted to go out alone on the river. He's been trying for weeks now. How many times have we intervened?"

"We should have taken the boat out of the water. We should have hidden the key. We should have locked his bedroom door . . ." Hallie listed all the should-haves, and of course there were more.

"I should have checked on the noise in the middle of the night." Colleen raised her hands in the air. "Me. I should have gone and made sure that it was Hallie looking at the stars. Me. I'm the *big* should-have in the scenario."

Dr. Matthews cleared her throat. "This is a tragic situation and when we're dealing with Alzheimer's these terrible things happen. There is only so much a family can do to keep their loved one safe. Blaming each other or yourself is not helpful."

"Yes." Shane took his dad's free hand from beneath the blanket, held it in his own. "Now what?"

"We have a few more tests, but . . ."

"You don't hold great hope."

"Your dad is surrounded by love and the

best medical care possible. There is always hope."

"Until there isn't," Hallie said, dropping her face into her hands.

"Stop it!" Colleen said.

"You're the one who's always telling me to look at the truth, Lena. 'Look at reality, Hallie. Look straight at it,' you told me. That's what I'm doing."

Dr. Matthews took two steps toward the door. "I'll be back. Meanwhile, I'm sending a social worker to come talk to you. A chaplain if you'd like one."

"A chaplain?" Shane asked.

"Yes, if you'd like. We have an interdenominational chaplain on-site. He's quite comforting and . . ."

"No, thank you." Shane walked with the doctor to the door, where he then said something Colleen couldn't hear before the door swished shut behind her. The three of them stood alone with their dad.

"We will not leave him alone." Hallie rolled her shoulders back and exhaled before speaking with more force than usual. "Someone will always be here talking to him until he comes back. Until he wakes up. I can't bear the thought of him being alone on that water, running out of gas, floating on the waves."

Colleen sank to a seat. "I won't leave him."

"Lena." Shane came to her side, placed his hand on her shoulder. "You need your wrist X-rayed, and you must get some food. I know you hid it from the doctor, but your suffering won't wake him up."

"I will not leave him."

"Okay . . ." Shane said. "I won't either."

"They won't let us all stay in here." Hallie began to pace the tiny room in a four-foot square, walking an outline. "Only two at a time they told me."

"I don't see them coming to remove us." Colleen placed her hand on the end of the bed, hanging on to it like a life preserver.

"But you can't have food or drink in here, in ICU." Hallie looked directly at Colleen. "Go get food now. And water. If you pass out you're no good to any of us."

Hallie was right of course. Colleen felt dizzy and untethered, the throbbing in her wrist telling her it was more than just a sprain. She needed food — how long had it been since she'd eaten? It was ten at night now, so at least twenty-four hours. Colleen took a few steps toward the door and then ran back to kiss her dad's flaming cheek. "I'll be right back. You stay right here and don't move."

It was something her dad had said to her

a thousand times, or maybe more, as he walked away to speak to a customer or grab a box from the back of the pub. He'd set Colleen on a bar stool next to a friend or neighbor. *I'll be right back. You stay right here and don't move.*

And she never had. She'd always waited there, her legs swinging off the stool, knowing he would return.

Colleen emerged from her visit to the ER downstairs with a cast on her arm and wrist, a bag of fluids in her veins for dehydration and a prescription for pain pills that she refused to take, not wanting to miss a moment with her dad. The night brought fitful sleep sitting straight in hard chairs, taking turns by Dad's side. Only one at a time during the night, they were told. The other two stretched out on the vinyl couch in the waiting area, where more than fifteen minutes of sleep could be had at one stretch.

When Colleen dozed off for more than two minutes, she dreamed of heat and thirst, of broken bones. She felt the waves beneath the boat, a slow rolling that brought the hospital cafeteria cheeseburger to rise up in the back of her throat. She prayed. She prayed to the One whom Dad believed watched over them. His god lived in and on the river; he lived in everything everywhere.

Once — Colleen wasn't sure what time it was — when she was alone with Shane, he placed his arm over her shoulder and pulled her close. "Mother must have forgiven Dad. They had such a beautiful life."

"She must have, yes." Colleen rested on her brother's shoulder, her broken wrist throbbing against the hard cast. "But I don't think she ever forgave me."

"For what?"

"For being the daughter of another woman. I think she wanted to, and I think she tried, but I'm not sure she ever did."

"Oh, Lena. I don't think that's true."

"Well, whether it is or isn't, I know where you're going with this: you want me to forgive Hallie. And I do. And I will. It will be a forgiving that has to happen in new ways every day. We have to find a way to trust each other in even the smallest things."

He squeezed her tight and for a few moments they both fell asleep.

Colleen was startled from sleep when Gavin departed. He woke Colleen when he left them, and later no one could ever convince her otherwise. She didn't tell anyone about the sensation of his hand on her forehead, about his voice saying he loved her, about the pungent aroma of the river washing over her. She sat bolt upright on that sticky vinyl couch, hearing the code blue call on the intercom, and she didn't need to be told her dad was gone.

When they came to tell her, she was already bent over onto her knees, Shane by her side, and they were both weeping, already weeping. It was his heart, they told the Donohue siblings. It couldn't survive the harm done that day by the seawater coursing through his veins and into the cells of his heart muscle.

Hallie joined Shane and Colleen, and then the chaplain, the one they'd never requested, and the social worker and the doctor. The siblings didn't see or notice anyone but one another as they were hustled into a private room.

"We'll never even know what his last words were," Hallie said, her hands twisting the Kleenex she held into a knot.

"It only matters what his last words were to you. Or me. Or Colleen," Shane said.

" 'Do not settle for the mediocre to avoid pain.' " Colleen recited the words her dad had said to her.

"What?" Hallie looked up.

"That's one of the last things he said to me."

Hallie propped her hand onto the side

table. "I have no idea of the last thing he said to me. No idea." Then she groaned. "How am I to tell the girls about this? They are already facing enough loss and change." Her voice cracked and Colleen found herself wrapping her arms around her sister, pulling her close.

" 'Don't forget the fiddle player,' " Shane said. "Those were his last words to me after I took him home. I guess he meant to tip him, but there wasn't even a fiddle player that night."

"It was Colleen, his other love," Hallie said. "The fiddle player. Remember? He said she was playing the fiddle when he first saw her."

"Oh . . . yes." Shane sat back in a padded chair in a posture of defeat, spine bowed and shoulders slumped.

Hallie blew her nose and wiped her face. "What if he was calling for us? Crying out for us on the ocean? What if he . . ."

Colleen stood. "You're making this worse. I can't bear to think of him in misery. I can't bear to think of him gone. I can't." She shoved open the door and burst into the hallway, running past the beeping rooms and hushed nurses' station, shoving open the door to the emergency stairwell and taking those stairs two by two as she held on to the railing, until she blew outside. She took in long deep gulps of the air her dad would never breathe again, that of his beloved Lowcountry.

Colleen sank onto a wooden bench in the hospital garden and stared in a trance at the tiny manufactured waterfall that cascaded over fake rocks covered in mildew and moss.

It wasn't supposed to end this way — before his party, and before they'd given him the memory book. Before she'd chosen her last words and held his hand. It wasn't supposed to end this way.

Did anything ever end the way we wanted it to end?

With a shattered champagne bottle? Or a stroke? Or an Alzheimer's-induced delusion?

With a jolt, she sat upright. Had he done it on purpose? Deliberately taken his life, with the sea in his veins, by powering his boat as far as he could toward the other side of the ocean, the other side of his memory?

He couldn't have.

Or he could have.

What had the social worker said about closure — that it was a myth?

Colleen must admit that she had no idea of her dad's intentions. This was a man she knew with all her heart and somehow didn't know at all. Perhaps some things weren't ever meant to be known; perhaps questions were all anyone was ever truly left with.

CHAPTER THIRTY-THREE

Time is veiled eternity.
John O'Donohue, *Anam Cara*

One Day Before the Party . . .
Far off, a clang of metal on wood, a boat coming into the dock, startled Colleen awake in her childhood bedroom, her heart pumping fast and hard in fear. Dad — he was back. He'd known where he was going; he knew what to do and how to do it. It had all been a bad dream: the search; the hospital; his failing body.

Colleen bolted upright and a searing pain shot through her wrist; a thick weight held her arm to the bed, and when she looked she saw why: a bright blue cast.

It hadn't been a dream at all.

A shudder of grief took her breath and she stood, steadied herself with a hand on the bedpost and shook her head free of confusion. A pain pill — Hallie had convinced her to take one when they'd finally left the hospital. They'd arrived home and her brother and sister had tucked her into bed as though she were a child. Beckett had been there, too, with soft words and a cup of chamomile tea. She'd tried to drink it, but then willingly succumbed to the cottony haze of Percocet.

Now the sunburn on her shoulders and collarbones stung like a horde of bees had set themselves on her in sleep. Her body couldn't decide whether to cry or flop back to bed or run screaming into the living room, where she heard the rise and fall of voices — her brother, her sister, the little girls and one other voice . . . Walter's. She didn't glance in the mirror, she didn't brush her teeth or hair; she bolted from the bedroom and rushed into the living room.

"Get out!" She pointed at Walter, who sat on the couch as though he belonged there. She had thought losing him was the worst thing? What a joke. It was the best thing.

He sat there in faded khaki shorts and a stained construction T-shirt, his hair curly and his sense of ownership grievous. Colleen stood in front of him before he'd even turned to her.

"Lena."

"Don't put my name in your mouth. Get out."

"Are you okay? My God, you're so sunburned."

Colleen touched the skin on her face, felt its heat. "You need to leave right now." She hadn't even looked at her brother and sister, at her nieces.

"Lena, please — the girls." That was Hallie's voice, but Colleen didn't acknowledge it. Instead she turned to her nieces, quiet and holding their magic wands, snuggled together in one chair, frightened and wide-eyed.

"My magic ones. Will you do Aunt Lena a favor and run to the bedroom and grab my magic wand?" She tried to smile at them, but smiling didn't feel like something she would do for a long, long time.

"You just want us to leave so you can be mad at Daddy," Sadie said.

"Yes, that's true." Colleen turned back to Walter.

"Please don't," Hallie interjected.

But the girls ran off, holding hands and skirting past Colleen, who kissed their cheeks.

Colleen lowered her voice. "This is family business. And you aren't family."

Walter stood, his true self a dark cloud.

How had she *only* seen the charming Walter? How had she *not* seen what was so evident to her now — how his personality changed in a quick flash as soon as his daughters were gone from the room?

"I am their father. This is my family, too. Just because I'm not yours doesn't mean I'm not part of the family. Someday, Lena, you will get over your anger. It's not attractive."

Colleen stared at him, her stomach lurching, and her grief a stone in her chest, her wrist throbbing. She lifted her other hand, the one without the cast, and slapped him hard and fast across the face. The sound, skin on skin, reverberated as Walter let out a strained grunt and raised his fists in automatic defense.

Colleen stepped back, unsure of what he was capable of doing in anger. "What you did to me — it might have been the best thing you could have done, but if I'd seen then what I know now, if I'd really known, I would never have left my sister with you but instead continued to love her, which might have allowed her to leave you a long time ago."

Hallie burst from her chair and stood between Walter and Colleen. "Stop. Follow me now." She motioned for Walter and Colleen to leave the living room, to follow her into the kitchen. Which they both did.

Hallie's cheeks were as red as the sunburn on Colleen's shoulders. "Walter, she's right. It's best that you're not here right now. We can discuss this another time, but you need to leave. Okay?"

Walter spun around to face Colleen, his lips almost drawn back from his teeth in rage. My God, had she really wasted all these years wanting and missing this man? What a waste of time and energy.

"It would have never worked with us, Lena. You know that." He glanced at Hallie, weighing the words he might not want her to hear. "She is a better fit. We get each other. You would have wanted more than I could ever give to you. Look at you traveling the world, always doing something new. You wouldn't have been happy here with me. Couldn't you have just left us to be happy?"

"That should have been my choice, Walter. Mine." She glanced at Hallie, who had tears running down her face, her hand held over her chest in a protective move.

"What?" Hallie asked. "You chose me because I don't want as much as Lena does? You think I'm . . . easier to handle, to deal with? What the hell, Walter?"

"No. No." He took a step toward Hallie as she took two back. "I love you. You know that."

Colleen slammed her hand on the kitchen table. "Look what you've done to her. What you've done to us. Now leave."

Walter looked at Hallie, holding his hand on the growing red mark on his cheek. "Hallie, I'm their father. I'm your husband. I will not just disappear."

Hallie stepped closer to Walter, holding her hands in a tight knot in front of her. "Right now you will leave. Our dad, our precious dad, is lying in a morgue and all you can think about is defending your rights as a family member. All you can think about is telling my sister why it was better that you married me and cheated on me instead of her. You have no empathy. No heart. Right now you *will* disappear."

Walter passed his gaze from one sibling to another and yet did exactly as they'd told him to do. He left.

Hallie and Colleen looked at each other, but neither spoke a word. There was altogether too much and too little left to be said. They returned to the living room, where Colleen collapsed into a chair and brought her cast to her lap as Shane brought her a glass of orange juice and another pain

pill. "I'm sorry." She spoke the words robotically, speaking to both siblings but looking at neither. "I couldn't have him in this
room with this grief."

"Thank you," Hallie said. "Honestly,
thank you."

"Lena," Shane said very quietly, "Mr.
Lister dropped off the will a couple hours
ago."

"Dad's lawyer. The one who does all the
pub business?"

"Yes. It seems he also did the will and
estate for Dad."

"And?"

"There's nothing stunning in it. Everything he owns is split between the three of
us, and the pub is mine to manage. We can
figure that out later, but the one thing that
is urgent is this — he asks for cremation
and that his ashes be scattered in the river.
Our river." Shane motioned to the back
window where they could each see the
water. "I'd never heard him state this belief
out loud, but he wrote that the Irish believe
that where you are buried, that is where you
will one day resurrect again. And he wants
to be in the river."

"Not with Mother in the cemetery?"
Hallie's voice was low and quiet.

"I don't think it's about not being with

her," Colleen said and paused to guzzle large gulps of the orange juice, brush her hand across her face, clearing her thoughts. "He spent his life with her. It seems obvious that the water is where he forever wants to be."

Hallie shook her head, her hair falling across her face. "It's too awful to understand. I can't understand." She looked between her brother and sister as the girls reentered the room, Sadie holding out the wand and handing it to Colleen. "Do you think he took his life?" Hallie asked in a quiet whisper.

"What does that mean?" Rosie asked, and her eyes scanned the faces of the adults.

Shane held out his hand. "Not now, Hallie. We have to fulfill his wishes, notify the rest of the family and organize a memorial. We have to get through this together."

"Together," Colleen said and twirled the wand. "Well, sadly, because there is a party already planned, it can now be his memorial."

Hallie shuddered. "So many people will show up for that, and I won't have enough food or drink . . ." She trailed off. "I need to hire more people."

Shane rested his hand on her shoulder. "I'm going to tell Hank to take it from here.

He will find servers and bartenders, food and drink. You stop now, Hallie. Just stop."

Rosie moved next to Colleen, slipped under her arm and rested her head against her chest. "I miss Grandy."

"Yes, love, we all do." Colleen drew her niece closer and felt warm wet tears sear across her sunburned cheeks.

CHAPTER THIRTY-FOUR

In the end, we'll all become stories.
Margaret Atwood, *Moral Disorder*

Day of the Party . . .
The day before Gavin's memorial had passed in surreal hours of visits by friends and family, of decisions made and an obituary written by Colleen. They notified the entire guest list about the change — how a celebration was now a memorial at Dad's sacred place. As Colleen surveyed the scene of the gathering in full swing, she figured that if there was anyone in town who hadn't shown up, she didn't know who it could be.

It was Rosie and Sadie they worried about most — losing Grandy and moving away from their dad into a new home, both within a few days, would be overwhelming for anyone. It was all too much, Hallie had said over and over. *Too much.* But they'd surrounded the girls; let them cry and held them close. Now they ran through the crowd of people handing out the poppers that were meant for a different kind of celebration, for a birthday party. The guests took the brightly colored party favors and patted the little girls on the head as if they were puppies.

Colleen scanned the room for her sister and brother and found them on opposite sides of the pub. Each time she tried to move, another person came to offer condolences or tell a story about Gavin. Over and over again, as Colleen balanced her weighted arm with the cast, she thought of life's tenuous threads, of the easy snap of that thread that tied us to the people and places we love the most. In the middle of things, when all was stable, it felt like nothing would ever change. But it always did and always does and always will.

The band played on as background music one hardly noticed above the din of voices until it stopped and the room fell silent. Yes, it was the absence of something — music or a loved one — that brought one to attention, that raised the gaze and focused the mind on the present moment.

Silence shimmered in the room and a deep, resonant male voice began to sing "The Lark in the Clear Air." *"Dear thoughts* are in my mind and my soul soars enchanted . . ."

Time paused, breath slowed and the room filled with the presence of Gavin Donohue. Colleen scanned the crowd for the source of the singing and found Bob standing on the makeshift stage with his eyes closed and a hand over his heart. His voice rose a cappella above those gathered. It seemed to soar above the building and higher still. She'd never known Bob possessed this gift — how much hidden and unknown remained to be revealed?

When Bob finished the song, the room broke into applause with hollers and stomping feet, and although the gratitude was for his singing, it was also for the life and gift of Gavin Donohue.

Shane's voice then reverberated through the room as he spoke into the microphone. "I'd like to give everyone a chance to speak if they'd wish. But first, my sister Colleen will say a few words."

The sounds of murmuring voices and clinking glassware fell away. The room became as silent as in the hours after closing when Colleen had walked through the pub with Dad as he locked up.

She froze. Hallie had made a schedule for the memorial. Music. Food. Speeches. And yes, Colleen knew she was supposed to represent the family and speak for all of them, but now she had no idea why she'd agreed. She hadn't written a speech. She hadn't thought much about it past the idea that she would tell everyone how much she loved her dad, how much they all did. But now that wasn't enough. She wanted to honor him. She wanted everyone in the room to understand who he was in the world, how his very presence was a spark of light, a wave of wonder.

What would she say now that she knew she had a mother she never met, and a dad she understood in deeper ways; now that she understood the story-rivers running beneath her dad's life, how the invisible was as influential as the visible? How the river had been his metaphor, his internal landscape surging behind their home in external form.

"Colleen?" Shane's voice made the microphone squeal, a high-pitched sound that shook Colleen from her frozen place. She walked toward the front, winding her way through the crowd, seeing no one, hearing nothing, her ears buzzing with fear.

Shane hugged her and said, "You've got this."

She shook her head. "No."

"Yes."

"I can't. I'm not ready. I'll write it down later."

"Sometimes we have to do things because we must, even when we don't believe we're ready," he said.

Colleen took the microphone from Shane and stared out over the crowd, her throat constricting and her eyes burning with both fear and fatigue. This was a terrible idea. Then her gaze stopped scanning, snagged and stayed on Beckett's gaze. Yes, she'd been looking for him, moving toward him instead of away, and spoke to him.

"Our dad, Gavin Aengus Donohue, was a bright light in this world. There is no speech I can give and no story I can tell that will allow you to know who he fully was, that can convey his infinite qualities. For weeks now, my sister, brother and I have been gathering stories about Dad, wanting to surprise him at this party, at his birthday party. And what I have come to see is that he was loved by everyone he knew. He was the same man and yet somehow a little bit different with each of you. The stories we collected have shown us that his integrity and his grace and his charm were widely shared and real, and yet there were parts of himself that only we, his family, knew, and

464

more still that were secret only unto himself. You each carry your own Gavin Donohue with you.

"I'd like to share a few stories about what made Dad special to me." She had no time to thoughtfully choose what she shared, but the stories flowed out of her: of how Gavin took his kids to work and taught them the pub trade; of how he showed them how to fish and what spending Sundays together on the water meant to his wife, his children and grandchildren; of his bad jokes and his ill timing and of his abiding love for his family and the river that ultimately carried him away. And then she told them of her great love for him.

"I am sure that for all our life, my brother and sister and I will miss him as achingly as we do now. But his life runs through us just as the river does this town."

Colleen put down the microphone, set it on the stool. There came the hushed sound of muffled sobs and murmur of voices. Shane dropped his arm over her shoulder and pulled her close as he lifted the microphone. "If anyone else . . ."

But already a line had formed, those wanting to tell their version of Gavin, wanting to share who he was in the particulars of their life. Same man, infinite facets.

An hour or more passed as men and women took turns at the microphone. They talked of how wonderful Gavin and Elizabeth were together, of their teamwork and spirit. And with each telling Gavin's soul shone brighter, his presence became known. His children were struck again and again that no matter how much they knew him, there was so much they did not know. There was the woman he saved from an abusive man at the pub; the money he gave to local charities; the hours he spent listening to patrons' troubles.

When the speeches were finally finished and the singer reclaimed the microphone, Colleen stood between Hallie and Shane. "Did we really know him?" she asked.

"Of course we did," Hallie said. "We knew him as our dad, as the man we loved. We knew him as ours."

"But no one can ever *really* belong to just you. Listen to these people." Colleen pointed at the stage. "Maybe deep down we're all unknowable, even to those who love us most."

Shane pulled her close. "Maybe. But we knew his heart and that means we knew him."

"Know him," Colleen corrected Shane.

"Because he is always here and he is always in us."

"Yes." Hallie glanced around the room and then back at her siblings. "Have you seen the girls?"

"Last I saw them they were devouring the shamrock cupcakes," Shane said and pointed to the empty table at the far end of the room.

"Just great, now a sugar high." Hallie wandered off to find her daughters as Shane went to check on the back bar.

Colleen stood alone in the middle of the crowd, feeling the heat and pulse of grief. Voices blended until one stood out. "Lena."

Colleen turned to face Walter Littleton, his face twisted in grief, his eyes red with both whiskey and regret — quite the combination, as she well knew. "Walter."

"I am so sorry," he said, wiping sweat from his forehead with a crumpled napkin. "I'm sorry you lost such a great man. But I lost him, too, Lena; I loved him." His voice was broken, fragments of it cracking with the words.

"It's the whiskey talking," Colleen said flatly.

"No." He shook his head. "You don't have to punish me anymore. I loved your dad and I am so, so sorry."

"Loved?" Colleen stepped closer to him, and he didn't smell like alcohol, but only of sweat and dirt. "How can you say that?"

"Because I do. Because I did." He took a step back. "I'm not the monster you think I am, Lena."

Somewhere below the clammy and oppressive grief for her dad, Colleen felt a sense of sadness for this broken man losing his wife and daughters in ways he hadn't expected. "Not a monster," she said quietly. "But a man who is capable of causing great pain in one small family. A selfish man."

He cringed, his eyes closed as though she'd hit him in the face with her words. "I know, but I'm not going anywhere." He exhaled and spoke quietly. "You've never let me explain what happened . . . what . . ."

Colleen closed her eyes so she wouldn't have to look at Walter, but his voice continued.

"I hadn't had any plans to leave you at the altar. I loved you. I might even still love you if you weren't so merciless to your sister. But you know, and I know, and you have to admit, we are a better fit — me and Hallie. You just wanted . . . so much."

"What is wrong with wanting so much?" Colleen opened her eyes and stared at the man she might have married and felt a flood of relief that she hadn't. "No! Don't answer that. Not here. Not now."

"Someday?" he asked quietly. "Let me try and explain."

She shook her head. "No. Not ever. It's past that time, and explanations don't matter so much anymore. It can't change things. It can't unbreak my heart, or Hallie's, or bring back Dad."

Walter rubbed the bridge of his nose and closed his eyes so tightly that Colleen could see where the lines of age would eventually appear. "You're right." And with that he walked away.

Colleen remembered words of C. S. Lewis she once read, "No one ever told me that grief felt so like fear." And for the first time she understood it was fear, quivering and moving below her chest. Fear of the future without her dad. Fear of loss. Fear of unknowing. It took her breath and kept it captive beneath her throat until she was dizzy and ran for the door, needing air.

Outside, the crowd just as thick, Colleen felt a hand on her back and turned to Beckett. "Lean on me," he said.

And she did, and she caught her breath. "It's so final," she said. "There's no more 'I'll fix it later. I'll call him later.'"

"I know."

She rested on his chest and waited for her breathing to slow.

"You know," he said, "I told you it wouldn't be ready but I did have a surprise for tonight. For your dad."

"What's that?" She lifted her head.

"The state did offer approval for the historic site status of the pub. I was going to surprise him."

"This is . . ." She stopped, unable to find the words she wanted or needed. "It's wonderful. And sad. And a fitting tribute even though he's not here. Thank you, wonderful Beckett. Thank you."

Beckett nodded, emotion clouding his face as he took her hand and they eased their way back inside. The microphone screeched and a high-pitched voice broke a soprano note and Colleen stopped. "What the . . . ?"

Beckett laughed. "It appears the speeches are over, but the songs are not. Patrons are each singing what they believe was Gavin's favorite song."

"Well, this is *not* it." Colleen felt laughter bubble up as Winnie Byers sang "Amazing Grace" in a key it had never been sung in before.

And then came "Danny Boy" and "When Irish Eyes Are Smiling" and "Molly Malone." Not one of them Dad's favorite song, but what each friend wanted to sing in his honor. Each song was worse than the one before until the band took back the microphone.

Later, in the back room, Colleen found Hallie hiding from the crowd, her hands covering her face as she silently cried, her shoulders moving up and down in the same but opposite motion of laughter. Colleen went to her sister, wrapped her arms around her. "I know. I know."

"I don't know how to do this, Lena. I don't know how." Hallie looked up at her. "What now?"

"I don't know either. But look what an amazing party you gifted our dad."

"It was supposed to be a birthday party! And so many things have gone wrong. The banquet people didn't show up with the green chair covers, the balloons were never delivered and my girls gave out the poppers too early. Nothing is right."

"Everything is right. Everything except Dad's absence." Colleen held her sister tight and regretted every moment she had been away. What a waste, a death in its own right.

Soon, the night grew long into darkness, not one guest wanting to leave this paradoxically joyous and grief-filled place where Gavin's presence was so strongly felt, not wanting to leave even as the food ran out.

Beckett whispered in Colleen's ear, "You doing all right?"

"I think I am." She pressed against his strong body, against the solid goodness of him, and felt no need to run. "Can one be emptied out and filled at the same time?"

"Yes." He kissed her forehead and held her closer. "Absolutely."

Still later, there was the hullabaloo when Garrett Miller passed out at the bar, and when a woman tried to take over the Guinness tap. There were jokes told and more hugs and stories than Colleen could count and file away — all of them blending into one.

Finally, after the pub had emptied, in the shadowed time between one day and the next, Colleen, Hallie and Shane gathered together preparing to head for home, taking Rosie and Sadie, who had fallen asleep on the benches of the corner booth.

Once their vehicles had arrived in the Donohue driveway, and the little girls had been tucked into bed, in silent assent the three siblings walked outside, past the broken tree house to the edge of the dock to sit. It was Hallie who said what they'd all been thinking. "Dad will never be able to read his memory book."

Colleen stared out over the water, where one day soon they would scatter his ashes. "He didn't have to read it; he lived it."

Hallie cleared her throat to break through the grief gripping them all. "It's been killing me, trying to remember the last thing he said to me. You" — she turned to Colleen — "had these profound last moments and conversations with him and I couldn't remember. And I felt like I never would."

"And you did?" Shane asked Hallie.

"I did. But it wasn't until I quit trying so hard and realized that I might never remember. I thought so much of how it must feel for Dad to lose memories, to be so lost. He had to try hard to remember things, only to realize he couldn't, and not just little things but things that mattered."

Colleen watched her sister carefully. "What did he say to you?"

Hallie paused. "I said good night to him before tucking the girls into bed. I told him I hoped one day you'd be able to forget about the church and the kiss. He said that no, you should never forget. That would be the worst thing because it's memories that make us who we are. Forgiving perhaps, but no, not forgetting — he was nearly shouting — never the forgetting."

"So what was the last thing?" Colleen

almost whispered.

Hallie lifted her face to the stars. " 'Never the forgetting.' "

Shane began to hum "The Lark in the Clear Air." "I researched the song," he said after a while. "I was going to tell the story at the party." He stared off over the river. "It was a poem first, written by Sir Samuel Ferguson. His wife . . . get this" — he paused for effect — "was part of the Guinness family. The poem was then put to music on a harp to an old Irish air called 'Kitty Nowlan.' The song has as rich a history as Dad did."

"That is so beautiful," Colleen said.

"As Dad once told me," Shane said, " 'my body will live longer without food than I can live without meaning.' Maybe he knew that. Deep down maybe he went out on that boat . . ."

"Don't say it, Shane." Colleen rested her hand on his leg. "We can't guess. We can't know. Don't."

"We were prepared to deal with taking care of him." Hallie's voice sounded choked. "We had our lists and I'd moved in." Her voice broke at the end and Colleen knew what they had prepared for, and she would have chosen that, chosen that deterioration over this loss. But would their dad?

In silence together they returned to the house, to their dad's house, to sleep and then to wake to another day filled with his absence.

The next morning, their eyes swollen and bleary, the sisters sat on the back stoop of the house under the fluttering awning, watching Shane begin the tree house renovation. They'd offered to help him, but he'd shooed them away. The pub would be closed for at least three days, and Shane had decided that now was the time to mend and replace what had been destroyed by years of neglect.

Rosie and Sadie ran through the yard perfecting their cartwheels.

Colleen slipped her hand into her sister's. "Dad's ashes," she said.

"We'll have them tomorrow." Hallie said this so quietly it might have been a secret. "Shane picked out a beautiful wooden box for now, until we decide when to . . ."

"Scatter them." Colleen finished the sentence for her.

"Yes."

"I've been thinking about it and I think we should wait." Colleen released her sister's hand and shifted to face her.

Hallie lifted her eyebrows. "For how long?"

"For as long as it takes us to settle into this grief, and for all of us to be together again."

"Again?" Hallie broke eye contact and turned away, glancing across the water as a kayaker paddled past, disturbing the water into silvery rays of light.

"Yes. I don't know how long I'll be gone."

"I thought you might leave again." Hallie shifted to stand and Colleen stayed her with her hand.

"I'm not running away, Hallie. I'm not leaving you or the girls or Shane. I've been asked to write a memoir based on my ten travel tips and I've agreed."

"Why would you need to leave to do that? Isn't this just about the most perfect place to write?"

"The last tip is about going home. I have to figure out what that word means to me, what home *really* is."

"How can you even ask? It's here. Right here in Watersend."

"That's true in so many ways. But now that I know about Dad's time in Ireland, now that I know about the first Colleen . . . my birth mother . . . I need to go to the

476

place where I was born. You get that, don't you?"

"Yes." Hallie nodded and her gaze wandered to her daughters. "I admit it is easier for me. My home is here. Home for me is now defined by wherever my girls are."

"Promise me this. Please don't make plans for Dad or his ashes until I return. Okay?"

"I promise."

Colleen stared at her sister, weighed the words inside her mind before she said them, making sure she meant them. "I trust you."

They sat quietly for a long while, listening to Rosie's and Sadie's sweet shouts, to the splash of the river against the dock and to Shane's sawing and hammering. Eventually car tires crunched the gravel drive and they turned to see Beckett's old Audi pull in and park. He climbed out tentatively, realizing as he glanced toward the yard that the family was watching him. He waved shyly but didn't come forward.

Colleen stood shakily, exhaustion weighing her down, her heart beneath a slab of grief. She went to him and hugged him. "Thanks for coming by." She kissed him lightly. "You've been so kind."

"You act like I'm here to say good-bye, which I'm not." He smiled and then he shook his head. "Wait, it's you. You're the one saying good-bye?"

"I am but just for a little while. I'm going to stay and help Hallie and Shane for a couple days, get things settled, but then I've decided I'm going to Ireland. To the O'Shea pub." Colleen held her casted arm level in her opposite hand, relieving the swelling in her fingers.

"It's my fault." He grinned with the joke. "I showed you that photo of that pub and now you have to go see it."

Her laugh was light. "Yes, your fault."

He gazed at her for a few moments. "You don't have to do this." He brushed the hair from her forehead. "You don't have to run. You know that, don't you? Please don't leave, Colleen."

"I just told Hallie — I'm not running away. I'm really not. This is different."

"If you're leaving the grief and loss, try to see that there is also love here. Can't you see that there can be both?" He touched her cheek and she leaned into his palm.

"What are you saying?" She kissed his palm and lifted her gaze to his as she took his hand in hers.

"That I am quite possibly falling in love with you? Yes. I have no idea what will happen with us, but please don't leave when it's just starting."

"I'm not leaving for good, Beckett, or at least I don't think I am. I'm going to see what I can find there. I can't start the book or this journey with myself unless I go. Does that make sense?"

"And you believe Ireland will help you forget and move on? You believe Ireland will fix things?"

"No. Not forget. Never that. And it won't fix anything; I'm sure of that. But Ireland is where I began. And how can I know where I'm going until I know where I started?" She paused. "Dad once told me that it was the memories that made his story, but that he was the only one who could find *meaning* in that story. Maybe that's what I'm trying to do. Go to where it all started to find meaning, or at least understand the best I can."

Beckett kissed her then. "You believe that getting close to someone will destroy you. I know that. But it won't. Don't go."

"I must." Colleen rested her head on his shoulder and spoke the truth. "My first travel tip was, Know where you are going. It was meant to mean be prepared, be organized, plan outfits, buy maps and stop by the bank for the right currency. But I now know it means so much more. It's also about a future." She smiled. "*How it starts is*

479

how it ends. That's what Hallie said to me last week. And I think she might be right. I need to go to the place where I began."

They kissed lightly and he held her. "Then go if you must. When you come back, I'll be waiting right here."

CHAPTER THIRTY-FIVE

Your feet will bring you
where your heart is.

Irish proverb

Colleen glanced out the airplane window —
the clouds were tumbled and gray, appearing impenetrable until the plane burst
through and the Emerald Isle appeared
below. The plane banked left and dipped;
Colleen gasped as the green patchwork-
quilted landscape appeared below. In a
quick scribble in her open notebook, she
wrote, *I arrive in a place where all the greens
in the world were born.*

She hadn't slept at all on the seven-hour
transfer flight from New York's JFK, where
she'd connected from Savannah. Instead,
she'd been writing as furiously as she ever
had. Her notebook, a small green one she'd
bought for the trip, was now one-quarter
full with notes and little sketches to remind

herself of other times and other trips — a shorthand she'd come to use in her travels. While other passengers slept with their eye masks on, and the flight attendants wandered up and down the aisle talking in subdued tones, Colleen wrote and wrote. While her seatmate — a British woman who wore too much perfume and chewed her food with the noises of a grinding machine — watched movie after movie, Colleen wrote and wrote.

Her work kept the grief at bay until she let down her pen, let down her guard, and it crashed into her as a blindsided punch. But still she kept writing — the work wasn't profound, she knew that much, but it was honest. It conveyed some small truths. She wrote about how she'd squelched her hurt with travel and adventure; about how she'd avoided intimacy by finding fault in others; she understood slowly and quietly that she could not wait for a man to save her life just as she could not blame a man for ruining it.

After they landed, she moved dreamlike and sleep deprived through the customs line, making small talk with a tall man and his son headed to a golf trip. Colleen felt both untethered and elated as she looked for her bag. Although she hadn't yet stepped her feet onto the green earth, the mantra *I am in Ireland; I am in the land of my birth* wound around and around her thoughts like yarn binding her close and safe.

After cashing in her U.S. dollars for euros at the exchange stand, she exited the airport and stood in the soft air of Ireland. It was just another airport, another city, just like the hundreds of others she'd found herself cast upon after a long flight, and yet it was anything but *just* another city. She stood still for a long while, breathing in and out, wishing she'd slept on the plane, and trying to catalog everything in her sight: sunlight creeping along the grass; the varied accents like musical notes; the soft scents of fresh-cut grass; the gray industrial buildings that might belong to any airport.

"May I help you?" A thin man in a fisherman's cap startled Colleen and she jumped, dropping her backpack onto the sidewalk as her cast banged against its edges.

"No. I'm good." She leaned over to pick up her pack and then smiled at the older man with wrinkles on his face like fissures, but pleasant in the creases of his smile. "Just needing a taxi."

"Well, then you're in luck." He tipped his hat and spoke in a brogue so lovely Colleen thought she wanted to record that simple sentence. He pointed at the black taxi directly behind him. "Where would you be needing to go, miss?"

"County Clare." Colleen rattled off the address of the pub, which she'd already memorized. There was no use in wasting time. If she'd traveled this far to see the place, then she would go straight there.

"Well, that's grand, let's be on our way."

She knew a taxi was extravagant, but she wasn't ready to drive the windy roads on the wrong side, and she planned on staying in the small town until she decided what to do next. No need for a car . . . yet. Her destination was only an hour away, but by the third curve in the road, Colleen's head lolled to the side and she was fast asleep. She awoke as the driver lurched to a stop and with a laugh asked, "You'd be liking the pub this early on a Tuesday morning?"

Colleen sat upright and rubbed her eyes, confused for only a moment as she re-adjusted both her gaze and her thoughts. Outside the window was a view as stunning as any she'd ever seen — Galway Bay glinting in the sun. She opened the door and stepped out, wondering vaguely if she were dreaming.

Here was a land she'd only imagined or seen in photos, a land so green and a sea so blue and a marsh so lush that it seemed to be an animated movie formed of hyper colors and sounds. Gulls cried, a donkey brayed and the bay water splashed and swished on craggy granite boulders that lined a boggy area so bright green it was almost neon. She knew it would take days, maybe weeks, for her eyes to see all there was, to absorb and understand the landscape. This was her geography, a place where she'd been conceived in love and born in trauma. This was the place of herself.

The taxi driver climbed out of the car and stood next to her. "You okay, miss?"

"I don't know that I've ever been better." She turned to take in the pub behind her, a simple facade next to a restaurant facing the bay.

"Are you sure you're wanting to be dropped off at O'Shea's? It doesn't open until six tonight."

Colleen glanced back at the driver, and his smile was concerned. "I'm staying only a couple doors down from here. I'll walk when I'm ready. I just wanted to see it straightaway."

He pointed at her cast. "You're sure now? You don't need help?"

She grinned. "Fit as a fiddle." She knocked on the cast with the knuckles of her free hand. She quickly paid the man and he drove off.

Colleen's backpack was flung over her shoulder and her small suitcase sat at her feet like an obedient dog. She didn't move, but cataloged the details of the pub as though she intended to paint it, needed to memorize it. It was just like the photo she'd seen in the historical office back in Waters-end.

It was as though the old photo had shimmered and shaken itself, and then come to life. The side windows and dark green door; the gold lettering above the door stating the name in proud letters; the pots brimming with multicolored flowers of anemone and foxglove; and the window displaying various kinds of whiskey and photos of local towns-people. The structure was simpler and smaller than the Lark — a double door in the middle and windows on either side in perfect symmetry. Colleen felt that if she opened the door she would find the décor to be similar to the Lark, all dark wood and low lanterns, sparkling glassware and taps poking above the lacquered bar. She might find old friends sharing a pint, sharing their lives in the intimate way of pub life.

Sauntering down the sidewalk, an older man approached Colleen. He carried a bag and he walked deliberately toward the bay. He was short and a cigarette dangled from his lips, his face hidden under a cap. As he neared her, she saw that he was even older than he'd appeared, and had a kind face. He stopped and smiled. "Hello, ma'am, are you lost?"

"Not at all," she said. "Just enjoying the view."

He nodded at her suitcase and then dropped the cigarette, crushing it beneath his leather boot. She noticed that the bag he carried was in fact a guitar case. "You arriving or leaving our fair town?" he asked.

"Arriving," she said. "And just now." She pointed at his case. "A guitar there?"

He glanced down as if he'd forgotten he was carrying it. "Ah, yes. Practice with the band." He nodded toward the pub.

"You're going into the pub? I thought it wasn't open."

"It isn't except for setup. You needing a drink?" He laughed and glanced at his wrist, which didn't have a watch but she got the point.

"Not quite yet. I just want to meet the owners, or the family who owns it."

He stared at Colleen for a moment, the silence stretching toward the bay and back again to the pub.

She smiled at him. "It's a lovely place. My dad used to work here . . . a long time ago."

The man stood still and placed his guitar case next to her suitcase so it appeared that they'd been traveling together. "Your da?"

"Yes. Well, I was hoping someone might remember him, although I know it's a long shot."

"Well, you'll be coming back tonight then." It was not a question.

"I will."

"That'll be grand. You'll find all the stories you'll be wanting to hear."

Colleen brushed the hair from her eyes as the man picked up his case. "Do you know any O'Sheas?"

"I do indeed. I'd be one."

Colleen stared at him then with new eyes. The fine smile, the pale skin and the jaunty pose. "So am I," she said. "I'm an O'Shea."

She hadn't, until that moment, thought this truth in words. She was, though. She was an O'Shea.

"Well, that is grand." He smiled and slapped his hand on his thigh. "You'll be finding quite a number of us here. Too many to count. Have you been doing that ancestry tree all the Americans are doing to find your ancestors?"

"No. My mother, well, I thought the family didn't own the pub anymore. I thought . . ." Although this stranger might be somehow related by blood, Colleen would not yet share her full story with him. Dare she mention her mother's name? "I thought Colleen O'Shea was the last one of the family to own it and when she passed . . ."

"God rest her beautiful soul." The man crossed himself and closed his eyes for a moment before gazing again at Colleen. "Aye, you'd be right about that. She was the last direct descendant, but her second cousin Shawn swooped in to save it after she passed on. And God bless him for that." The man smiled. "My name is Sully."

"Nice to meet you, Sully." She held out her hand. "Colleen."

The man shook her hand and held to it, his fingers entwined in hers. "Well, well, you are Colleen, aren't you?"

"You mean . . . ?" She clung to his hand and he to hers.

"Well, here you are now. This is the land where stories come alive. And you, Colleen O'Shea, have always been part of a love story." He released her hand and picked up his guitar case with a smile so wide Colleen wondered if it hurt his cheeks.

"A love story?"

"Well, yes, you are. Welcome home. Tonight shall be grand." And with that, he was gone, disappearing around the back of the pub.

She gazed toward the water and realized that if she were to put in one of the sailboats moored to the concrete dock a few hundred yards away, and steer it west and slightly south, she could eventually land at her own dock in Watersend. She would find herself again at the water's edge in her backyard with the tilting tree house and the one-story home where her sister and nieces now lived, where her childhood had unfolded and where a man named Beckett had told her that he just might be falling in love, if he allowed himself, or if she allowed him to do so.

Colleen gripped the suitcase handle and began to walk the few blocks to her rented cottage, the wheels popping on the cobblestones and uneven sidewalk.

The pub crowd pressed in on Colleen as she stripped off her raincoat. It was nine at night and the place was packed to the walls. During the day she'd walked around the town, napped for hours and wrote her first impressions of the town. She found a place for fish and chips and gobbled as though she hadn't eaten in weeks. Now she stood near the entranceway taking it all in, cataloging it as she would any place she'd be writing about. The hoppy aroma of beer mixed with the scents of rain and warm bodies. The wooden bar was dark and formed an L shape at the end of the room. Men and women were bellied up, placing orders in their thick accents and slapping one another on the back. It seemed everyone knew everyone else and Colleen wondered if this was how a stranger might feel entering the Lark. The room looked and felt as she'd thought, but also deeper and richer, just as though she'd imagined it in three dimensions and found instead four.

The dark wood-paneled walls were nearly covered with framed photos of men in uniform, men in groups, women at the bar or the bay, families and parties, priests and bartenders. And just as in Watersend, there were posters for bands and musicians.

With her raincoat draped over her arm, Colleen moved through the room, not looking at those around her but at the photos. Was her dad here? Her mom? As she wiggled and wound her way to the back of the room, she saw it — a photo of her dad as a much younger man, exactly as he'd appeared in the photo back in Watersend, the one where he was sitting on a stone wall, dressed in a suit with a flower pinned to his lapel. Here, though, there was a woman at his side. She wore a simple white dress with lace sleeves and a short lace veil pinned to her wild curly hair, both of which seemed alive in the wind. She clung to Gavin, both her arms looped through one of his as she leaned against his shoulder. He gazed at her and she at him, and it was clear they were both laughing. All was right with the world for this couple — they had no idea what was coming. Does anyone ever?

Colleen backed up and bumped into an older man. His shock of white hair sprouted in all directions and his Guinness was half-empty. He smiled kindly and stepped out of the way.

"I'm sorry. Did I make you move from your spot at the bar?"

"Aye, no, you didn't. But I'm afraid if I stay here I'll be falling in love with you." He bowed his head and laughed, then ambled off to join another white-haired gentleman at the far end.

Colleen grinned at the flirtation and backed up to take his vacated spot, still gazing at the photo. Her mom, or the woman who had given her life. The laughing woman in the white dress on her dad's arm looked like her. Curly dark hair, large wide-set eyes, a smile that reached high onto her cheekbones. Yet, this Colleen had a face full of freckles, a smattering across her nose and cheekbones like sprinkled stars.

"You know those people?" a voice asked behind Colleen and she turned, her hand reflexively coming over her heart. She faced a gentleman, most likely her dad's age, holding a tray teetering with beer and whiskey glasses.

"Partly, yes."

He nodded his head toward the wall. "This is the wall of O'Sheas."

Colleen took in the man's kind blue eyes and furrowed forehead. "That's my dad." She pointed at the photo.

The man set the tray on the bar and threw his hands in the air. "Sully told me you might be coming tonight. You're Colleen."

She blushed, feeling the heat of it in her face and under her arms. "Yes."

"Welcome." He took her right hand in both of his wide callused palms and pumped her arm up and down. "Let me take your coat." Which he did, and hung it on a hook behind the bar. "Expect you'll be staying awhile?"

"I think so, yes."

"Sit." He pulled out a bar stool and then

placed two fingers in his mouth to emit a loud whistle. The bar crowd was silenced and he hollered out, "We have Colleen O'Shea with us here tonight. Now you make her feel welcome."

The remainder of the night was loud and blurred and she felt as if she were in a lucid dream. The accents, deep and rich, carried her along. She sipped whiskey and met second cousins and a slew of townspeople who had all adored her mom, and a few who remembered and loved her dad. Colleen O'Shea had been an only child, they said, and look now, they exclaimed, her only daughter here at last. "We knew you'd come back one day," almost all of them said. "This land draws people home."

There were the few, a pair of sisters who'd been Colleen's best friends, who blamed Gavin for the loss of Colleen. And they told her so. "If your da had just stayed where he was meant to be, and married the woman he was meant to marry, none of this would have happened." After all of the backslapping and hugs, Colleen was speechless at the sudden turn of tide, at the implications cast as quickly as a slap across the face.

"But," she said to the one sister, Maury, her hair feathered with gray and piled high in a bun that was springing loose from its bounds. "But there would have been no great love and there would have been no me."

"Well," said the second sister, Elana, younger but wearing the same hairstyle, her lipstick too orange and too thick, "that very well might be true, but we'd have our best friend and we'd have never known about you at all."

Colleen gripped the edges of the bar and nodded at the sisters, feeling the sink of despair, of the irreversible despair, of death. "My dad is gone now, too," she said. "And I'm so sorry you lost your best friend, my mom."

They seemed to soften but not enough to answer. They turned in unison and bowed their heads close together as if discussing a plan of action. Colleen turned away and took the few steps toward the left side of the L-shaped bar, where she could see the sisters' faces as they looked at only each other. Loss and time dug long trenches in every life, and memories, regrets and pain filled in the deep furrows. The sisters had filled their troughs with bitterness, and Colleen felt, quickly, out of the corner of her heart, that she had a choice, that they all had a choice of how to fill those long empty places — with forgiveness, with bitterness, with rage or with, above all, love. She'd made some wrong choices and some right, if there was any right or wrong about it all. She would choose differently if she had the chance to rewind, but she was here now, in a land across the sea where she could begin again. Choose again.

The pub was overflowing with life, and every life its own universe of joy and pain, of love and loss. This was a mirror to South Carolina. This was the same and it was different and it was her dad and mom's pub, and it was where she began.

Soon, Colleen showed off her prowess at the Guinness tap and bowed at the applause. When the owner, a second cousin named Millie Walsh, closed the bar hours later, Colleen was met at the front door by Sully, who offered to walk with her to her rented room.

As they ambled side by side in the darkness, a sliver of moon blurry beneath the cloud cover, he asked, "Was that to your liking?"

"If it wasn't, there would be something wrong with me, I believe." Colleen laughed. Jet lag, whiskey and beer made her feel as though she were half floating above the sidewalk.

He, too, laughed and then stopped so that

Colleen did also, turning to face him a block from her cottage. The streetlight lit his face, the furrows of his wrinkles casting shadows across his smile. "May I tell you a story about your mum?"

"I'd like that." Colleen's heart raced and she took a step closer.

"When your mum was a little girl, she wanted to travel the world. She kept a globe in her bedroom and when I'd come to see her da, my uncle, she would bring it out to me. She would spin it and spin it, pointing to the places she meant to one day visit. When her parents died together in that accident, she knew that those plans were to be put aside, that she must run the pub, possibly for a long while. And then she met your da. We here in town weren't so happy at first, thinking she'd run off to the States with this American. But she didn't. Your da, he became one of us quick as a wink. He did his best to learn some Gaelic and most of all he honored and loved your mum. When she discovered she was to have you, she told me, 'This is the one who will see the world.' "

Colleen's breath caught in her chest and her hands flew to cover her mouth as a cry threatened to erupt. Light rain began again, misting them both.

"Did I go making you upset? I didn't mean to now." Sully took her good hand in his and kissed her cheek. "That story was meant to make you happy."

"Sometimes I cry when I'm happy," Colleen said and squeezed his hand.

Sully nodded. "Aye, I think the Irish know a thing or two about that."

Colleen allowed the misty rain to settle on her face, on her hair and hands. "She never left here, though. This was her home. It was where she was born, and where she died."

"It was." Sully nodded. "Which means that in many ways it is also your home. Although you must find your own place to settle and live because we all know that home must be a place that shelters your life."

"A place that shelters your life." Colleen repeated the words and stared at the man for a long while with the bay behind him, the soft rain and the whitewashed thatch-roof cottages surrounding them.

"I will see you tomorrow, then?" Colleen asked. "I think I'd like to stay awhile in this place and hear some more stories about my mom."

"Indeed." Sully bowed and began to amble along the sidewalk for the last block to Colleen's cottage.

The clouds above Galway Bay puckered, tumbling toward each other and away. The whip and whistle of the wind gathered at the edges of the night and blew Colleen's hair around her face, into her eyes and the corner of her lips, carrying the past and the future all together.

EPILOGUE

The people we most love do become a
physical part of us, ingrained in our
synapses, in the pathways where
memories are created.
> Meghan O'Rourke,
> *The Long Goodbye*

Three Months Later . . .

Half-hidden in the high branches and Spanish moss, the tree house appeared like a
small cottage that had been built snuggly
into the nook of the oak. It sat steady and
level, the metal roof shimmering in the
November sunlight. A ladder, much larger
and safer than the one Colleen, Hallie and
Shane had climbed long ago, had been attached to the trunk, pink ribbons hanging
off the sides, fluttering in the wind. Behind
it, the river was flat and calm at ebb tide.
Colleen heard her nieces' voices, muffled
and laughing in the branches, their voices

blending with the afternoon frog croaks and birdsong.

Colleen gently closed the door to the taxi and dropped her backpack at her feet next to her suitcase. She inhaled the river-soaked air and smiled. She hadn't told anyone but Beckett that she was returning today. He would arrive soon, but she wanted to surprise her nieces and Hallie first, then Shane.

For three months she'd rented a white-washed cottage with a thatch roof, hiked the land of West Ireland, met distant relatives of her Irish mom and written an outline and first chapters of the travel memoir. She'd had her cast removed after seven weeks and begun to type even faster. She hadn't traveled much, but instead had become deeply familiar with the small town and its people.

She'd kept in touch with her family, sending letters and texts, updating them with photos and e-mails. She'd sublet her apartment in New York, and hadn't promised anyone when she'd return because she hadn't known. As time had stretched out in Ireland, there came a moment when she understood why her dad had decided to stay, reasons that went beyond his love for his wife Colleen. It wasn't one quality of the land or the people, one person or pub or house that attracted her; it was the mix and mash of it all, a seductive quality not unlike the Lowcountry. A land alive and surreal, changing with each tide and wind. A land where the trees seemed as old as the earth, and the water had spent a lifetime thrashing against the tide and rocks, begging her to dance with it. A lush land, of every shade of green, that surrounded her and asked her quietly, in the night air, in the stormy sea, in the curved roads, green pastures and fairy circles ringing the trees, if she would stay and allow it to make her its own.

For a little while Colleen, too, had thought she might stay. She befriended her neighbors and became involved in the community. She found enough friendship to sustain her and enough solitude to write. In the midst of her writing, the realization flowered — since she'd arrived she hadn't known what to *do* about home, but the in-between space allowed the decision to grow and become what it must until she was certain — the pulse of the water and the heartbeat of her family on the other side of the sea drew her home — a place she chose.

As she wrote, and as the stories spread across the pages, she understood that there is and always would be heartbreak. Always.

It was the cost of love. To live her life in fear would not do. Walter hadn't only destroyed her faith in love but had also offered her a new belief: that getting close to anyone would destroy her. Getting close to Walter wasn't the same as becoming close to anyone else. The world was not made solely of Walters — to believe the lie kept her in bondage to fear. "Don't move on anymore," Hallie had cried out when she left. "Don't move on."

As the cab backed away and honked, two little faces appeared in the window of the tree house. Colleen couldn't make out one from the other, but she waved.

"Aunt Lena!" Rosie's voice called out clearly and then Sadie's voice joined in.

With loud squeals of delight two little girls scurried down the ladder, both jumping before the last step to land in the soft grass and run toward Colleen. They flew into her, arms and legs flying, their voices rising still higher.

"You're home!"

"Did you bring us presents?"

"Are leprechauns real?"

"I lost another tooth."

"Will you stay in our room with us?"

They talked over and above each other while Colleen tried to hug them both, two squirming little girls. They fell to the grass in laughter.

The commotion brought Hallie to the back steps, one hand on her hip, the other shading her eyes as she looked up toward the tree house, where her girls were supposed to be. She wore a pair of jeans and a white linen button-down fluttering in the breeze. Her hair, shorter and loose around her face, touched her shoulders. Not seeing what she meant to see, she shifted her gaze to the lawn, where Colleen and the girls were now tangled together in a heap.

"Lena?" Hallie asked in a quiet voice, walking toward them slowly as if she might make her disappear.

Colleen stood up and brushed off her jeans. "Hey, sis." She smiled at her sister and reached for a hug.

Hallie came into her arms, holding tight. "You didn't tell me you were coming home. I would have made you a nice dinner. I would have . . ."

Colleen let go and kissed her cheek. "Maybe that's why I didn't tell you. I don't want you to *do* anything."

Sadie and Rosie bounced around like pogo sticks, wanting Colleen's attention.

"Are you really home?" Hallie asked.

"It looks like it." Colleen spread her arms

wide, hugging the property, the river, the house and all its inhabitants.

"I was afraid you'd stay there. I was afraid you'd be just like Dad and not come back."

"Ah, but Hallie, Dad did come back."

"But not for a long time and only because of tragedy." Hallie shook her head and smiled. "I'm so happy you're here. We saved your bedroom for you."

"There is so much to tell you." Smiling at her sister and then her nieces, Colleen felt a fullness that could only be happiness. "But there's plenty of time for that."

The sound of a car made them both turn to see Shane's Jeep rattle up the driveway and pull to a stop. Out of the driver's side he emerged and from the passenger side stepped Beckett. She knew they'd become close friends while she was away and Beckett had brought Shane along, knowing he'd want to be part of the reunion.

Colleen didn't know where to rest her eyes — on her brother or her friend — but they approached together and hugged her tightly between them. She laughed and pushed them both away. "You're squashing me. Stop."

Shane spoke first. "Lena," he said and then paused. "Colleen, welcome home. I am so damn happy you're here."

"Lena is good with me," she said and smiled at her brother, gently nudged his shoulder with hers. "I'm very happy to be home."

She turned to Beckett and gave him her full attention. They'd been writing to each other and talking on the phone, long conversations. She'd found herself saving moments and thoughts of the day to share with him each evening. But no promises had been made, no plans solidified. He kissed her, softly and quickly with everyone watching. She touched his cheek. "Hi there, Beckett."

"It's mighty fine to see your face, Colleen Donohue. Mighty fine."

"Yours, too." She kissed him again.

Silence fell and into it Hallie asked the question they all might have asked. "Did you find out what home is?"

Colleen held Beckett's hand and looked directly at her sister, allowing their gaze to hold, allowing everything they were and had been and would be to settle between them. "I think so, yes. I believe home is a land that calls for you, a place that shelters. It's a family with all the complications that a family can be." Colleen looked at her brother and nieces and then at Beckett. "This is my home." She kissed Beckett, and then smiled at her family. "Because now I understand

— home is more than a place, it's a love story."

ACKNOWLEDGMENTS

I have long been fascinated by the role of memory in our lives — how it both allows us to look back in fondness and yet is also capable of keeping us captive to pain or loss. Who are we without our memories? How do they define, center and hold us? I attempted to answer these questions — as I do most inquiries that keep me awake — in story.

Although the pages must be written alone, the story unfolded with the input, help, brainstorming and encouragement of many others. First, I want to acknowledge and thank Dr. Jim Ray (son of the brilliant writer Cassandra King) of the Neurodegeneration Consortium at MD Anderson Cancer Center for allowing me to interview him ad nauseam about Alzheimer's research and treatment. Dr. Ray is on the forefront battling this horrific illness and yet spent time with me to help me understand how it affects both the patient and the families. Any errors are mine alone.

My writer tribe was there with me to brainstorm and carry me through when the story seemed to be falling apart. I love *all* of you. Thank you most directly to Mary Alice Monroe and Kathy Trocheck (aka Mary Kay Andrews), who worked through the plot tangles with me, who helped me name the pub and title the book, and who were there through the dark night to help me find the heart of the story.

My friends — all of you — God bless you for having to put up with me through the heads-in-the-cloud phase, through the on-the-road phase, through the I'm-overwhelmed phase. I love you each and all.

My agent, Marly Rusoff, has been there to strengthen and encourage. My stellar team at Berkley/Penguin Random House continually offers unwavering support. I offer over-the-top gratitude to my editor, Danielle Perez; my publisher, Claire Zion; Danielle Keir; Craig Burke; Roxanne Jones; Fareeda Bullert; Betty Lawson; and my sales team. You are the dream team in so many ways.

To Meg Walker at Tandem Literary, whose calmness and insight only make this a better journey from beginning to end.

To Ellen Edwards — we have worked on over seven books now together and your keen eye, compassionate spirit and steady hand always make my stories more than they would be without you.

And always to my beloved family, I love you and would not and could not do this without you.

WOMEN'S ALZHEIMER'S MOVEMENT

CHANGING THE FUTURE FOR ALL MINDS

DID YOU KNOW

Every 65 seconds someone in the United States develops Alzheimer's; 2/3 of them are women

5.8 million people in the United States have Alzheimer's

Women make up 2/3 of the caregivers taking care of those with Alzheimer's

Alzheimer's can begin to develop 20–30 years before diagnosis

TIPS FOR A BRAIN-HEALTHY LIFE

- ***Exercise — Get moving!*** Studies show that through exercise you'll improve blood flow to the brain, release hormones that make you feel good, and stimulate growth factor to help create new neurons and synapses in your brain. Be consistent, mix it up, and don't forget to move anywhere and everywhere.

- ***Nutrition — What's good for your heart is good for your brain.*** Research shows that it improves every aspect of your health to switch out old-fashioned meat and potatoes for the healthier Mediterranean and MIND diets. That means less red meat and bad fats — and loads more fruits and vegetables, avocados, fish, legumes, beans, whole grains, and healthy fats, such as olive oil, seeds, and nuts. Fill your plate with colorful fruits and vegetables. Lose the refined sugar. Hydrate!

- *Move Your Mind — Challenge your brain.* Research indicates that mental activity offers benefits to brain health. Learn something new to create new neural connections. Study an unfamiliar language or take up an instrument. Other ideas include playing, singing, and listening to music. Changing up your daily routines will also help. And give your brain a break from multitasking all the time — by focusing on too many things at once, you are compromising your ability to store information over short periods of time.

- *Sleep — Rest your busy mind.* Sleep is essential in the formation of memories and also in cleaning out amyloid deposits that can lead to Alzheimer's and other dementias. Your brain needs 7–9 hours a night, so don't cheat yourself of sleep's many therapeutic benefits.

- *Well-Being — Take good care of your precious body.* Put out the cigarettes. Practice mindful meditation. Reduce stress and anxiety. Laugh! Stay positive, and find places in your life to rest. Research shows that spending time in nature lowers cortisol — a stress hormone — and is linked with longer life in women, so take a long, silent walk outside.

- *Social Connection — Love your friends and family.* Research shows that social isolation is dangerous to your health — and that people who stay connected and have regular social interaction with friends and family maintain brain vitality. Share your concerns and grief; engage with others, and reach out to new friends. Remember your stories and share them with others! **Memories are the connective tissue that make us and our relationships unique.**

*For more information about the groundbreaking work of the **Women's Alzheimer's Movement,** please visit:*
www.thewomensalzheimersmovement.org

@thewomensalzheimersmovement
@womensalzmovement
@womensalz

ABOUT THE AUTHOR

Patti Callahan Henry is a *New York Times* bestselling author whose novels include *The Bookshop at Water's End, The Idea of Love, The Stories We Tell,* and *Driftwood Summer.* As Patti Callahan, she's the author of the *USA Today* bestseller *Becoming Mrs. Lewis.* Short-listed for the Townsend Prize for Fiction, and nominated multiple times for the Southern Independent Booksellers Alliance (SIBA) Book Award for Fiction, Patti is a frequent speaker at luncheons, book clubs, and women's groups.

CONNECT ONLINE
patticallahanhenry.com
facebook.com/authorpatticallahanhenry
twitter.com/pcalhenry
instagram.com/pattichenry
pinterest.com/patticalhenry